Piers Anthony's
Robot Adept
Book Five of the Apprentice Adept Series

"It's fun and games time again with the Gamemaster himself, Piers Anthony . . . always entertaining in everything he writes!"
—*Rave Reviews*

"A world inhabited simultaneously by two separate spheres of being: the science fictional Proton's technological Earth colonists and the fantasy Phaze's magical natives including dragons, demons and goblins . . ."
—*Publishers Weekly*

"Piers Anthony is as facile as he is prolific. He creates and populates realms with fanciful creatures from mythology (unicorns and werewolves), fairy tales (ogres and trolls), and his own imagination."
—*Cincinnati Post*

"One of those authors who can perform magic with the ordinary!"
—*A Reader's Guide to Science Fiction*

By Piers Anthony

Bio of an Ogre
Chthon
Phthor
Anthonology
Macroscope
Prostho Plus
Race Against Time
Rings of Ice
Triple Detente
Steppe
But What of Earth?
Hasan
Mute
Shade of the Tree
Ghost

Series by Piers Anthony

THE APPRENTICE ADEPT SERIES
Split Infinity • Blue Adept • Juxtaposition • Out of Phaze • Robot Adept

INCARNATIONS OF IMMORTALITY SERIES
On a Pale Horse • Bearing an Hourglass • With a Tangled Skein • Wielding a Red Sword • Being a Green Mother

BIO OF A SPACE TYRANT SERIES
Refugee • Mercenary • Politician • Executive • Statesman

THE MAGIC OF XANTH SERIES
A Spell for Chameleon • The Source of Magic • Castle Roogna • Centaur Aisle • Ogre, Ogre • Night Mare • Dragon on a Pedestal • Crewel Lye • Golem in the Gears

TAROT SERIES
God of Tarot • Vision of Tarot • Faith of Tarot • Tarot

THE CLUSTER SERIES
Cluster • Chaining the Lady • Kirlian Quest • Thousandstar • Viscous Circle

OF MAN AND MANTA SERIES
Omnivore • Orn • Ox

BATTLE CIRCLE SERIES
Sos the Rope • Var the Stick • Neg the Sword

PIERS ANTHONY

ROBOT ADEPT

ACE BOOKS, NEW YORK

The author gratefully acknowledges permission from the Society of Authors, on behalf of the Bernard Shaw estate, to excerpt from the play *You Never Can Tell* by Bernard Shaw.

This Ace book contains the complete text of the original hardcover edition. It has been completely reset in a typeface designed for easy reading and was printed from new film.

ROBOT ADEPT

An Ace Book/published by arrangement with
the author

PRINTING HISTORY
Ace/Putnam edition/April 1988
Ace edition/March 1989

Cover illustration by Darrell Sweet.
Author photograph by Carol Jacob.

For information address: The Berkley Publishing Group,
200 Madison Avenue, New York, New York 10016.

ISBN: 0-441-73118-X

Ace Books are published
by The Berkley Publishing Group,
200 Madison Avenue, New York, New York 10016.

PRINTED IN THE UNITED STATES OF AMERICA

10 9 8 7 6 5 4 3 2 1

Contents

1.	*Phaze*	1
2.	*Proton*	23
3.	*Agape*	50
4.	*Fleta*	66
5.	*Spy*	97
6.	*Amoeba*	114
7.	*Troll*	130
8.	*Tourney*	153
9.	*Masquerade*	185
10.	*Filly?*	218
11.	*Magic*	237
12.	*Oracle*	254
13.	*Pole*	272
14.	*Chase*	289
15.	*Table*	312
16.	*Decision*	326

Giants
Goblins
Yellow Demesnes
Ogres
Black
Demesnes
Oracle's Palace
Green
Demesnes
Harpies
Orange
Demesnes
Animal Heads
Dragons
Purple Mountains
© 1987 STORRINGS

White Mountains
Brown River
Red River
White
Demesnes
attice
Vampires
Red
Demesnes
ake
Blue
Demesnes
nicorns
Werewolves
Mound Folk
Brown
Demesnes
Trolls
PHAZE

Giadom
Gobdom
West Pole
Lake
Anidom
Hardom
Purple Mountains
© 1987 STORRINGS

White Mountains
Snodom
Vamdom
Lattice
East Pole
Trodom
Unidom
Weredom
Moudom
Gnodom
PROTON

1

Phaze

Suchevane stood in the canoe. She was obviously fatigued to the point of collapse, and in a misery of mixed emotion, but she remained such a stunningly beautiful figure of a woman that the rest hardly mattered. "I must needs fly home," she said. "I may not, I think, associate with ye folk longer."

"I understand, vampire maiden," Mach replied, looking up from his place at the rear of the canoe. "I thank you for your great service, and hope that we may at least remain friends."

"Mayhap," Suchevane agreed. "I did it mostly for thee, Fleta, and glad I am that thy life be safe and thy love secure. Would I had such love myself." She gazed for a moment at the fading brightness around them. "Would that any man evoke such splash for me!"

The woman in Mach's arms lifted her head, gazing at her friend through tear-blurred eyes. "Wouldst thou had such love thyself," Fleta agreed. "Fare thee well, dearest friend!"

Then Suchevane lifted her arms like wings, and with effortless elegance even in her fatigue became a lovely bat, and flew into the haze. Exhaustion made her flight ragged, but she would get where she was going.

The watery bubble floating beside the canoe bobbed gently. "I be not partial to vamps," the face of the Translucent Adept said within it. "But that one might almost tempt an Adept." The bubble spun, so that the face reoriented on the canoe. "I will, an thou wishest, provide thy craft a tow to my Demesnes."

"Accepted, Adept," Mach replied. Then he lowered his face again to Fleta's face, and lost himself in her.

The watery bubble moved, and from it stretched a watery line that touched the prow of the canoe. Bubble and canoe floated through the air, gaining speed, traveling through the closing night.

Mach and Fleta, victims of forbidden love, were on their way into the power of the Adverse Adepts.

Mach woke to the sound of lapping water. He looked, and sure enough, their canoe was on the surface of a large lake or small sea. "How strange!" he exclaimed.

Fleta woke. "Art well, my love?" she asked, concerned.

"We're on water," he explained.

She laughed. "It be strange to see a boat on water? Mayhap in thy frame, rovot, but not in mine!"

He smiled ruefully. "I enchanted this canoe to float in air, that's all. I was surprised."

The watery bubble ahead of them rotated so that the face in it faced back. "Willst be yet more surprised, youngster, in a moment."

Fleta stretched, arms bent, her breasts moving against him. "Must needs I call on nature," she said. "Let me change." She drew away from him.

"Don't leave me!" he protested, abruptly wary. "The last time you did that, I almost lost you forever!"

She abruptly sobered. "I thought only to spare thee evil, then," she said. "Fear not, I shall return to thee very shortly." Then she leaned into him and kissed him with such passion that his burgeoning doubt was sublimated into joy.

While he sat half-stunned by the delight of her, she stood much as Suchevane had, and abruptly became the hummingbird. The bird was glossy black, with golden little legs and beak; it darted forward to muss his hair with its wings, then shot away.

Mach shook his head, half in rue; he was a bit jealous of her instant shape-changing ability, and wished he could simply change and fly like that.

That gave him pause for thought. He was a novice Adept, wasn't he? He had managed to perform magic on occasion. What were his limits? The real Adepts could do amazing things; could he do likewise, if he only mastered the magic?

The more he considered, the better he liked the notion. He had conjured this air-floating canoe that had given him such good service; that was by any reckoning competent magic. He had nullified the suicide spell on Fleta by the force of his declaration of love: the triple Thee. While that was not an ordinary type of magic, neither had the spell on her been ordinary. She had asked the Red Adept to give her an amulet that would cause her to lose her ability to change forms, so that when she dived off the mountain she would be unable to save herself by changing to hummingbird form and flying away. The Red Adept, reluctantly, had granted her this. Mach had reversed Adept magic! Surely shape-changing himself would be a comparatively minor enchantment. All he had to do was work out the appropriate spells.

Fleta returned, humming up to perch on the canoe's front seat, then shifting to girlform. She had evidently completed her business. That was another advantage of shape-changing: the nectar of just a few flowers could feed her, and she remained fed when she shifted to a far more massive form. Similarly, one bird dropping could clean out her system, for the human form as well. Magic took little note of scale.

"Going down," the Translucent Adept's voice came from ahead. Then his bubble dipped under the surface—and the canoe followed. In a moment they were sinking through the greenish water, but breathing normally; the water seemed like air.

Fleta moved back to take his hand. "Adept magic spooks me," she confided. "I wish—"

He silenced her with a kiss. He knew what she wished: that they could be together without the intercession of the Adept. But it seemed that this could not be, for their union was opposed by her kind and his, so they were constrained to accept Translucent's hospitality.

They continued down. Fish swam by, gazing with moderate curiosity at the canoe; apparently they had seen things like this before. Then the bottom came into view, and it seemed again as if they were floating through air, with the rocks and seaweed and sea moss like the terrain of some jungle land.

Now that land turned strange. Orange and blue-green sponges spread across it, and corals reached up like skeletons, and peculiar flowerlike, tentacled things waved on yellow stalks. At first these were small, but as the canoe progressed they grew larger.

Mach looked down below the canoe as they passed a long log. No, it was a pipe, with a spiral band wrapping it, getting larger in diameter as they traveled along it. Then they came to its end—and there was a big round eye gazing up at him. The thing was a living creature!

"A giant nautiloid," the Translucent Adept exclaimed from ahead. "Creature o' the Ordovician period o' Earth. I have a certain interest in the paleontology o' the seas."

Beyond the eye were about eight tentacles, which reached for the canoe but stopped short of touching it. Mach was just as glad. "It looks like an octopus in a long shell," he remarked.

"That might be one description," Translucent agreed. "It is related, in the sense that the nautiloid is an order o' molluscs, as are modern octopi and squids. But these are far more more ancient examples; the Ordovician was approximately four hundred million years ago."

"You sound like a scientist!" Mach remarked. "Yet you are an Adept."

"No incongruity there! The separation o' magic and science on this planet occurred only a few centuries ago; prior to that, our history is common. The magic is employed in restoring ancient creatures who exist no longer on Earth or elsewhere. All Adepts be scientists in their fashion; it be merely that we specialize in the science o' magic, and turn it to our purposes exactly as do our counterparts in the frame o' Proton."

A creature vaguely like a monstrous roach swam across the canoe, startling Fleta. "A trilobite," Translucent said, evidently proud of the creatures of his domain. "And see, here comes a sea scorpion."

Indeed, the thing resembled a monstrous scorpion, almost a meter long. Fleta shrank back from its reaching pincers. "At ease," Translucent rapped, and the scorpion flipped its tail and swam quickly away. It was evident who was master here.

They came to a hill rising from the ocean floor, and the canoe bumped to a halt. "Here is thy honeymoon isle," Translucent announced. "Secure from all intrusion, guarded by the trilobites and scorpions and nautiloids."

"Does that mean we be prisoners?" Fleta asked nervously.

"By no means, mare," the Adept replied. "I promised ye both a haven for love, and freedom to do as ye pleased. Ye be free to depart at any time—but naught can I promise an ye depart mine Demesnes, for my power be limited beyond."

Mach's powers of doubt came into play. "What is it you hope to gain from this?"

"There be only one known contact between the frames, now," Translucent said. "That be through thy two selves, in the two frames. An thou use thy power o' communication on our behalf, we shall establish liaison with our opposite numbers, the Contrary Citizens o' Proton, and gain advantage. An we use this lever to unify the frames for full exploitation, our wealth and power will be magnified enormously. It be straight self-interest."

"But I can contact only Bane, who is the son and heir of Stile, the Blue Adept of this frame," Mach protested. "He opposes you, I'm sure, as my father Blue of Proton opposes the Contrary Citizens. If I work for you, as I think I must do in return for your hospitality, that is no guarantee that Bane will cooperate."

"Aye, none at all," Translucent agreed. "Yet it be halfway there, and mayhap for the sake o' his love there he will elect to join with us as thou has done. We prate not o' the nebulous good o' future generations that may or may not come to pass; we proffer honest self-interest, ours and thine, and believe that this be the truest route to success in any endeavor."

"I question this," Mach said. "But for the sake of what you offer, which is the fulfillment of my love for Fleta, I will make my best effort to contact Bane and relay those messages you wish. I regard this as a deal made between us, not any signification of unity of interest beyond the deal."

"Fairly spoken, rovot man," Translucent said. "We require not thy conversion, in language or in mind, only that thou dost betray us not."

"I will deliver your messages without distortion; my word on that is given. But I may not have complete control. If I should exchange again with Bane—"

"Then thine other self will be in my power, here," Translucent said. "But I will not hold him; he hath no deal with me. He will be free to rejoin his own, and thy filly too. But thy loyalty in this lone respect will be mine. My messages, when it becomes possible to pass them through."

"Agreed," Mach said shortly. He was not completely

pleased, but then he looked at Fleta and knew he had no choice. Their union would never be sanctioned by Stile or Neysa or any of those associated with them; only here with the Adverse Adepts could their love be honored.

The love between a robot and a unicorn.

The island—for so it seemed, though it was entirely under water—was a marvelous place. It was defined by a transparent dome similar to that of the cities of Proton, in which the air was good and the land dry. The dome held out the sea, and the creatures of the sea stayed clear because they were unable to swim or breathe here. Indeed, Mach and Fleta learned to make frequent circuits just inside the barrier, to spot sea snails, starfish, small trilobites and sea scorpions that had fallen through and were dying in the dryness. Mach fashioned a heavy pair of gloves so that he could handle such creatures safely; he simply picked them up and tossed them back through, for the barrier was pervious to matter other than air and water.

Once a fair-sized nautiloid blundered through, its two-meter-long shell lying dry, its eye and tentacles barely remaining in the water. Mach picked up the front section, and Fleta took the rear point, and they heaved it back into the sea. The nautiloid sank slowly through the water, as if not quite believing its luck, then jetted away, shell-first, its tentacles trailing. It was heavy enough in air, but a bubble of gas filled much of its shell, making it buoyant in water.

"Funny that there are no fish," Fleta remarked.

Mach checked through the files of his memory. He had been educated in paleontology along with all the rest, but it had been a survey course, scant on details. "I think true fish did not develop until the late Silurian, perhaps 330 million years ago," he said. "So this is about 70 million years too soon for them."

"Latecomers," she agreed wryly. "And how late be we, then?"

"Well, in the Mesozoic 200 million years ago the reptiles evolved, culminating in the dinosaurs of about 75 million years ago. Only after they passed did the mammals really come to the fore, though they had been around for 100 million or more years before. Man dates from only the last 10 million years or so."

"We be very late!" she concluded.

"Very late," he agreed. "And of course man's expansion into space occurred within the past half-millennium, and his discovery of magic in the frame of Phaze—"

"Yet surely magic existed always," she said. "Only we knew naught o' its reality until we found the frames."

"Perhaps so," he agreed. "There have been legends of magic and magical creatures abounding on Earth for many thousands of years. We believe that the development of the vampires and werewolves—"

"And unicorns," she said, shifting to her natural form. She was a pretty black creature, with golden socks on her hind legs and a long spiraled horn.

"And unicorns," he said, jumping onto her back and catching hold of her glossy mane.

She played an affirmative double note on her horn. Each unicorn's horn was musical, resembling a different instrument, and hers resembled the panpipes. This enabled her to play two notes at once, or even a duet with herself. All unicorns were natural musicians, but her music was special even for the species. She had had competitive aspirations, before her association with Mach caused the Herd to shun her.

"I wish I could change the way you do," Mach said, reaching forward to tickle one of her ears.

She flicked her tail, stinging his back, and walked toward a grove standing in the interior of the island. There she abruptly lay down.

"Hey!" Mach exclaimed, tumbling off, still hanging on to her black mane.

But she changed back to girlform, so that he had a

hold on her hair, and was not crushed by her mass. "No hay in this state," she said, rolling into him.

He used his hold to bring her face in to his. He kissed her. "How glad I am that I rescued you!" he exclaimed.

"And glad I be that thou didst rescue me," she responded. Then she tickled him on a rib.

They rolled and laughed and made explosively tender love, then sought a fruit tree for food. This island, however magically crafted and maintained, was a paradise, with many bearing trees. It was always moderately bright by day, with the sunlight coming down as if diffused by beneficial clouds, and moderately cool by night, for comfortable sleeping. There was a house on it, but they hardly used this, because Fleta had no need of it and Mach had no desire for what she did not share.

But as time passed, their satisfaction waned. "No offense to you," Mach said cautiously, "but I find myself increasingly restive. Maybe it is because I am not accustomed to being alive."

"Dost miss those naked girls o' thy frame?" she inquired teasingly. She was naked herself, having no use for clothing, here. She could appear in girlform clothed or unclothed, as she chose. Her equine coat translated into a black cape, her socks to stockings, and her hooves to shoes. What happened to these items when she appeared naked, Mach had never ascertained; and she, teasingly, had never explained.

"No, that means nothing in Proton, only that they are serfs. But with you—"

"Have I not done my best to please thee, thy way?" she asked. "To have sex with thee when I be not in heat?" For she, being a unicorn mare, normally sought such interaction only when the breeding cycle demanded, and then with such intensity as to wear out any man. Her shape might be completely human, for this, but her underlying nature remained equine. The unicorns owed more to animal lineage than to human.

"Indeed you have!" he agreed. "But I want more."

She frowned. "Mayhap another filly? Be thou eager to start a herd?"

He laughed. "No, of course not! You are all I want, and all I love! But—"

"Thou dost want me in other shape? I thought—"

"No, Fleta!" he exclaimed. "I want to marry you!"

She considered. "As the humans marry? Mating restricted one to the other, for all o' their lives?"

"Yes."

"But this be not the animal way, Mach. We have no need o' such a covenant."

"I think I do. I think of you as human."

"I be not human," she said firmly. "That be why thy folk—Bane's folk—oppose our association o' this manner. And my dam, Neysa—ne'er will she accept our union."

He sighed. "I know it. And I think we cannot have a valid marriage without the approval of your kind or mine. So we are forced to cooperate with the Adverse Adepts, whose policies I think I should oppose."

"I tried to free thee from this choice," she reminded him.

"By suiciding!" he exclaimed. "You almost freed me from the need to exist!"

"Aye, I know that now," she said contritely.

"So here we are in paradise, with no future."

"Mayhap we could have a future, o' a kind, if—"

He glanced sharply at her. "You know a way to persuade our relatives?"

"Mayhap. If we could but breed."

"Breed? You mean, have offspring? That's impossible."

"Be it so?" she asked wistfully. "Not for aught would I dismay thee, Mach, but how nice it would be to have a foal o' our own. Then might the relatives have to accept our union."

"But human stock and animal stock—you may assume human form, but as you said, that doesn't make you human. The genes know! They deal with the reality."

"Yet must it have happened before. Surely the harpies derive from bird and human, and the vampires from bats and human, and the facility with which we unicorns learn the human semblance and speech suggests we share ancestry."

"And the werewolves," he agreed, intrigued. "If it happened before, perhaps it is possible again."

"I really want thy foal," she said.

"There must be magic that can make it feasible," he said, the idea growing on him. "Perhaps Bane would be able to—"

"Not Bane!" she protested. "I want *thine!*"

"Uh, yes, of course. But I am no Adept. I'm a fledgling at magic. I don't know whether—"

"Thou didst make the floating boat," she pointed out. "Thou didst null the spell the Red Adept put on me. That be no minor magic."

"In extremes, I may have done some good magic," he admitted. "But I was lucky. For offspring I would need competence as well as luck."

"Then make thyself a full Adept, as Bane is growing to be," she urged. "Enchant thyself and me, that we may be fertile together. Success in that would make up for all else we lack."

"You're right!" he said with sudden conviction. "I must become Adept in my own right!" But almost immediately his doubt returned. "If only I knew how!"

"My Rovot Adept," she said fondly. "Canst thou not practice?"

"Surely I can. But there are problems. No spell works more than once, so I cannot perfect any particular technique of magic without eliminating it for future use. That makes practice chancy; if I found the perfect spell, it might be too late to use it."

"Yet if thou didst seek advice—"

"From the Adverse Adepts? I think I would not be comfortable doing that; it would give them too intimate a hold on me. I mean to do their bidding in communications between the frames, but I prefer to keep my personal life out of it." Yet he was conscious as he spoke of the manner his personal life was responsible for their association with those Adepts; he was probably deluding himself about his ability to separate that aspect.

"Aye," she agreed faintly. "Methinks that be best. Yet if thou couldst obtain the advice o' a friendly Adept—"

"Who opposes our union?" he asked sharply.

"I be not sure that all oppose it."

"Whom are you thinking of?"

"Red."

"The troll? He's not even human!"

"Neither be I," she reminded him.

"Um, you may be right. He did help you try to suicide." Mach had mixed feelings about that, too, though he knew the Red Adept had no ill will in the matter.

"He urged me not, but acceded to my will. If thou shouldst beseech him likewise—"

"It's worth a try, certainly. But would it be safe to go there? Once we leave the protection of the Translucent Demesnes, we might have trouble returning. Our own side might prevent us."

"I think not so, Mach. It be thy covenant they desire—thy agreement to communicate with thine other self. Thou wouldst no more do it for one side as for the other, an the agreements be wrong."

He nodded. "Let's think about it for a few days, then go if we find no reason not to."

"Aye." She kissed him, enjoying this human foible. Unicorns normally used lips mainly for gathering in food. The notion that human folk found the seeming eating of each other pleasurable made her bubble with mirth. Sometimes she burst out laughing in mid-kiss. But she kissed remarkably well, and he enjoyed holding a laughing girlform.

• • •

Before they decided, they had a visitor. It was a wolf, a female, trotting through the water to the island and passing through the barrier. Mach viewed her with caution, but Fleta was delighted.

"Furramenin!" Fleta exclaimed.

Then the wolf became a buxom young woman, and Mach recognized her also. The werebitch had guided him from the Pack to the Flock, where the lovely vampiress Suchevane had taken over. The truth was that all Fleta's animal friends were lovely, in human form and in personality; had he encountered any of them as early and intimately as he had Fleta, he might have come to love them as he did her. He accepted this objectively, but not emotionally; Fleta was his only love.

"I come with evil tidings," the bitch said. This appellation was no affront, any more than "woman" was for a human female. Indeed, the term "woman" might be used as an insult to a bitch. "The Adept let me pass, under truce."

They settled under a spreading nut tree. "Some mischief to my Herd?" Fleta inquired worriedly. She was tolerated by the Herd, but no longer welcome; still, she cared for the others, and they cared for her.

The bitch smiled briefly. "Nay, not that! It relates to thy golem man."

Fleta glanced at Mach. "The rovot be not true to me?" she asked with fleeting mischief.

"He be from Proton-frame. The Adept Stile says it makes an—an imbalance, that grows worse the more time passes, till the frames—" She seemed unable to handle the concept involved.

"Till the frames destroy themselves?" Mach asked, experiencing an ugly chill.

"Aye," Furramenin whispered. "Be that possible?"

"I very much fear it is," Mach said. "In the days of our parents, many folk crossed the curtain between frames, and Protonite was mined and not Phazite, generating an imbalance. They finally had to transfer enough Phazite to restore the balance, and separate the frames permanently so that this could not happen again. That depleted the power of magic here, and reduced the wealth of Proton there, but had to be done. Too great an imbalance does have destructive potential. But I would not have thought that the mere exchange of two selves would constitute such a threat."

The bitch looked at the mare. "Be he making sense?" Furramenin asked.

"I take it on faith that he be," Fleta replied.

"If Stile says it, he surely knows," Mach said. "I realize that the two of you are not technically minded, but I have had enough background in such matters to appreciate the rationale. They must be able to detect a growing imbalance, and I must be the cause."

"But what does that mean for thee?" Fleta asked.

"It means that every hour I remain in Phaze, and that Bane remains in Proton, is bad for the frames, and could lead to the destruction of both frames. We must exchange back."

"No!" Fleta cried. "I love thee; thou hast no right to rescue me from suicide only to relegate me to misery without thee! Didst thou speak me the triple Thee for this?"

"The triple Thee?" the werebitch asked, awed. That was the convention of Phaze; when spoken by one to another and echoed by the splash of absolute conviction, it was an utterly binding commitment.

"No right at all!" Mach agreed, feeling a pang. "Yet if remaining with you means destruction for us both, and the frames themselves, what can I do? We lose each other either way."

"Nay, there be proffered compromise," Furramenin said. "That be the completion o' my message: an thou agree to exchange back for equal periods, that the frames may recover somewhat, truce will be extended for that."

"The families accept our union?" Fleta asked eagerly.

"Nay. They merely recognize an impasse, and seek to prevent further damage while some solution be negotiated."

"If I return to Proton for a time, they will accede to equal time here with Fleta?" Mach asked. "A month there, a month here, with no interference?"

"Aye, that be the offer," the bitch said.

"That seems to be a good offer," Mach said to Fleta.

She gazed stonily into the ground, resisting the notion of any separation at all. Unicorns were known to be stubborn, and though Fleta was normally the brightest and sweetest of creatures, now this aspect was showing. Her dam, Neysa, was reputed to be more so.

Mach looked helplessly at Furramenin. The werebitch responded with a shrug that rippled the deep cleavage of her bodice. "Mayhap thou couldst offer her something to make up for thy separation," she murmured.

Mach snapped his fingers. "Offspring!" he exclaimed.

Fleta looked up, interested.

"Grant me this temporary separation from you," he said, "and on my return I shall make my most serious effort to find a way to enable us to have a baby, and shall pursue it until successful."

They waited. Slowly Fleta thawed, though she did not speak.

Mach addressed the bitch again. "What of the Adverse Adepts? Do they accede to such a truce?"

The watery bubble appeared, floating at head height. "Aye," the Translucent Adept said. "Our observation in this respect matches that o' the other side. The frames are being eroded. We profit not, an the mechanism o' our contact destroy our realm. But the two o' ye can communicate regardless o' the frames occupied. Hold to thy agreement with us, and we care not which frame thou dost occupy."

"I cannot implement that agreement unless my other self concurs," Mach reminded him.

"And the other side cannot profit from the connection unless thou dost concur," Translucent agreed. "The impasse remains—but an Bane appear here, mayhap we can negotiate with him."

"I suppose that is the way it must be," Mach said. "I must seek my other self and offer to exchange with him. I hope I can devise a spell to locate him."

"Surely thou canst," Translucent agreed, fading out.

"I must return to my Pack," Furramenin said. She became the wolf, and exited at a dogtrot.

Mach pondered. To do magic, he had to devise a bit of rhyme and deliver it in singsong. That would implement it, but the important part was his conception and will. If he wished for a "croc" verbally, he could conjure an item of pottery or a container of human refuse or a large toothed reptile, depending on his thought. He had very little experience with magic, and was apt to make awkward errors, but he was learning.

What he wanted was an unerring way to locate his other self. He did not want to risk any modification of his own perceptions, because if that went wrong, he could discover himself blind or deaf or worse. But if he had an object like a compass that always pointed to Bane's location on Proton, he could follow it, and if he made some error in crafting it, he could correct it when the error became apparent. Was there any type of compass that rhymed with "self"?

He quested through the archives of his Proton education, but came up with nothing. How much easier it would be if that word "croc" fit! Rock, mock, smock, lock, flock—

Then it came to him: delf. Delf was colored, glazed earthenware made for table use in the middle ages of Earth. A kind of crockery, not special, except that it proffered the rhyme he needed. If he could adapt pottery to his purpose . . .

He worked it out in his mind, then tried a spell: "Give me delf to find myself," he singsonged, concentrating on a glazed cup.

The cup appeared in his hand. The glaze was bright:

brighter on one side than the other. Mach turned the cup, but the highlight remained on the east side.

"I think I have it," he said, relieved. He had been afraid he would have to try several times before he got it right. Apparently the effort he had made to work out both rhyme and visualization ahead of time had paid off. He could do magic adequately if he just took proper pains with it.

"All I have to do is follow the bright side, and I should intersect Bane." For Bane's location in the frame of Proton would match the spot indicated in the frame of Phaze; the geography of the two worlds was identical, except for changes wrought by man. The separation of the two was of another nature than physical; the two overlapped, and were the same in alternate aspects, just as many of the folk were the same on each. Otherwise it would not have been possible for Mach and Bane to exchange identities, with Mach's machine mind taking over Bane's living body in Phaze, and Bane's mind taking over Mach's robot body in Proton.

Fleta did not respond. She was evidently still pensive because of the prospect of even a temporary separation. But he believed she could accept it in due course. Even unicorn stubbornness yielded on occasion to necessity.

Or did it? The following day did not ameliorate her reservation. Fleta did not want to go. She agreed that the compromise was valid and the measured separation necessary, but she made no effort to mask her dislike of it. "How can I be sure thou willst return, once thou art gone?" she grumbled.

"Of course I will return!" he protested. "I love you!"

"I mean that the Citizens or Adepts will not let thee back. They interfered before; hast thou forgotten?"

"It was the Adverse Adepts and the Contrary Citizens who interfered," he reminded her. "Now they support us."

"Until they find some other way to achieve their purpose," she muttered. "Mach, I like this not! I fear for thee, and for me. I fear deception and ill will. I want only to be with thee fore'er. E'en if we must constantly kiss."

"So do I," he said. "But I am willing to make some sacrifice now, in the hope that things will improve. Perhaps our families will agree to our union, in the course of this truce, so that you will be able to return to your Herd without being shunned."

A glimmer of hope showed. "Aye, perhaps," she agreed.

"Now I must follow the highlight on the delf. I hope you will come with me, so that our separation can be held to the very minimum."

She tried to resist, but could not. She converted to her black unicorn form, proffering a ride for him.

Mach mounted her, and for a moment reached down around her neck to hug her. "Thank you, Fleta."

She twitched an ear at him in an expression of annoyance, but it lacked force.

They left the island, passing through the water as the bitch had. The Ordovician flora and fauna ignored them, having gotten to know them. Mach knew that it would have been otherwise, had the Translucent Adept not invited them; these creatures might be several hundred million years old, geologically, but this was their realm, and they were competent within it. So Fleta's hooves avoided trampling the sponges and fernlike graptolites, and the squidlike nautiloids watched without reaction. Translucent had promised a place where Mach and Fleta could dwell safely together; this was certainly that!

They emerged to the normal land, and the past was gone; it existed only in Translucent's Demesnes, and these were in water. Now Fleta could gallop freely, knowing the general if not the specific terrain. They traveled for a day, avoiding contact with other creatures, and camped for the night by a small stream. Fleta changed to girlform so that they could make love, having thawed to that extent, then returned to mareform to graze while Mach slept alone.

She was avoiding him, he realized. Not overtly, but significantly, by spending most of her time with him in her natural form. She denied the implication by assuming girlform for his passion, but he knew that this was tokenism; she felt no sexual need when not in heat, and did it only to please him. So he was left with no complaint to make, yet the awareness of their subtle estrangement.

She didn't want him to return to Proton. She had agreed to it, knowing the necessity, but not with her heart. Perhaps she felt he had compromised in this respect too readily. She lacked the type of training he had had in Proton, that made it easy for him to accept the rationale of frames imbalance. She was a creature of the field and forest, while he was a creature of city and machine. Perhaps the root of his love for her lay in that. Her world represented life, for him, and that was immeasurably precious.

She thought he sought some pretext to leave her, after having won her love. How wrong she was in that suspicion! He sought a way to make their liaison permanent, recognizing the barriers that existed.

He gazed out into the night, where she grazed in pained aloofness. How could he satisfy her that her hurt was groundless? He realized that the differences between them were more than machine and animal, or technology and magic; they were male and female. He had assumed that rationality governed; she assumed that emotion governed.

And didn't it? Had he acted rationally, he would never have fallen into love with her!

"Thee, thee, thee," he whispered.

A ripple of light spread out from him, causing the very night to wave and the stars overhead to glimmer in unison. It was the splash, again, faint because this was not its first invocation, but definite.

Suddenly Fleta was there, in girlform, in his embrace.

She had received it, and must have flown, literally, to rejoin him. She said no word, but her tears were coursing. There was no separation of any type between them now.

On the third day they caught up to Bane. He was evidently in Hardom, the Proton city-dome that was at the edge of the great southern Purple Mountain range. In Phaze it was the region that harpies clustered. Thus the Proton name, reflecting the parallelism: HARpy DOMe, Hardom. But there were no harpies in Proton, of course, other than figuratively.

They paused to pay a call on the harpy they had befriended during their flight from the Adverse Adepts and their minions the goblins. That had been before the Translucent Adept's intercession and their change of sides. This was Phoebe, who had by virtue of Mach's fouled-up magic gained a horrendous hairdo that she liked screechingly well. It had enabled her to assume leadership among her kind, having before been outcast because of an illness. Fleta had cured that illness, which was the real basis of the unusual friendship; harpies generally had no interest in human or in unicorn acquaintance.

Phoebe was perched in her bower. Her head remained the absolute fright-wig that Mach had crafted, with radiating spikes of hair that made her reminiscent of a gross sea urchin. "Aye!" she screeched. "The rovot and the 'corn. I blush to 'fess it, but glad I be to see ye again!"

"We were passing, and thought we would pay our respects," Mach explained. "I must return to my own frame for a time."

"So? Methought thou didst have a thing for the 'corn."

"I do. I will return to her. But there is business I must attend to meanwhile."

"Be there any aid I can render?" Phoebe asked. "Ye be mine only friends among thy kinds."

"You have done more than enough for us. We merely wished to greet you again, and be on our way."

"As thou dost wish," the harpy said, shrugging. "But let me give thee another feather to summon me, in case thou shouldst have need o' me." She plucked it from her tail with a claw and extended it to him.

"Thank you," Mach said, touched. Harpies were in a general way abominable creatures, but this one they had befriended seemed quite human. Probably the others would be too, if the animosity between species could be overcome. He tucked the feather into a pocket.

"Yet it be late," Phoebe continued. "The night be cool, and my nest be warm. If ye two would stay the eve—"

Mach exchanged a glance with Fleta. This nest had fond memories for them. They decided to stay.

In the morning they continued to the spot where Bane was, on the edge of the plain just north of the Purple Mountains. The glow on the delf cup became so bright it was as if the sunlight were reflecting from it, but the sky was overcast. When the glow spread to circle the cup, Mach knew that this was where he could overlap his opposite self.

He turned to Fleta, who now changed to girlform, wearing her cape and shoes. Her mane became her lustrous black hair, a trifle wild and wholly beautiful. He embraced her and kissed her. "You must explain to Bane, if he doesn't already know," he said.

Mutely, she nodded. They disengaged.

It was time. But though he had to leave her, he sought some way to make the parting less absolute. He wanted to say something, or to give her something. But he could think of nothing to say, and had nothing to give.

His hand went to his pocket, reflexively. His fingers found the feather.

"Fleta—this may be foolish—but I want to give you something in token of what I will try to give you in the future. I have nothing, but . . ."

"There be no need, Mach," she said bravely.

"This." He brought out the feather.

She looked at it. Suddenly her laughter bubbled up past her bosom in the way it had, and burst out of her mouth. "A dirty harpy pinion!" she exclaimed.

"Well, technically it's a tail feather. A pinion is from the wing."

"Only a rovot would be thus at a time like this!" she exclaimed. She flung her arms around him and kissed him fiercely. Then she withdrew, and gravely accepted the feather. "But it be a good thought, Phoebe's and thine. Mayhap I will have need o' her. Certainly Bane will not." She tucked it into a pocket in her cape.

It was foolishness of a sort that he would not have indulged in, as a robot. Therefore he valued it now. "Farewell—for now. My love."

He stood where the cup indicated, and concentrated. Yes—he felt the presence of his other self. Now all he needed was to will the magic for the exchange, assuming that Bane joined him in the effort. "Let me gain the body of Bane," he singsonged, knowing that the doggerel was only a token, hardly necessary for this act.

He felt the magic of the exchange taking hold. Bane was cooperating. In a moment they would—

Fleta flung herself back at him, clasping him tightly. "Thee, thee, thee!" she cried, her bravery abolished.

There was a ripple around them. Then the exchange happened. There was something strange about it; this was no ordinary event. But it was too late to reverse it; whatever was to happen, was happening.

2

Proton

They took their places on either side of the console. Bane's screen showed a grid with sixteen boxes. Across the top was written 1. PHYSICAL 2. MENTAL 3. CHANCE 4. ARTS, and down the left side was written A. NAKED B. TOOL C. MACHINE D. ANIMAL. The numbered words were highlighted, which meant that he was supposed to choose from among them.

But his mind drifted, conjuring different interpretations for the terms.

Physical: He looked across at Agape, who was naked in the serf mode of Proton, as was he. She was beautiful, with curling yellow tresses, wide-spaced eyes with yellow irises, and erect breasts. It was hard to believe that she wasn't human.

She met his gaze. Her hair lengthened and turned golden, then orange. Her eyes nudged closer together, as did her breasts, and her nipples brightened to match the new hair and eye color. She smiled.

Mental: "Thou hast no need to change for me," he murmured, smiling back. "I be smitten with thee regardless." But now it was easier to believe that she was alien. Agape, accented on the first of the three syllables, meaning "love."

Her hair continued to grow, becoming red, and it curled down across and around her breasts, which were gaining mass. "Make your move, Bane," she said.

He looked again at his grid, pondering. His mood was lightening, as perhaps she intended, but it was not easy to set aside the gravity of their situation.

Chance: Bane was with the creature he loved, but he had little joy of it, because she would soon be leaving the planet and his life. Citizen Blue had made it plain: as long as Mach and Bane represented the only contact between the frames of Proton and Phaze, and the Contrary Citizens and Adverse Adepts desired such contact, the boys were probably safe. But their girlfriends were at risk, because they could be kidnaped and used to put pressure on the boys. Therefore the relationships had to be sundered, lest much worse occur. It was risky for them to maintain their association.

Agape had agreed to return to her home planet, Moeba. But the Contrary Citizens were watching, and would surely try to intercept her at the port and take her captive. So for the nonce she remained with the experimental group, and Bane had the benefit of her company. Every day might be the last together, so they did their best to make it count.

Arts: Today they were playing the Game. They had had a bad experience with it on the estate of Citizen Purple, but now they had the chance to play it as it should be played, unrigged, for fun instead of for life. It was fairly new to each of them, because Bane was from another frame and Agape was from another world. Neither was what either appeared to be; each was fashioned artistically to be on the appealing side of ordinary.

Her breasts caught his eye again, just above the level of the console. Now they were huge and purple.

He laughed. "Thou be trying to distract me!" he accused her. "So I may make a bad choice!"

"Curses, foiled again," she muttered. She had studied hard to learn human idiom as well as custom, and seemed to enjoy showing off her increasing mastery of both.

"I want to make love to thee," he said, experiencing a reaction.

"You did that this morning," she reminded him. "Have you forgotten already?"

"Nay, I remember! That be why I want it again."

"Well, defeat me in the game, and you can do with me what you will."

"But what if I lose?" he asked.

"Then I will do with you what *I* will."

He reflected on that, and his erection doubled its growth. A passing couple noticed. "I'd like to know what game *they're* getting!" the man said.

Too late, Bane remembered that he was now able to control such reactions. He thought the correct thought, and his member subsided. But his desire remained, for he could not control his mind as readily as his body.

He touched the number 1. PHYSICAL. He wanted to get physical with her, in or out of the game.

She had already made her selection. It was B. TOOL. Was she teasing him with another idiom, because of the reaction he had just quelled?

He grimaced. The way his thoughts were going, he would have preferred A. NAKED. Of course that wasn't literal; it simply meant that the players were relegated to their bare hands. All serfs of Proton were unclothed; that had no significance here. It had taken him some time to get used to this, but now he accepted it.

A new set of boxes appeared on his screen. This was the Secondary Grid, and its numbers across the top were labeled 5. SEPARATE 6. INTERACTIVE 7. COMBAT 8. COOPERATIVE. Down the side were E. EARTH F. FIRE G. GAS H. H_2O. The letters were highlighted for him this time.

He looked at her again. She had reverted to a more normal figure and color, except for her nipples and eyes, which were now electric green. What would she choose? 8. COOPERATIVE? Maybe he could still get close to her. "Earth" meant a flat surface, as opposed to the variable or discontinuous surfaces of the following options, or the liquid surface of H_2O. Cooperation on a flat surface—that might be good.

He touched the E panel. Again, her choice was ready.

She had chosen 5. SEPARATE. So much for that. Was she teasing him again? No, she was merely playing the game, unaware of his thoughts. They would do what they would with each other after the game; they had no need to do it *in* the game. He was being foolish.

They were in 1B5E: the category of tool-assisted physical games, individually performed on a flat surface. That did not sound very appetizing to Bane.

This time the grid was only nine squares, with the numbers 9, 10 and 11 across the top and the letters J, K, and L down the left side. There were no words there, but there were a number of choices listed to the right. These consisted of ball games, wheeled games, and assorted odds and ends games that had perhaps been lumped into this category because it was the least irrelevant place for them.

Bane hesitated, not sure where to go from here. "Now we place games," Agape explained. "May I have the first turn?"

Bane shrugged. "Thou mayst."

She put her finger to her screen and evidently touched KNITTING, for that word brightened on his screen. Then she must have touched the center square of the grid, for abruptly the word was there.

"Knitting?" he asked. "What kind o' game be that?"

"A woman's game," she said smugly. "I am not good at it, because we do not have it in my society, but I had to learn its basics in order to come here. I suspect that you, being arrogantly male, have never had experience with it."

Bane opened his mouth, and shut it again. She had him dead to rights.

"Now you place one," she said.

"Ah." If knitting was a tool-assisted physical game of the female persuasion, there were many others of the male persuasion. He put his finger on BALL: Throwing. She would have trouble throwing a ball as far as he could! He touched the upper left square, and the expression appeared there.

She put SEWING beside it in the top row.

He scowled. If she got three lined vertically, then got to choose the numbers, she would be guaranteed one of her choices! But no, he remembered now that the turns alternated; the last person to place a game, which on this odd-numbered grid would be her, had to yield the choice of sides to the other. So he could choose the vertical and avoid that.

All the same, he played it safe. He put ICE SKATING in the middle of the bottom row.

She put BAKING in the left center, or 9K square.

He quickly filled in the other end of the K row with BICYCLE RACING so that she would not have a horizontal line. He was beginning to enjoy this; he had thought they would not play the game until the grids decided what it would be, but realized that they were already in it. This was the aspect of strategy, where the game could be virtually won or lost, depending on the player's cleverness in choosing and placing.

Agape put COOKING in the lower right corner.

Bane put SHOT PUT in the lower left.

She put SOAP BUBBLES in the upper right square, the final one. The grid was complete.

He chose the numbers, though there did not seem to be much difference. Then he wrestled with the decision over which column to choose. If he took the first, he had two chances to win one of his sports: Ball-throwing or Shot-putting. But she would anticipate that, so take the middle row, winning her choice of Baking. So he should take one of the other columns . . . where the odds were two to one against him. Except that if she figured him to take the first column, so she chose the middle row, he obviously should take the third column, putting them in Bicycle Racing. So the odds weren't really against him. Unless she realized this, so took one of the other rows, so as to win. So he should—

He shook his head. He was getting confused! There was no way to be sure of victory; it was an endless maze of suppositions.

He decided to go with the odds. He touched Column 9.

This time she had not chosen before him, for the chosen box did not illuminate. His row highlighted; that was all.

At last she chose. The 9K square lighted, then expanded to fill the full screen. She had won it after all: they would play the game of Baking.

"Do you concede?" she asked.

It was only part of the ritual, but he was tempted. What did he know of baking? His mother, the Lady Blue, had always handled that. But he didn't like quitting, even when it was only a game. Even when it really didn't matter who won or lost. "Nay."

"Will you accept a draw?"

That was a generous offer! He knew he should take it, but he decided to take his loss like a man. "Nay."

She sighed. "I thought to bluff you," she admitted. "I know nothing of baking."

"Then methinks we both should learn," he said. "The loser must eat the winner's effort."

"But you don't even need to eat," she reminded him.

"Aye, but I can. Mayhap I will not have to."

She looked at her screen. "Oh, there is a list of baking choices. What do we want?"

"Something simple," he pleaded. "Something we ne'er can mess up too much."

"I agree." She addressed the console. "What is simple, and tastes all right if poorly made?"

BROWNIES, the screen replied.

Agape looked at Bane. "Do you know what brownies are?"

"Nay, if they be not a species o' the elves."

"Neither do I. So we're even. Let's do it."

"Aye."

There was a message on the screen: ADJOURN TO KITCHEN ANNEX, BOOTH 15.

They had committed themselves. They made their way to the kitchen annex.

The booth was ready for them. Two chairs were at consoles, their screens lighted.

Agape took one seat, Bane the other. Both consoles faced the wall. Bane's screen said: TOUCH WHEN READY TO PROCEED.

He reached out and touched Agape on the shoulder.

"It means the screen!" she exclaimed. But she leaned over and kissed him.

He had known that. Satisfied, he touched the screen. Nothing happened. "Thou hast to touch thine too," he reminded her.

"There's someone watching us," she murmured. "You can see him in the reflection of the wall."

He looked. It was a middle-aged serf, apparently one of the caretakers or troubleshooters of this section. He ran it through his brain's storage bank, and culled a positive reference. The serf was legitimate. "He be an employee, likely assigned to watch lest some minion o' a Citizen molest us," he murmured back. "Blue be not one to let us be taken hostage again."

"Oh, of course," she said, relaxing. She touched her screen.

Now the game was on. A menu appeared on his screen:

1B5E 9K BAKING BROWNIES MACH (R) VS AGAPE (A)

1. GENERAL INSTRUCTIONS
2. OPTIONS
3. RECIPE
4. LIST OF INGREDIENTS
5. TERMINATE

"What be 'R' and 'A'?" Bane inquired.

"Robot and android," she replied.

"But—"

"This is a standard unit. It cannot distinguish between a robot and a human being inhabiting the body of a robot. See, you are also listed as 'Mach.' Similarly, it cannot distinguish between an android and an alien; it knows only the distinction between Human, Robot, Android and Cyborg. So I count as an android."

He smiled. "Yet we be two other people."

"Two aliens," she agreed. "From Phaze and Moeba. That is what brought us together."

"I would not change it."

"Nor would I." She returned his smile. They were doing a lot of that, now. "But let's get cooking."

"Aye." He returned his gaze to the screen.

He did not understand much of it, so he decided to start at the beginning: GENERAL INSTRUCTIONS. He touched the number 1.

The original menu contracted and retreated to the upper right corner of the screen, evidently remaining functional. New words took over the left and center:

> MOST COOKING AND BAKING IS DONE BY REMOTE INSTRUCTION. ALL DIRECTIVES INDICATED ON THE SCREEN WILL BE IMPLEMENTED IN THE ACTIVITY CHAMBER IMMEDIATELY BEYOND THE CONSOLE. IF YOU ARE FAMILIAR WITH YOUR OPTIONS AND RECIPE, PROCEED DIRECTLY TO THE LIST OF INGREDIENTS AND MAKE YOUR SELECTIONS. IF NOT, PROCEED TO 2. OPTIONS.

Well, that was clear enough. Bane touched 2. OPTIONS in the corner. He wondered how Agape was doing. She had come to Proton only a day before he had, but had been better prepared for it.

OPTIONS: YOU MAY GO DIRECTLY TO THE LIST OF INGREDIENTS IF THE RECIPE IS ALREADY FAMILIAR.

YOU MAY SPECIFY THE SYSTEM OF MEASUREMENTS EMPLOYED IN THE RECIPE AND LIST OF INGREDIENTS.

YOU MAY SPECIFY A MULTIPLE OF THE STANDARD RECIPE. WARNING: THIS MAY AFFECT THE BAKING TIME AND THE QUALITY OF THE PRODUCT.

YOU MAY SPECIFY VARIANTS OF THE STANDARD INGREDIENTS. WARNING: THIS IS NOT ADVISED FOR NOVICE PRACTITIONERS, AS IT MAY AFFECT THE QUALITY OF THE PRODUCT.

YOU MAY SPECIFY VARIANTS OF OVEN TEMPERATURE AND DURATION. WARNING: THIS MAY AFFECT THE QUALITY OF THE PRODUCT.

The list of options continued, but Bane had seen enough. He decided to stick with the standard recipe and ingredients. He touched 3. RECIPE.

There it was: the listing of the materials that were to go into the production, with brief instructions on integration and processing.

60 GRAMS UNSWEETENED CHOCOLATE
60 CUBIC CENTIMETERS BUTTER

Oops! He was in trouble already! He was not conversant with the metric system used in Proton; he thought in terms of ounces and pounds and cups and quarts.

But he had the solution. He touched OPTIONS again, and when its listing reappeared, he touched SPECIFY SYSTEM OF MEASUREMENTS. A sublisting of measurements options appeared: the various systems used by the other planets and peoples and creatures of the galaxy. That wasn't much help either!

However, there was at the bottom a place for OTHER. He touched that, and when it asked him to

PLEASE SPECIFY, he said, "The system used in the Frame o' Phaze."

The screen blinked. For a moment he was afraid that this was not a viable choice, but then it replied OLD ENGLISH SYSTEM OF WEIGHTS AND MEASURES INVOKED.

Well! This was just about like doing magic in Phaze.

He returned to the RECIPE. Now it listed:

2 OUNCES UNSWEETENED CHOCOLATE
1/4 CUP BUTTER
1 CUP SUGAR
2 MEDIUM EGGS
1/8 TEASPOON SALT
1/2 CUP WHEAT FLOUR
1/2 CUP WALNUT FRAGMENTS
1 TEASPOON VANILLA FLAVORING

This he was able to make some sense of. He glanced across at Agape, and saw that her activity chamber was in operation: things were happening in a lighted box in her section of the wall.

He read the assembly instructions. He was supposed to melt the chocolate and butter together, then stir in the other ingredients. He should be able to manage.

He touched 4. LIST OF INGREDIENTS. This turned out to be the master list of everything available. There were dozens of types of chocolates, and similar variety for the others.

He returned to INSTRUCTIONS and read beyond the point he had before. Sure enough, it mentioned that there were several types of options, including automatic selection of standard variants. He went to OPTIONS, found the place, and touched STANDARD VARIANTS. Then he returned to INGREDIENTS.

Now the listing was much contracted. There was only one type of chocolate. He touched that, and the screen inquired QUANTITY? followed by a graduated scale of measurements. He touched the scale at the two-ounce point.

Now his activity chamber came to life. Two ounces of chocolate landed in its floor.

Um. Perhaps he had overlooked another instruction. He reviewed, and found it: he needed a container. He specified one of suitable capacity, then specified in a SPECIAL INSTRUCTIONS option that the available chocolate be placed in the container. The chamber turned dark, then lighted again: the chocolate was in the pan. The mess on the chamber floor had been removed.

He added the butter, then instructed the chamber to heat it to 400 degrees Fahrenheit.

Almost immediately the mixture started boiling violently. Goo splatted on the window of the chamber. Oops!

He turned off the heat and reviewed his general instructions and his recipe. He discovered that at this stage he was only supposed to heat enough to melt the chocolate and butter, not to bake it. He decided to start over.

ERROR the screen blazoned. It seemed that he had to make do with what he had; no second starts. He should have known; no one would ever let any mistakes stand if restarts were permitted. He could have gotten in trouble with his first loss of chocolate; evidently the system tolerated that amount of spillage.

Meanwhile, Agape's project was well along. She might be an alien creature, but she had a much better notion of cooking than he did!

His start was a mess, but a good deal of the chocolate/butter solution had been saved. He marked 100° F heat, and got the degree of melt he needed. Then, following instructions, he stirred in the remaining ingredients. The sugar was no problem, but the eggs were in translucent packages, and he had to do spot research to discover how to open these by remote control. He managaged to bungle it, getting half an egg splattered across the outside of the pan.

When he had everything stirred in, he had a rather

thick brown mass in the pan. Now he set the heat for 400° F and let it bake for a nominal half-hour. Actually it didn't take that long; the game computer used microwave energy to do the equivalent in just a few minutes, because otherwise the booth would be tied up too long for each game and would not be able to accommodate all the game players.

The two finished products were brought out, and for the first time Bane and Agape could smell and touch their brownies.

His was burned, so dry and hard that it would be a real effort to consume it. Hers was underdone, resembling a pudding; she had evidently set the heat too low, and perhaps included some fluid by mistake.

"Who wins?" he asked.

"We can get the machine to judge," she said unhappily.

"Nay, no need," he decided. "Thy concoction resembles thee: amoebic. I like it best."

"But yours resembles you," she countered. "All leather and metal. I like it best."

"We'll eat each other's," he said. "We both have won."

"We both have won," she echoed, smiling.

They leaned into each other and kissed again. Then they had the machine pack their wares in plastic bags, so that they could leave the booth for the next players. As they departed, both their activity chambers were in chaos; the game computer was trying to get them clean, and on this occasion that was a considerable challenge.

They retired to the private chamber they now shared, and opened the bags. Bane took a bite of pudding, but found it tasteless. This was not because it lacked taste, but because his body, having no need for food, had no taste sensors. What he chewed and swallowed went to a stomach receptacle that he could evacuate subsequently, either by vomiting or by opening a panel and removing the soiled unit. Eating was a superfluous function for a robot, but the ability had been incorporated in order to enable him to seem completely human. He was glad of it; he wanted to reassure her by eating what she had baked. Digestibility was irrelevant.

Her mode of eating differed. She set the brownie lump on the table, leaned over it, and let her top part melt. Her features blurred and became puddingy, indeed resembling the consistency of what she had baked. She drooped onto the food, her flesh spreading over and around it. Her digestive acids infiltrated it, breaking it down, and gradually the mound subsided. When all of it had been reduced to liquid and absorbed into her substance, she lifted her flesh from the table. Her head formed, and her shoulders and arms and breasts. Her eyes developed, and her ears and nose and mouth, assuming their appropriate configurations and colors. She had a human aspect again.

"I hope it doesn't poison thee," Bane said, not entirely humorously.

"It was solid and burned, but not inedible," she reassured him. "You made it; that is all I need to know."

He took her in his arms. "I have never before known a creature like thee."

"I should hope not," she said. "I am the only Moebite on this planet."

"I wish I could love thee in thy natural form."

"I have no natural form," she reminded him. "I am merely protoplasm. I assume whatever shape pleases you."

"And I am pleased by them all. I never loved an alien amoeba before."

"And I never loved a terrestrial vertebrate before. But—"

"Say it not!" he protested. "I know we must part, but fain would I delude myself that this moment be forever."

"If we continue speaking of this, I will melt," she warned him.

"And thou leave me, *I* may melt," he said.

"Perhaps, when I am safe among my own kind, you could visit?" she asked hesitantly.

"Let me go with thee now!"

"No, you must remain, and communicate with your opposite self, and return to your own frame. Our association is only an interlude."

"Only an interlude," he repeated sadly.

"But we can make it count. Tell me what to do, and I shall do it for you."

She was not being facetious. She had come to Proton to learn human ways, including especially the human mode of sexual interplay, because the Moebites wanted to work toward bisexual reproduction. They understood the theory of it, but not the practice. They believed that their species development was lagging because they lacked the stimulus of two-sex replication, and they wanted to master it.

But in the pursuit of this quest, Agape had run afoul of another aspect of such reproduction: she had fallen in love. Now she had much of the information, but lacked the desire to return to her home world and demonstrate it to others of her kind. She wanted only to remain with Bane.

Now that it was feasible to do, Bane found that he had lost the desire for sexual activity. Part of it might have been her sheer accommodation; no challenge remained, when she was completely willing and malleable. But most of it was his foolish gut feeling that once Agape had learned all that he might teach her in this regard, there would be no need for her to remain with him. Thus he wanted to conserve the experience rather than expending it, to keep her with him longer. He knew this was nonsensical, but it unmanned him for the moment.

"Let's play another game," he said.

She gazed at him in surprise. "Another game? But I thought—"

"Thou didst think rightly! But I—I find I be not ready. I want to experience more things with thee, a greater variety, while I may. I want to build up a store o' precious memories. Or something. I know not exactly what I want, only that I want it to be with thee."

"I see I have much to learn yet about the human condition," she said, perplexed.

"Nay, it be not thee, but me," he reassured her. "Only accept that I love thee, and let the rest be confused."

She spread her hands in a careful human gesture. "As you wish, Bane."

They went out to play another game, and another, and another, the victories and the losses immaterial, only the experience being important. So it continued for several days, with physical, mental and chance games of every type. They raced each other in sailcraft, they played Chinese checkers, they bluffed each other with poker, they battled with punnish riddles. Sometimes they cheated, indulging in one game while nominally playing another, as when they made love while theoretically wrestling in gelatin. Whatever else they did, they lived their joint life to the fullest extent they could manage, trying to cram decades into days.

They found themselves in machine-assisted art: playing parts in a randomly selected play whose other parts were played by programmed robots. Each of them was cued continuously on lines and action, so that there was no problem of memorization or practice. It was their challenge to interpret their parts well, with the Game Computer ready to rate their performance at the end. They had specified a play involving male-female relations, of a romantic nature, with difficulties, and the computer had made a selection from among the many thousands in its repertoire.

Thus they were acting in one by George Bernard Shaw titled *You Never Can Tell,* dating from the nineteenth century of Earth. Bane was VALENTINE and Agape was GLORIA CLANDON. They were well into the scene.

"Oh, Miss Clandon, Miss Clandon: how could you?" he demanded.

"What have I done?" she asked, startled.

"Thrown this enchantment on me . . ." And as he spoke the scripted lines, he realized that it was true: she had enchanted him, though she had not intended to.

"I hope you are not going to be so foolish—so vulgar—as to say love," she responded with uncertain feeling. According to the play, she had no special feeling for him, but in reality she did; this was getting difficult for her.

"No, no, no, no, no. Not love; we know better than that," he said earnestly. "Let's call it chemistry . . ." And wasn't this also true? What was love, really? But as he spoke, he became aware of something that should have been irrelevant. They had an audience.

"Nonsense!" she exclaimed with more certainty.

They had not had an audience when they started. Several serfs had entered the chamber and taken seats. Why? This was a private game, of little interest to anyone else. ". . . you're a prig: a feminine prig: that's what you are," he said, enjoying the line. "Now I suppose you've done with me forever."

". . . I have many faults," she said primly. "Very serious faults—of character and temper; but if there is one thing that I am not, it is what you call a prig." She gazed challengingly at him.

"Oh, yes, you are. My reason tells me so: my experience tells me so." And his reason and experience told him that something was wrong: there should be no audience.

". . . your knowledge and your experience are not infallible," she was saying, handling her lines with increasing verve. "At least I hope not."

"I must believe them," he said, wishing he could warn her about the audience without interfering with the set lines. "Unless you wish me to believe my eyes, my heart, my instincts, my imagination, which are all telling me the most monstrous lies about you."

"Lies!"

Yet more serfs were entering the audience chamber. Were they players waiting for their turn? "Yes, lies." He sat down beside her, as the script dictated, but wasn't sure he did it convincingly. "Do you expect me to believe that you are the most beautiful woman in the world?"

Now she was evidently feeling the relevance! "That is ridiculous, and rather personal."

"Of course it's ridiculous . . ." His developing paranoia about the audience was, too! He wished they could just quit the play here, and get away; he didn't trust this at all. But as they exchanged their lines, his apprehension increased. Suppose the Contrary Citizens had managed to divert Blue's minions, so that there was no protection for the moment?

"And I'm a feminine prig," she was saying.

"No, no: I can't face that: I must have one illusion left: the illusion about you. I love you."

She rose, as the cue dictated, and turned. Then she spied the audience. She almost lost her place. "I am sorry. I—" Now she did lose it, and barely recovered. "What can I say?"

What, indeed? Now it seemed sure: the Citizens were about to make their move. But how could he get away from here with Agape, without setting off the trap? They needed a natural exit, to get offstage, out of sight.

". . . I can't tell you—" he was saying.

"Oh, stop telling me how you feel: I can't bear it."

And he saw that the scene was coming to a close. Here was their chance! "Ah, it's come at last: my moment of courage." He seized her hands, according to the script, and she looked at him in simulated terror, also scripted. But their emotions were becoming real, for a different reason. "Our moment of courage!" He drew her in to him and kissed her. "Now you've done it, Agape. It's all over: we're in love with one another."

Oops—he had used her real name, not her play name! But he couldn't change it now. It was time for his exit.

"Goodbye. Forgive me," he said, and kissed her hands, and retreated.

But now the men of the audience were advancing on the stage. Bane ran back, grabbed her arm, and hauled her along with him offstage.

"It is happening!" she exclaimed as they ran for a rear exit.

"I think so. We must get back to the main complex, where Citizen Blue is watching." For this particular chamber was outside the region of the Experimental Project of humans, robots, androids, cyborgs and aliens living in harmony. Most facilities were set within it, but when particular ones were crowded, the Game Computer assigned players to the nearest outside ones. Thus it seemed that Bane and Agape had inadvertently strayed beyond the scope of Citizen Blue's protection, and the Contrary Citizens had seized the moment.

There were serfs in the hall outside. They spotted Bane and Agape and moved purposefully toward them.

They retreated back into the play complex. But they could hear the serfs in pursuit here too, coming through the stage region.

"The service apertures," Agape said. "Go there!"

Bane obeyed. Maybe there would be an escape route there.

There was not. The service door led only into a chamber in which an assortment of maintenance machines were parked.

"We be lost!" Bane exclaimed.

"Maybe not!" She hurried to a communications panel, activated it, and tapped against it with a measured cadence.

"Approach the cyborg brusher," the speaker said. The lid lifted on the top of a huge cleaning machine.

"Come, Bane!" she said, running toward the device.

"What—?"

"The self-willed machines are helping us! Trust them!"

Bemused, he followed her. "Remove the brain unit," the speaker said.

There was a pounding on the door. Evidently it had locked behind them, barring access by the serfs. That could not last long, for all doors had manual overrides.

Bane saw that there was a complicated apparatus just below the lid, with wiring and tubing and plastic-encased substance that looked alive. He took hold of the handles at either side and lifted. He had to exert his robotic strength, for the unit was heavy, but it came up and out.

"Set it here," the speaker said. A panel slid aside, revealing a chamber set in the wall.

He carried the brain unit across and shoved it into the chamber. The panel slid shut. Evidently this was a servicing facility for the living cyborg brain.

"Stand for dismantling," the speaker said. Another machine rolled toward him.

Bane hesitated. Then he heard an ominous silence at the door. They were setting up for the override! He stood for dismantling.

Quickly, efficiently, and painlessly the machine removed his arms, legs and head. It carried these to the big cyborg husk and installed them in the bowels of it. Then it stashed his torso in a refuse chamber in its base. Finally it separated his head into several parts, and his perceptions became scattered. The chamber seemed to wave crazily as one of his eyes was carried across and set into a perceptor extension. He had no idea how it was possible for him to see while his eyes were disconnected from his head, or to remain conscious while his head was apart from his body, but evidently it was. The machines of Proton had strong magic!

Meanwhile, Agape was doing something; he heard fragments of the instructions to her. It seemed she was required to melt into a new brain-container that was being set into the machine.

All this occurred extremely rapidly. In less than a minute the two of them had been installed into the cyborg. His accurate robot time sense told him it was so, despite the subjective human impression.

The entrance to the chamber opened. Bane saw this with his two widely separated eyes, and heard it with his buried ears. Six serfs charged in.

"Search this room!" one directed the others. "They have to be in here!"

They spread out and searched, but could not find the fugitives. They did find a panel that concealed a service tunnel leading to another drama complex. "Check that complex!" the leader snapped. "They must have crawled through."

Four men hurried out. But the leader was too canny to dismiss this chamber yet. "Check these machines, too," he snapped. "Some of them are big enough to hold a body."

They checked, opening each machine and poking inside. They checked the cyborg, and found only its brain unit and operative attachments. At length, frustrated, they departed.

DO NOT REACT. Bane saw these words appear briefly on a wall panel, and realized they were for him. The hunt remained on; this could be a trap.

After a few minutes the speaker said: "Cleaners ten, twelve and nineteen to the adjacent drama chamber for cleanup."

"We are nineteen," Agape's voice came faintly to him. "I will direct you; you must operate the extremities."

So they were now a true cyborg: a living brain and a mechanical body! Bane discovered that when he tried to walk, his legs were wheels. He started a little jerkily, but soon got the hang of it, and propelled them after the other contraptions toward the door.

Outside the serfs were waiting. Obviously they expected Bane and Agape to walk out, thinking that they were safe.

He took them around and into the drama suite the two of them had vacated. "Brush the floor," Agape said.

Bane tried to reach with an arm—and extruded an appendage whose terminus was a roller brush. He lowered this to the floor and twitched his fingers. The brush spun. He started brushing the floor.

DO NOT REACT, a panel flashed.

Then a serf wearing the emblem of Citizen Blue entered. "Good thing I got here in time!" he exclaimed. "They had us blocked off. Come on; we're going home."

Bane continued brushing.

"Hey, you're safe now!" the man said. "At least, you will be when we get you to the Citizen's territory. Come on!"

Bane ignored him, playing the dumb machine.

Disgruntled, the serf departed.

They continued brushing the floor. In due course the job was done. The two other machines had cleaned off the chairs and dusted the walls. "Return to storage," the speaker said. They returned to the storage chamber. There they parked and waited for another hour. What was going on? Obviously the self-willed machines were protecting them, but could the chase still be on? Where was Citizen Blue?

The panel flashed. REACT.

Then Citizen Blue walked in, followed by Sheen, his wife. "Is this chamber secure?" Blue asked.

"Yes, Citizen," the speaker replied.

"I owe you."

"No. Your activities benefit our kind."

Blue faced the cyborg brusher. "Are you in good condition?"

Now at last Bane felt free to answer; Blue was evidently legitimate. "Yes," he said through his mouth-speaker, which was now set near the top of the apparatus.

"This is a respite, not the end. You will assume our likenesses. Keep alert."

Then the dismantling unit approached, and reversed the prior procedure. It extracted Bane's arms, legs, torso and head and assembled them, so that soon he was back to his original condition. Agape was removed from the brain chamber, as a mound of jellylike flesh, and she stretched out and up and became herself in human form.

"You will assume our forms," Blue said. "We shall not be challenged in the halls, but you would be."

Agape began to change again, orienting on Sheen.

"No," Blue said. "Emulate me. The sensors can distinguish between flesh and machine."

"But I am alien," she protested. "They will know I am not human. I can emulate only an android, if they test."

"They distinguish human from android by fingerprints," Blue said. "The self-willed machines will give you my prints."

She nodded. She shifted until she looked so much like him that Bane was startled. Then she went to a unit in the wall where a unit overlaid her blank fingertips with pseudoflesh molded in the likeness of Blue's prints. Blue got out of his Citizen's robe and set it on her. The emulation was complete.

Meanwhile Sheen was attending to Bane. She simply had the dismantling unit remove her brain unit and exchange it with his. Abruptly Mach was in her body, and she was in his. This one would certainly pass inspection!

"Go to my private residence and remain there until we return," Blue said. He was applying pseudoflesh the self-willed machines provided, remolding his face and body to resemble Agape's. He had done this before, when he had rescued Bane from the captivity of Citizen Purple; he was good at emulations himself.

"But thou—when they find thee and take thee for Agape—" Bane protested.

"They will discover they are in error," Blue said. "Sheen and I will serve as diversion until the two of you are safe. This is a necessary precaution; they want you very much."

"Do not be concerned for us," Sheen said from his body. "We are immune to molestation."

Bane hoped that was the case. He faced the door.

"And let her do the talking," Blue said from Agape's apparent body.

Bane had to smile. It would not do to have the seeming Sheen speaking the dialect of Phaze!

They left. There were serfs, but those stood respectfully aside, eyes downcast. The two of them walked down the hall to the nearest transport station. Agape, as Blue, lifted her right hand to the panel. The prints registered. In a moment the panel slid to the side to reveal a blue chamber: Citizen Blue's personal conveyance. They stepped in.

The chamber moved, first rising, then traveling horizontally. There was no challenge, no delay; they were being transported to the Citizen's residence.

Bane wanted to take Agape in his arms and kiss her—but even had this been in character in their present guises, he would have found it awkward when she looked like Citizen Blue, who almost exactly resembled his own father Stile.

She looked at him and made a wicked smile. Then she took him in her arms and kissed him. Any watcher would have sworn that it was male kissing female, rather than vice versa.

The transport delivered them directly to Citizen Blue's suite. There were no servants there, so no awkwardness about identities.

Should they maintain their emulations? They realized that they had to, because Bane had Sheen's body. It was strange, seeing himself in the mirror, looking so like his other self's mother! So they settled down and watched news features on the screen, and waited.

An hour passed. Then the entrance chime sounded. The entry vid showed Bane and Agape.

"They're back!" Agape exclaimed, hurrying to the entrance. She touched the admit button as Bane came up behind her.

Suddenly Bane froze. His body had gone nonresponsive; it was as if it had been disconnected. He couldn't even speak.

Agape stepped forward—and the two figures jumped up to take her by the arms. Astonished, she tried to draw back, but they put a bag over her head.

Bane realized that these were not Citizen Blue and his robot wife, Sheen. They were impostors, similar to the serf with Blue's emblem—but he could not act.

"When you are ready to cooperate, send word," the Citizen figure said to Bane. "Then you may see her again."

Appalled, he watched them haul Agape back to a waiting vehicle. They had used a ruse to capture her after all!

Then a new figure showed up—and this one also looked like Citizen Blue. "Now there are two ways we can do this," he said.

The Sheen-figure whirled and leaped at him.

A net shot from the wall and wrapped about her, lifting her up and suspending her in the air.

"That was the second way," the Blue figure said.

The first Blue figure tried to run, but another net trapped him similarly.

Bane recovered use of his body. "Agape!" he cried, running to her.

Serfs appeared. They hauled away the two netted figures. "I wanted to catch them in the act," Citizen Blue explained. "Now I have proof."

Agape had dissolved into jelly, but when she felt Bane's touch she recovered and reformed, this time assuming her normal female shape.

Sheen appeared. They returned to the suite, and a machine servitor approached to transfer computer-brains. Bane had his own—or rather Mach's—body back.

"We have been watching, but until they made their move, it was pointless to act," Blue explained. "They were watching all the planetary ports, and indeed, all the exits from Hardom; there was no chance to get Agape out. But they gained nothing by keeping her bottled up here; they had to gain direct possession of her. So we tempted them by arranging a game beyond the protected region, and they finally took the bait."

"The bait!" Bane exclaimed, horrified.

"The seemingly vulnerable pair," Blue said. "Unfortunately, they were more determined than we expected; they arranged to send false signals of normalcy, so that we believed they had not struck. It was a good thing you thought to seek the help of the self-willed machines."

"They helped us," Bane agreed, feeling somewhat dazed as he remembered. "I knew not that this body came so readily apart!"

"Now that they have made their move, they will be trying more openly," Bane continued. "They have shown a certain cleverness in their efforts. We shall have to hide Agape until we can get her offplanet."

"Then hide me with her!" Bane exclaimed.

"Yes. But you may not enjoy the manner of concealment."

"I enjoy not the need for separation," Bane said. "Needs must I be with her while I can."

"I believe we have worked out a situation in which you can be together without suspicion," Blue said. "But you will have to be careful and alert, because it is risky."

"It be risky just acting in a play!" Bane exclaimed, and they laughed.

"We shall set the two of you up as a menial robot and an android girl," Blue explained. "You will be substituted for the ones assigned to go to a common location. The self-willed machines control placements;

they will arrange it. Such assignments occur constantly; there should be no suspicion."

"But won't they be watching us?" Agape asked.

"They will. They will continue to see you here."

"Oh." It had been demonstrated how facile such emulations could be.

So it was that the two of them were smuggled out, while another robot and android took their places as guests of Citizen Blue. They found themselves assigned to a young Citizen who was opening a new office in the city and required a humanoid robot and humanoid android to maintain it during his absences. It promised to be a routine and rather dull matter. But at least they would be constantly together, and in the off hours no one would care what kind of relationship they had. It was possible that they would never even see the Citizen himself.

The employer turned out to be Citizen Tan. Bane felt a shock when he learned of their assignment. Perhaps the self-willed machines considered this citizen to be a harmless nonentity, as Citizens went. But Bane suspected that he would be parallel to the Tan Adept in Phaze, and that meant he was in the Adverse or Contrary orbit.

If Citizen Tan caught on to their true identities, they would be already in the power of the enemy.

And Citizen Tan very well might, for if he was the other self of the Tan Adept of Phaze, he had the potential for a most devastating ability: the Evil Eye.

But they had no choice, now; they had to go. And it seemed they were lucky, for Citizen Tan made no appearance. They ran his office, with Agape receiving messages and smiling at vid callers—naturally her features had changed, so that she did not resemble the girl he had known—while he handled mechanical chores. He, too, no longer resembled the original Mach; his brain unit had been set into another body.

At night, when no business was to be done, they lay together and made love. They knew that permanent separation could occur at any time; that made love constantly fresh.

Then, in the early morning, Mach contacted Bane. Mach had amazing news.

Stile, Bane's father, had ascertained that their exchange was generating an imbalance that was damaging the frames. They had to exchange back—but the Adverse Adepts had welcomed Mach and Fleta to their Demesnes. So now Mach represented them, as far as communications between the frames were concerned. When they exchanged, Bane would not be pursued by the Adepts; he could go where he wished. But they wanted to talk to him, to try to persuade him to their side. He could trust the Translucent Adept.

All this was transferred on one gob of thought and impression; it would take him hours to digest the ramifications. Meanwhile, he was sending his own information back: how he and Agape had agreed to separate, though they loved each other, and the Contrary Citizens were trying to abduct her to use as a lever on him. How they were now hiding in a place the Citizens should not suspect, until Agape could be smuggled offplanet.

"Don't leave me!" Agape cried, realizing what was happening. She clapped her arms around him and clung close, almost melting into him. "I love you, Bane!"

Then the exchange occurred.

3

Agape

Agape realized that she had lost consciousness for a moment, for she found herself sagging in Bane's embrace. She lifted her head, and saw an open grassy plain. It was chill early morning outdoors, with no pollution in the air.

She blinked, and tried to shape her eyeballs more carefully, as they were evidently malfunctioning. It didn't work; her flesh remained fixed as it was.

Bane put his hands on her shoulders and set her gently on her feet. "We have exchanged, Fleta," he said. "I be not Mach."

There was a little pop in the air behind him, and a bit of vapor seemed to center on him for a moment. Then it dissipated.

Agape stared at him. Then she took one of his hands and squeezed it. *The hand was flesh, not plastic!*

"You are alive," she breathed.

"Aye, filly!" he agreed. "Now canst thou tell me more o' the truce Mach made with Translucent? Fain would I have stayed with my love in the other frame, but not at the price of destruction for all."

"Destruction for all?" she echoed blankly.

"In our contact, he told me that our exchange made an imbalance that needs must be abated. So he sought me, though he loved thee and wished ne'er to be apart from thee."

She looked again at the plain. Could it be?

"Where are we?" she asked.

He laughed. "Where thou hast always been, mare! In Phaze, of course."

"In Phaze?" she repeated.

"Aye. Surely thou dost not mistake this for Proton-frame!"

Suddenly she realized that this could be yet another trick of the Contrary Citizens. Citizen White had attempted to fool Bane into thinking he was back in Phaze, by putting him—and Agape—into a setting resembling Phaze, and emulating the magical effects. But he had caught on, because his magic did not operate quite as usual, and the vampire-actors had not correctly identified one of the vampires he named. Then Citizen Purple had hunted them in a setting resembling the Purple Mountains of Phaze, but stocked with robots in the forms of dragons and such. The Citizens were very good at emulations, as their narrow escape from the pseudo-Citizen Blue and Sheen had shown.

"Are you sure this is Phaze?" she asked. "Not another trick?"

He smiled. "I know my living body from Mach's robot body, without doubt," he said. "There be no question in my mind." Then he glanced sharply at her. "But thee, my lovely animal friend—why dost thou ask this?"

He was living flesh, certainly. But was he Bane?

"Please—do some magic," she said. "Just to be sure."

"Gladly, Fleta!" He made an expansive gesture, then sang: "Bring me fare, for the unicorn mare!"

A basket of oats appeared: feed for a horse—or a unicorn. Certainly it was magic—or a clever illusion.

"I am not the unicorn," she said abruptly.

He smiled. "Thou canst hardly fool me, Fleta! I have

known thee long, and sometimes intimately. Who art thou, if not my friend?"

"I am Agape."

He stared at her. "Be thou joking, mare?"

"I am your lover in Phaze. We are hiding from the Contrary Citizens until I can get offplanet and return safely to my home world, Moeba. I don't want to go, but the Citizens want to use me as a hostage against you, so I must flee."

He considered for a moment. Then he asked: "Exactly where were we hiding?"

She started to answer, then stopped. If this was another pretend-Phaze, then he was not Bane, and he was asking not to verify her identity, but to find out where the two of them were. If she told, the Citizens would immediately pounce and take them both captive, and this time they might be unable to win free. "Ask some other question," she said.

"Thou dost doubt me?" he asked, surprised.

"You are doubting me."

He smiled. "Aye. Then tell me aught that Mach could not have told Fleta."

She launched into a detailed description of their recent history before the final hiding: the brownie-baking game, the sex in the gelatin, the rendition of *You Never Can Tell* and their pursuit by the minions of the Contrary Citizens.

"Enough!" he exclaimed. "I be satisfied! Thou art my love! But how came thee here?"

"I am Agape," she agreed. "But how do I know I am in Phaze, or whether you are Bane?"

"But I am flesh, here, in my natural body!"

"Many human folk are flesh, in Proton as well as in Phaze."

"But I conjured feed for thee!" Then he looked embarrassed. "Which thou canst not eat. Unless thou canst change as Fleta can?"

That might be a valid test! Agape concentrated, trying to change form. She could not; her flesh remained firmly human. "I cannot. But that's not the point. Conjurations can be arranged, and other special effects. How do I know that any of this is genuine, or that you are not some Proton actor?"

He nodded gravely. "I could tell thee what we have done in our most intimate moments, and where we were hiding a moment ago, but I think these things could be known to the Contrary Citizens and used to deceive thee. I know I be in Phaze, but thy presence here be strange, and I think I have no way to convince thee of its validity. I understand not its mechanism myself. But I can show thee my world, here, and then mayhap thou willst believe."

"I want no guided tour calculated to persuade me!" she flared. "I love Bane, but I am not at all certain you are he. If you are not he, then you are trying to get information from me that will hurt him or enable his enemies to deceive him in some way." And she turned, ready to walk away.

"Nay, wait, my love!" he cried. "Phaze be dangerous to the uninitiate! Fleta can take care o' herself, but thou couldst get hurt or killed in short order. I cannot let thee go alone!"

"I cannot stay with you, until I'm sure," she said. "And I am not sure."

"I see thy problem," he said. "But I love thee, and cannot send thee into danger. I can protect thee, but I must be with thee."

Uncertainty buffeted her. He did seem exactly like Bane! But so would a clever actor, and if she fell into a trap fashioned by the Contrary Citizens, she could do the real Bane terrible damage. Her only proper course was to resist any blandishments he might make, until and if she was sure of him. The real Bane would understand; a fake one didn't matter. "I must go my own way."

He sighed. "I see the justice in thy position, Agape. But an thou shouldst die—" He shook his head. "I know thou canst not afford to accept new information from me, but I beg thee to listen while I remind thee of what thou dost already know. In that way I may help thee to survive the rigors o' this frame, and if thou be not here, it matters not."

"There is justice in that," she agreed, wishing she could simply hug him and believe him.

"Thou dost now occupy the body of Fleta the Unicorn, whom mine other self Mach loves. She has three forms: human, hummingbird and her natural equine one. She has many friends among the 'corns, weres and vamps. Such as Suchevane." He said the name with special emphasis. "An thou dost go to that person, mayhap thou canst satisfy thyself."

Agape nodded. Suchevane, he had told her before, was the most beautiful of female vampires. The setting of Citizen White had foundered when Suchevane had been identified as a male. Bane was giving her a chance to meet the vampire girl now; he had carefully refrained from identifying her sex.

But the minions of Citizen White could have listened to Bane's prior comment, and learned their mistake. They could be using it now to convince her of the lie. "No."

"Aye," he said sadly. "Then must I leave thee to thine own devices, that thou mayst satisfy thyself of the validity o' this frame, and therefore of mine own validity too. But one thing I needs must ask, that thou accept a spell o' protection, so that thou goest not naked into danger."

"But anything like that would mask the reality of it," she protested. "Exactly as would be required to conceal an artificial setting."

"I know it. But on this must I insist, else must I remain with thee myself. I love thee, and shall not allow thee injury or risk that might be avoided. The spell be this: an invocation thou mayst utter that will make thee fade from the perception of those near thee. When danger threatens, say thy name three times, and it be done. But use it not capriciously, for a given spell be effective only once, and it will protect thee not a second time. An thou try it again, I will perceive the effort and come to thee, and woe betide who chastises thee." Then he sang an invocation of his own, and there was a faint glimmer in the air; that was all.

"Thank you," Agape said, feeling guilty for her intransigence. Yet if this were all an exceedingly artful device, she would be foolish to let it move her.

Bane walked away. Then, at a brief distance, he vanished. He had evidently invoked some other spell, and conjured himself to other parts. Or so it was meant for her to believe.

She was alone with the basket of oats. She was sorry to waste them, but they were in their hulls; it would be a difficult chore to consume them.

Difficult? Perhaps impossible! She seemed to be unable to melt or change her form. She tried it again, with no success.

Wasn't that an indication that she was in a different realm, and a different body? No, not necessarily so; the Citizens could have given her medication to fix her in her present format, as part of the illusion.

Exactly what was her present form? Bane had called her Fleta the Unicorn, but she seemed to be thoroughly human. A mirror would have helped, but even without it she could tell that this was not her normal human semblance. Indeed, it seemed to have fixed flesh, with bones and digestion differing from her own. She wore a black cloak and orange slippers, and had a bony knob set in her forehead. That last detail suggested the unicorn form; it certainly seemed genuine. But surgery could have implanted it.

And, in one pocket, she found a somewhat grimy feather. Why would the unicorn have saved this?

The unicorn? Already she was accepting the appearance as valid! But if this was a Citizen setup, why would they have given her a dirty feather?

Well, she could throw it away. But if she did so, and this really was Phaze, she would be discarding something of evident value to Fleta. That did not appeal. So she repocketed the feather and reconsidered her situation.

She stood not far from the great Purple Mountain range. It really was purple, rising in the southwest. In Proton they were barren peaks; here they were clothed in verdure. She had had some experience in the Purple Adept's mock-up of a section of these mountains, so they seemed familiar. If this were a larger mock-up, perhaps she could discover it by exploring that region of the range.

She started walking. She soon felt hot; the air was warm, and the sun was shining, and the grass was so thick she had to forge through it, so that she was expending energy and heating herself internally. She was tempted to take off the voluminous black cloak so as to let the brief breezes cool her body. Actually, she would feel better without it, because all of her time on Planet Proton had been spent without clothing; she was, here, a serf.

But on Phaze serfs wore clothing. Bane had been clothed. She had been so distracted she had hardly noticed! So nakedness might be an error here. If this really were Phaze.

She didn't know, so after brief consideration, she removed her cloak. She had nothing on beneath it, other than the orange socks; her body was lithe and well formed, and seemed designed to be free of constraint. She walked on, feeling better.

But after a time she felt the heat on her shoulders, and realized that the sunlight was damaging them. Nakedness was a privilege available only to those in protected environments, such as the domes! With regret, she unfolded the cloak and donned it again; it was better to sweat than to burn.

Sweat? She didn't sweat! Moebites dissipated heat by extending thin sheets of flesh to radiate excess calories, and by reducing activity. Only true human beings exuded moisture from their skins for the purpose of cooling. And horses. And androids.

Was she a true human being now? If so, she had to be in Phaze. No—she could be an android in Proton, so that was not definitive.

Yet how could her mind have been transferred to another living body? She was not a robot or cyborg; her mind was a part of her entire physical being, inseparable from the flesh. If she had accompanied Bane to Phaze, it would be an aspect of the exchange; Fleta the Unicorn would now be in Proton with Mach the Robot. But that might be just what the Citizens wanted her to think. Perhaps they did have a technique for transferring consciousness of an android body, perhaps maintaining an electronic link to her natural one. How could she tell the difference? Or they could simply have drugged her and given her hypnotic suggestion, to cause her to dream a programmed dream and believe that her body as she now found it was real. In that case, there would be no real danger to her—but the Citizens might go to extremes to make her think there was danger.

As if on cue, a great hulking shape appeared in the air: some monstrous flying creature. It looked very like a dragon.

Should she try to hide from it, or should she ignore it? If this were a setup, it wouldn't matter. But if this were real, she could be in serious trouble.

She decided to play it safe. She ducked, trying to hide in the high grass.

But the dragon, evidently questing for prey, had already spotted her. It flew directly toward her. It came close, circled her once, then made a strafing run. Fire shot from its mouth, coming straight at her.

She threw herself aside. The fire ignited the grass behind her, and scorched her backside. Indeed, her cloak was burning, and she felt the flame as if it were roasting her own flesh. She threw herself down flat, to roll, to crush the blaze out, but it continued stubbornly.

Meanwhile the dragon was looping about, readying

itself for a second run. This time she knew it would not miss.

Then she remembered the spell that Bane had given her. Maybe it was all part of the fakery, but she would have to use it! "Agape, Agape, Agape!" she cried.

The dragon, orienting on her, hesitated. It peered down, perplexed. It flew over her without firing, then looped back and searched again. It sniffed the air. Then, frustrated, it flew away, trailing a small, angry plume of smoke.

The spell had worked—or had seemed to. The dragon had not been able to see, hear or smell her. But she was perfectly perceivable to herself, and she still cast a shadow. So if the spell was genuine, it operated only on the perceptions of the predator. If it was fake, then the dragon, or dragon mock-up, had simply been feigning.

That fire was real, though! There was a smoldering patch of grass, and her cloak had a hole in it near the pocket. Indeed, the feather had been scorched.

"Who calls? Who calls?" someone screeched.

Agape looked up, startled. It was another flying creature. This one was much smaller, being a gross woman-headed bird. She smelled awful, and had a fright-wig head of hair or feathers. She was a harpy, one of the creatures in the human pantheon.

Was Agape still unperceivable? How long did the spell last?

"I smelled thy signal, but I see thee not!" the harpy screeched. "Where dost thou be?"

Smelled her signal?

The harpy circled. "Damn!" she muttered. "Mayhap the dragon got him, ere the smell of my burned feather reached me!"

Burned feather? That was the signal? If Fleta had kept that feather, knowing it would summon the harpy when burned, that harpy must be a friend.

"Here I am," Agape called, almost before she realized she was doing it.

The harpy whirled in air and peered down at her. "Ah, now I see thee, mare! Glad am I thou wast not hurt! Yet why didst thou summon me, an thou escaped the dragon?"

"The dragon's fire burned the feather," Agape explained.

The harpy screeched so violently with laughter that she practically fell out of the air. "Aye, don't that beat all! An accident! But how camest thou to run afoul o' a dragon? Why not change form to thy natural state and pipe it off?"

This harpy, however gross of humor and person, seemed friendly, so Agape decided to speak frankly. "I am not Fleta. I can't change the way she could."

"Not Fleta?" the harpy screeched, amazed. "How can that be? Thou hast her body, and the feather!"

If this was Phaze, the truth should not hurt. If Proton, it was known already, such as it was. "I am Agape. I exchanged with Fleta. I have her body, but do not know how to use it."

The harpy peered cannily down at her. "It be true thou dost speak not like her. But Mach! Where be Mach?"

"He exchanged too. Now Bane is here."

"Then how came a dragon near? Mach be a burgeoning Adept! He prettified my hair! Next to that, banishing a dragon be mere chick's play, and Bane be more than Mach."

"I sent him away."

The harpy flapped heavily in place, considering that. "Nay, I can make sense not o' that! Why send him off, an thou helpless 'gainst a dragon?"

"So I could learn where I am, by myself."

"Surely thou knowest where thou art! Canst not see the mountains? This be the fringe o' the Harpy Demesnes, and I be queen o' the dirty birds, for now, so long's my hairdo sustain itself. I be Phoebe, befriended by the mare not long agone. There be no mystery here!"

"If you did not know whether you were in a strange

land, or had had a spell cast on you to make you think you were there, what would you do?" Agape asked.

"Why, I'd go out and look!" the harpy screeched. "I'd know soon enough—" Then she paused. "Belike thou hast a point. But thou must chance not Fleta's body to dragons! She will need it when she returns."

"If I had any portion of her abilities, I would use them," Agape said. "But I am not a unicorn; I cannot change forms in her manner."

The harpy came down for a bumpy landing in the grass. "Thou hast her body; thou must needs be able to change."

"I don't know how. On Proton I can change form, but the mechanism differs."

"Mayhap thou dost just need encouragement. Here, take my claw, and when I fly, do thou likewise." She extended a filthy foot.

"But I don't know how to begin!" Agape protested.

"Nonsense, alien lass. Knowing be no part of it. Just *do* it!" She shook her foot invitingly.

Bemused, Agape took hold of the foot. Then Phoebe spread her greasy wings and launched into the air, her dugs bouncing. Agape willed herself to do likewise.

Suddenly she was flapping her own wings. But she was out of control; she went into a tailspin and plunged back to the ground.

"Thou didst it!" Phoebe exclaimed, hovering. "Thou hast her hummingbird form! But why beest thou not flying?"

Agape tried to answer, but all that emerged was a peep.

"Well, change back to girlform and tell me," the harpy said, coming down for another crash landing.

Agape tried, but nothing happened.

"Mayhap I shouldn't've messed. I fear thou art stuck in birdform, and know not how to fly!"

Agape nodded her tiny head affirmatively. Magic was definitely not for novices!

The harpy considered. "It be my fault; I told thee to

try. Needs must I take thee to a shapechanger. The werewolves be not too far, and methinks Fleta has friends among them. Come, bird—let me carry thee there, and we shall see." She reached for Agape.

Agape shied away, suddenly terrified. The claw was huge, larger than her whole present body!

Phoebe paused. "Aye, I see thou be afraid o' me now, and 'tis true my kind preys on thine, or at least on true birds. But I mean thee no harm; remember, I be friend to Fleta."

Agape realized that she had to trust the harpy. She hopped toward her.

Phoebe reached out again, slowly, and closed her claws about Agape's body. That foot could have crushed the life from her, but it did not; it merely tightened to firmness. Then the harpy lurched back into the air.

She flew east, carrying Agape. The air rushed past, though the harpy did not seem like a particularly effective flyer. Probably the flight was boosted by magic. Well, it was one way to travel!

As they moved across the plain, Agape wondered how it was that she had been able to change form from a woman to a hummingbird, instantly. There was a question of mass: the woman had hundreds of times the mass of the bird. Where had it gone? When Agape changed form, in her own body, she never changed mass. Had she sacrificed any significant portion of her mass, she would have lost her identity.

She realized that magic was the only explanation. Magic took no note of the laws of science; it had its own laws. Apparently mass was not a factor. But it was still a strange business!

"Uh-oh," Phoebe screeched under her breath.

Agape twisted her neck, which was marvelously supple, and saw lumbering shapes closing in. More harpies!

"List well, alien," Phoebe said urgently. "My filthy sisters think I've got prey I mean to hide away, so they mean to raid it from me. I can escape them not; must needs I hide thee till they leave off." She swooped low. "Come to none ere I call to thee, for they will snatch thee and chew thy bones in an instant! Now hide, hide!" And she let go.

Agape fell into the grass. It was less than a meter, and she was so small and light that no damage was done. She half flapped, half scrambled on down through the tangle, getting out of sight.

But another harpy had seen her. "Haa!" she screeched, and dived, claws outstretched.

Agape scooted to the side, and the harpy missed. But the ugly bird had not given up; she looped just above the grass and came back, more agile than she looked. "Come here, thou luscious morsel!" she screeched.

Agape tried to scoot away, out of reach, but the harpy loomed over her, about to pounce.

"Mine!" Phoebe screeched, zooming in and colliding with the other, knocking her out of the way. Just in time!

Agape found a mousehole and scrambled down it. She did not like going into darkness under the ground, but it definitely was not safe above!

Then she heard the sound of scratching, or of excavation. A harpy was trying to dig her out!

Fortunately the mouse tunnel had been constructed with exactly such tactics in mind. It branched and curved and extended forever onward. She scooted along it, hoping she didn't encounter the proprietor, leaving the harpy behind. Then she settled down to wait.

When silence returned, she crept back the way she had come. She was not constructed for crawling, but was so small that she could pretty well run two-legged along the tunnel. That was one advantage to tiny size!

"Agape! Agape!" a harpy screeched. "They be gone now. Come to me!"

It was Phoebe! No other harpy would know her true name. Agape made her way out of the tunnel, and gave a peep.

Phoebe spied her. "Ah, 'tis a relief!" she screeched.

"I thought sure I'd lost thee! Come, we must to the weres 'fore else amiss occurs!" She took Agape in her claw again, and lunged into the air.

They reached the Were Demesnes without further event. Three husky wolves veered toward Phoebe the moment they spied her, evidently meaning business. The harpy was tired from her long flight, and could not achieve sufficient elevation to avoid them. Their teeth gleamed.

But her voice was enough. "Halt, weres!" she screeched. "Slay me not, for I bring a friend of thine for help!" She lifted her foot, showing Agape.

One of the wolves became a buxom young woman in a furry halter. "That be Fleta in birdform!" she cried. "What dost filth like thee do with her?"

Phoebe flopped tiredly to the ground. "Bitch, I be friend to Fleta; she cured my tail-itch, and her friend Mach gave me this spectacular hairdo. But this be not the 'corn; she be her other self from Proton-frame, who knows not how to change form. So I brought her to thee, 'cause thou knowest the art o' shape-changing and mayhap can help her."

The young woman reached down to pick Agape up. "Be this true? Thou be not Fleta?"

Agape nodded her beak affirmatively.

"Then mayhap we owe thee, harpy," the woman said. "Choose a tree and roost, and we shall let thee be in peace."

"I thank thee, bitch," Phoebe said. "Do thou help her if thou canst; Fleta will need her body, an she return. This be Agape, an alien creature, but not inimical." Agape realized that the harpy was not being insulting to the werewolf girl; the female of the species was called a bitch.

The girl held Agape up at face level. "I be Furramenin. I talked with thee at the Translucent Demesnes not long ago."

Agape shook her little head no.

Furramenin laughed. "Ah, yes, that be right! It was

Fleta I talked to, not thee! Thou art Agape! Come, let me instruct thee in form-changing. Let me shift to bitch-form, and then do thou take my paw and shift to girl-form with me. Understand?"

Agape nodded yes. The girl set her down.

The wolf reappeared. Agape hopped across to touch a front paw. Then the girl manifested—but Agape remained a bird.

They tried it again, and again, but with no success. "Must needs it be with a flying creature," the woman concluded regretfully.

"Aye, bitch," Phoebe called from the branch she had chosen. "I got her to birdform, but could get her not back."

"Then will I take thee to Fleta's friend Suchevane," Furramenin decided. "In the morning."

Suchevane! Agape knew that name! That was the one the Citizens had not known, whom Bane had recommended.

Then she felt faint, and fell the tiny distance to the ground.

"What be the matter?" Furramenin exclaimed. "Be thou sick?"

"I know, I think," Phoebe screeched from her branch. "She be locked in hummingbird form, and the bird has high metabolism. She has eaten not in hours. She be starving!"

"Of course!" the werebitch agreed. "We must feed her! But what do such birds eat?"

"Nectar, methinks," the harpy replied.

They ranged out and gathered fresh flowers and brought them back. Furramenin held the flowers up for Agape, but she did not know how to eat. Her long bill poked through the delicate petals, getting little nectar.

"This be trouble," Furramenin muttered. "An we could get her to girlform, we could feed her, but she may starve before we succeed!"

They consulted with the Pack leader, who it seemed was a wolf named Kurrelgyre, who told them to take her to the vampires and the Red Adept. "Start now, tonight," he said.

So it was that Agape found herself tied to the back of a running wolf, moving rapidly through the night. She was too weak to react, but was conscious, except when she slept. The motion continued interminably, across what she took to be plains, and through what seemed to be forest, and past some dark river. Furramenin seemed indefatigable in her bitchform, but Agape could tell by the lather that leaked from the corner of her mouth that she was straining.

She faded out, and in, and it was morning. Then out, and in again, and it was deep into day, and they were arriving at the caves of the vampires.

There must have been dialogue and explanations, but Agape was too far gone to assimilate them. She was in the process of dying; she knew it. Her foolish attempt to go out on her own had led her inevitably to harm. It was hard to disbelieve that she was in Phaze, now, but it was too late; her belief no longer mattered.

She woke briefly to find herself in the air again, carried by a larger creature. Phoebe? No, the smell was not the same. Then she faded out again.

4

Fleta

The world shimmered, and she felt an ineffable change. Then things steadied, and she found herself still in Mach's embrace.

But it was different. She looked up at him—and his face had changed. It was similar to its normal configuration, but somehow less flexible. His arms, also, were somehow less yielding.

She glanced to the side, and discovered that they were in a chamber. What had happened to the field?

"The exchange has been accomplished," he said. "We had better disengage."

He still sounded like Mach! But this was definitely not the same body. Now she noticed that their clothes were gone, too. "Where be we?" she asked.

"In an office maintained by a Citizen, he informed me. Citizen Tan, I think." Then he drew away from her, surprised. "But you already know that, Agape."

She was startled. "I be Fleta!"

His startlement mirrored her own. Then he laughed. "Don't tease me like that, Agape! I love her."

"Tease thee? I tease thee not! What magic hast thou wrought, Bane, to conjure us so swiftly here?"

He gazed at her, evidently sorting things out. Then he spoke slowly and carefully. "This is the frame of Proton. I am Mach, a self-willed humanoid robot. Are you telling me you are not Agape, but Fleta of Phaze?"

"Aye, I be Fleta of Phaze," she repeated. "If this truly be Proton-frame, and thou truly be Mach, then must I ha' traveled here with thee. Be that possible?"

Again he considered. Then he touched his bare chest, and a door opened in it, showing odd wires and objects. "I am the robot, as you can see; this is my own body, not Bane's." He closed the door, and his chest looked normal again. "Let me question you briefly. Who was the last person we met, on the way to the exchange?"

"Phoebe," she said promptly. "The harpy whose hair thou didst ruin, and she takes it as elegance. But she be decent, especially for her kind. I have her feather in my pocket—" But her hand found no pocket, for she had lost her cloak.

"And then we made love," he said.

"Nay, we followed the delf till the glow was brightest, and only kissed, and then—"

"Then, as I sang the spell of exchange—"

"I spake thee the triple Thee, as thou didst do when—"

He stepped into her and crushed her in his embrace. "You *are* my love!" he said. "I tested you, but no other person could have known—"

"This really be thy rovot form?" she asked uncertainly.

"It really is. But let me prove myself to you, so that you know you can trust me. I came for you in a canoe I fashioned to float in air, with Suchevane, the most dazzling of vampires, and saved you from your suicide. Then the Translucent Adept appeared, and offered us sanctuary, and the splash of truth supported him, so I agreed—"

She put a finger against his lips. "It be enough, Mach; I know thee now. Methinks in my desire to stay with thee, I worked a bit of magic of mine own, and came with thee to thy frame."

"A double exchange!" he said, awed. "You are in Agape's body."

She looked down at herself. "Aye, this nor looks nor feels like mine! Let me see whe'er I can revert to natural state." She tried to shift to her unicorn form, but nothing happened. "It happens not."

"You cannot change that way, here," Mach said. "Magic doesn't work in Proton. The laws of science are enforced; mass must remain constant. When Agape changes, she does so slowly, melting from one shape to another."

"Melting?" Fleta asked, repelled.

He smiled. "I suspect Agape finds your method of changing form awkward, too!" Then he made a soundless whistle. "And she must be there, with Bane! Experiencing magic for the first time!"

"In *my* body?" Fleta asked, disturbed.

"I'm sure she'll try to treat it as well as you treat hers," he said with a smile.

She relaxed. "Mayhap 'tis fair. But this body—I want to be locked not in human form fore'er! How does it work?"

"I can't tell you directly, because I have had no experience in it, or in any living body other than Bane's. She just melted and reformed. Here, maybe we can do it small-scale first, so you can discover the technique." He took her left hand. "Concentrate on this, and try to turn it into a hoof."

She tried. Her instant change did not exist, but gradually the outlines of her fingers softened. Then they sagged into each other, and melted together. Then they assumed the form of a hoof, and the nails expanded and fused to make it hard.

She looked at the rest of her. "I be girlform—w' one hoof!" she said, amazed.

"So you can do it," he said warmly. "But for now, I think it is best to maintain your human form. I gather from what Bane thought to me that we are two serfs serving in this office, and the Citizen does not know our identities. We had best keep it that way, for if Citizen Tan is the same as the Tan Adept, we could be in serious trouble!"

"The Tan Adept," she repeated, chagrined. "He o' the Evil Eye."

"The evil eye? That's his magic?"

"Aye."

"Exactly how does that work?"

"We know not, save that it makes others do his will."

"I think we are lucky that magic is inoperative here; the Tan Adept cannot affect us that way. Still, we should take no avoidable risks. I had better drill you in office procedures—which I fear will make little sense to you, at first."

"They make no sense to me already," she admitted.

"The first thing to do is conceal your Phaze mode of speech. That would give you away in the first few seconds. Can you speak as I do, if you try?"

She giggled. "I can try. But thou dost—you do speak so funny, mayhap—I may burst out laughing."

"It isn't funny for Proton. Look, Fleta, this may be a matter of life and death." He paused, reconsidering. "I had better call you Agape, too, so *I* don't give you away."

"At times you are idiotic," she said carefully.

"What?"

"Are we not in hiding? Call me Agape, and Tan will know instantly I be his prey."

He knocked his head with the heel of his hand. "There must be a gear loose in my circuitry! You're right! We surely have artificial names!"

"Yes," she said, in her measured way, resisting the urge to say "Aye." "Can we find out those names?"

"Have to." He went out to the desk in an adjacent chamber. "There have to be records." He activated the desk screen and spoke to it: "List authorized office personnel."

Words came on:

PROPRIETOR: CITIZEN TAN
EMPLOYEES: TANIA—SUPERVISOR—HUMAN
AGEE—DESK GIRL—ANDROID
MAC—MENIAL—HUMANOID
ROBOT

"There it is," he said. "You are Agee, and I am Mac. Evidently they set us up with names as close to our own as feasible, so we would identify more readily." He smiled. "Your name means 'One who flees'; that seems appropriate in the circumstance."

But she was staring at the screen. "I am glad Bane taught me to read your language," she said, with the same measured care. "This magic slate is fascinating. But—"

"It's called a screen," he said. "You simply tell it what you want, and read its answers. It is simple enough for an idiot to operate, because most androids are idiots. When you encounter something you don't understand, you should just smile and look blank, and it will be dismissed as android incompetence."

"That, too," she agreed. "But—Mac—what of Tania?"

"If she comes to the office, you just do whatever she tells you to do. Androids must always obey humans, outside of the experimental community. Evidently she doesn't bother to come in much; this office must still be on standby status. We're just caretakers."

"Tania," she said carefully, "is the Tan Adept's daughter. Stile was minded to marry Bane to her, but feared she would dominate him with her evil eye."

Mach stared at her. "And this is parallel!" he exclaimed. "Of course she has access to this office! If she comes in, we're in trouble!"

"That were my thought," she said.

He addressed the screen again. "Status of Tania."

The screen answered: TANIA—SISTER OF CURRENT CITIZEN TAN, DAUGHTER OF FORMER CITIZEN TAN, RETIRED. EMPLOYED BY HER

BROTHER AS RANKING SERF. DESIGNATED AS HEIR TO TAN CITIZENSHIP.

"That's her, all right," he said. "Her brother inherited the Citizenship, so she is the next in line, should he retire or die. That was evidently fixed by their father. She will be very like a Citizen, in all but legality." He glanced up. "Bane was going to *marry* her?"

"They want an heir to the Blue Demesnes," she said. "Tan wanted a suitable match, too. She is about four years older, but is pretty if you like that type."

Mach glanced at the picture of Tania the screen showed. The average man would like that type.

"And if they married, the Blue Demesnes would have its heir, and the Adverse Adepts would have a permanent hold on Stile," Mach said. "I can see why Bane balked!"

She smiled. "He never saw her. He refused to get close to her, because of the evil eye."

"Smart person, my other self. Let's just hope she doesn't show up here."

Mach drilled her on office etiquette. He evidently hoped that there would be no calls to this office soon, but at least she was minimally prepared.

She saw him looking at her. His body and features were different, as were her own, but she knew that look. "Dost thou wish to make love, thy way?" she asked quietly.

He sighed. "I do. But it occurs to me that though it may be known that Bane and I have exchanged back, it may not be known that you and Agape exchanged also. Therefore it would seem that I am with the wrong female, and if I wish to be consistent, I will not make love to her."

"But who will know?" she asked.

"That's the irony: perhaps no one. But just as you must adopt the speech of this frame to conceal your identity, I think I must adopt a loyalty to an inapplicable principle, to further conceal your identity. We shall have enough trouble hiding from the Contrary Citizens, without adding to it this way."

"But be they not the analogues o' the Adverse Adepts, whom we have joined?" she asked.

"Yes. But we are now standing in for Bane and Agape, who have not joined them. The truce is a compromise that leaves us in the Adepts' hands, and Bane and Agape in Citizen Blue's hands. I'm trusting Bane not to interfere with that situation in Phaze, and I shall not interfere with it in Proton. I think that is the equitable course."

"It all be too complicated for me," she said. Then, reverting to the local dialect: "I need some rest."

"Rest," he agreed. "I don't need it, in this body."

"For my mind, not my body," she clarified. "I deal not—I don't deal in alien frames every morning."

"I will see what else I can learn of our situation."

"What will you do?"

"I will activate a circuit within myself to ensure that no electronic device can spy on me without alerting me, and another to give me access to a secret connection via the phone."

"This must I—" She broke off and tried again. "I must see this."

Soon he had it. "This is Mach," he said to the screen, and gave a code sequence that identified him. "What is my status?"

"Citizens are canvassing the city," a self-willed machine replied. "They seek the alien woman, not you. They have narrowed it down to this sector, and will close in on you within three days."

"What is the contingency plan?"

"We have a chute with meshed valves, for liquid wastes; the alien must melt and flow down that, and we shall convey her to the Tourney, which commences in six days."

"The Tourney? She is not qualified for that!"

"She must enter and lose. She will then be required to depart the planet, without interference."

"Now I understand," he said. "The Contrary Citizens cannot hire a Tourney loser, and cannot prevent that loser from departing the planet unless there is a question of a crime to settle. Any such charge against Agape would put her under the authority of the courts, which also would protect her from them. This is a practically foolproof way to get her safely offplanet and back to Planet Moeba, where the Citizens have no power. All that is necessary is to keep you hidden until the Tourney begins, and qualify you for it; thereafter you will be safe. Obviously Citizen Blue, my father, has taken a hand and acted effectively to save Agape and his own position."

"What is the Tourney?" Fleta asked, confused.

"An annual tournament whose first prize is Citizenship. It is run by the Game Computer, by the rules of the Game. It is very popular with serfs, though all losers are deported."

"Like the Unilympics?" she asked.

"The what?"

"A big contest for status. Each species has its own: the Werelympics, the Vamplympics, the Elflympics—"

"Maybe so." He frowned. "But the Citizens are liable to locate you in two days. That leaves a gap of three. Also, you are unqualified for the Tourney. Theoretically you would have those three days to qualify; if you fail, or if the Citizens capture you in that period, all will be lost."

She realized that Agape, with her lively intellect and special powers of adaptation, might have found a way to qualify. Fleta, in Agape's body, would hardly have a chance. This unexpected exchange of the two females could prove to be extremely costly!

Still, now they knew the challenge: get her through to the Tourney, and get her qualified. If they accomplished that, she would be shipped to the completely alien Planet Moeba.

And what would she do there? She had only vague

knowledge of Proton, and none of Moeba. Even success was disaster!

Mach pondered, and told her that he would have to modify the plan in one detail. He would have to get Fleta exchanged back to Phaze before she was exiled to Moeba. That meant he had to locate Bane, and intercept him, and catch him in the company of Agape, and bring Fleta in for another exchange. He was sure the girls could not exchange unless the effort was made in the company of the boys. It seemed an almost impossible act of juggling, considering the pursuit by the Contrary Citizens and the demands of the Tourney, but somehow he had to manage it. Because however he might be constrained to act personally, Fleta was the creature he loved, and he could not allow her to suffer exile to a completely alien world, with no prospect of return to her homeland.

"Aye," she whispered, loving his determination though she hated the threat that hung over her.

"I have accepted sanctuary with the Adverse Adepts, in Phaze, for the sake of our love. If I had no other way, I would seek similar sanctuary with the Contrary Citizens. But integrity requires that I make every other effort first, before giving the Citizens the complete victory they seek."

"Aye," she agreed again. Now at last she could relax.

Except for another problem: food. This was morning, and her body was hungry. Fleta had no idea how to operate the food dispenser, and no idea how to make Agape's body eat. Mach could operate the food machine, but when she took food into her mouth, she discovered that she had no mechanism for swallowing; indeed, she had no throat. The body possessed a bellows mechanism for the inhalation and exhalation of air, for which the amoebic body had a need similar to that of the human body. Thus her chest rose and fell naturally, and she could speak normally. But that was all; she had no internal digestive system.

"She dissolves herself and covers the food," Mach

explained somewhat lamely. "When she's done, she reforms her head and face."

"Yuck," Fleta said.

"Maybe you could dissolve the inside of your mouth, so you could digest a bite of food there, and then reform tongue and teeth afterward."

"If I can't see it, I doubt I can get it right," she said. "I had better stick to what I have."

"Maybe your feet, then. Dissolve them over the food, where no one else can see, and take your time."

She tried that. He brought a bowl of mush, and she sat at the desk and put her feet on the mush. Soon they melted into shapelessness, and spread over the mush. Her flesh seemed to know what to do; she felt the effort of digestion and assimilation, and then the vigor of new energy traveling through her body. It was working!

When the mush was gone, she concentrated on reforming her feet, shaping them back into humanoid extremities. She had a fair idea how to do this, because of her practice in learning the human form as a unicorn. In due course her feet had been restored, and it was even possible to walk on them again. It seemed that Agape's body had a design for bones and flesh, or the equivalent, and this was what she was drawing on.

That problem had been solved. Now she should be able to function. She sat at the desk and began her day's work.

They were fortunate: no one came to the office that day, and there were no calls. Mach was able to brief her on many further details, so that she was beginning to feel halfway competent. It was true: an idiot—or a unicorn—could fill this position. She also developed better facility in eating, and learned how to eliminate by forming a ball of wastes inside, then softening her flesh to let it pass outside at the appropriate time and location.

But the effort had wearied her. By day's end, she was eager to sleep.

She lay down to sleep. But as soon as she relaxed, she started to melt. Alarmed, she reformed herself and approached Mach. "I'm melting! I can't sleep—I might dissolve away!"

He smiled reassuringly. "That's why there is no camera coverage in that chamber; the machines saw to it that Bane and Agape were sent to an office that did not yet have full equipment. Agape is an amoeba; her natural form is a blob of protoplasm. Only when she is awake can she maintain humanoid form. Do not be concerned; you can reform when you wake."

"But I be not sure I can find this exact shape again!" she wailed.

"I think the body has memory devices that enable it to return to prior forms, just as you have them for your unicorn forms. I will inform you of any deviance."

"But what if I melt into the bed?"

"I don't believe that will happen. Your surface retains its skin, which contains the fluids. Also, I suspect that the amoeboid form does not relinquish consciousness completely; it probably shores up its surface at need, to prevent seepage. Human beings perform similarly in sleep, not falling off beds and not releasing urine during sleep. Maintenance circuitry."

Moderately reassured, she returned to the bed and let herself dissolve. Sure enough, she neither flowed off the bed nor released fluids into it as she slept. She woke after a few hours, refreshed.

Next day the worst happened: Tania stopped by the office. She was a buxom woman of about twenty-one, her somewhat plain face enhanced by an artful framing of luxurious hair. She was technically a serf, so was naked, but she carried herself as if clothed.

Mach stood absolutely still, a machine out of action, in an alcove in the wall. Fleta was at the desk, where she belonged; it was her duty to handle whatever tasks were required, such as providing information about the location of her employer, Citizen Tan. Fleta was of course aware of Tania's identity; the woman had given it for admission to the office, and she matched her picture.

Tania eyed Fleta. Her eyes possessed a peculiar intensity; obviously in Phaze that would manifest as the evil eye. "Any news?" she asked curtly.

"No, Tania," Fleta said, as Mach had told her.

The woman eyed her. Her eyes were the color of her hair and nails: tan. "Android, you will address me as Tan."

"Yes, Tan," Fleta said obediently. Mach had warned her that this woman might be imperious, and that though she could not be addressed as "sir" she probably wished she could be. She knew from her own knowledge of Adepts in Phaze that the utmost caution was in order.

"Stand, android," Tania snapped. "Come in front of the desk where I can see you."

Fleta stood and went around to the front. Serfs were not supposed to answer Citizens unless an answer was called for, and Tania was to be treated like a Citizen.

"Turn around."

Fleta turned, while the woman's eyes probed her body. "You aren't very intelligent," Tania remarked.

Fleta was tempted to reply that most animals weren't, but stifled it. Mach had explained that she was passing for an android, and that few androids approached the human level of mental performance.

"What is the nature of ultimate reality?" Tania asked.

Fleta stared at her, needing no effort to feign confusion. She smiled and looked blank in the approved manner. "Should I ask the screen, Tan?" she asked at last.

"Don't bother, android." Tania glanced around the office. "Robot, come forth," she commanded.

Mach stepped out from his alcove, silently. She eyed him as she had Fleta.

"Have you kept this office clean?"

"Yes," he said.

"Did you hear me tell the android to call me Tan?"

"Yes."

"Well?"

Mach didn't answer. Fleta had to suppress a giggle; he was playing dumb. Tania had not asked a comprehensible question, so he hadn't answered.

"Address me as Tan," she said coldly. "Is that a functional penis?"

"In what manner, Tan?"

"Sexual."

"Yes, Tan."

"What's it doing on a menial?"

"Whatever my employer directs, Tan."

"Android," Tania snapped without turning. "Put in for a replacement menial robot. This one's too smart."

Oops, trouble! If they replaced Mach, how would she get by? But she had no choice. She returned to the desk, sat, and addressed the screen. "Requisition replacement menial rovot for Citizen Tan, this office," she said, perversely pleased that she had managed the strange formula without hesitation.

"Requisition entered," the screen replied. "Allow forty-eight hours for delivery."

Tania was already on the way out. In a moment they were alone again.

Mach said nothing. He simply marched back to his alcove and resumed his inert stance. By that signal Fleta knew that it was not safe to talk. He knew when they could be overheard; she depended on his judgment.

She had passed Tania's inspection, but Mach had not! What an irony! Then she had to stifle another giggle: irony for a metal man! But she was not happy.

But as she pondered the matter further, she realized that the Contrary Citizens were closing in, and so there would be trouble within two days anyway. This might make no difference. They would have to get away from here before Mach's replacement came.

She finished out the day, answering the occasional incoming calls in the routine manner: Yes, this was Citizen Tan's office. No, the Citizen was not available at the moment. Yes, she would enter a message for the Citizen, and he would return the call if he wished to. When she was hungry, she ordered Mach to fetch her food from the food machine. As an android she ranked the robot, and naturally used every bit of what little authority she possessed. This nicely concealed the fact that she still had no idea how to use the food machine. Mach had set that up, too. She wished she could hug him. Instead she set some food on the desk, and took a careful bite, so as to seem to be eating normally; the rest she put on the floor, so she could melt her feet over it.

Proton was a dreary frame! No wonder Mach liked Phaze better!

In the evening, when the office officially shut down for the shift, Mach came out. He checked to be sure they were not being spied on, then opened his arms. She hurled herself gratefully into them. "Methinks the boredom be the worstest torture o' all!" she whispered.

"You did well," he murmured. "I only hope Tania didn't notice your one slip."

She felt a chill. "Slip?"

"You referred to me as a 'rovot.' The screen has an interpretation circuit, so passed it through because of the context; you were merely echoing her command, which it had heard. But if she noticed—"

"Ro-bot," she said. "Ro-bot, ro-bot. I can say it if I try. But is that an error Agee would make?"

"No. Since there should be no suspicion that you are here, instead of Agee, and that is not typical of her speech, it should pass unnoticed. Actually, you passed the real test: Tania knew that if you had any emotional attachment to me, you would have had trouble putting through that requisition. You showed no hesitation."

"I dared not hesitate," she said. "But oh, Mach—"

"This may have been a routine verification," he said. "But the Citizens are looking for us, and we were assigned within the key period. It could have been a preliminary to the pounce."

"The pounce?"

"If you were looking desperately for a person, and suspected that that person was already in your power, would you alert that person?"

"Nay."

"The threat to replace me could even be a diversion. They want me with them, not away from them. But you are the real target; if they have you, they have me. You must be the one to escape. I must show you how to incapacitate a human being, and how to melt and reform."

They worked on it. He pointed out the vulnerable places on the human body, male and female: the spots that could be pressured to bring pain or unconsciousness or death. "If I give the word, you do that to whoever bars your way," he said. "Then get to this waste chute and melt into it as fast as you can."

They drilled on melting, until she could do it with fair swiftness. She practiced moving in the melted state: flowing like goo across the floor, then reforming into something that could climb. "The self-willed machines will help you at the other end, but you have to get through that screen yourself," he said. "Remember: wait for my signal, then act without question when I give it. Have no concern about me; I am not threatened. Trust the machines. Their forms vary widely, but they are with me. I am a self-willed machine."

"Aye," she agreed, frightened.

Next day Citizen Tan himself stopped by, in the voluminous tan cloak or robe that identified him as a Citizen: a member of the only class privileged to wear clothing in Proton. He was the same age as his sister—they were twins—and similar of feature, especially in the eyes. Their tan irises and intensity were eerie. Fleta was afraid of him. Did he suspect her nature, either as Agape or as Fleta? If so, they were lost!

The Citizen asked a number of routine questions. He seemed gentler than his sister, but there was a sureness about his manner that continued to strike alarm in her. What was he up to?

Then, abruptly, she found out. He reached out to catch and squeeze one of her breasts. "Android, I like your look," he said. "Enter the sleeping chamber with me."

She followed him into the chamber where the bed was.

"Lie supine, spread your legs," he said, as he opened his robe. Then, to Mach in the other room: "Robot! Come here and take my robe."

Mach entered the room and took the robe. He stepped back, watching the proceedings, showing no expression.

Serfs had no rights with respect to Citizens; she had known that as a bit of otherframe folklore all her life. Just as animals had none with respect to Adepts. Power made the only law. But how could she tolerate this? He was going to use her sexually!

If she protested, she would give herself away. If she did not, what would Mach—or Bane—do?

But Mach had told her to wait for his signal before acting. She had to rely on his judgment. She lay down on her back and spread her legs.

It was another irony, she thought, that the sexual act as human beings performed it had no inherent meaning for either her or Agape. She normally would indulge in it only when in heat, for the sole purpose of breeding; only her association with Mach had educated her to the joys of sex as an act of entertainment or of love. Agape, with her completely alien body, would neither breed nor entertain herself in this manner; she surely did it only to please Bane. But now it was a matter of principle: this act should be done only with the one she loved. That, too, was the human way.

Naked, Tan sat beside her, running his hands along her body and up between her legs. "If you like it, I will make you a household serf," he said. "Your body has a certain distinction from that of other androids. I am not sure exactly what it is. That is what intrigues me about you. Would you like to be a household serf?"

This was a direct question, and required an answer. "No, sir," she said.

A tan eyebrow elevated in supposed surprise. "Why not? It is an exceptionally easy life, for an android."

"I am not that kind of android."

Now his gaze became so intense that she was sure he had penetrated her disguise. "Exactly what kind of android are you, Agee?"

She had no answer she could give to that without giving herself away, so she did not answer.

"Well, let's give you more experience on which to base your attitude," Citizen Tan said. He climbed onto the bed, on hands and knees, his body above hers. "Now you will, regardless of whatever personal reactions you may or may not have, smile and emulate delight as I proceed." He lowered himself.

Mach stepped forward, starting to speak. He froze.

"Ah yes, the robot," Citizen Tan said. "Tried to act on its own, and got zapped by the shorting field I just turned on. So it's self-willed, and quite possibly the one we seek." He glanced down at Fleta. "But are you the female we seek? If so, this will be a special pleasure for me. I have never before indulged with an alien creature." He resumed his positioning, about to proceed with the act.

Fleta decided that Mach must have been about to give the signal, before the field enchanted his body. That meant it was time for her to act.

She melted the flesh of her central region. In fact, she had started to do this before consciously making her decision, for the process was well along now. The Citizen's probing member encountered only mush. Then that mush rose up and gripped adjacent and very vulnerable flesh.

Tan opened his mouth to scream, as that grip closed. But Fleta slapped a hand across his mouth, and melted it to cover the lower part of his face. "An thou dost say anything, Adept, then will I squeeze, hard," she whispered, and gave him a small sample. This was a pretty good body, for special effects!

Tan's eyes glazed with pain. Fleta continued to melt. "Lie down, roll over," she said.

He dropped on her and rolled over, carrying her around so that she was now on top of him. As she melted, her flesh spread across and around him. Only her head remained humanoid. "Turn off thy magic field."

When he hesitated, she began to squeeze again.

"I'm free," Mach said. "We're off-camera here, but those in the front chamber remain operational, and you must pass through that. Form into his robe and make him take you there."

She obeyed without question, knowing that only he understood the nature of the magic that surrounded them. She spoke once more to the Citizen: "I will become thy robe. Carry me to the waste chute and dump me there. Else will I squeeze. An thou do it right, thou willst be free o' me. An thou balk, then will I kill thee, caring naught for my fate thereafter, for it be anyway sealed. Dost understand?"

The Citizen nodded. Then she melted her head, and spread herself over Tan's body, and changed her color, becoming tan. She was getting good at this!

"Longer, with folds," Mach murmured.

She thinned herself and lengthened herself, until she matched the length of his original robe. Then, as the man sat up, she flowed around to fill in the back. But she never released her constriction around his generative parts. Her freedom and life were at stake, and this was the other self of an Adept; she knew she could afford no error at all.

Tan walked to the other room. Fleta could no longer see or hear, because she had melted her eyeballs and ears, but she could feel the orientation and motion of his body, and she knew that Mach was following, a nominally servile robot, actually making sure nothing went wrong. She had to trust that the Citizen dumped her correctly.

Tan reached down and lifted the hem of her substance. She let herself be lifted, like flexible material. She finally had to relinquish control of his nether anatomy, but she tightened her closure around his neck so that he could feel it. She could still hurt him, and he knew it.

She was being stuffed into the hopper; she could feel its cool metal. She melted, letting her substance flow down inside it. She had a head start, because of the form she had assumed; the melting was swift. When all of her was in the chute except the neck circlet and one "sleeve," she released the neck but tightened about the arm, sliding down to encircle and grip the fingers, bracing them apart. She could break them if she chose. This body was completely malleable, but when it formed bonelike sections, they were strong enough to exert considerable force.

Finally there was nothing left of the connection except the hand. All the rest of her was a liquid string. She had already negotiated the mesh; it was no trouble in her present state. She let go the hand and slid down and away.

If the Citizen then sprang into action, she didn't know. Mach remained in his power, but she knew that without her as hostage, they could not make him cooperate, they could only kill him, or whatever it was they did to golems. To rovots. Ro-*b*ots! She hoped he was correct that they would not do that.

Now she was in free fall down the chute. It became a pipe, with a blast of air to carry its contents along. If it led to a furnace to burn the garbage—

Then she slurped into a tub. The moment she was all in, something moved it, carrying it elsewhere. She was being loaded into a motorized vehicle; she felt the vibrations. Then she accelerated; it was taking her very swiftly to somewhere else.

Mach had told her to trust the machines. She was trusting them, but she hoped there was no error!

The acceleration eased, but vibration continued; she was still traveling. It was hard for her to judge time while in this state, and she didn't dare shape into another form until told to; she knew that the machines were hiding her from what was bound to be a determined search by the Contrary Citizens. She did form a masked eye, so she could perceive light and vague outlines, and a masked ear, so she could hear somewhat, in case the machines addressed her.

The tub slowed, then stopped. It lurched, evidently being loaded somewhere. Then it was still.

Was it time to emerge? How could she know? She formed a pseudopod—this body was really quite versatile, as she learned its capabilities!—so that she could peer out.

She made an eyeball on the end of the pseudopod, and peered through a vent in the top of her container. All she saw was other containers, similar to her own. She started to extend her eye farther, so as to see more.

"Unsafe," a voice said immediately. "Wait. Hide."

She dissolved the pseudopod and settled down. If the Citizens were tracing the possible routes of her shipment from the waste chute, it would be dangerous to manifest now. They must have her stored in a warehouse, until the search passed. She would be lost among all the sludge containers. That was good.

She had nothing to do, so explored her own parameters further. She discovered that there were patterns in her memory for a number of set forms, and that she could fairly readily modify these for specific effects. Thus she could emulate a human being, the pattern being for the form she had found herself in when she exchanged to Proton, but could also change that form so that she remained human but did not resemble the original form. She could become almost anyone, if she had a representation to copy from.

Agape was very like a unicorn, slower in her changes,

and limited to a fixed mass, but more versatile within that mass. Of course Fleta preferred her own body—but here in Proton, the amoeba body might be better.

Time passed, and nothing happened. She grew bored, and then sleepy. This was actually the sleep format of this body, and this time she didn't have to worry about melting off the bed.

She was awakened by the resumption of motion. She started to stir. "Remain quiescent," a machine voice ordered.

She did so, but was alert. Her container was loaded onto another vehicle, which then moved a short distance and stopped. She was unloaded and wheeled to yet another chamber.

Then at last the directive came: "Form into humanoid semblance."

She invoked the process of human body formation, which included the hardening of columns of flesh into the equivalent of bones and joints and the development of the key apparati of perception and communication, as well as the humanoid skin tones. Agape must have worked hard to develop this pattern, and had done an excellent job! Fleta never would have been able to do it, had she had to develop the pattern herself. Soon she stood as Agee, the office android.

She was in another warehouse chamber, much like the prior one, alone.

"Modify to male," the speaker said. It was a grill set in the ceiling.

Fleta spluttered as the import registered. "Male?"

"Affirmative."

She had never thought of such a thing! But she realized that probably the pursuing Citizens had not thought of it either. She discovered that there was a pattern for humanoid male, so she invoked it.

Her breasts shrank, until they were mere nipples set in her chest. Her hips melted and reformed, contracted. Her genital region became jelly, then drooped. It formed a penis and scrotum, neither functional, but similar externally to those of male serfs. Her shoulder-length mane shrank into briefer tonsure.

"Modify to this image," the grill said. An image formed in the air before her, of an unfamiliar man.

She studied the details of the man, changing her configuration to match. The hair was yellow, the body slender and tall, the chest hairy, the eyes blue.

"Less buttock," the grill said.

Oh. She worked on that region, shrinking the dual masses further.

"Follow the line to the Game Annex," the grill said.

"But where is Mach?" she asked. "I need his advice!"

"Mach is being watched. You must qualify alone. You will be secure as long as your identity is not suspected. If you qualify for the Tourney, you will be secure until you are eliminated."

And thereafter, if she returned directly to Moeba. Theoretically. She hoped Mach intercepted her before that happened!

She walked along the line. It led her from the warehouse and through a passage and into a concourse where other serfs walked. They were following lines too; it seemed that this was a standard way to show them where to go, as they went to the Game Annex.

She remembered the Lympics of Phaze, in which the various major species competed for honors. She had hoped to enter the Unilympics, for she was fleet of foot, and also could play her horn well. She had been working on a duet with herself, accompanied by an intricate hoof-tap pattern, that she thought could be a contender in the marching music division. But now, in Proton, in an alien culture and an alien body, none of that applied.

If she won entry to the Tourney, she would in time find herself confined to the alien planet. If she lost, she could be caught and tortured by the Contrary Citizens, to make Mach do their will. Or Bane, because they thought she was Bane's love; they already had Mach's cooperation, if they but knew it. What a complicated confusion!

She arrived at the Annex. Her line led to a console. A young man stood at the other side: her assigned opponent.

He reached over, extending his hand. "Hi! I'm Shock. My hair, you know." He gave his dark mass of head hair a shake, so that it fell across his face, then flipped it back out of the way.

She took the hand, remembering how human beings clasped digits in greeting. She concentrated on the correct dialect, so as not to give her origin away. "Hi. I'm Fleta."

Then, stunned, she realized what she had said.

But the other seemed not to have noticed. "Welcome to the Leftover Ladder. I'm second from the bottom. I love the Game, but I'm no good at it, so I'm easy to beat."

"Ladder?" she asked, still appalled by her slip.

"Oh, you new here? From another world?"

"New," she agreed. "From another world." Both quite true, but not the way he would take it.

Shock grinned. "Say, that's great! I'm a Koloform myself. Well, I mean my folks came from Kolo, so it's my blood. I was born here, but I can only stay till I'm twenty-one, next year, you know. Then I'm either a serf, or I have to go to Kolo. What're you?"

"A unicorn," she said.

She had done it again!

"I never heard of that planet!" he said cheerfully. "But what do I know? There's thousands of planets. Well, c'mon, let's play before the next pair need the console."

"Yes," she agreed.

Her screen had words printed:

PLAYER ONE: SHOCK OF KOLO
PLAYER TWO: FLETA OF UNI

Below was a sample grid. He had the numbers, she the letters. Mach had explained this, but still it was confusing. She had to pick something she thought would get her into a game she could win.

Her choices were A. NAKED B. TOOL C. MACHINE D. ANIMAL.

That was easy enough! The only thing she really understood was ANIMAL: being one herself. She touched D.

Shock was still making up his mind, for though her column highlighted, none of his numbered rows did. That gave her a chance to look around.

She hadn't paid attention to her surroundings; she had just followed the line in. She saw that she was in one of a number of open chambers, each of which contained a console, and most of the consoles had players standing by them. Many folk were playing this peculiar game! But that might be because they were doing what she was supposed to do, qualifying for the Tourney. Mach had said that only the top ten in each age group, among the males and the females, would qualify. So now they were trying to get into the top tens.

She realized that that must be what the ladder was for. Shock had mentioned a ladder, that he was near the bottom of. A ladder was a thing that human folk used to climb up onto higher places. So she was trying to get on the ladder, starting near the bottom, which was the way with ladders.

But how was she to get to the top, if she had to win games against experienced players to climb each rung? The Tourney was only a few days away, and even if she could win every game, there would hardly be time for them all!

A row illuminated. Shock had finally made his choice. It was 1. PHYSICAL. The two highlights overlapped at 1D.

Then the 1D square expanded to fill the screen. ANIMAL-ASSISTED PHYSICAL appeared across the top, and new sets of choices appeared. This time she had the numbers, and he had the letters.

She looked at her choices: 5. SEPARATE 6. IN-

TERACTIVE 7. COMBAT 8. COOPERATIVE. She wasn't certain how these applied, but the safest seemed to be the first, because it seemed to mean that she could do her own thing. She touched it.

Again she had played ahead of Shock. That encouraged her, though it might be that he was making more intelligent choices. His options were E. EARTH F. FIRE G. GAS H. H_2O, whatever those meant.

When he chose, it was E: EARTH—FLAT SURFACE. So that was it: Earth, as in a plain someone could run on. That was fine with her; unicorns understood running room.

The 1D5E square expanded to fill the screen, and a new, slightly smaller lattice appeared, with nine squares. Down the right side was a list of activities.

Shock whistled. "I don't know how to do any of these things!" he exclaimed. "Well, let's see where it goes." The words BRONCO-BUSTING appeared in the top left box.

Fleta realized that he must have touched one of the words at the side, because it had disappeared from the side when it appeared in the square. So she touched her favorite: HORSEBACK RIDING. It wasn't that she liked riding horses, but that she, being a related animal, understood them better than any of the others listed, and in her human form certainly could ride one of them.

He put BULLDOGGING in the third square, so she put GOAT MILKING in the fourth one. There were not many goats in Phaze, but they were easy enough to get along with.

They continued with DOG TRAINING, COW MILKING, CAMEL RIDING, BULL FIGHTING and CHICKEN SEXING. "That's not what it sounds like," Shock explained. "It's telling the chicks apart, you know, male or female, so they know who'll grow up to lay eggs. A good chicken sexer can make a pile, on a farm planet. Well, let's choose up; this is it. I got the last placement, so you get choice of numbers or letters."

She chose the letters, and touched B, the center column, because that had the horse riding in it. She was lucky; he chose 1, and the highlights overlapped at HORSEBACK RIDING. She had her first choice, which meant a good chance.

ADJOURN TO RIDING AREA, the screen said. FOLLOW THE LINE.

She looked at the floor. A new line showed, leading away from the console.

They followed it. It brought them to a corral where a number of people were riding horses. It terminated at a check-in office.

The bored attendant glanced up. "Whatcha into—easy, rough or show?" he asked.

"I don't mind losing, but I don't want to get dumped," Shock said candidly. "I bruise easily."

"Easy," the attendant said. "Saddle or bareback?"

"Your turn," Shock said.

So they were still taking turns on choices. "Bareback," Fleta said.

In due course they found themselves on two sedate horses, bareback, with reins. The one who guided his horse most accurately along a set course would be the winner.

Fleta didn't like reins, so she dismounted, went to the horse's head and removed the bit and the reins. The man who had brought the horses looked surprised, but did not comment.

She remounted, and they proceeded along the course. Shock was evidently barely familiar with horsemanship; had the course not been long familiar to the animal, he would soon have been lost. Fleta leaned low, embraced her horse with legs and arms, and spoke to it in its own language: a low whinny. Her body might be alien, but her nature was equine, and now it came strongly through. She felt a sudden surge of homesickness for her homeland, and knew that this captive horse felt the same.

The horse's ears perked. She stroked its neck, reassuring it, explaining by pressures of her legs how it should react. Soon she had it responsive, and the horse obeyed her commands when they were neither verbal nor visual. She really did understand horses.

Thereafter, the horse stood tall and proud, and moved so precisely along the course that others stopped to look. One of the keepers, alarmed, challenged this: "You do something to that animal? No tether, no halter, no bit, no reins—you drug it?"

"No drug," Fleta said.

"Bring it over here; I want the vet to see."

So they had to interrupt the contest, while the horse walked to the side where the robot vet rolled up. The machine ran sensors across the horse's skin and flashed little lights in the animal's eyes and mouth. "This horse likes this rider," the robot said, and rolled away.

"You sure have the touch!" Shock said. "Or did you just get a happy horse?"

"We can exchange horses if you wish," Fleta said.

"Yes, let's do that!"

So they dismounted and exchanged. Fleta addressed the new horse as she had the first, and removed the bit and reins, and soon it was as cooperative, while the first, feeling the ignorance of the new rider, became surly.

By the time they finished the ride, there was no question of Fleta's victory. "Serf, you're new on the register," the corral manager said, hurrying up. "You looking for employment? You've got a touch with those animals I never saw before!"

Fleta dismounted, put her arm up around her mount's head, and kissed it on the nose. "I do relate well to animals," she agreed. "But I am trying to qualify for the Tourney."

"But once you enter that, you're gone, unless you win!" the manager protested. "Look, this spread is owned by a pretty savvy Citizen. If he sees how you are with his animals, he'll give you good employment and treat you right. It's a lot better risk than the Tourney!"

It surely was—for an ordinary serf. But Fleta knew that she could not remain in this guise indefinitely without being discovered, and then she would be in instant trouble. "I wish I could do it," she said with genuine regret. "But I am committed. I must enter the Tourney."

They left the corral. "I think you should have taken it," Shock said. He shrugged. "Well, you bumped me down a rung on the ladder; you're number one-four-two on the Leftover Ladder."

"Why is it called the leftover? I thought there was a ladder for each age group."

"There is, and the top ten of each ladder qualify. But some don't fit well, being underage or overage or alien or handicapped or whatever, so there's a special ladder for us. I guess they sent you here because you're too new to know the ropes."

That was not the reason, Fleta realized. It was because she was an alien creature masquerading as an android of the opposite sex. She could not qualify for a regular ladder without giving herself away, so the self-willed machines had set her up with this all-inclusive one. They did know what they were doing.

But she was on the 142nd rung! How could she ever make it to the top ten rungs?

Shock showed her where to verify her ranking: the Game Computer had a special screen that would show the placement of whomever approached it. Sure enough, FLETA was now listed 142 on LEFTOVER. SHOCK was 143. He shrugged and departed, satisfied.

"Report to alcove for special instructions," a low voice murmured from the speaker.

Surprised, she went to an alcove, where there was slightly greater privacy.

"Challenge the player on the eighth rung," the speaker said.

"But don't I have to climb step by step?" she asked.

"Not in this case. You are permitted two free challenges: one in the lowest ten, to register on the ladder, and one elsewhere, to establish your regular position. Thereafter you can ascend or descend only rung by rung, and need accept only a single challenge each day. If you win Rung Eight, and limit subsequent challenges to one a day, you can lose on the following two days and still qualify for the Tourney. You must achieve the rung now; pursuit is closing, and you will be protected while you remain at the qualifying level."

She felt like melting. She had almost forgotten the danger she was in. "How do I challenge?"

"We shall enter it for you. Follow the line."

She looked. The new line was there on the floor. "Thank you," she said, but the speaker did not respond. She hadn't known that the Game Computer itself was cooperating with the self-willed machines; probably it could get in serious trouble itself, if the Contrary Citizens learned of its part in this. That had to be why her double slip in naming herself and her nature had not given her away: the computer already knew her identity, and was covering for her.

She followed the line, still intrigued by the magic of this realm. It led to another console, where an older woman stood. She had only one arm. This, it seemed, was Number Eight on the Ladder.

"Fleta of Uni," the woman said disapprovingly. "You breeze here from offplanet at the last minute and want to enter the Tourney and maybe win Citizenship, just like that?"

Fleta looked at the name on the screen. This was Stumpy of Proton. A cruel name for a long-time serf. "Citizenship?" she asked, alarmed. If the Citizens were already closing in . . .

Stumpy looked at her with open incredulity. "You don't *know?*"

"Know what?" Fleta asked, confused.

"Oh—you're an android," Stumpy said.

Fleta did not argue, as she was impersonating an android. A reputation for stupidity was an asset, for her. She smiled and looked appropriately blank.

"Well, let's get this charade over with," Stumpy said. She slapped her hand down on her screen.

Fleta had the letters again, so she took D. ANIMAL again. Immediately the screen showed Stumpy's choice, 3. CHANCE. The square expanded.

Instead of a new grid, there was a message: BETTING ON ANIMAL CONTESTS. SELECT AN INCIPIENT CONTEST. ONGOING LIST FOLLOWS. Below was a grid in which many animal contests were listed: races, fights and performances, between horses, dogs, fowl or other creatures.

Bemused by this approach, Fleta touched the column that contained horses, but immediately the chosen square brightened, and it was 1D7E: DOG FIGHT.

Well, she had watched werewolves fighting each other for status. Because she was the foal of Neysa, the friend of the entire local Pack, she had been privileged to witness rites that were ordinarily barred to outsiders. That was how she had become friends with Furramenin; she had been a foal and the werewolf a pup together. Dogs were similar creatures, though inferior; they bore about the same relation to werewolves as horses did to unicorns or monkeys to human folk. She should be able to judge a dog fight.

Now the screen became a picture, startling her. It showed a pit, with two snarling dogs being held by trainers. Fleta saw at a glance that one dog, though slightly smaller and leaner, had a more savage temperament; it would be more serious about the fight than the other.

SELECT VICTORIOUS DOG, the screen directed.

Fleta touched the screen where that dog was portrayed. But in a moment a message appeared: BET-

TORS SELECTED SAME ANIMAL. SELECT TIME OF DECISION: CLOSEST MARK.

A scale of times appeared, delineated in seconds and minutes and hours.

Fleta judged that the larger dog would quickly be cowed, and try to break off. Would the fight be halted at that point? Since the horses were owned by a Citizen who wanted them treated well, perhaps the dogs were similarly owned, and the fight would not be allowed to proceed beyond the point of evident advantage. That would keep it short. She touched the scale at one minute, ten seconds.

Stumpy's mark showed: four minutes even. Now they had a viable bet.

The picture of the dogs reappeared, with the scale retreating to the bottom of the screen. Both bets were marked, and a pointer pointed at 0: the elapsed time of the fight.

Then the dogs were released. They sprang at each other, the larger one confident of the advantage. Indeed, for a few seconds he had it. But then blood flowed from grazing gashes, and the smaller dog went berserk. He attacked with such ferocity that the other was first surprised, then dismayed. Suddenly the other tried to break free—and nets came down, incapacitating both animals, and the fight was over.

The time was fifty-four seconds.

Stumpy looked at Fleta with new appraisal. "You weren't guessing," she said flatly.

"I understand animals," Fleta said.

Stumpy turned and walked away.

Fleta walked back to the Ladder screen. There was her name, on the eighth rung, with Stumpy just below it. She had qualified for the Tourney.

5

Spy

Bane felt the girl in his arms sag. He steadied her, realizing that Fleta had been in Mach's embrace, just as Agape had been in his own embrace, at the time of his exchange with Mach. Fortunately this had not disrupted the process.

Bane looked out over the grassy plain. It was good to be back in Phaze, after the horrors of the pursuit by the Proton Contrary Citizens! Mach had told him briefly of the discovery by Stile, his father, that their exchange was causing a dangerous imbalance, so they had to spend more time in their own frames. Thus he was back for that reason—but the love of his home frame smote him, and he knew he was glad that this need had developed. It was early morning, just as it had been in Proton, but here it was beautiful.

Except for his separation from Agape. He loved her too, and wanted to be with her—and could not, here.

The girl blinked, recovering equilibrium. "We have exchanged, Fleta," he told her. "I be not Mach."

There was a little pop behind him, and a trace of vapor passed, evidently lingering from the mist of the dawn.

She stared at him. "You are alive!" she breathed.

"Aye, filly." Then he asked her about the nature of the truce Mach had told him about, but she seemed confused.

"Where are we?" she asked.

He laughed. "Where thou hast always been, mare! In Phaze, o' course."

Still she seemed perplexed. "Please—do some magic," she said.

He realized that she had suffered some kind of shock, perhaps because of her proximity to the exchange he had made with Mach. He conjured a basket of oats for her.

"I am not the unicorn," she said. "I am Agape."

"Be thou joking, mare?"

She claimed she was not. There followed some confusion, as each doubted the other's identity, but soon she convinced him that she was indeed Agape. He could not, however, convince her that he was Bane. Finally they compromised: he gave her a spell she could invoke for protection and left her. He would know if she used the spell, so he could check on her, for it was his magic.

Then he conjured himself to the Blue Demesnes.

His mother, the Lady Blue, welcomed him, of course. It was his father Stile he was concerned about.

He need not have been. They met privately in Stile's office, protected from observation by a careful spell. "I made a mistake in judging you," Stile said, speaking in his original dialect, as he was apt to do when serious. "Or perhaps in judging your other self, Mach the Robot. I should have remembered how Sheen was—and how Neysa was. Their offspring—" He shrugged. "I shall not err like that again."

There was a faint ripple in the air. Bane was startled. The statement had seemed incidental, but that was the splash of truth. Stile was deadly serious.

"As you may know, Fleta sought to kill herself," Stile continued gravely. "And Mach rescued her in a manner reminiscent of my own Oath of Friendship to Neysa, proving his love and his nascent power. Were you aware that he overrode an Adept's spell in the process?"

"I had not much time for news," Bane said. "Trool's spell?"

"Trool's spell. He always was too decent for his own good, and when he couldn't talk her out of suicide, he gave her what she asked, reluctantly. It was incidental magic, for him—but no ordinary person overrides *any* Adept magic! The doing of it shook the frame, and suddenly all of us knew that a new Adept was in the process of coming into being. Translucent pounced on the opening, and won Mach's trust, leaving us in a very bad situation."

"Aye," Bane agreed. "Dost know that I have found love in Proton-frame?"

"The parallelism of the frames made that likely. We were so blinded by our concern for the continuation of our line that we lost sight of other realities. Our opposition to your union as such is at an end. Do what you must do; I'm sure you have found a worthy companion."

"As such?"

Stile laughed. "We still must oppose it—for different reason. You cannot remain in Proton without aggravating the deadly imbalance."

"Ah, aye," Bane agreed. "So it be the same." He grimaced. "I sought not love there," he continued. "I knew not I was going there, when first it happened. But e'en as thou didst find love across the frames, so did I."

"I was concerned about the future," Stile said. "Now I am concerned about the present. The Adverse Adepts are marshaling their forces, seeking to use their advantage to achieve complete victory. If they can establish communication between the frames, merging Proton analytic techniques with Phaze magic, they can dominate this frame. You and Mach are the key; if you cooperate in that, the power is theirs."

"I seek not to give them that!" Bane protested.

"But if they take possession of your woman?"

"Aye, they tried," Bane said. "We seek to return her to her planet of Moeba, then she will be safe. But it be difficult; the Contrary Citizens be alert."

"You will accept separation from her?" Stile asked, surprised.

"Aye, because though I love her, so also do I love the frame. I would not take her at the cost of all else I value. So I am with thee, my father; I know our romance can be not permanent."

"I had thought you would oppose me in this," Stile said. "But if you give her up, will you then—?"

"Aye, I will find a woman of Phaze and make an heir," Bane said. "An she be amenable to the knowledge that I love her not."

Stile, not normally the most demonstrative of men, simply extended his hand. Bane shook it. Again a faint splash was evoked. There was no quarrel between them.

"I thought to give up my own love similarly," Stile said, "for the good of the frame. But I got her back—and if there is any way I can find to do the same for you, I will do it, regardless of the heir."

Bane smiled. "But there be a development they know not: Agape be now here in Phaze."

"She crossed the curtain with you?" Stile asked, amazed.

"Aye. She was embracing me, and Fleta embraced Mach as we exchanged, and methinks we carried them with us."

"But where is she now?"

"In Fleta's body, girlform. She feared a trick by the Citizens, and they have been most devious before. She be seeking her answer alone."

"But there is danger for the uninitiate in Phaze!"

"Aye. I gave her a spell. More can I not do, an I wish to keep mine agreement to let her be. When she accepts Phaze, then can we be together again."

"This is apt to aggravate the imbalance," Stile said.

"I sent word to Mach and Fleta. Trool identified it; your exchange is wreaking mischief of a cumulative nature. The Adverse Adepts verified it, once we identified it; they know that both frames can be pushed to destruction, if we ignore this imbalance. We can halt it only by returning you to your own frames."

Bane sighed. "And our loves be in the opposite frames! Mischief indeed!"

"Mischief indeed," Stile agreed. "But it does not solve the problem of dominance in the frames. The two of you can continue to communicate from your own frames, and if you do it for the benefit of the Adverse Adepts, they will prevail."

"And if the Contrary Citizens gain power o'er Agape, I can promise not that I will not do their bidding," Bane said.

"And the same for the Adverse Adepts," Stile said. "You don't want them to catch on to her presence here. As long as they believe she is Fleta, they will leave her alone, so as not to give Mach cause to change his mind."

"Aye. That were in my mind as I left her: that she be in no danger from them, only from natural creatures."

Stile walked around the chamber, his blue robe swinging out as he turned. "I do not trust the Adverse Adepts to wait passively for you to fall into their hands. They seem to be honoring the truce, perhaps because they fear that any violation here will bring a countermove in Proton, or will alienate Mach. But as Mach discovers that the Lady Blue and I have withdrawn our opposition to their union, and realizes that he no longer needs sanctuary with Translucent, the Adepts will seek to consolidate their advantage by more forceful means. It would facilitate my preparation if I had a better notion what they might be planning."

"And thou canst not simply go and ask!" Bane said with a wry smile.

"They keep aware of me as I do of them," Stile agreed. "They know where I am at any given moment, just as I know where they are. I fear they use their minions for their dirty work, but I don't want to seem to be spying on the goblins or ogres or demons either, lest I alert them to my suspicions."

"But if I were to use similar magic to do some spying—"

"I could cover for you," Stile concluded. "They surely have a tracer on you, too, but I could enchant a humanoid golem to resemble you and divert their awareness to it. Then you would be unsuspected."

"Aye," Bane agreed, liking the challenge. "But e'en so, I could go not in mine own form."

"You have been studying blue magic for several years. I think you're ready for full Adept-level techniques, such as form-changing. I have long since used up most of the best forms for me, and cannot assume them with the same spells. But those spells will still be good for you, and perhaps it is time for you to use them."

"Aye," Bane said, gratified. This was a tacit promotion to adult status. He realized that his decision to favor the welfare of the frame over his personal love had won his father's respect, and this was an immediate result.

"The main problem with form-changing is the reversion," Stile said. "Blue magic is spoken, or sung, and other forms cannot duplicate the human sounds. What is required is a translation of the spells to the language of the other form. Once you have that, you can always revert to human form. But then that form is done for you; the magic will not work a second time."

"Aye."

"Therefore you will need a form that the Adverse Adepts will not suspect, that you can remain in until you are done, and will not need again. It is true that there are many available forms, and a variant of the original spell will work as new for changing into similar species. Still, caution is best."

"Aye." Bane was really pleased; his father had never before trusted him with magic of this nature.

"Select a form that you find suitable, and when you assume it, I can conjure you to one of the Adverse Demesnes," Stile said. "Thereafter you will be on your own. If you get in trouble, you will have to revert to your natural form, then conjure yourself back here. You should be able to handle that."

"Aye," Bane agreed. He had devised many conjuration spells, so that he could jump from one spot to another at any time, as he had done to come here from the region of the harpies. "But—methinks a trial run first?"

Stile laughed. "A sensible precaution! We'll try something innocuous, and complete the full process; then you will know what to expect. What form would you like to try?"

"I think for observation, something small and unnoticed. An insect, perhaps a bee."

Stile had the spell. He spoke it, and it had no effect on him because he had already used it for himself. Then he described the reversion spell in bee-buzz, making sure Bane understood it. "If you confuse it, you could change back into the wrong form," he warned. "I could devise a spell to correct the error for you, but I think it best that you handle it yourself."

"Aye." For when Bane became the Blue Adept, there would be no one to rescue him from his own errors.

Agape, Agape, Agape!

Bane jumped. "She invoked the spell I gave her!" he exclaimed. "She be in danger!"

"Your spell should protect her," Stile said. "But you don't want to interfere before she is ready. Still, you want to be sure she is safe."

"How canst thou know my thought so perfectly?"

"I knew it when I first loved your mother. Change now, and I will conjure you to her vicinity; this is an ideal test situation."

Bane realized it was true. He wanted, in effect, to spy on Agape, to be sure she was safe without intruding on her presence. He sang the bee spell, and in a moment was crashing to the floor, unable to fly.

"Think bee," Stile said, looking down at him. "Rev up your wings gently, until you have the technique and the balance."

Bane followed directions, and in a moment was hovering somewhat unsteadily, a few inches above the floor.

"Now I will conjure you to her vicinity," Stile said. He sang a spell—and Bane was back at the open plain, still struggling to maintain equilibrium in air.

He flew in a wobbly circle, and ascended. His bee senses informed him that this was indeed the proper region. A bee wasn't smart, but did have excellent positional awareness.

Not far distant a dragon was snorting. That was reason enough for concern! He put forth more energy and buzzed toward it, gaining proficiency in flight.

There was no sign of Agape. That was as it should be, for his spell made her undetectable by ordinary means. It was really a rhyming invocation, her name rhyming with itself as the inflections differed, and it was not her magic, but his; her speech triggered his performance. It was one of the useful devices he had mastered in his years of study: the Blue parallel to the Red amulets or the Brown golems, operating away from the creator. Most Adepts could do similar magic; only the forms of it differed.

The dragon was casting about, trying to find its vanished prey. Soon it flew away, frustrated. Bane relaxed; Agape was safe, and after a while the spell would wear off.

Then another shape winged in. It was a harpy! That was another kind of danger. But how did the harpy know where Agape was? For the ugly bird was definitely orienting on something. "Who calls? Who calls?" she screeched. "I smelled thy signal, but I see thee not!"

Smelled her signal?

"Damn!" the harpy fussed, mildly enough for her kind. "Mayhap the dragon got him, ere the smell o' my burned feather reached me!"

Now Bane remembered. Mach had made friends with a harpy! There had been a passing thought about it. The harpy must have come to help.

"Here I am." That was Agape's voice. The spell allowed her to make herself known when she chose, and of course it was fading anyway.

Bane hovered nearby long enough to verify that the harpy was called Phoebe, and that she was helping. While it was true that the harpies were among the most dirty and vicious of flying creatures, it was also true that hardly any other creature sought to interfere with one. Agape should be safe enough for a time in the company of Phoebe.

He flew to a reasonable distance, then buzzed out the spell for the return transformation. He got it right; in a moment he was a man again. He stood in his normal clothing: part of the magic was the transformation of apparel into fur or skin, in the fashion of the unicorns or werewolves. Quickly he conjured himself back to the Blue Demesnes.

"She be safe for now," he reported, vastly relieved. "She has a harpy friend."

"Fleta made that friend," Stile agreed. "I think I learned from my experience with Trool the Troll that any species, no matter how vile seeming, can have good representatives, if correctly approached."

"I think I be ready now to spy on the Adepts," Bane said. "The test was a success."

"First rest a day," Stile said. "Then we'll send you out in the morning."

Bane realized that much had happened recently, and he was tired. "The morning," he agreed.

Thus it was that the next day he found himself in butterfly form—the flying mode of this creature was easier to relate to than that of the bee—near the Orange Demesnes. He had taken the precaution of becoming well adapted to his form before being conjured to this vicinity, so that he would not flutter about inadequately and perhaps call attention to himself. But in getting that practice he had used energy, and now in the presence of the many exotic blooms of the Orange Demesnes he was hungry. So he flitted from flower to flower, sampling as many as he could and thoroughly enjoying himself.

However, he did not forget his mission. He wanted to spy on the Orange Adept, and learn if he could what mischief the Adverse Adepts were plotting. Stile was not paranoid; if he suspected trouble, then trouble was surely in the making.

The Adept lived in a tiny shack in the center of an overgrown vale in a jungle forest. Bane fluttered closer to the shack, but it showed no sign of life. The Adept was either asleep or absent. In either event, Bane was not accomplishing much. It had not occurred to him that spying would be this dull!

Then a bird swooped down. Oops! Bane plunged for the tangled ground, avoiding the predator. But the bird swerved to follow, with marvelous accuracy. It had far more speed and power than Bane did, and was evidently determined to snap up this morsel.

Bane could not do other magic in this form. As the bird took his body, he invoked the conversion spell in butterfly language, and became a man.

The bird, startled, winged immediately for distant parts. Bane was safe—except that he now stood in his normal form in the heart of the Orange Demesnes. That was dangerous!

He took a step—and encountered ferocious brambles the butterfly hadn't noticed. Indeed, they were coiling about his legs, nudging their thorns into position for best effect. No easy way out of this!

There was no help for it: he would have to conjure himself out, and hope that the Adept *was* absent, because magic of this magnitude would surely alert him otherwise. That could make him, and therefore all the Adverse Adepts, aware that they were being spied on by someone, and it would not take them long to guess whom.

He conjured himself to the center of the Purple Mountain range. He hoped that if Orange were aware of the conjuration, and traced it, he would assume that another Adept had stopped by. This might not be the best of ploys, but it was all he could think of in the pressure of the moment.

He was tempted to check on Agape and the harpy, if they remained together, but resisted the impulse. If an Adept were tracing his course, he hardly wanted to lead that hostile man to Agape!

He conjured himself to the White Mountain range, and finally home. He had expended a number of valuable spells, but it seemed a necessary precaution, doubly hiding his true destination.

"I think he was asleep," Stile said. "My magic indicates he is at home; he seldom leaves it. I don't think you alerted him. What happened?"

"A bird," Bane said, disgruntled.

"Next time make it a poisonous species."

"Aye." Bane grimaced. "I be not much good at spying, methinks."

"Who among us is? Evidently there was not much to be learned there."

Bane resolved to do better next time. That afternoon he transformed into a brightly colored, highly toxic species of butterfly, whose blue and yellow wings advertised its nature; no sensible bird would touch it. Stile conjured him to the Tan Demesnes.

He fluttered near a monstrous banyan tree, whose branches spread so far horizontally that they could not support their weight and dropped new trunks to the ground as buttresses. Thus this single tree seemed rather like a forest, with lesser plants growing in the shadows and arches of it. Bane studied it with his butterfly senses, but could not fathom its extent; it was a labyrinth!

Odd that the Adept whose magic related to plants lived in a wilderness hovel, while the one whose magic related to people lived in the most elaborate vegetative structure. The Adepts as a whole seemed to honor no sensible pattern.

He fluttered into the shadows of the tree, seeking flowers, but there were few here; the light was too dim. He flew up to see whether there was more above the lower branches, for he needed flowers as a cover for his presence.

There was a pavilion above, built into the upper sections of the tree. A woman was reclining there, sunning herself in the nude, or perhaps merely enjoying the breeze. Her eye fell on him.

"A blue-striped zinger!" she exclaimed. "I need a pair of those!" She jumped up and fetched a net from a hook on a trunk-post.

It was Tania, the Adept's daughter—and it seemed she was a butterfly hunter! This was a bad break.

He fluttered down and away, but the woman pursued, the net poised competently. He barely managed to get out of its range beyond the pavilion; Tania could not follow, because she was ten feet above the ground.

"Damn! I'll have to use magic," she muttered.

She gazed intently at him, and the evil eye struck. Bane was abruptly paralyzed. He fell to the ground, unable to fly. Because he was an insect, not a man, he landed lightly, unhurt. Because he was a nascent Adept, the effect did not last; Adepts could seldom hurt each other seriously by their magic, being naturally immune. Had he been in manform, she would have had to work much harder to achieve the same effect. He could fly away before she descended a ladder to the ground.

But if he did, she would know he was more than an ordinary butterfly. He did not want to arouse suspicion. It was better to play the role, and let her capture him, and escape when he could do so in the natural butterfly manner. If no opportunity came, then he would have to do it in an unnatural manner.

Tania arrived. She slid a bit of paper under him and picked him up, carefully. "Come on, you pretty little prize," she said. "I have just the place for you."

That did not sound good. Should he have bolted?

She carried him to a garden set within the far fringe of branches that was entirely surrounded by fine netting. Within it were scores of butterflies. She opened a small section and set him inside. "You will recover in a moment, zinger," she said. "Just find yourself a perch; I'll find a mate for you as soon as I can." She withdrew.

He waited a suitable period, then righted himself and flapped his wings. He flew to a spot on a thick bush and perched there, as directed.

Tania returned to the pavilion and resumed her sunning. But she faced the caged garden, and she was watching him; it was probably because she was pleased to have come this providently on a rare acquisition, but it meant he could not do anything contrary to butterfly nature. He was still captive.

He just did not seem to be very good at spying!

Since he had nothing else to do, he watched her. He had known her occasionally as a child; she had been about ten when he was six, and the Tan Adept had brought her when he came to the Blue Demesnes to confer on this or that. Stile had not gotten along well with the Adverse Adepts, but they *were* Adepts and had to be accorded the respect due that status. Tania had seemed insufferably snotty from the vantage of his youth, but he learned that it was in Tan's mind that he, Bane, might make a suitable match for her, when he became adult. He had rejected that notion out of hand; he would have no truck with any of the Adverse Adepts or their ilk.

But in Proton, and now in Phaze, he saw from the vantage of his sexual maturity that Tania was an attractive young woman. Her body was tanned all over, and her matching hair and eyes had their own peculiar appeal. Physically, she was now a creature he could have been attracted to.

Then a wren appeared, a tiny bird flitting along a lateral branch, checking it for edible insects. Tania's eyes moved to follow it, as it reached the edge of the pavilion. She concentrated—and the bird gave an anguished peep and flopped onto its back, its legs kicking frantically.

"Suffer, creep, before I kill thee," Tania said, watching it with satisfied malice. "Didst think to prey on my butterflies?"

But the bird had not been after the butterflies, Bane thought. It had been looking for crawling bugs in the bark of the huge tree and could not have gotten into the garden cage anyway. She was torturing it without proper reason, evidently enjoying the process. Indeed, she licked her lips as she watched the wren, and her face seemed to glow.

After a time the wren showed signs of recovering from the effect of the evil eye. Its kicking and fluttering slowed and stopped, and it started to right itself.

Then Tania got up, fetched her butterfly net, reversed it, and smashed the handle down on the hapless bird. When she was sure it was dead, she nudged the body off the edge, so that it fell to the ground beyond.

And that completed the picture on Tania: he could never have been attracted to her mind. She was a true example of the nature of the Adverse Adepts.

In due course her brother arrived. "How goes it, Tannu?" Tania asked.

"Indifferently," he replied, plumping into another deck chair. "The rovot and the unicorn traveled to the Harpy Demesnes, where he switched with Bane. Then Bane went to the Blue Demesnes, leaving the 'corn."

"He sported with animals, but does no more," she remarked. "Bring him to me, and I will bind him to our cause."

"Can't, under truce," Tannu said.

"Truces exist only for convenience," she said disdainfully.

He grimaced. "Needs must someone inform Translucent o' that," he said. "After Purple botched the job, Translucent won o'er the rovot, and his word governs. Methought Translucent was crazy and would hang himself, but he did not."

"Yet," she said. "He has hanged himself not yet. He were lucky, but his luck will turn. It be crazy to let Bane run loose."

"We be preparing for the time Translucent comes to his senses," Tannu said. "The ogres, goblins and demons be alerted; they be marshaling their forces."

"For what? Bane can be held not by goblins!"

"But the 'corn can," he replied. "An the rovot return and change his mind, we want that unicorn captive."

"Where be she now?"

"We know not. She set out afoot in girlform for the mountains, but vanished."

"Belike she took birdform and flew away," Tania said. "An she come to me in that form, I know how to deal with her!" Her gaze flicked to the butterfly net.

"Save thy strength for Bane," he advised. "It will require it all to make him do thy will."

She shrugged, her breasts moving. "He be a man. I have practiced the Eye to stun the higher functions. An I hit him with that, he will not know he be changed; he will see only a body he lusts to possess. By the time he spend himself on that, he be mine."

"Just make sure he is, an that time come," Tannu said seriously. "Meanwhile, we marshal the animals."

"Speaking of which—there be a bird below. Do thou get it away from here before it stinks."

He shook his head. "Thou must cease wasting thy power on nonentities, Tania."

"Well, bring me something worthy of mine effort!" she snapped. "Like Bane. Methinks I could have amusement of him; he be a fair young man now."

"All in good time," he replied, and got up, evidently to take care of the dead bird.

Bane realized that he had scored as a spy after all. By being made captive, he had remained close enough to overhear the enemy dialogue. Now he had confirmation of the treachery of the Adverse Adepts—and some notion of their interest in him, too. Could Tania really use her evil eye to enchant him? He would have thought no, before, but now he was not sure. She seemed too confident, and her approach was insidious. Stun his higher sensitivities, and tempt him with sex. If he succumbed to that, it would play havoc with his relationship with Agape, as perhaps Tania intended. More likely, she merely wanted the challenge of taming an apprentice Adept, and of fashioning a sexual plaything.

He did not think she could do it. But he wasn't sure, and did not care to take the chance. He would stay well away from her!

The day slowly passed. Bane flew to a number of flowers in the cage, satisfying his hunger, but did not dare try to escape. He was sure he could get away by reverting suddenly to manform and immediately conjuring himself away, but that would give away his identity and ruin the validity of the information he had gleaned. It was important that he escape without being suspected.

At night, when Tannu and Tania had settled for sleep elsewhere in the tree, he made his move. He flew to a firm spot in the garden, and reverted to his natural form. Then he walked carefully to the fastened flap of netting that Tania used for her own entry, opened it, and stepped out. Then he climbed a branch overhanging the garden and broke off a dead projection. He brought this down to the net and used it to tear a small hole in the fabric, directly below the spot from which the branch had been taken. He set it down just beside the net. In the morning, when Tania found her prize butterfly gone, she would discover the hole evidently made by the falling branch, and realize how the insect had escaped. She would be annoyed, but not suspicious. He hoped.

Then he climbed down a trunklet to the ground, and made his way out of the tree. He walked some distance into the night, putting distance between the sleepers and his conjuration, making it less likely that they would be aware of it. Then, finally, he conjured himself home.

In the following days he spied on the goblins, ogres and demons that Tannu had mentioned. Sure enough, they were organizing as for battle. But where did they plan to strike, and when, and with what forces? The break he had had at the Tan Demesnes turned out to have been his best; butterflies could not get close enough to the decision makers at the right times to spy out anything critical.

Then he learned that the Adverse Adepts were suspicious of the unicorn. They had managed to trace her to the Red Demesnes, and saw little reason for the unicorn to go there. But if it were another person in her body, who needed help learning the magic, that could account for it. So they were alert for her, in whatever form. They knew their strongest possible hold on him, Bane, would be through the creature he loved, just as it was with Mach.

"I must go to her, to protect her," he told his father.

"No," Stile said. "They aren't sure. If you do that, they will be sure, and her danger will be increased. Let Trool handle it; he can protect her readily enough."

Bane knew that his father was right. So, reluctantly, he continued his spying missions, hoping for the break that would give them the rest of the information they needed. In time he would be reunited with Agape. That was what he lived for.

6

Amoeba

Mach found himself naked in a chamber, embracing the alien female, Agape. "The exchange has been accomplished," he said. "We had better disengage." For Bane had conveyed to him that this was the office of one of the Contrary Citizens. What a place for them to hide!

"Where be we?" the woman asked.

He started to explain, then realized it was pointless, because she had been here all along. "But you already know that, Agape."

"I be Fleta!" she said.

"Don't tease me like that, Agape," he said. "I love her."

"Tease thee? I tease thee not," she protested.

They discussed the matter, and soon she satisfied him that she really was Fleta, who somehow had managed to exchange with him, and was now in the body of the alien female. What a development!

"This really be thy rovot form?" she asked.

He was glad to have his love with him, however unexpectedly, but this was decidedly awkward. Fleta had no notion of the ways of Proton, or even of the management of her strange body. She would quickly give herself away, if he didn't indoctrinate her immediately. Her language alone . . .

They worked on it. Fleta adapted to the language fairly readily, and with some difficulty learned how to reshape her amoebic body. Learning how to cope in the frame of Proton would be a longer task; he had to settle for the minimum.

In the course of their discussion, he learned from her that Tan was the Adept of the Evil Eye, and that he had wanted to marry his daughter to Bane. How fortunate that Bane had resisted!

Teaching Fleta to eat the amoebic way was a challenge. Getting her through the night was another, because Agape's body melted when it lost consciousness and puddled on the bed. But they squeaked through it, and in daytime Fleta was at the front desk as Agee, the android receptionist.

Meanwhile he researched their situation, and learned that the self-willed machines were helping, and had a plan to enter Agape in this year's Tourney, which was about to begin. That would protect her from the Contrary Citizens until she washed out, when she would be shipped back to Planet Moeba, no interference brooked. Good enough; all she had to do was hide for three days, and she would be safe.

Except that it wasn't Agape with him now, it was Fleta, and Fleta knew nothing about the Tourney, and less about Planet Moeba. It would be complete disaster to ship her there.

He would have to get her exchanged back to Phaze before she went to Moeba. That could be difficult. He would have to think about ways and means.

Tania stopped by the office: the very thing he hoped would not happen. She was striking in her fashion: a face that was removed from the ordinary by its tan eyes and framing of tan hair, and a well-developed body. Obviously she could be a beauty when she chose to be. At the moment she was too cold and Citizenlike despite her nakedness to be attractive, however. Serfs learned early to treat the bodies of Citizens as objects of veneration, not of interest, unless directed otherwise.

She reviewed Fleta in a cursory manner, then Mach. She wasn't satisfied. She curtly ordered Fleta to requisition a replacement menial robot. Then she was gone. Perhaps it was a test; if so, Fleta passed it nicely, except for the single error of referring to him as a "rovot."

Then Tania's brother appeared. In Phaze it seemed that this young man had not yet assumed the office of the Adept, but in Proton he was evidently Citizen Tan. Parallelism was approximate, not perfect; otherwise Mach and Bane could not have been alternate selves.

Did the Citizen suspect? Mach watched with increasing apprehension as Tan questioned Fleta, then handled her, then took her to the sleeping chamber for a sexual exercise. Obviously a true android serf would be thrilled to have such attention from her employer, while an alien female in love with a robot would not. Could Fleta tolerate this intimacy for the sake of concealment of her nature? He feared she could not, and tried to interfere on a pretext.

And his body was abruptly shorted out. Now he knew, too late, that Tan suspected; he was helpless.

But Fleta, primed to act when he gave the word, decided it was time. She wrapped her amoebic flesh about Tan's more sensitive parts and forced him to obey her. She made him free Mach, then deposit her in the waste disposal chute. The self-willed machines would guide her from there. She had escaped.

Leaving Mach with a hurting and humiliated Citizen.

It would not be smart for Tan to do anything to Mach, because Mach was the key to communication between the frames that the Contrary Citizens so very much desired. But Mach wasn't sure that Tan was in a mood to be smart at the moment. He made a hasty retreat from the office, and with a speed that only a machine in a frame whose details were run largely by machines could manage, became lost in the service network. He knew Tan would not give the alarm; this would be a private grudge. Citizens did not take lightly to depradations on their dignity.

He consulted his brethren, the machines. He learned that there was indeed a search on for Agape (Fleta), and that it would be dangerous for her if Mach were to try to approach her before she was safely qualified for the Tourney.

Yet she would want and need his support. How could he provide it, without putting her in peril? How could he resist the natural urge to go to her prematurely?

He knew how. He requisitioned a unit and programmed a dialogue. He dictated an opening statement that would satisfy her as to his authenticity, and left the rest to interactivity. It would seem just like him, and give her comfort. He left it with the self-willed machines, who would use it when appropriate.

But when he set foot in the halls, and sought to lose himself among the walking serfs as he made his way to the estate of Citizen Blue, an android turned abruptly and threw an object at him. Mach dodged it, and it struck the wall beyond him, detonating in a flash and report like that of a small bomb but doing no harm. Apparently it was a toy, a mock explosive.

Mach took off after the android, who was trying to duck around a corner. He wanted to know who had sent him, and what the mock-bomb was supposed to do.

The android, like most of his species, was clumsy. Mach reached him easily, catching him by the shoulder.

The man whirled, flipping another bomb toward Mach's face. Mach intercepted it with his left hand, his reactions much swifter and better coordinated than the android's.

The bomb exploded in his hand, and the pieces of it fell away. It might have harmed a flesh hand, but not his. "What are you trying to do?" he demanded.

"Mark you," the android said.

Suddenly Mach understood. That had not been a damage-bomb, but a marker-bomb! It had impregnated his hand with radiation that would enable him to be traced.

"Who sent you?" he asked.

"Citizen Tan." The android was not even trying to evade; evidently his attempt to flee had been part of a ruse to get Mach close.

Mach let him go and ran on toward his destination. But he saw suggestive motion ahead, and realized that others were already closing in. They knew his destination, and his location, and would intercept him before he reached safety.

He had been right about Citizen Tan: the man was angry. Tan intended to capture Mach, regardless of the Contrary Citizens' desire to get him to work for them. Injured pride was more immediate than long-term power. Fleta was safe because Tan could not find her—but Tan could get at her through Mach, reversing the ploy.

This situation had developed so quickly that Citizen Blue was not aware of it. Mach needed to get back to the self-willed machines, who would alert his father. But the minions of Tan were cutting him off from that contact too. Also, his contact with them now would serve as proof of their complicity. He had to find some other avenue of escape.

Mach charged back the way he had come. This happened to be the hall leading to the spaceport; he had entered it from a service aperture, which he did not dare use now, as the tracer radiation would betray his private contacts.

The spaceport? That was a dead end! They would close in on him there, and spirit him away before he could alert his side. Unless—

Why not? Their tracer would do them no good, if he were offplanet!

He hurried to the waiting shuttle. Ships did not actually land in the dome city; the shuttle conveyed passengers to the orbiting station, where they boarded the interplanetary vessels. He stepped in just as the port was starting to close; the shuttles departed on a rigid schedule every few minutes. He was safe from pursuit—for those few minutes.

He checked the screen for the imminent listings. Ships arrived and departed from and to a dozen planets every hour. There should be somewhere convenient, from which he could alert his father. It was ironic that they had been having so much trouble getting Agape offplanet, while he was doing it on the spur of the moment!

The name leaped out at him from the list: MOEBA. The very planet!

Mach laughed, internally. He would visit Planet Moeba.

Mach had been on interplanetary flights before; it had been a deliberate part of his education. He understood about the temporary blackout of Feetle (FTL—Faster Than Light) travel and the necessary adjustment of time to synchronize with that of the planet being approached. But he was surprised by the passengers.

It seemed that they were all from other planets; Proton had merely been a mail-stop, and he was the only new traveler. One individual resembled a molding green cactus. Another seemed like a living plate of spaghetti with olives for eyes. A third was rounded and furry, with half a dozen whistle-pipes poking out. The others were somewhat stranger.

Mach ran through his geography program, identifying the various species and cultures. They were all legitimate; the surprise was in finding such a varied assortment on a single ship. Their languages were all different, too, and he had no programs for these, so could not communicate.

He did have a program for Moebite, because of his association with Agape. He had never used it, but he automatically set up for likely eventualities. He had thought that Bane might find it useful; in the rush of events, he had neglected to inform his other self. How fortunate he had it now!

That jogged a little alarm circuit. His acquisition of that program was on record, which meant that Tan must know about it. Tan would not have known that it was for Bane; he would have thought it was for Mach himself. Tan might have concluded that Mach planned to go to Moeba at some time in the future.

Why, then, had Tan not acted to prevent it? Tan's minions had tried to intercept Mach on the way to Citizen Blue's estate; they had left an avenue to the spaceport open. That was the kind of error Citizens seldom made.

The timing had been remarkably convenient. Tan's minions had struck just when the next ship out was the one to Moeba.

Mach had no further doubt: Tan had wanted him on this ship. That meant that there would be a welcoming party on Moeba. Away from Proton, Mach could not turn to his father for help. Perhaps a trap had been set for Agape, so that if she succeeded in departing Proton safely, she would still be taken captive. Now Tan had elected to use it on Mach. It could have been serendipitous for the Citizen: a trap set for one used to catch the other.

Now he was on the way to that trap, and he could not detour. The ship terminated at Moeba; it would undergo inspection and preparation for its next voyage, and only service crews would be permitted to remain on it. Mach would have to go to the planetary surface—where he would be vulnerable to whatever the Citizen had in mind. How could he escape it?

He smiled. There were ways. Bane, in this body, might have been helpless, but Mach was not.

First he had to eliminate the marker. He knew that his left hand was hopeless; once impregnated with radiation, it would remain so until the radiation faded, which could be years. So—

He opened his chest cavity and brought out a small tool. He used this to pry under the pseudoflesh of his left wrist and access the circuitry there. He nulled it, and separated the physical locks. Soon he removed the hand and sealed over the wrist.

Another passenger noted this procedure. "Most interesting," the creature murmured. It was a serpentine form, with a dozen handlike projections along its sides. Perhaps its interest was professional.

Mach realized that the creature had spoken in Moebite. It must have learned the language for its visit. He held out the hand. "Would you like to borrow it?" he asked in that language. "I must warn you that it has been impregnated with marker radiation: harmless to living flesh, but a beacon for the party seeking it." He held out the hand.

The creature took it. "I would like to study this. I regret I cannot detach one of my own. May I proffer some other item or service?"

"Perhaps a service. I believe that some party on Moeba intends to take me captive, identifying me by this hand. Would you care to lead that party astray?"

"I would be delighted!" the creature said.

Thus expeditiously was the deal made. Mach was gambling that the party would use the radiation to do the identification, not considering the physical appearance of the subject at all. It was evident that many strange creatures visited the planet, so appearance meant little.

He would have to do without his hand, but that seemed a necessary price for his freedom.

Now all he had to do was decide on a legitimate mission, since he would have to remain on the planet at least until another ship traveled back to Proton—and until he could safely return. That might be a while.

Actually, he had a mission: to learn how a robot might breed with a Moebite. This was the occasion to investigate the prospects.

In due course the ship arrived at the planet of the

Amoeba and established orbit. The passengers were shuttled down on a winged craft that swooped onto a dark marsh. A submersible bubble took them to a chamber some distance below the surface.

It turned out that the other passengers were Moebites, returning from their various interplanetary missions. They had maintained their discrete disguises as a matter of principle while away from home, but now dissolved with relief into their natural jelly forms. They had assumed that Mach was another Moebite, and were evidently surprised when he did not melt.

The individual with the marked hand went immediately to another chamber, as if trying to escape detection. There was no immediate sign of pursuit, but Mach was sure some would soon manifest. There was no chance of losing track of that hand!

A Moebite formed into a vaguely human outline and approached him. "You have business here?" it inquired in its own language; Mach understood it only because of his language program.

"I have come to inquire about your nature and culture," Mach said. His actual words were only approximately analogous to the ones he would have used on Proton.

"We are always glad to exchange information," the Moebite said. "Do you wish a cultural tour?"

"Yes." His preliminary research had indicated that this was the proper mode of introduction.

"I shall summon a guide."

"Thank you."

In a moment the guide appeared, in the guise of a naked human being, except for one distinction: it was neuter. "A greeting, man-being," it said in Moebite. "I am Coan. Have you a preference?"

Mach considered. The creature was sexless, and could assume the appearance of either sex, just as Agape could. Agape had chosen to be female, and had then conformed psychologically to that image. He de-

cided not to get involved with any other alien female.
"Male, if you please. I am Mach."

Coan's midsection melted, then shaped into penis and scrotum. His hips thinned down slightly. He had made the requisite cosmetic adaptation.

"Our habitat is dry, but we handle wet well," Coan said. "These are melt channels through which travelers normally pass." He indicated several holes in the floor. As Mach looked, he saw one in use: semi-fluid substance was squeezing up from it and pooling around it. Soon the Moebite was through, and sliding toward a waiting region, evidently early for its ship.

"I hope there is an alternative exit," Mach said. "My body is not flexible in this manner."

"Our facilities for aliens are limited, but sufficient," Coan said. "We shall utilize a capsule." He showed the way to a port that could accommodate a man. He touched it and it opened, revealing the small transparent bubble beyond. They climbed in and sealed the bubble's lock. Then the little craft moved through the water, dropping slowly to the sea floor and extending fibers that traveled along its nether side, moving it gently forward.

"What was the business of the other travelers?" Mach inquired.

"They are representatives to other planets. They assume the forms of the creatures whom they visit and learn their modes of communication. We are studying the galaxy, and wish to know as much as we can learn about the ways of other sapient species."

"Because you have no technology of your own," Mach said.

"True. We had no need of it until we made contact with other species. Now we realize that we are retarded in this sense, and we wish to make progress. We prefer not to be entirely dependent on other planets for our interplanetary contacts."

Mach could appreciate why. Any aggressive planet could exploit Moeba unmercifully, and surely in time that would occur. "So you are studying technology, and trying to learn sexual reproduction, so that your species will evolve as effectively as others do."

"You have an unusual comprehension of our effort," Coan remarked.

"I am not a normal individual of my species," Mach said. "I am a machine—"

"I had noted that. But you are self-willed."

"Who is in love with a living creature of another species."

"I begin to perceive the nature of your empathy."

"I also represent, in a manner, the interest of another individual who is in love with a Moebite, and who I believe would like to breed with her."

Coan considered a moment. "I believe we have some common interest. We must explore it in greater detail."

"Agreed."

The bubble reached the shore and crawled onto land, then stalled; its fiber-propulsion was unable to sustain the weight on land. The port opened, and they climbed out.

Coan escorted him to a building that appeared to have been constructed by natives of another planet. That made sense; the Moebites had had no technological culture of their own. This was the limitation they were trying to surmount.

"In the beginning, our culture was without form and void," Coan said, showing a setting of deep water. "We were amoeba, but small, floating in the current. We were victim to other species, and to each other. Predator species were dominant." And in the setting, little amoeba were engulfed by larger ones.

"We retreated to the least hospitable realms, the shallows and the rivers," Coan continued as they moved to the next exhibit. "Conditions were more extreme here, and we had to develop tougher membranes and tougher protoplasm. But the predators did the same, and followed us. We retreated to the fresh water, developing membranes to contain our vital solutions, and finally to the land itself." The settings showed this progression.

"But here the climate was truly savage. No amount of fleshly adaptation could sustain us against the alternate desiccation of the summer sunlight and freezing of the winter. But we discovered how actually to shape our environment somewhat for our comfort, by crafting deep pools in hollows on the land that the predators could not reach, or by walling off sea inlets so that predators had difficulty passing. Food was a serious problem on land, but we learned to cultivate simple cells and feed on them.

"The most important breakthrough was the development of linguistic communication. It enabled us to form, in effect, a larger entity, that was better able to cope with inclement conditions. We now dominate our planet, and no other species preys on us. But when the first shuttle from an alien planet landed, we realized that a great deal more remained to be mastered."

"But how do you reproduce?" Mach asked.

"By fission. We grow to sufficient size, then divide into clone entities, each the same as the original."

"But this should result in the continual fragmentation of the species," Mach protested.

"No. When two of us have need, we flow together, and the dominant genes establish a new entity with traits of each of the contributors. Then we fission, and the clones are similar. This process maintains a unified species."

"But each individual loses its identity when mergence occurs," Mach protested. "A new individual is formed, a compromise creature."

"Yes. This is why our leading scholars avoid mergence as long as possible. Unfortunately, mergence is our nature; aging and weakening occur if it is postponed too long. Thus we are unable to maintain a truly discrete intellectual stratum in the fashion of the creatures of other planets. This, we now perceive, is a liability."

"Sexual reproduction allows individuals to reproduce

in a species-unifying way without sacrificing their individuality," Mach said. "That is an asset."

"Yes. That is why we seek to master this style of reproduction. We are devising a mechanism of uneven fission, so that the clones are not of the same size."

"But the merging entities must still form new individuals," Mach protested. "The size should not affect that."

"True. But it enables one of the clones to retain identity."

"I am a machine. My thinking may be limited. I don't follow this."

Coan showed him to another exhibit. This was an expanded view of two amoeba. "Each adult fissions unevenly," he explained. As he spoke, the models divided, each forming one large and one small daughter cell. The amoeba, of course, were single-celled, despite their size. "But this is contrary to our nature; the smaller individuals cannot survive alone, being too small to sustain the sophisticated processes of our advanced state. They must merge immediately, while the larger ones are able to survive independently." The two small ones merged, forming a new individual of about the size of the parent amoeba.

Now Mach understood. "The two parents survive unchanged; together they have generated a new individual, without sacrificing their identities!"

"Yes. This is our analogue of sexual reproduction. By this device we can retain our memories and culture, without sacrificing succeeding generations. But problems remain. The fission into uneven clones is not natural to us, and there is little individual incentive to do it. We need to make it sufficiently rewarding so that every one of us has an incentive to do it this way instead of the old way."

"And so you are studying the other species of the galaxy, seeking the secret of sexual attraction and fulfillment," Mach said. "That was what Agape was doing, when she encountered—" He hesitated, then continued. "Me."

"Yes. It appears that she was successful."

"I believe so. Not only did she learn the physical pleasure of sexual union, she learned the emotional pleasure of love."

"We have had difficulty with the latter concept."

"I am sure you have! But Agape will try to explain it to you when she returns to this planet. Meanwhile, if I might offer a suggestion—"

"We are seeking suggestions from all sources."

"I am a robot. I have no natural emotions or pleasures. All that I am is unnatural: the result of programming for specific effects. Yet I do have pleasure, and I do love. Perhaps you need to program artificial inducements for your artificial process of reproduction."

"How can you, as you say a machine, know that your feelings would have meaning for living creatures?" Coan asked. "You have had no living experience."

Mach decided to be open. "I have had living experience. My identity has crossed over into the body of a living male. I found the sensations and emotions more intense, but of the same general nature. I had not understood them before that experience, but when I returned to my machine body, so did the emotions, and I know they are the same, only reduced somewhat in strength. Enhancement of my programming could correct that. If you could arrange for genetic programming of similar emotions—"

Just then two others barged into the chamber. "My pursuers!" Mach said. "I must flee or fight!"

"But there can be no violence here!" Coan protested.

Mach ran for the far exit—and encountered a third intruder, a Moebite in the form of a giant legged ball, with two tentacles at the top holding the poles of what he recognized as an electronic shorting device. One touch of that, and he would be turned off. They had come prepared!

But they were amoeba, not robots. They lacked his

strength and ferocity of reflex. He dived below the dangerous tentacles and slammed into the ball-body. It squished. He reached up to grasp the insulated handle-end of a pole and ripped it out of the flaccid grasp. He jammed the point against the opposite point.

There was a flash. That shorted out the shorter; it was now useless. He dropped it and scrambled on out of the chamber.

Soon he found himself outside, on land. But the others were following, and he knew they would not be careless again with their shorters. He had to get farther away.

The water! He could handle it, and the shorter could not. He would be safe there. He ran for it, and plunged in.

In a moment he was in the wilderness of uncivilized Moeba. Life was thick, here in the sunlit shallows, and he discovered to his surprise, also beautiful.

Some shapes were like yellow ferns, waving gently in the warm current. Some were like patches of blue gelatin, spread across the warm rocks. Some were like pink puffballs clinging to vertical surfaces, and others like the thick brown bristles of scrub brushes. Some were like flowing syrup, and some like puffy white mold—which they just might be. Many were like large ant eggs standing on end, and many others were like dewed spider webs.

This was the realm from which Agape had sprung. He made a file of photographs of it, so that Bane would be able to recall this information and see it all, exactly as Mach was seeing it now, when Bane returned to this body. Mach knew that his living other self would be pleased.

He was safe, now, walk-swimming through the water. But how was he to return safely to Proton? By this time Citizen Blue would have secured things there; all Mach needed to do was get there, and see how Fleta was doing.

He decided to wait a reasonable interval, then return

to the museum, where the Moebite authorities should have dealt with the intruders. As Coan had said, violence was not tolerated there; they would do whatever they did to criminals. Then he would be able to return to the space station in the normal manner and take the next ship for Proton. It should be straightforward, now that he had triggered the trap and escaped it. Agape, too, should be safe, when she came here; the Contrary Citizens' fangs had been pulled, at least on this planet.

Meanwhile, he would explore this realm further, recording as much of its beauty as he could for Bane.

7

Troll

When she recovered full consciousness, she was in a cage. She scrambled up in alarm.

Immediately a bat leaped into the air beside her cage. The bat became a woman of extraordinary beauty, wearing a light cloak resembling the folded wings of the bat. "Adept!" she exclaimed. "She wakes!"

An extraordinarily ugly man appeared. "Aye," he agreed. "The amulet restored her somewhat. Now must thou teach her to change her form."

The woman reached up and opened the cage. "Come to me, hummingbird," she said. "I be Suchevane, and I did promise my bitch friend to help thee. She says thou art not Fleta, but her other self, unable to use her body well."

So this was Suchevane! Bane had been right; there could be no lovelier creature than this! Agape hopped onto her hand.

"The Red Adept caged thee with an amulet to restore thy strength, but thou must also eat," Suchevane said. "Now shall I revert to my natural form. Do thou take my paw and change back to girlform with me. Dost thou understand?"

The routine was becoming familiar. Agape nodded agreement.

The woman set her down on the floor. Then the bat reappeared, beside her. Agape touched the bat's paw. Then she willed herself to change when the bat did.

The room reeled. She found herself being supported by the bat-girl. She was human again!

"I thank thee, Suchevane," the Red Adept said. "Now can I help her, and thou be free to return to thy flock."

"Will she be well, Adept?" Suchevane asked anxiously. "She be—her body be my friend too."

"She will be well," the Adept assured her. "It will take time for her to recover completely, for much vitality was lost in the birdform, but I will see to her recovery."

The bat-girl smiled at him. "Much do I appreciate this, Adept. An thou dost need me for aught else, thou needst but ask."

"For naught but dreams," the man muttered. Then, with ordinary volume: "Thou has done more than enough. I must not hold thee longer."

"Then do I take my leave," Suchevane said. She became the bat, and flew away.

The ugly man turned to Agape. "I be Trool the Troll, otherwise known as the Red Adept. I see thou art repelled by mine appearance, as all normal damsels be. But fear not; I gave up trollish ways when the Blue Adept befriended me. I mean thee no harm, but only to restore thee to proper health and the use o' thy body, so that thou mayst go thy way without danger. It was needful to convert thee to thine human form so that thou couldst eat normally." He walked to a chest and brought out an armful of fruits and breads. "Do thou eat thy fill, and then I will show thee where thou mayst rest. The cage were but to protect thee from injury, an thou shouldst wake and be affrighted."

Agape gazed at him, becoming reassured. "You like her, don't you."

The Adept paused, taken aback. "Does it show so much? I wish to make not a fool o' myself."

"No, not at all," Agape said quickly. "She is stunningly beautiful, and I—I am an alien creature who loves a human man. I think I tune in to this sort of thing, now."

"An old troll has no business dreaming," he said. "Now do thou eat, for thy present well-being is but temporary, the result o' mine amulet. I will leave thee now; do thou snap thy fingers when thou wishest aught." He turned away.

Agape realized that she was ravenous, but she had a doubt. "Adept, if you will—if it is not an imposition—would you stay?"

"Stay? I thought to relieve thee o' my presence whilst thou dost eat."

"Your presence is no affront to me. I recognize that for a man you are ugly, but I realize that you are not a man, and in any event, my standards are alien. I am not certain I can eat, here, so may need your further help."

"The food be good," he said quickly. "The vamps provide it—"

"I am sure it is good. It is that my normal mode of eating may not work, here, and I am not sure I can eat the human way."

"Thou dost become more interesting by the moment," the Adept said. "Do thou make the attempt, an this suit thee not, I will fetch other."

Agape made the attempt. She put her face over a chunk of bread and tried to melt into the digestive format. Nothing happened.

Trool fetched a chair and sat opposite her. "Exactly how dost thou eat, in thine own fashion?"

Agape described the process.

"But thou dost know how human beings eat?"

"I have seen it happen," she admitted.

"Thou art now in human form, and not merely in external emulation," he said. "Do thou imitate me, step by step." He took a chunk of bread, and brought it to his face.

She imitated him. He opened his mouth, baring his teeth, and bit into the bread. She bit likewise. He tore free a piece of bread and closed his mouth over it. She did the same. He closed his mouth and masticated, and she did too. Finally he swallowed, and she copied him as well as she could.

The sodden mass of chewed bread went down inside her neck and into her main torso.

"That be it," he said. "Thy body will take care o' it from here. Do thou continue eating." He took another bite.

"You mean—that's all?" she asked, amazed by the revelation. "I don't need to melt into it?"

"That be all," he agreed. "Thy digestive processes be now entirely within thy body."

"I—I thought it was like—would be the way it is with Bane—with Mach's robot body. He can eat, but not digest, so must open a panel and remove the food before it spoils."

"That be one fancy golem body!" Trool remarked. "Nay, it be not that way for thy present body." Then he angled his head, struck by another thought. "Hast thou had experience with elimination?"

"Only of my own type, which is not the same."

"It be not meet for me to try to teach thee that. Suchevane can instruct thee, when she comes to practice thee on form-changing."

Agape practiced her eating, finishing the chunk of bread, then tackling a large pear. Juice slopped down her chin; this was a new challenge! But gradually she learned to do it more neatly and efficiently. She even managed to drink a cup of grape juice without spilling very much down her front.

Finally, her stomach full, she stopped. She lay on the bed the troll had provided, and slept.

• • •

In the afternoon Suchevane arrived. Trool explained briefly the need, and the bat-girl escorted Agape to a shed that smelled of manure. "Do thou sit on this hole and let it go," she said.

"Let what go?"

Suchevane cocked her head. "Thou has truly done this not before?"

"Nor seen it done," Agape agreed. "Human beings are secretive about the details, and Bane—the robot had no need. He showed me sex, but not elimination."

"He showed thee sex," the girl repeated. "Aye, and he showed that me, too; men be eager enough for that."

"Bane showed you sex?"

"We were young, and curious. He had no human female friend, so he played with us animals, and we be friends since. Fleta, Furramenin, me—we told not the adults, o' course."

"He played with me too," Agape said. "In the frame of Proton. But why didn't he marry one of you?"

The girl laughed. "The son o' an Adept marry an animal? That were never in the cards! Nay, it be play only, and long o'er now."

"Did he tell you that he loved you?" Agape asked, concealing the tightness she suddenly felt.

"Nay, o' course not! Bane ne'er deceived others; he spoke only truth." Then she looked sharply at Agape. "He told thee that?"

"Yes."

"And Mach told Fleta!" Suchevane shook her head. "Oh, did he e'er tell her! He spake her the triple Thee. I was there, and ne'er saw the like! The air, the cliffside, indeed all the world it seemed turned sparkling clean, and she—" She shook her head. "I envy both!"

Agape remembered the way the Red Adept had reacted to this young woman. "Adepts don't marry nonhumans?"

"Ne'er! Why should they, an they have anything they want o' us anyway? They marry seldom at all, and then only human women, as did Blue."

"Forgive me if I am speaking inappropriately—but would you marry an Adept if he asked you?"

Suchevane shrugged. "That be entirely theoretical. Any animal would marry any Adept, an he asked her. Or any decent human man. I would have married Bane, an he e'er wished. But an Adept ne'er would."

"But what about a nonhuman Adept?"

"There be only one, and he be Trool the Troll. He be separated from his own kind since he adopted human ways, and he be kind to my folk. An he wish to take one o' us for play, she would do it readily enough."

"Even you, the most beautiful of creatures?"

"Aye, especially me! I tired early o' handsome males; fain would I settle with one like him, with decency and power. But he has no interest." She looked at Agape. "But this be a diversion. I must show thee how to eliminate."

True enough. Agape was suffering some discomfort but was unable to relieve it in her natural fashion. "Is it like eating?"

"Nay, not precisely. Here, mayhap I can show thee. Let me take the hole."

Agape moved off, and Suchevane moved on. She lifted her cloak out of the way to reveal her bare posterior. "Here do the solids come out, and here the liquids."

"Oh—either side of the—"

"Aye. The major functions be set close together, for convenience."

"I recognize it now; I have seen anatomical illustrations. I made surface emulations, with only the aperture required for the sexual congress. On Proton, I mean. I suppose the others are functional now. I should have realized."

"It be hard at first to learn the nuances o' a new form," Suchevane agreed. "I had trouble learning the human way, when I had practiced only the bat way as a cub. Now there be muscles here, and thou dost normally keep them tight, but now thou must let them relax. See, when I do, it comes out." A stream of yellow liquid jetted from her, down into the darkness below the hole.

"Let me see, that muscle should be about here," Agape said, lifting her own cloak and touching her body. "If I relax it—oops!"

Suchevane leaped from the hole, put her hands on Agape's shoulders, and swung her around and down on it. Liquid splashed on the board. "Thou hast it now!"

"But there is substance in the other—"

"Let that out too! This be the place for all o' it."

Agape let it all out, and her body felt much relieved. Then the vampire showed her how to use paper to clean herself up, and how to wash where necessary. The process took some time, but now she had learned what she needed to. She would be able to handle it herself in the future.

Suchevane also showed her how to change forms from human to flying, and back. There were a number of misstarts, but when Agape finally got it straight, she realized that she could have done this at any time, had she only known how. It was a matter of concentrating on the right form in the right way: a talent which, once learned, she knew she would never forget, as with the elimination. Now she could change freely from girl to hummingbird, and from birdform to girlform, as Suchevane put it.

But flying was more complicated. Agape could flap her wings, but this only resulted in disaster. They decided to leave this aspect for another day.

Suchevane went home, and Agape settled down to another big meal. Trool joined her, at her request; she realized that he was not a busy man, but a creature with time on his hands, and lonely.

"If I may say something personal . . ." she said between mouthfuls.

"Speak, Agape," he said. "It has been long since I

have had company o' any kind, other than momentary business."

"I think that if you were to ask Suchevane to stay here, she would."

He grimaced, and on him this was a phenomenally grotesque expression. "Aye, and so would any animal! I crave that kind o' company not!"

"Because you are an Adept?"

"Adepts be the leaders o' Phaze," he explained. "Each has his mode o' magic, but each has power o'er any other creature. This power be easy to abuse, and I mean not to do that. I would not take a woman, human or animal, because she feared my power—and that be the only way a woman would come to me."

"I think she might come voluntarily."

"Aye, she would say that. But fear be the motivator, not preference. Look at me." He spread his arms, his left hand holding a plumb. "I be ugliest o' all Adepts, and unversed in manners. I deceive not myself on this."

Indeed, he spoke truly! He was catastrophically ugly, considered as a man. But not completely. "You are ugly in appearance," she agreed carefully. "But not in manner, and I think not in intent. Some women appreciate those other qualities."

He shrugged. "So it would be nice to believe."

She realized that further pursuit of this subject would be pointless. Any overture would have to come from the other side. So she dropped it, and worked on her eating, and her elimination, and her form-changing, and grew steadily stronger and more talented in her use of this body.

Suchevane came daily to help her, and soon she mastered the intricate balancing and motions of flying, and was able to use this form too as it was made to be used. But she could not assume the unicorn form; neither the vampire-girl nor the Red Adept could tell her the way of that.

She realized that somewhere along the way her doubt had faded. She now knew that this was Phaze—and that she was in love with Phaze, as she was with Bane. So many of its folk had been kind to her, in such understanding ways.

"Thou'rt recovered," Trool informed her in due course. "Thou canst now go thy way. What dost thou seek?"

"I have found what I sought," Agape told him. "I was in doubt whether this was really Phaze; now I know it is. Now I can return to Bane."

"Dost know his location?"

She shook her head. "No."

"Mayhap thou shouldst go to the Blue Demesnes; he will surely be there soon or late."

"Yes. I would like to meet his folks."

"They be a piece distant from here. Best that thou not go alone."

Agape now appreciated the wisdom of such advice! "I might fly, if Suchevane were willing to fly with me."

"Aye, that seems best. There be a matter thou shouldst know: the Adverse Adepts be looking for thee."

"They are? Why?"

"We know not. But it be known that Mach and Fleta took sanctuary with Translucent, which gives the Adverse Adepts half o' what they need to establish contact between the frames, to their advantage. An they discover that now Bane and Agape be here, they might wish to offer further sanctuary."

"But we support the existing order!" Agape protested.

"Aye. Therefore it be a stalemate, till Mach return to us or Bane join the Adverse Adepts. If they possessed control o' thee, that might be a lever 'gainst Bane."

"That's why I was leaving Proton!" she cried. "The Contrary Citizens were after me! We were hiding when Bane and Mach exchanged back—only Fleta and I exchanged too!"

"Aye. Stile noted that the imbalance is abating not, and knew that either the boys had exchanged not, or that other had exchanged. Bane went to him and proved his identity, so then it was known. Now the Adverse Adepts be searching, and we think this be their likely reason."

"I must exchange back, and get away from Proton!" Agape exclaimed. "But I can't do it by myself! I think that only with Bane, and with Mach and Fleta together—"

"Aye. But methinks the Adepts be watching. They cannot molest thee here, and I think know not thy location, for Fleta's friends would not tell. But they may intercept any unusual traveling. Therefore, let me give thee an amulet thou canst invoke at need, to protect thee from revelation o' thine identity, and mayhap from molestation an it be suspected." He went to a cabinet and brought out a fine silver chain with a small foggy stone.

Agape accepted it. "This—how do I—"

"Merely hold it and say 'I invoke thee' and it will mask thine identity. No one will know thy nature. But use it not except at need; it be an unpretty spell, and it wears off not swiftly."

She remembered Bane's warning about his spell of undetectability. This seemed similar. Indeed, she would not use it unless she had to! "Thank you, Adept. I appreciate all you have done for me."

"Thou hast been good company," he said deprecatingly.

He was also a good person, she knew. She resolved to do him a singular favor, when the occasion presented itself.

Suchevane readily agreed to travel with her. The two changed to their flying forms and set out, heading southwest toward the Blue Demesnes. Agape's practice and restored health stood her in good stead; she now flew well and swiftly.

But a hummingbird was no hawk, and a bat was no dragon. They were unable to make the full distance in one day, and had to descend, to revert to human form and eat and rest for the night. They could have remained in their winged forms, but these were relatively small and weak, and it seemed safer to assume the more massive human forms for sleeping. They landed in an oasis, a clump of trees near a spring, and plucked fruit for their supper.

"I thought vampires ate human blood," Agape remarked.

"Nay, not ordinarily," the girl demurred. "Only for special occasions, such as the onset o' flying. Then we seek not human beings, but animals o' the unintelligent variety."

"Something I've been meaning to tell you," Agape said. "Trool thinks that no attractive woman would associate with him voluntarily, and he doesn't care for anything involuntary. If you were to ask him—"

"Ask an Adept?" Suchevane exclaimed. "I would not presume!"

"You do like him?"

"Aye. But that has no bearing."

"You showed me how to do the things I need to do to survive," Agape said firmly. "Now let me show you how to do this. You must find a pretext to approach him, and then say, 'Adept, I would stay with thee and be thy companion, an thou not be offended.' I tell you, he will not be offended."

"But I could ne'er—"

"I couldn't fly, either."

Suchevane paused. "Thou really dost think—?"

"I don't think, I *know*. If he expresses doubt, tell him that you came to him because you have come to know him and respect him, and would like to share his life until he finds some better woman. I assure you, he will not find that, or even look for it. But if he declines your company, what have you lost? How can it be wrong to speak honestly of your desire? I am an alien, but I do not think the way of the folk of this planet differs that much from that of mine."

"Thou dost make it sound so easy!" Suchevane said. "But he be an Adept, and I an animal!"

"He is also a lonely old troll, and a decent person. He helped me substantially, and now I would like to help him—by sending him something I know he would really like. You."

Suchevane stared into the closing night. "I cannot believe—"

"I couldn't believe this was Phaze, either. But now I do, for I have come to know it. Reality is similarly waiting for you, if you care to grasp it—and it would be a shame not to. You risk only a little pride, and stand to gain so much."

The woman's face turned toward her. "I think now I see how Bane came to love an alien creature."

"Alien creatures can love, too."

"Aye, aye! They can! And animals too!"

"And animals too," Agape agreed. "And trolls."

Then they leaned into each other, and hugged each other, and wept together.

Agape woke to discover herself enmeshed. Lines were closing around her, and suddenly there was yelling and scrambling, and weight on her as something small and awful pounced. Earth-smelling hands clamped on her head, and more of them clamped on her breasts. "Got her! Got her!" someone screamed, almost in her ear. "Get the other!"

Agape tried to change to hummingbird form, but couldn't. The transformation spell just didn't work.

Suchevane's form beside her vanished, and the bat was scrambling out through the netting. "Hey, I told you to hold her!"

"I did, but she changed!"

"A 'corn can't change with a hand on her horn!"

"She's not a 'corn, she's a bat!"

Then Suchevane was up and away, flying into the moonlight. She had escaped, but Agape was captive. Because, it seemed, the button in her forehead was the vestige of her unicorn horn, and that had to be unfettered for its magic to operate.

"Well, this one's a 'corn," a voice said. "Come on, let's have at her before the chief comes."

Hands pulled up her cloak, exposing her body. Agape struggled, but there were too many hands on her, grasping her head, her arms, her breasts, her legs and her bottom.

They were little men, no, goblins, with huge ugly heads and big hands and feet and small, twisted, knobby bodies.

They worked the net off, and the rest of her cloak, their hands taking new and more intimate holds. They held her spread-eagled, while one came at her with bared member.

"Hey, who said thou dost go first?" another goblin cried. "*I* be first!" He shoved the other aside.

"No way, Snotnose!" the other returned, shoving him back.

Snotnose punched him in the belly. The two exploded into a fight, landing on Agape's exposed torso. Three other goblins hauled them off, while a fourth made ready to rape her. But this left nobody holding her legs. She brought them up kicking, scoring on the face of the would-be rapist.

Ouch! His head was like rock. He seemed not to notice the kick, while her toes were smarting in her slipper. He threw himself down on her, trying to get into place.

She hooked her feet behind him and applied a scissors squeeze. His body was relatively puny; now she was managing to hurt him! But other goblins were piling on again, and in a moment her feet were unhooked and her legs wrenched apart.

"What's this?" a new voice cried.

All goblins froze. This was evidently their leader, the chief whom they wished to avoid until they got their business done.

"We are supposed to capture the 'corn unharmed,"

the chief said. "Remember, her body's the same as the friendly one. Damage it, and we'll alienate the friendly one, when she returns."

"We weren't going to damage her," the goblin between her legs protested. "Just have a little fun with her."

"Well, 'corns have funny notions about damage," the chief said sardonically. "Tie her—and don't let go o' her horn."

Grudgingly, the goblins tied her, finally wrapping a strip of cloth about her head to cover her forehead. Then they let her go, with a few final pinches at succulent portions of her torso. If she hadn't known before why Bane hated goblins, her understanding was improving now.

Trool had warned her that the Adverse Adepts were searching for her. This was confirmation.

Then she remembered the amulet. Her hands were tied, but the chain remained around her neck; the goblins hadn't noticed it, having been paying too much attention to the flesh of her body.

"I invoke thee," she said to it, hoping it didn't have to be actually in her hand.

Nothing happened.

She felt a surge of dread. If the amulet couldn't help her, then she was lost, for they had already made her captive. At least Suchevane had escaped. If only they had perched in their flying forms, out of reach of goblins! But had some hungry night-hunting hawk spotted them—

"Very well, 'corn," the chief said. "Who be ye?"

Agape didn't answer.

"Speak, or hurt," the goblin warned.

"Go soak thy snoot in a sewer," Agape replied. Then she was amazed; she had not intended to say that, and it was not the way she talked!

"Speak, or we shall bite thee on the tender feet!" the chief said.

"Hear me well, fecal-face," she said evenly. "An

thou put one foul toothmark on my tender foot, the Adept'll put sixteen handsome teethmarks in thy foul bottom. Thou canst not touch me!" What was she saying?!

"She talks like a harpy!" one of the other goblins said, impressed.

"An thou beest the creature we seek, that be true," the chief admitted. "An thou turn out other, we shall chain thee spread o'er an anthill while we take turns raping thee to death. Now answer: what be thy name?"

"An I tell thee aye, I be the one thou dost seek, an thou dost take me to thy employer, an he know I be not, then willst thou rue the day and night that thou didst set thy smelly posterior on this globe," she said grimly. "An I tell thee nay, and thou dost set thy minions at my body, an the Adept learn I after all be the one, then willst thou rue the very thought that sent thy sickly sire slumming to conceive thee on the stinking slut that bore thee."

Even the chief took stock at this point. This was evidently not the precise language he had anticipated from the captive. Certainly it was nothing she had intended ever to say to anyone! What had happened to her mouth?

Then it came to her: the amulet! She had invoked it, and it was working! Already she had talked the goblin into a situation in which he dared neither to take her in nor to maltreat her.

The goblin pondered. He grimaced. "There be no help for it except I take thee in," he decided. "That be the lesser gamble."

"Not so, thou son o' an infected slug," she retorted. "Thou canst save thy putrid skin only by releasing me unharmed and reporting that thou didst discover naught in these parts."

He stared at her. "Truly, do I wish we had found thee not!" he exclaimed. "Yet an I free thee, and thou dost turn out to be the one, then there be no spot under the earth safe to escape the vengeance o' the Adept!

So needs must I bring thee to him intact, and tell him thou art but a suspect, and my punishment then may be slight."

"Until I tell him how thou didst have thy minions hold me whilst thou didst shove thy puny thing in me," she said. "Then I think I had better be not the one thou seekest, for an I be the one, thou willst find thyself suspended by that thing from the nether moon." She had not even realized that there was a nether moon! This was obviously hyperbole, but nonetheless effective.

He looked glumly at her, not commenting.

"An if I be not the one, as it be needful for thy health that I be not, then why bring me in at all?" she concluded persuasively. "I be nothing but mischief for thee, either way."

"I shall take thee to my superior," he decided. "The decision be his. Let him free thee or ravish thee; it will be out o' my domain."

He had figured out a way to pass the buck, she realized. She was stuck with captivity. Still, the tainted tongue foisted on her by the amulet had bought her some time, and perhaps it would befuddle the superior goblin as readily as it had this one. She had never before realized what a weapon a tongue could be! Trool had warned her that this was not a pretty spell; he had known whereof he spoke.

They left her tied, and spent the remainder of the night in the oasis. Then, in the morning, prompted by her harpy-tongue, they gave her some bread and water and leave to relieve herself. Then they started on their way to the goblin headquarters. They gave her back her cloak, and some food, and did not molest her. But it was a wearying walk, hours in the rising sun, bearing north.

Then something appeared on the horizon to the southwest. The goblins looked back over their shoulders, alarmed.

And well they might be, for it was a huge wooden

figure, striding rapidly toward them, its face fixed in an ominously neutral expression. Obviously it intended them no good.

"A golem!" the chief muttered. "We'll have to fight it."

The goblins lined up, drawing weapons: sticks, daggers, and the net. The golem strode up without pause. What did this mean?

Then Agape saw the form of a bat perched on the figure's head, and understood. Suchevane had brought help!

The golem arrived. The goblins attacked it. Their weapons had no effect; its wooden limbs were impervious. Then it swept its hands around in a double circle, at the goblins' head level, and knocked over every goblin within range. Its wooden arms were like clubs!

Very quickly the goblins had had enough. They fled. The golem stopped, the bat hopped down—and Suchevane stood there. "Agape!" she exclaimed, as she hurried to remove the bindings. "How glad I be that thou be not hurt!" She paused. "Or did—?"

Agape opened her mouth to reassure her friend. "Whom dost thou think thou art talking to, guano brain?"

Oops! The spell was still in operation!

Suchevane looked startled. Quickly, Agape lifted off the amulet and threw it away.

The vampire smiled with understanding. "The amulet! Thou didst invoke it to befuddle them!"

Agape smiled agreement. "And thee, thou quarterwit! Now let me be!" Then she closed her mouth, appalled.

But Suchevane understood. "Thou canst not abate a spell by throwing away its origin," she said. "Needs must it pass of its own accord. Come, change form, and the golem will take us to the Blue Demesnes."

Agape was glad to keep her mouth shut and comply. She became the hummingbird, and Suchevane the bat, and they both perched on the golem, who strode purposefully for its home.

Before long the blue turrets of the castle appeared. The Blue Demesnes! A lovely older woman, also garbed in blue, came out to meet them as they arrived.

They changed back to girlform. "This be Agape, Lady," Suchevane said. "She whom I told thee of."

The Lady Blue extended her hand. "I am glad to meet thee at last," she said graciously.

"Well, I be not pleased to meet thee, thou harridan," Agape snapped. Then, appalled anew, she slapped both hands over her mouth.

"She be under geis!" Suchevane said instantly. "The Red Adept gave her an amulet, to conceal her identity—"

The Lady Blue smiled with comprehension. "Mayhap my son can abate it somewhat," she said. "I have heard much about thee, Agape."

Agape's mouth opened. She stuffed her right fist into it, stifling whatever it had been about to say.

Suchevane turned to Agape. "Mine alien friend, I must haste to my Flock before I be missed. I have business . . . and the Lady Blue knows thy situation and will keep thee safe till Bane return."

Indeed she had business! She wanted to go to Trool the Troll and speak her piece. Agape could not trust herself to talk, so merely nodded, then embraced the vampire tearfully.

Suchevane became the bat and flew to the northeast. Agape gazed after her, abruptly lonely.

"Fear not for her," the Lady said, mistaking her mood. "I gave her a packet o' wolfbane, which she can sniff when she tires; it will buoy her to complete the journey in a single flight, so that naught can befall her aground."

And that was the concern that Agape should have been having: for her friend's safety after a tiring night. She felt ashamed.

The Lady put her hand to Agape's elbow. "Come into the premises, my dear. Thou surely dost be tired after thine experience, and will require food and rest.

My son be absent yet, but will return in due course, and then thou canst be with him."

Agape suffered herself to be guided into the castle, but she glanced askance at the Lady. Didn't Bane's parents oppose this union?

The Lady laughed. "I see that thou dost have concern o'er thy status here, Agape. Do thou make thyself comfortable, and we shall have a female talk ere my husband return."

Agape did that. She was glad that she had learned how to take care of this body, so that she was able to clean up and empty her wastes without complication.

In the afternoon, after a meal and a nap, she joined the Lady for their talk. The geis remained on Agape; the Troll had been right about its lasting effect! Thus it was pretty much a one-way conversation, with Agape merely nodding agreement at appropriate intervals.

"The opposition o' factions o' Adepts be longstanding," the Lady said. "Adept ne'er liked Adept, till Stile came on the scene. Then he did what was necessary to separate the frames, for by their interaction they were being despoiled, and so he evoked the enmity o' the despoilers. That be the origin o' the Adverse Adepts; they liked each other not overly much before, and very little now, but they league in common interest. One did he befriend, Brown, and one did he replace, Red; all others be 'gainst him, to lesser or greater extent. But Stile, who be also the Blue Adept, be strongest o' Adepts, save for the one he promoted, Trool the Troll, who has the Book o' Magic. So did he prevail, and the frames were parted."

She looked at Agape, and Agape nodded. She had learned some of this from Bane, before, but knew that the Lady was merely establishing the background for her point.

"After the parting, the force o' magic in Phaze was reduced by half," the Lady continued. "Because o' the transfer of Phazite to Proton, to make up for the Protonite mined there, that had caused the dangerous imbalance. But since the reduction was impartial, affecting all alike, it made no difference in the relative powers o' Adepts, and things seemed much as before. But the Adverse Adepts resented this wrong they felt Stile had done them, and conspired 'gainst him. They stifled his programs for better relations between man and animals, and wrought mischief in constant devious ways. Gradually their power increased, for they were many and we few. We knew that we needed new magic to hold them off, and our great hope was in our son, Bane, who showed early promise. An he grow, and marry, and have an heir like himself, belike we could hold off the Adverse Adepts indefinitely, and maintain a fair balance in our land, that evil not o'ertake it."

The Lady sighed. Agape wanted to speak, for she had known of this too, and understood, and intended to act to free Bane for that future his parents wished for him. But the geis constrained her, and she only nodded again.

"But there were no suitable young women," the Lady said sadly. "The village girls were poisoned 'gainst our kind; e'en I, a generation ago, would ne'er have married Blue an circumstances not been unusual. The only truly eligible woman is the daughter o' the Tan Adept—one o' the hostile ones. Bane played with animal friends, but o' course these were not suitable for marriage. It be not that we be prejudiced 'gainst the animals, for many be fine creatures, and we work closely with them and like them well. It be that they cannot breed with man. Therefore the future o' our good works came into peril. It seemed we would have to deal with Tan, and be compromised accordingly; but the alternative was to lose all. It were not a happy position."

This was new to Agape. She kept her mouth shut and listened.

"Then the boys made their exchange, and Mach came to our frame, and Bane went to thine. We had not believed such possible, and were caught unprepared. We saw that the exchange was but mental only, not o' the bodies. Mach became attached to Fleta, the unicorn, and Bane to thee, the alien. We understand; there be not a finer person than Fleta, and we know our son would bestow not his love on an unworthy creature. But we opposed such union, because it meant the loss o' all we planned on, and incalculable damage to the frame, owing to the lack o' the continuation o' our line.

"That were our error. We appreciated not how true Mach's love was. Fleta understood our position, and resolved to disengage—but she knew what we did not, that only her death would accomplish it. So she arranged to die—and Mach came to her, and spake her the triple Thee, and such was the force o' it he overrode Adept magic and saved her."

The Lady found a handkerchief and dabbed at her eyes, for she was crying now. "We ne'er meant Fleta to die! Ne'er did we wish her ill! We thought their love but an infatuation that would pass. How wrong we were! So were we cast as the villains, and they took refuge with the Adverse Adepts, and our ruin did we bring upon ourselves. Fain would we undo the mischief we did, but it be too late; the two be alienated from us."

As she spoke, there was a faint ripple of light in the air. Agape glanced about trying to fathom its curious nature, but it was gone almost before she was aware of it.

Then she realized that this was the splash of truth that she had heard about. The Lady Blue had not noticed it, but it authenticated her statement.

Agape did not dare speak, but she had to act. She stood, and went to the Lady, and embraced her, and cried with her, silently.

After a moment, the Lady continued. "We resolved to make not the same error again. We knew that the parallel o' the frames meant that Bane would find similar love in Proton. Our cause be lost, but not necessarily our son. We accept his choice, and we accept thee. We can do not other. That be the root o' thy welcome here. When Bane came home not long ago and told us more o' thee, we knew it was right. Thou dost be the one we would have chosen for him, an the choice been ours. An our circumstance not blinded us—"

The Lady could not continue, but hardly needed to. She had made her point.

But how awful it was, that the acceptance of the romances of the two boys had to come in the face of such a loss. Even for Agape, who faced not death but separation from Bane, it seemed hopelessly difficult. What was the use in going home to Moeba, if Mach and Fleta remained together and the family of Blue was denied an heir? Was her sacrifice after all pointless?

"There be one other thing," the Lady said after a fair pause. "Stile discovered that the exchange leads to new imbalance, so that the frames be headed for destruction, an the imbalance be not corrected. That be why we sent the messenger. E'en now, the Adverse Adepts be verifying it. So it may be that all else becomes moot. But I wanted thee to know that this be no device we made to deceive thee; we discovered it after accepting thee. We think the communication between the two can continue, but that actual exchange must be limited. What this means for thy future we know not."

Agape was satisfied at this point not to speak, because she had no answer either.

That evening, as the two of them were gazing out across the dark plain, and admiring the nascent stars and moons, there came another ripple in the air, a gentle passing glow from the east that slowly faded.

The Lady Blue glanced at Agape. "Methinks Suchevane reached the Red Demesnes," she murmured.

Agape could only smile. How glad she was that she had spoken as she had!

Agape remained with the Lady for several days, and gradually the geis wore off and she was able to engage in halting dialogue. Now she loved Bane, and Phaze, and the Lady too—and knew she had to give them all up. Unless some accommodation were discovered that would enable her to remain with Bane, and even to visit Phaze again . . .

She had to cling to the faint hope that this was possible. But her dread was that it was not.

Then at last Bane arrived. He appeared just beyond the moat and called out: "Anybody home?"

The two of them went out to meet him. Agape did not have to say a word; she stepped into his embrace.

He entered the castle with them, and had news of his own. "The Adverse Adepts be preparing for war. I spied on them and verified it; they be organizing their minions, the goblins and demons, ready to take by force what they may not accomplish by negotiation. They mean to have me join them, and to use thee as a lever against me, as the Contrary Citizens did."

"I know," Agape said. "I am not safe here either."

"I would have come for thee sooner, but it be tricky spying on Adepts, and they were far more watchful than I expected. But news came to me that thou wast with Trool, and I knew thou wouldst be safe there."

"I was." It was so good to be with him again!

"But we must exchange thee back, and get thee to thy home planet! I love thee, and would not have thee taken hostage. I will visit thee on Moeba, later, when I exchange."

"But we are going together!" she exclaimed.

"Nay. First must thou exchange, and I not, for there be much for me to do yet here. But ne'er doubt I will join thee when I can, nor Adepts nor frames will hinder me."

He continued talking, reassuringly, but Agape hardly paid attention. She just hugged him forever.

8

Tourney

A serf hurried toward her. "I am empowered by my employer to take you to—"

The Ladder screen blinked. Then its speaker spoke: "This serf has qualified for the Tourney. Until disqualified, Serf Fleta is ineligible for reassignment."

The serf's brow furrowed. "But Citizen Tan says—"

So Tan had caught up to her—just too late!

"The Citizen has no authority over the Tourney," the speaker said.

The serf stepped forward, reaching for Fleta's arm. "He won't take no for an—"

There was a flash. The serf staggered, evidently jolted by something. "Interference in the Tourney is not tolerated," the speaker said. "Serf Fleta to report to Game accommodations until further notice. Follow the line."

"Yes, sir," Fleta murmured, awed. The Adepts of Proton-frame did not mince words or actions!

The line led to a small residential chamber, complete with a screen and food machine. The door panel clicked behind her, and she realized that she was confined.

She was suddenly alarmed. Could the Contrary Citizens have tricked her again, and led her to—?

Then the screen came on. "Don't worry, Fleta," Mach's voice said.

She whirled to face it. There he was, back in his normal guise. Still, it was only a picture, and she was coming to distrust those. "How do I know—"

He smiled. "When we first met, in Phaze, I was rescued from the swamp by a unicorn. She took me to a dead volcano crater, where I encountered a lovely young woman. It took me some time to realize that the two were the same, and that I was in love with an animal. But of course I was only a machine myself." He eyed her body. "It is almost as difficult to realize now that this stranger is that same bubbly nymph whose foal I mean to sire, when we return to Phaze."

It was Mach, all right! "I qualified for the Tourney!" she exclaimed gladly.

"I know. So you are being confined until it starts, so that no one can get at you. Now you can revert to your own girlform, and I will join you soon."

"They are not watching you?"

"They are watching me, but I am not in danger. They lost their chance when they lost you."

"Then we need fear them no longer?"

He grimaced. "Not so. They have our cooperation, in Phaze; we resist them here only because we are standing in lieu of Bane and Agape. Similarly Bane and Agape in Phaze may have a different status; the Adverse Adepts may be trying to capture them and convert them now. We must preserve their independence, by protecting yours. It's a funny situation, but this is the way I interpret the truce. In Proton we are against the Citizens, until the situation changes, if it does."

"I wish we were against the Adverse Adepts, too," she said.

"Had Bane's folks only been able to accept our love—"

"They want an heir," she said.

"And they shall have it!" he said. "I have been thinking about that, and researching genetics here in Proton. I believe the Book of Spells now in the Red Adept's possession will have information on the magical meshing of species, and I am going to research there the moment I return."

"Then willst thou need not to support the Adverse Adepts!" she exclaimed, lapsing into her natural dialect.

"That does not follow. We made a deal, and I must deliver what I promised, unless the truce is modified. But perhaps the objectives of Stile and the Adepts are not mutually exclusive. If we could somehow forge a compromise—"

"A compromise!" she repeated. "A mating of their differing desires!"

"Yes. Therein lies our true hope. Now you get some rest; I have further research to do before I join you."

"Do thy research!" she exclaimed, gladly. "An it mean our foal—"

"This is one advantage of exchanging between the frames," he said. "I have the advantage of pursuing both lines of research. If I can't see it through, I doubt anyone else can."

Then he faded out, and she, relieved, melted onto the bed and slept, feeling exhilarated.

There were no challenges in the two days. Mach joined her, and now they were free of the need to hide or to conceal their identities; they had found temporary sanctuary here at the Game Annex. Now, for the first time, they were able to make love in these other bodies.

Then she learned that Mach had not really been talking to her, before their physical reunion. He had set up what he called a responsive emulation. "Damn thee!" she cried, furious at this deception. It had fooled her completely.

"But I could not approach you," he protested. "It

would have been dangerous for you. Then I had some trouble, so I went to Moeba."

Curiosity caused her to rein her fury for the moment. "Agape's planet? What did you there?" And by the time he explained, she had decided to forgive him.

"So when Bane returns, my research may help him," he concluded.

"I like Phaze better," Fleta said.

"So do I," he agreed. Then he looked at her, becoming grave. "We have been assuming that we will return together. But if you wash out of the Tourney, and go to Moeba, will exchange be possible for you?"

She was stricken. "If I be not with thee, and they two together, how can we exchange?"

"I think we cannot. Therefore we must be sure that all four are together. If not, we must not exchange."

"We cannot search for them, as we did in Phaze," she said. "Needs must I remain in the Annex."

"Yes, they must come to us. But when Bane contacts me, I will make this clear."

"Aye." She pondered a moment more. "Meanwhile, methinks I had best stay here until then. I must win my games."

"Fleta, you are not trained in the games! You were lucky, and your opponents were selected, for the qualifying ladder. The Tourney is different; you will be up against experienced players, each of whom is desperate to win."

"And I lose thee, and Phaze, if I lose. I too be desperate to win," she said quietly.

"I'd better drill you in strategy."

"Aye."

So for most of their waking time, he indoctrinated her in the ways of the Tourney, trying to prepare her for a competent performance. The object was not to win the Tourney and become a Citizen, but to remain uneliminated long enough for Bane and Agape to come and make the exchange.

The details of the Tourney varied from year to year. Sometimes only the top five or six on each ladder qualified; this year it was ten, making it a large one. That meant that the authorities had concluded that there were too many serfs, and so were using the Tourney as a device to prune them back voluntarily. There were other ways, but this was considered to be the gentlest.

On the other hand, this was single-elimination. Normally it was double-elimination, which meant that each contestant had two chances. This year, one loss was all, and that made players nervous, though their chances for final victory were unchanged.

One thousand and twenty-four contestants would start the Tourney: ten males and ten females from every age ladder from Age Twenty-one through Age Sixty: eight hundred in all, plus two hundred from the Junior and Senior ladders (those below and above the normal range) and the Leftover Ladder, and a dozen or so slumming Citizens, aliens and such. Each round would cut the number in half, until the tenth round produced the single winner. Because the number of consoles and the extent of the game facilities were limited, Round One would require four days for completion, and Round Two two days; thereafter single days would suffice. Thus the complete Tourney was scheduled for fourteen days, and that schedule would be kept. Any player who failed to show up promptly for his match would lose by default. Audiences were permitted, but no interference would be tolerated.

Fleta had already seen enough of the game system to appreciate how intolerant the Game Computer was of interference. That reassured her.

"Of course that doesn't apply to Citizens," Mach said. "They set their own schedules. But most who have the interest to play, also have the pride to do it properly."

"But if the prize be Citizenship, and the cost of loss be exile, why do Citizens play?" Fleta asked.

"Mere entertainment. Victory gains them nothing, and loss costs them nothing. They are immune. But those they play against are bound. If you come up against a Citizen, call him sir and play to win. He cannot hurt you, here, except by beating you."

"Not e'en Citizen Tan?"

"Not even he," he reassured her.

Then, seemingly suddenly, the Tourney started, and she was summoned to her first game. "I am not allowed to help you, here," Mach said. "But I will try to tune in on Bane. If I can find him, I can tell him what we need."

"Do thou do that," she said, kissing him.

She followed the line to the console. She was the first there, which made her feel better, though she knew it made no difference.

She looked at the screen.

TOURNEY ROUND ONE: FLETA VS JIMBO

She hoped Jimbo was a duffer.

He turned out to be a man in his fifties. There were no ladders in the Tourney; they were for qualification only. He nodded at her, then took his stance at the console.

Her numbers lighted. That meant she could not select ANIMAL. But she had discussed this with Mach, and knew her best route. Without hesitation she touched 4. ARTS.

It settled on 4A: Naked Arts. The choices were Poetry, Stories, Singing, Dancing, Pantomime and Drama, with distinctions between recitative and creative. They assembled the nine-square subgrid and chose, and came up with Original Story telling.

JUDGING: the screen printed. COMPUTER PANEL AUDIENCE.

This was new to Fleta. Should she touch one of the words? But there was no grid.

"We can do it by agreement if we want," Jimbo said. "Me, I don't like a machine deciding how I rate, or a panel of experts either."

"A living audience," Fleta agreed, relieved. She

touched that choice, and evidently he did too, for that one highlighted.

SUBJECT: the screen continued. SELECTED BY COMPUTER RANDOM AUDIENCE.

Fleta hadn't realized that a subject had to be chosen; she had assumed that any story would do. She wasn't certain how she would do if she got a bad subject. Since she could not choose it herself, and shared her opponent's distrust of impersonal decisions, she asked "Audience?"

"Agreed," Jimbo said immediately.

ADJOURN TO STAGE. And a line appeared, showing the way.

They followed it to the stage. There was a small dais and an audience section with seats for about twenty-five.

Now they had to wait for the audience to arrive. It seemed that a number of Tourney spectators had registered for audience purposes, and were on tap awaiting assignment. The Computer was making a random selection and notifying the selectees of this assignment. They were now following their lines to this chamber.

In a few minutes exactly twenty-five people arrived. They were all serfs, male and female, ranging from young to old. They took their seats in silence.

A note sounded at the large screen set in the wall behind the stage. All eyes fixed on it.

> AUDIENCE WILL SELECT SUBJECT FOR STORYTELLING. THE FOLLOWING SUBJECTS ARE AVAILABLE; TOUCH <SELECT> BUTTON ON CHAIR WHEN CHOICE IS HIGHLIGHTED.

Then the screen was filled with an alphabetical listing of subjects, beginning with ABANDONMENT and ending with ZOOLOGICAL. The Computer gave the audience a moment to consider the list, then the first word was highlighted. In a second the next was, and then the third, the lighting continuing at one-second intervals until the list had been covered, several minutes later.

THE LEADING CHOICES ARE, the screen announced, ILLICIT WEALTH UNTIMELY DEATH FORBIDDEN LOVE. TOUCH <SELECT> WHEN CHOICE IS HIGHLIGHTED.

The highlight made its tour. Then: SUBJECT IS FORBIDDEN LOVE. AUDIENCE WILL <SELECT> FIRST STORYTELLER.

Then a light illuminated Fleta, and moved across to Jimbo. JIMBO SPEAKS FIRST.

Fleta did not know on what basis the audience decided, but she was relieved; this was proceeding so efficiently that she had not been able to organize her thoughts. She was, after all, an animal; she knew she lacked the versatility of a human being. What story of forbidden love was right for this audience?

"Uh, well," Jimbo said, evidently also somewhat at a loss. He did not seem to be any better prepared for this than Fleta was, which made her wonder. Maybe he had just gotten into a bad area, for him.

Then he shrugged, as if deciding something private, and began his story.

"There was once this serf, and he wasn't much, he was forty when he came to Proton, but all they let anybody have is twenty years anyway so maybe that didn't make much difference. He was a message carrier—any time the Citizen wanted a note delivered personal, so it wouldn't be in the records, this serf would hand-carry it to wherever it was going. It wasn't a bad job; he got to travel all over Proton, just taking messages, and got to sleep over at some pretty fancy Citizen estates while waiting for the reply-message to be ready. It went along like this for about nine years, and then the Citizen died and his daughter inherited it."

Jimbo paused. Fleta saw some knowing smiles in the audience, and realized that they were guessing what was coming next. This seemed to be Jimbo's own story!

"This woman, the new Citizen, was maybe twenty-nine years old, and she was the damned loveliest creature in the dome. Her hair sort of rippled when she walked, throwing off highlights, and her eyes were like twin headlamps, they were so clear and bright. But because she was new, she was uncertain, and she didn't want to make any fool of herself, putting on the wrong airs in the wrong place, you know, specially when it came to handling serfs. So she sort of asked this serf for advice, because he'd been with the estate for nine years and kept his mouth shut, because sometimes the messages he carried were verbal and he would've been fired if he ever breathed a syllable of them to any but the designated party, so he just didn't say much of anything to anyone, just to be safe. She liked that, so she said, 'I want a message, only to me,' and then she asked how she should handle this other serf who sort of did things wrong but didn't mean to. And the message serf, he delivered his message, only it was really just his advice, that she should maybe reorganize her household a little, and move that clumsy serf to another position without saying why, so no feelings would be hurt and nobody had to be fired. And she did that, and it worked out just fine, and after that she asked for other messages like that.

"And then one time she sort of forgot where she was, only it didn't really matter because Citizens make their own rules and serfs just do what they're told. She was getting ready for a party, and she'd sent her personal maid for something, and the messenger man was there, so she just told him to take off her robe and put on the new one she had selected. So he put his hands on her shoulders from behind, and pinched the fabric, and lifted it up, and it came right off her and she was naked. Then he folded it and set it down and fetched the new robe from its hanger, only it was really more like an evening gown, and she turned and lifted her arms so he could put the gown up over her, and she had the body like only an android or robot made for that sort of thing ever has, only on her it was real, I mean natural, and he like to have goggled, because mostly Citizens don't take much care of themselves and even when they look good in a gown it's mostly corset stays and foundation creme and whatever, or maybe a fresh rejuve treatment, but she didn't even use underwear, her body was genuine throughout. And then she was mostly dressed, and looking just as good, only better, because he knew it didn't just come with the clothing.

"Then the maid came back, and took over, and he went back to his chamber. But it was like that image of that body was burned into his retinas, because he kept seeing it every time he blinked. And suddenly he lost interest in the android gal who would be with him any time he wanted, because she was like a cratered moon, and the Citizen was like the sun. And every time he saw the Citizen, she was clothed but he saw her naked like a serf, and her skin shining, and her eyes sort of looking at him, and it was like a fire inside him, but she never noticed. Sometimes she'd bring in these men, Citizens, and have sex with them, and they were jaded but they got hot for her in a hurry when they discovered that her body didn't come off with the clothing, and sometimes she'd just hire a robot to do it exactly the way she liked it. Only she didn't like to have to tell a robot how, that was maybe too much like masturbation, so she'd have the messenger tell the robot, and make sure the robot had it right. And the messenger—"

Jimbo paused, again, and it was clear that every member of the audience understood his hesitation perfectly. He had conceived a passion for a Citizen: forbidden love indeed! What was he going to do about it?

"Then one day she had a new robot, and maybe there was a circuit not properly integrated, because it wasn't getting it quite right, even though it had the instructions down pat and could repeat them verbatim. 'Damn it!' she swore, irritated. So she called in the messenger and told him to show the robot how to do it right. He was moving too fast and heavy, when she liked slow and light. So the messenger, he got down on her—"

He paused again, but the audience did not object. Evidently he was uncertain about how much detail he should provide, and what was relevant to the assigned subject, and how to phrase it for this mixed audience.

Fleta, too, was thrust into thought, perhaps for different reason. Jimbo was telling how a male humanoid robot was routinely used for sexual purpose; apparently this was accepted in Proton. She had had relations with just such a robot. If she told her own story—and indeed, it was all she could think of to do—would this audience take it to be routine and therefore dull, and deem her the loser? What was the most wonderful experience of her life might seem, here, to be unworthy of mention.

If she lost, here in this first round, she would be shipped to Moeba, and would never be able to exchange back to her own body in Phaze. But if she won, she would have several more days before the second round, and maybe by then—

"He got down on her," Jimbo repeated, resuming his narration. "His heart was beating like a teenager's, because the Citizen's body was his ultimate dream, and all he wanted to do was be like this with her for real, and have her want him as a man. He knew this wasn't so, that she saw him only as a convenient source of minor information, and now as a device to demonstrate a minor technique to a machine, but his dream wanted to pretend it was something more.

"His flesh touched hers, lightly, and penetrated gently, moving with just that constrained urgency that she required. 'Yes, like that,' she said to the robot. 'Proceed exactly like that.' The robot nodded, understanding at last.

"Her face turned back to the messenger, and he knew she was about to tell him to get off, now that his job was done. But the folly of the forbidden dream overcame him, and suddenly he plunged on in, exactly the way the robot was not supposed to. Her mouth opened with surprise, the annoyance just beginning, and he put his mouth on hers and kissed her savagely as his loin thrust against her and his body exploded in rapture.

"Then, his folly of passion abating, he realized what he had done. *He had raped a Citizen!* He scrambled up and ran from the chamber, knowing that his life was forfeit. He did not try to flee, for there was nowhere to go; he simply waited for what was to come.

"After an hour the call came: to report to the Citizen's front office. He knew there would be a robot there to take him into custody. For one moment of bliss he had forfeited all that he had worked for for nine years. He went, but the Citizen was there alone, standing in total loveliness in a gown. 'I require a message, for one only,' she said. 'If a serf oversteps his bounds, what should a Citizen do?' He knew she was referring to him. 'Have him put to death,' he replied, determined at least not to be a coward in his termination.

"Her expression did not change. 'If he has otherwise given good service, and perhaps was overtaken by an aberration of the moment?' she asked. He had not even hoped for such generosity of response! 'Fire him,' he said.

"She turned away from him. 'If publication of the offense might cause embarrassment to the Citizen?' she asked. Then he dared indeed hope! 'Enter him in the Tourney without explanation,' he said.

"She nodded. 'Thank you,' she said. And so it was that he found himself in the Tourney, though he had always been a duffer in the Game and knew he would quickly wash out and be deported. But his years of service still counted (for he had not been fired) and would represent a very nice payment on his departure; he would leave with an untarnished record. He was duly grateful for this, knowing how much worse it could have been, and his respect for his employer was undiminished. But still in his dream he had the temerity to wonder: was it possible that in some tiny way the Citizen had returned his interest, and perhaps been flattered by his inability to hold back when given the opportunity to indulge his passion with her? Could she have been unable to admit any trace of an interest so far beneath her, yet not displeased to have had the indulgence of it forced upon her? Would that account for her uncommon generosity in dealing with the one who had ravished her?"

Jimbo gazed out across the audience. "I do not know the answer, but I would like to think I might guess it."

Fleta knew before she spoke that Jimbo had won this game. She had thought that her own crisis was unique, and that the others in the Tourney were merely competing for the prize of Citizenship. Now she saw that that was not necessarily the case; each contestant might have as good reason to be here as she. She did not begrudge Jimbo the evident sympathy he had evoked in this audience.

FLETA SPEAKS SECOND, the big screen announced.

Now it was upon her! Encouraged by her opponent's example of discretion and candor, she told her own story in similar fashion.

"There was once in the Frame o' Phaze a unicorn filly," she began. "She was happy in her Herd, grazing the plains and running with her companions and learning the ways o' her kind. She labored to master her transformations, choosing one original form and one common form to complement her natural one. Her dam could become a firefly, so the filly liked the notion o' a flying form, and chose the smallest o' the avians, the hummingbird. Most other unicorns chose fierce hawks or fast falcons or lovely feathered birds, or even flying dragons, and some were amused that she should aspire to such an insignificant creature, but she had no fear o' smallness, for her dam was the smallest o' mares yet well respected by all the members o' the Herd and o' the neighboring Pack o' werewolves too. Indeed, it turned out that she could feed more readily than others, needing only the nectar o' some flower, and hide well, and it was a good choice.

"The common form was the most challenging, however, because that was human. The form itself was not difficult, but just as she had spent more time learning to fly than she had learning the birdform, she had to spend far more time learning to speak like a human than she had achieving girlform. To speak, she had to learn to think like a human, and the ways o' human thought were marvelous and weird. So she sought help, first from acquaintances among the werewolves and vampires who came more naturally by girlform, then from the most feared o' human folk, one o' the Adepts. This was because her dam was oath-friend to one Adept, and he was friend to some other Adepts, and so one o' them was willing to help the filly o' the oath-friend. Thus it was that the filly spent some time as the guest o' the Brown Adept, serving her as a serf might serve a Citizen, but also learning from her the complete human language and much o' the social ways of the human species too.

"Then did the filly come to maturity, and learned the identity o' the herb that suppressed her cycle o' heat so that she would not be bred too soon, for the Herd Stallion was her uncle and banned from breeding her. She played with the human son o' her dam's oath-friend, and he showed her how his kind mated, though it were meaningless in the absence o' heat. E'en so, she came to like that young human man, and wished she could be truly human, that she might be always with him. But he, o' course, knew her for an animal, and while he treated her always as a companion and e'en friend, there was no way he saw her as one to breed with or, as the humans put it, marry. So she kept her desire for him hidden, knowing that any union between them was forbidden. He was after all the son o' an Adept, one year to be Adept himself; he was far beyond the aspiration o' a normal human woman, let alone a mere animal."

How neatly she had summarized the whole of her

first decade and a half of life! But now she was ready for the real story. "Then she came o' age to mate and bear a foal for the Herd, so she was sent to another Herd, that its Stallion might breed her without incest. But she dawdled, remaining near the place favored by the Adept's son, in case he should come there and need a ride or companionship. She knew the hope to be vain, but still she stayed, foolishly. Perhaps it was in her mind that if she arrived at the other Herd not in time for her heat, she would escape breeding, and be free a little longer. It might not make much sense, but she was after all only an animal.

"Then happened something strange. A man passed the region, and he smelled like the Adept's son, but he acted like him not. He was going naked, as men did not, and stumbling as if he had been ne'er there before. She kept her distance, wanting to approach, but uncertain. Finally he cried for help, and that was all she needed; she sounded a chord on her horn in answer, and galloped to his aid. He seemed surprised to see her, as if his memory was gone, but rode her away from that place. She had to back off a water dragon, but carried him to safety in the crater. It was especially strange that he used not magic o' his own to protect himself, and seemed almost wary o' her, despite their long acquaintance. He settled down to sleep in the crater, and she pondered, then yielded to her desire and changed to girlform and joined him there.

"Next morning it seemed he was playing a game, for his speech was strange and he seemed still not to know her. He insisted his name was other than what she knew it was. He claimed to know magic not, and he was loath to wear clothes. She persuaded him to try a spell, and he did, but it worked strangely. She also encouraged him to make some clothing. He said he was a rovot, a thing like a wooden golem, only made o' metal, and that he needed not to have natural processes. But o' course he did; he did just prefer to do it alone. And gradually she understood that he was not the same man she had known, but his other self, from Proton-frame, a stranger to Phaze and all that was in it. Yet was he very like the one she knew in appearance, and perhaps in other things too, and she liked him very well. Perhaps she liked him better, for that he needed her help constantly, lest he blunder into trouble. But he knew not she was an animal; he thought the girlform and the birdform and the unicorn different creatures. He liked the girlform, and therefore she spoke not o' her other forms, but stayed close to him and teased him and smiled at him, reveling in the companionship she had ne'er had recently w' the Adept's son.

"Then he, thinking her human, took her in his arms and kissed her, and her heart fled from her and became his captive that moment. She tried to tell o' her nature, and why love between them was forbidden, but O she could not; she did want the illusion to linger longer. Then demons attacked, and to save them both she had to change to her natural form and carry him to safety. The secret was out. But he was not appalled; he said he was a machine, a thing not alive, a creature without feeling, that could not love. Then did new horror loom for her, that she had lost her heart to one who could care not. But he was wrong; he did care for her. And so their forbidden love was born."

She paused, and looked at the audience, and saw them rapt as they had been for Jimbo's story. But such was the joy of her memory, for all its heartache, she hardly cared now whether they cared; she just wanted to finish it.

"Then did the Adverse Adepts make chase, seeking to capture them and use him for their purpose, and they had to flee and hide. Goblins were questing e'erywhere. But they traveled a route the enemy did not suspect, and managed to escape. Later she learned that their love was forbidden not because the Adept his father objected to unicorns, but because only a human woman could bear him an heir. The filly saw that this was valid, for though she could have sex with her lover she could breed with him not. So she decided to free him for his destiny, and to fix herself in human form and jump from a ledge to her death. But he found her, and cried out to her the triple Thee, the ultimate statement o' his love, and such was the power o' it that it saved her from the extinction she had sought and made them one again.

"But now that love be still forbidden, if not by humans, then by the situation, for he be a creature o' Proton, and she a creature o' Phaze, and they can ne'er cross o'er to each other's frames without making an imbalance that will harm all. So now they quest for some way to make it right, but know not w'er it e'er can be."

Then she felt her eyes melting, and knew that her story was done.

AUDIENCE WILL TOUCH <SELECT> WINNER, the big screen printed. Jimbo's name highlighted, then Fleta's.

JIMBO SIX VOTES, FLETA FIVE VOTES. ABSTENTIONS FOURTEEN.

"Hey, wait!" a serf cried. "I didn't abstain! I hadn't made up my mind yet!" There was a chorus of agreement.

MAJORITY VOTE OF ESTABLISHED AUDIENCE REQUIRED FOR DECISION, the screen continued imperturbably. AUDIENCE WILL BE REQUIRED TO CONTINUE VOTING UNTIL THAT MAJORITY IS REGISTERED. TWO-MINUTE RECESS FOR CONSIDERATION BEFORE NEXT VOTE.

Fleta looked at Jimbo, and found him looking at her. She walked across to him. "I liked thy story," she said, feeling an affinity for him. "Truly, thou dost know forbidden love as I do."

"Too bad we didn't fall in love with each other," he said. "Are you really a . . . ?"

"A unicorn. Aye. But an the Citizens catch me, that be meaningless."

"How so?"

"They mean to use me as lever against him whom I love. But the Tourney protects me—an I not depart too soon."

"Won't you be safe offplanet?"

"I be not in mine own body, here. An I depart this world before I exchange to mine own frame, methinks can I not exchange at all, and that be worse yet."

"So you would prefer to remain here a little longer," he said.

"Aye," she said sadly. "But that decision be not in my power."

He smiled. "But it may be in mine." He stepped to the front of the stage, waving his hands. "May I have your attention!" he cried.

Instantly a sour note sounded from the screen. ERROR! CONTESTANT MAY NOT ATTEMPT TO INFLUENCE AUDIENCE ON HIS BEHALF.

"I haven't finished my story," he cried. "There's something else I have to say."

ERROR! STATEMENT IS OUT OF ORDER AT THIS TIME.

A man in the audience stood. "Listen, who's deciding this game, us or the machine?" he demanded. "Aren't we like a jury, and we can hear more if we want?"

"Yes, and can't we judge for ourselves whether he's trying to change our votes unfairly?" a woman responded.

The screen hesitated. PROCEDURAL MATTER. AUDIENCE WILL INDICATE WHETHER TO HEAR MORE FROM CONTESTANTS. SELECT RESPONSE YES NO. The YES was highlighted, then the NO.

CONTESTANTS MAY SPEAK, the screen printed, yielding gracefully.

"Okay," Jimbo said. "We've got two people here, both probably on the way out regardless of this particular game. One can go any time; the Tourney is just a pretext to get him offplanet without being charged with anything. The other is here to protect her from trouble still brewing, and if she can stay a while longer, maybe things will work out a little better for her. So if I were voting, and I had trouble making up my mind, I think I'd boot the one with nothing to lose, and keep the one with maybe something to win. Now I'm not trying to tell anybody how he should vote, just saying the way I see it, and the damned machine can't object to that, can it?" He walked to the side, leaving the stage to Fleta.

She realized that she was supposed to say something, but she could think of nothing. She just stood there and started to melt again, which seemed to be this body's way of crying. She didn't want to melt in front of all these people, so she hid her face in her hands, overcome.

After a moment, the voting proceeded. Fleta forced her eyes back into shape and looked at the screen.

FLETA TWENTY-THREE VOTES, JIMBO TWO; FLETA PROCEEDS TO ROUND TWO.

Jimbo looked at her and smiled. She ran to him, hugged him, and kissed him. The members of the audience applauded.

Suddenly she felt much more at home in the frame of Proton.

She had two days before her next match, because of the time required for the remaining Round One games to clear. Mach came to her, after passing through a thorough screening by the Game Computer to ensure that he was whom he claimed to be, and they had a little additional honeymoon. She cherished this brief experience with his own body; she had come to love him in Bane's body, but this was his reality. If she managed to return to Phaze, this would be all she ever knew of the true Mach.

Then it was time for her Round Two match. This time her opponent was a young woman, of grim visage, and she knew there would be no courtly generosity. She had to win outright.

She got the numbers again, and chose ARTS again. The girl chose B, so they were in TOOL-ASSISTED ARTS: Painting, Sculpture, Costumed Drama, Decorative Sewing, Patterns with blocks, colored sand, grains of rice or whatever, Card Houses, Kaleidoscope, and Musical Instruments.

Fleta was encouraged; she understood most of these Arts. She played with confidence, and got Music. The other girl was plainly uncertain now. In the end they had to play music, each on her own instrument. The girl chose the piano, and Fleta chose the syrinx: otherwise known as the panpipes, her natural instrument as a unicorn. She had, as a matter of private challenge, learned to play the panpipes in girlform. This was difficult, because her girlfingers lacked the musical coordination of her horn, and her girlmouth could play only one note at a time, or adjacent notes. But fingers weren't really necessary for this; hooves would have done to hold this instrument firm. She was unable to play two themes simultaneously, but the underlying harmonics came naturally, so she could do a creditable job. Whether she could do it in this alien body she wasn't sure, but she thought she could. They followed the line to the appropriate chamber.

Again, they were to be judged by an audience. None of the listeners was the same as those of her prior game; the Computer was careful about that sort of thing.

Fleta had to play first. She took the instrument, which consisted of eight tubes of graduated lengths, bound together. She sounded each note by blowing across the top of the proper tube. She played a simple yet evocative melody that had given her pleasure as a filly at the end of a perfect day of grazing, as the sun settled slowly into the trees on the horizon, setting them afire, and the evening wind fanned the high fringe of the grass to be grazed on the morrow. As she played, Phaze seemed to form around her, so lovely, and then it seemed that Mach was there too, delighted by her music as he always was, and for this moment everything was perfect.

Then the tune was done, and it was Proton again. The audience was staring at her. Had she started to melt again? No, they merely liked the music, perhaps not having heard the panpipes as played by a unicorn before.

Her opponent looked at the piano. "I concede," she said shortly, and walked out.

FLETA PROCEEDS TO ROUND THREE, the screen announced.

Just like that, she had won!

The audience filtered out, though several serfs glanced admiringly at the instrument as they passed.

"Clear the chamber," the speaker said. "Citizen approaching."

Fleta looked wildly around. "But I'm supposed to be protected!" she cried. "I'm still in the Tourney!"

"At ease, filly," the Citizen said, entering the chamber. He stood somewhat shorter than she, but his bright-blue robe identified him as far above her. "Not every Citizen be thine enemy."

"The Blue Adept!" she exclaimed, astonished.

He smiled. "Now Citizen Blue. Thy secret has been kept; the Game Computer allowed news o' thine identity to leak not beyond its annex. But I was o' Phaze, and I know the music o' the unicorn when I hear it. Ah, the memories it brought!"

"Mach's sire," she breathed.

"Aye. And thou'rt Neysa's foal. Glad I am to meet thee at last, however briefly, though thou dost favor her not in this guise." He squinted at her. "Best abolish the horn, though."

Fleta touched her forehead. She had grown the button-horn! It must have happened while she was playing the panpipes. No wonder the audience had stared! Quickly she melted it; she was not trying to make a freak of herself, here.

"Mach be looking for Bane, now," Citizen Blue said. "Must needs I tell thee what we be about. He has made truce with the Adverse Adepts, in Phaze, but Bane remains with us, in Proton. We oppose not thy union with him, or Bane's with Agape. But the news he brought o' the imbalance—that have we verified, and so it be true that thou canst not remain here. We shall get the four o' ye together and make the exchange back—but with a change." He looked penetratingly at her. "Only thou willst exchange, not the boys. That will give Mach power here, and Bane power there, to seek some better compromise than this truce. Mayhap Bane, being bound to us rather than to the other side, can find a way through. We seek not to void the deal Mach made with Translucent, only to provide us opportunity to explore the situation when the Adepts be off guard. I think thou canst go along with that."

"Aye," she said. "But that means—"

"That thou willst find thyself with Bane in Phaze—and must make it seem that he be Mach."

"But—but I love Mach!" she protested, appalled.

"Aye. That be thy challenge, and why I speak to thee now. Agape must do likewise, here."

"I—I will try," she agreed faintly. What a position Blue was putting her in!

"Now let us play together," he said. He brought out a harmonica, and put it to his mouth.

Relieved to have the subject change, she lifted the panpipes. Then the two of them played an impromptu melody, and Blue was a master musician, almost as good as a unicorn in the finesse with which he handled his instrument.

When it was done, she was melting again. "Thou didst depart Proton before I was foaled," Fleta told him. "Yet do I feel I know thee well, now."

"It were thy dam Neysa mine other self Stile knew," he said. "So in any event, our acquaintance is based on that of two other folk. Yet be it good to renew."

"O Adept, may I hug thee?"

"Hug me, 'corn, and remember me to my homeland."

She hugged him, finding him much like Bane, only

older and smaller. His visit to her buoyed her immeasurably; now she knew that she and Mach were not fighting for their happiness alone. Stile had turned down her union with Mach, and for good reason; Blue was supporting it, and she hoped his reason was as good.

Then he departed, and she returned to her chamber. For the second time, the aftermath of a Tourney game had lifted her outlook. She no longer felt like a complete stranger here; indeed, her homesickness for Phaze was diminishing.

Two days later she had her Round Three match. This was against a humanoid robot who reminded her eerily of Mach, but he was not. She had the numbers again, but hesitated to choose ARTS, because the records of all prior games were available, and she knew that the robot could have looked up her games and discovered her preference, and calculated accordingly. So she touched 2. MENTAL. He chose A. NAKED, as she had thought he might; it could be tricky for a robot to use a tool, as robots really *were* tools in a manner of thinking, and even trickier for him to use a machine. He would naturally avoid her own strength, ANIMAL. So he depended on his own resources, as Mach tended to do. She felt a little guilty for using her knowledge of Mach to gain an advantage over this robot, but she knew she had to do it.

The secondary grid for MENTAL came up. She had the numbers again: 5. SOCIAL 6. POWER 7. MATH 8. HUMOR. What should she choose?

She looked at the robot's choices: E. INFORMATION F. MEMORY G. RIDDLE H. MANIPULATION. What would he take? It depended on his type; if he were a sophisticated model, like Mach, he would have an enormous store of information, and a sizable temporary memory, but would be weak on mental tricks such as riddles. If he were a simpler model, his information and memory capacity might be much smaller, but he would still be good at manipulating what he had:

numbers, for example. So she had better stay well clear of MATH!

She decided that her safest course was HUMOR. Mach had a sense of humor, though not on a par with hers, but other robots might not understand it at all. She touched the word.

Sure enough, he had chosen MANIPULATION, going for his strength. They were in 2A8H: SPURIOUS LOGIC. It came down to a contest in telling jokes, and topping them.

Again they had an audience. It seemed that most contestants resembled Fleta in this respect. They preferred to be judged by ordinary folk, not by the machine.

The robot was required to tell his joke first. He did so mechanically. "A smart humanoid robot was concerned that his employer was not satisfied with his performance and sought a pretext to fire him. The employer always assigned him the least rewarding tasks, such as supervising the maintenance menials. When the employer gave him an assignment to report to the robot repair annex, he feared he would be junked. So he tinkered with the wiring of a cleanup menial robot, an inferior machine, and caused it to respond to the humanoid's identity command. Thus the menial went off to the repair annex for junking, instead of the smart humanoid!"

There was a robot in the audience who found this very funny, and two androids who smiled. But the joke fell somewhat flat for the human beings.

Now it was Fleta's task to top it. If she could do so, she would nullify it, and leave her opponent scoreless. She had to think quickly: what would reverse the situation in a funny manner? She thought again of Mach. What would he say to a joke like this? That gave her the key.

"But it turned out that the robot was being sent to the repair annex not for junking, but for upgrading to superior status," she said. "When the menial robot returned, it was much smarter than the humanoid robot, and was made the new supervisor, bossing the humanoid himself."

Several humans laughed, and the two androids smiled. They liked that reversal. Only the humanoid robot in the audience failed to see the humor of it. Fleta had succeeded in topping the joke.

Now it was her turn to start. She remembered a little story she had imagined as a young filly, back when she was learning to assume girlform. "A mean man of Phaze caught an innocent young unicorn in human form, when she was trying to learn the human ways so she could handle the form perfectly. He grabbed her and clapped his hand over her forehead, covering her horn button, so she could not change. 'Now I won't let you go unless you teach me how to change form as you do,' he told her. 'Teach me, or I will do something terrible for you but nice for me.' She knew he would rape her if she did not agree, so she gave her word to help him change to equine form.

"He could not do it exactly the way she did, because he was not of her species, so she had to translate the magic to a verbal command that would work for him. Actually it was two commands: the second to change him back to manform. He tied her to a post and tried the first spell, and lo! He became his analogy of the equine form, which was a silly ass. Immediately he tried to change back, but he only brayed, because his assform was unable to speak in the human mode. He was stuck for the rest of his life as an ass."

There were a few smiles in the audience, but it seemed that most of the serfs had been expecting something like this, so were not suprised. It was after all a pretty weak joke.

It was the robot's turn to top it. Unfortunately, he had found the joke hilarious: man becoming ass! That was almost as funny as having a menial robot sent off to be junked in one's place. He tried to come up with an improvement on it, but his thought circuits were inadequate, and he could not.

But he was not completely dull. "Maybe there is no topper," he said. "If there is no topper, then it doesn't count!"

AGREED, the screen printed. TELLER MUST TOP OWN JOKE FOR VICTORY.

Oops! Fleta had not anticipated that! She had never devised a reversal of this one, having had no motive. If she was a human being, and wanted to turn the joke to human account, how would she do it?

The challenge brought the response, and she had it. It was in the form of her worst fear as a young creature. "Then the unicorn changed to her natural form, for she was just coming into heat and needed to be far from here before the mating urge took her. But she forgot that she was still tied, and the rope was too strong for her to break. She was trapped—and there was this ass, smelling her condition, eager to—"

She was drowned out by a surge of laughter. The serfs found that fate very funny!

She had won the match—but at the cost of allowing her secret self to be raped by an ass. She was not completely pleased.

Mach visited her again. "I have located Bane," he said. "I have explained what my father wants. He has agreed. But he says that Agape is far from here. He will have to go to her, and explain, and bring her here. It will take at least two days."

"Then needs must I win again on the morrow," she said.

"You have been doing very well," he said. "You have qualified for Round Four; you are one of the final 128 contestants. Almost 900 have been eliminated."

"That many!" she exclaimed in wonder. "But I be just lucky!"

He shook his head. "I'm not sure of that. I think you may be cut out to be a Game player. Your instincts have been good, and your play good. Considering your unfamiliarity with this culture and your inexperience with the Game, that suggests a very good potential."

"Nay, it be but luck," she protested. "I fear for each new contest, that I may muff what I might have played well."

"Which is exactly the attitude of a superior gamesman." He smiled. "In any event, you have to get through only one more, and then you can exchange."

"One more—and then be separated from thee," she said, with mixed emotions.

Her Round Four match was against a Citizen. Fleta saw him approaching the console with horror; how could she defeat such an opponent? Furthermore, she recognized him: he was the Purple Adept, here known as Citizen Purple.

Now she knew that the Contrary Citizens had caught on to her identity, and somehow arranged to get close to her within the Tourney. If she lost this one, Purple would have her, and Mach would be helpless. The alliance of Citizens and Adepts would have both sides of it, and Bane and Mach would have to work wholly for them. Their noose was closing.

Purple looked at her, and grinned. "I mean to have your hide, animal," he said. "You have led a charmed existence, but I have a score to settle."

Terror coursed through her. This man was serious—and deadly. Mach had said something about the way Agape had escaped captivity by this man, and Mach himself had escaped, in a violent confrontation. Certainly Purple had a score to settle—and she knew he was an evil man.

"Thou canst not touch me in the Tourney," she said with as much bravado as she could muster. She had to cling to the console, for her knees were melting.

"But the moment you wash out, as you are about to, I shall preempt the deportation process and take you with me," he said. "Citizenship hath its privileges."

Could he do that? She feared he could. The Game Computer had protected her from external threats, but could not bar a legitimate contestant, and Citizens did have special powers. She had to win! But could she? She greatly feared that this man had her number, as the serfs put it.

Her screen showed that she had the letters. That meant she could choose ANIMAL. But Purple would be ready for that, and have some devastating trap ready. What, then, was left? What she understood least was MACHINES, having had no experience with them prior to her meeting with Mach. Purple knew that too, and he was of course thoroughly conversant with the most sophisticated machines. It would be folly for her to choose that category.

So it was between NAKED and TOOL. In her own unicorn body she would have been confident with NAKED, but in this Amoeba body she was doubtful. It was a wonderful body, but she hardly understood it well enough to trust it to direct physical competition—and she was afraid that that was exactly what Purple would choose. TOOL? That could be anything, including weapons; he was surely skilled with those, while she understood only the weapon of her horn—which she lacked, here. She seemed to have no good choices!

But maybe she could surprise him! With sudden resolve, she touched the very worst of her choices: MACHINE.

He had chosen PHYSICAL, as she had surmised. Maybe Mach was right: she did have a touch for the Game, being able to judge her opponent's likely choice. But she was still stuck in a box she didn't like.

She hoped she would get the numbers, this time, so she could avoid INTERACTIVE or COMBAT and perhaps COOPERATIVE; she wanted no contact with this brutal man!

Luck did not help her. She got the letters again, and had to choose between E. EARTH F. FIRE G. GAS and H. H_2O. She had learned that EARTH meant a flat surface, such as a ball could roll on, and that FIRE meant a variable surface that a stick might help to cross, and GAS meant a broken surface, such as might have been carved up by a knife, and that H_2O meant water, where anything went. She didn't trust any of them, but as a unicorn she preferred the flat surface, such as might be grazed or run on. Therefore she avoided that, still trying to surprise the Citizen, to get into some combination that, however bad it might be for her, would be worse for him. So she touched FIRE, with a sense of futility.

He had chosen 6. INTERACTIVE. Thus they were in 1C6F: Machine-assisted physical activity on a variable surface, interactive. That, when they played through the choices, turned out to be SNOWMOBILE BUMPING.

"Well," Purple said, making a motion as of lathering his hands. "It will be a pleasure to return to this sport."

She realized that she had nothing to lose except the game, and her freedom. There was no point trying to placate the Citizen, but perhaps she could learn something from him. "Thou wast good at this?"

"I was good at everything, in my youth," he said. "But especially mountainside sports, because of my association with the mountain range."

The Purple Mountain range, of course. That made sense. She had after all walked into the worst of choices!

They adjourned to the Snow Sports range. The snowmobiles turned out to be machines that could cruise rapidly up and down slopes. A steeply banked track circled the central housing. The route was not long, but had plenty of variety, and because it circled, there was no end to it. The two would circle until one bumped the other out of the track.

Suddenly Fleta realized that this was very much like a game she had played with others of her Herd. They had gone up into the snowy regions and beaten out a track, then ran in it, trying to shoulder each other out of it. She had not been the best, because she lacked the mass and power of some of the others, but she had been good, because she was fast and sure. Had her physical assets matched the others', pound for pound, she would have been the best.

The snowmobiles were machines, all the same size and shape and power. The only difference in the contestants would be that of their own body masses—and their skills in the game. Fleta had never before used such a machine, but she suspected that once she became accustomed to it, she would be able to compete with anyone.

The Citizen thought he had an easy victory. He might discover he had no victory at all!

They donned heavy clothing, for the range was cold. This was one of the few occasions when serfs were permitted apparel. The attendant explained the use of the machines, which turned out to be simple: a wheel mounted sidewise for steering, and a pedal to set the speed.

They got into their mobiles and exited simultaneously on opposite sides. They would circle left. It was possible for the two to avoid contact by traveling at constant speed on opposite sides, but if too long a period elapsed without a bump, both would be disqualified, and both would be out of the Tourney, with a bye granted to whatever contestant would have encountered the winner in the next round. Purple might be satisfied with that, but Fleta couldn't afford it. She hoped that Purple's pride would require him to mix it up, and not go for the ignominious disqualification, just to get control of her.

As she moved out into the snow, she concentrated on attuning to the machine. She had only a little time to ascertain the range of its capabilities. How fast could it gallop? How quickly could it slow? How well could it maneuver? She had to get the feel of it, so that she could use it without thinking, exactly as she would her own body.

She pushed down on the pedal, and the mobile leaped

ahead, spewing out snow behind. She lifted her foot, and the thing stopped so suddenly that only her restraining harness prevented her body from being thrown forward and out of it, while snow flew up in a small cloud.

The machine was responsive!

That made her think of Mach, the most responsive of machines.

But Purple was overhauling her rapidly. She leaped forward again, lest he ram her and bump her out before she got started. As she did, she steered to the side, and the machine quickly swerved. This was an excellent unicorn!

Now she was ready, and barely in time, for Citizen Purple's mobile was upon her. It had maintained speed while she experimented, and she could not gain on it from a standing start. The Citizen was aiming to ram her, he being on the inside of the track and she moving more slowly on the outside. She would be out of control in a moment if he scored.

But she had a body that was close enough in principle to her own, and experience in exactly this kind of tactic. She gauged the likely point of impact, and as he speeded up to add more impetus to the bump, she cut suddenly left, crossing in front of him, and abruptly slowed.

Caught by surprise, he struck her right flank and caromed off to the right. She was already steering left again, countering the shove of her rear. Then, as he tried to compensate for his unexpected impetus, she cut right, accelerated, and bumped him hard from the inside.

He careened out of the track so violently that his vehicle collided with the outer retaining wall. A buzzer sounded: the contest was over.

Fleta had not only won, she had won decisively. She had made an experienced gamesman look like a duffer. "How dost thou like *that* manure, Citizen?" she called gleefully.

Then, realizing that caution was in order, she guided

her snowmobile quickly inside, and departed before Purple could get there.

As she returned to her chamber, she knew she had secured her chance to return to Phaze. But now, oddly, she wished she did not have to go just yet. After all, she had just qualified for Round Five, one of only sixty-four survivors! That was halfway through the rounds! Who knew how far she could go if she remained in the Tourney!

But Mach was waiting at the chamber. "Don't get notions, filly," he said severely. "You're safe, now—but if you play again and lose, we might not be able to coordinate the exchange before you got shipped off-planet."

That sobered her. "Agape will have to play in my stead," she said regretfully. "Mayhap she will win the Tourney and become the next Citizen!"

"Maybe," he agreed. Then they made love, for it would be their last night together for a time.

"Remember," he said in the morning. "Keep the secret. Bane tells me that the Adverse Adepts are raising an army. He has to learn more about their plans, and only he can spy on them without their knowledge; I am too much a duffer at magic, and if they mean to betray us and break the truce—"

"Aye," she said. "That other tourney be not over yet."

Then, before the call for the next game came, Bane arrived. There was no sign of him, but Mach could tell. "She's with him," he said. "Come, embrace me, and concentrate on Phaze: your desire to return."

"Aye," she repeated, embracing him with mixed emotions.

Now she felt the presence of the others. She willed herself to Phaze, to the lovely open plain that occupied this spot there, and the exchange took hold.

9

Masquerade

After a horrendous three-day stint with Stile, operating from a hidden retreat and spying on demons who tended to stomp butterflies on sight, Bane made contact with Mach and learned that it was time to return Agape to Proton. He explained his own plan, and they agreed.

He returned to the Blue Demesnes to discover a change. There was an evanescent glow about the castle that could only signify a rare happiness. If the Lady Blue was happy, she surely had good reason. He could think of only one likely event that would have this effect.

Was that why his father had decided to pursue his investigation elsewhere, instead of returning to the Blue Demesnes at this time? Stile had withdrawn his opposition to Bane's union with Agape, but the situation still prohibited it; perhaps Stile simply preferred to stay clear of the inevitable awkwardness.

"Anybody home?" he called.

His mother came out to meet him, smiling. With her was a young woman who looked like Fleta, but was not.

The woman stepped into his embrace. This was Agape,

all right! He did not need to ask; he knew she accepted Phaze, now. He had not realized how important that acceptance was to him until this moment. This was his world; he wanted her to understand it and approve of it, however surprising her introduction to it.

He summarized the news of his spying as they entered the castle. His mother knew it, of course, but would not have said anything; she was not one to speak carelessly. He wanted Agape to know why he had neglected her all this time. "They mean to use thee as a lever against me," he concluded.

"I know," Agape said.

Then he went into more detail about his recent activities as a spy and butterfly, but she just hugged him and seemed satisfied with that.

But there was one thing he had to be sure she understood. He took her for a walk outside the castle, and explained. "Mach contacted me, while I was in the field," he said. "Fleta be about to be shipped to Moeba."

That got her attention. "She can't go there! It's an entirely different world!"

"Aye. So thou must return tomorrow. It be not a strange world to thee." He took a breath. "And must needs I remain here. The Adverse Adepts watch me too closely; an they think Mach be back, their suspicion may diminish, so I can learn what we need."

She nodded sadly, understanding. "And I will not see you, after that."

"Nay, I joked not when I said I would visit thee there. Mach has been there, and promises to leave a program for me."

"A program?"

"In his brain. He has compartments, and in them are programs for many things, such as the speaking of alien tongues or the application of special skills. With his program, I will know all he has learned, and can survive on thy home world. Thou hast experienced mine; now will I experience thine. Our acquaintance be not at an end."

She hugged him again. Then: "We have been apart, and now have so little time together. I know this is not my own body, but—"

"I met thee in Mach's body," he reminded her.

"Do you think Fleta would mind, if—"

"Nay, she would mind not." Then he conjured them both to the private glade where he had first exchanged with Mach, and made a small screened tent there, and they made love, first savagely, then again gently, and then they slept.

Next day he brought her to the proper spot. He held her closely as they overlapped their opposites in Proton, and sang the spell to transfer her back.

Her body did not change, but its nature did. In a moment he knew that it was Fleta he was holding.

He put his lips to her ear. "Filly, dost know me?" he whispered.

"Aye, Bane," she whispered back. "I will help thee in thy quest."

"Thou knowest they watch us."

"Aye." She drew back her head and gazed into his face as if in love with him. "Can you speak Protonese?" she murmured.

He stared at her. It was not that her words were unreasonable; it was that he had never imagined her using that mode. "I can," he said. "But—"

"Methinks I can suffer this masquerade for a time, an thou canst," she said. "I like it not, but my love asked me, an if it helps put things right . . ." Then she lifted her lips and kissed him.

He was startled again. Of course she would kiss Mach! If he was to play the part, he had to play it, and she did too. That was why her cooperation was essential. He just had not anticipated this aspect. His days of experimentation with Fleta were long over.

But, this being the case, he would have to make love to her too! It would be an early giveaway if he avoided this aspect of Mach's relationship with her. But how did she feel about this? She had exchanged the triple Thee with Mach!

She brought her mouth close to his ear again. "I love another, but I hate thee not, and can play such games with thee as thy kind does. As I have done before."

"Then it be but sex," he whispered back. "Our hearts be in it not."

"Aye." Then she drew away from him. "But we dally, Mach!" she exclaimed brightly. "Didst thou not have enough o' manstyle play w' me in Proton?"

"I can never have enough," he replied carefully. But he let her go.

"We have been long away from our sanctuary," she said. "Let me carry thee there." And she became her natural self, the unicorn.

"Yes, of course," he agreed. He mounted her a trifle clumsily, as he judged Mach might. She set off westward. One thing about this: he did not have to say much or do much, so ran less risk of giving away his identity. The Adverse Adepts might be watching, but would soon become bored with this, and would not pay much attention.

While he rode, he pondered the plan that he and Stile had devised. Stile, in those last three days, had taught him an exotic technique that even most Adepts did not know: that of spiritual separation. This magic could send a person's awareness out apart from his body, so that he could perceive things that his body could not. It required a different spell each time, of course, but Stile had worked out several that had worked for him, and should now work for Bane. The effect was limited in time and distance, so it was necessary to get physically within range before invoking the separation. This restricted its application—but if Bane could find a way to get close without suspicion, it could be invaluable.

That was why he had sought Mach's cooperation. Mach could not spy in this manner, lacking the magic, and would not if he could. But Mach could get close to the Adverse Adepts. This switch of seeming identities should enable Bane to get close enough so that he could learn what they needed to know. The dominance of the frame might depend on his success in this mission.

And Fleta, bless her, was cooperating! Mach had a good match in her; she might be an animal, but some animals were more substantial folk than some human beings, and she was an example. Her friend the were-bitch Furramenin was another, and of course Such-evane—ah, the vampire was special indeed!

As evening approached, and the sun reddened behind a cloudbank before them, Fleta stopped, and Bane dismounted. She set about grazing, which was her most comfortable way to eat, while he foraged for nuts and fruits. He could have conjured food, but did not for two reasons: first, because Mach would not be good at such magic, and second, because magic was too valuable to waste on routine chores. If he was in danger of starving, then a conjuration would be in order; meanwhile, foraging would do.

As complete darkness settled in, Fleta assumed girl-form and came to him. The air was turning chill—but again, what point magic, when they could share body warmth? They removed their clothing, and spread her black cloak and his blue shirt and trousers over the two of them as blankets, and embraced. It made sense because of the warmth, and because they were supposed to be lovers. For all an observer could have told, they were being lovers now, and that was the impression they wanted to give. Bane intended merely to sleep.

But Fleta was as full of mischief as ever. "Canst guess how often I longed to get thee like this, an my heat approached?" she whispered.

Heat! Bane went rigid. When a mare came to that part of her cycle, she had to breed, or suffer terribly, and no mere man could satisfy her. "Thou'rt not—?"

"Nay, not this week," she said. "But when I learned the human way of it, for pleasure rather than naughtiness, I came to like it any time." She moved against him, breast against his chest, thigh over his thigh. She might be an animal, and a childhood friend, but she felt exactly like a woman at the moment.

"I made love to her, in thy body," he said, hoping to divert her. "We thought thou wouldst not mind."

"Nor do I," she agreed. "Oft did I do the same with him in thy body." She considered a moment. "How was my body?"

"Ne'er better," he confessed. "Now stop thy teasing, and let me sleep."

She decided she had gone far enough, and acceded. Her sexual urge was not at all the same as his; she just liked to demonstrate that she could make him react against his will. She had done that now, and was satisfied.

He relaxed. But he knew the time would come soon enough when, to preserve his secret, they would have to make it real. That might be just part of the game, to her, because animals had no proprietary concerns about sex, but it was no game to him. He felt guilty already for what would surely occur—and more guilty because he discovered that a part of him desired it. The act he could account for, when circumstance made it necessary; the desire he could not.

Bane had never been within the Translucent Demesnes before, and he found it fascinating. The underwater isle, the ancient creatures, the seeming ability to fly—what a realm the Adept had, here! He tried not to gawk as the unicorn carried him through the strange landscape to their refuge.

At last they passed through the dome-shaped curtain and walked on the "normal" land of the isle. All around this region the creatures of the archaic ocean could be seen.

"Must needs we tour the isle, to be sure naught be changed," Fleta said brightly, shifting to girlform.

"Yes," he said, keeping his language in character. This was her way of acquainting him with the details of this setting, so that he would not make any giveaway errors.

In this fashion she introduced him to the creatures she and Mach had come to know. "And here be Naughty, the same as ever!" she exclaimed as they encountered a creature like a squid in a shell longer than the length of a man. "Nay, chide me not, Mach; I know thou dost call him 'Nautiloid' from the Ordovician period o' Earth! But to me he be Naughty, for all the times he blunders through to land and we needs must heave him back." She reached through the dome-wall and petted the monster on the shell. A tentacle reached up and coiled briefly about her wrist, squeezing and letting go. Obviously the monster did remember her, and liked her.

In due course they completed the circuit of the isle. "All be in order," Fleta announced. "Now let me graze and sleep."

"But—" Bane started, concerned that he did not yet know enough about this region to avoid a blunder.

"Hast thou not had enough o' sex on the way here?" she chided him. "Canst not let me sleep in peace, after carrying thee all this distance?"

Oh. She was giving him a pretext to leave her alone, so that the Translucent Adept, who surely watched, had no reason to be suspicious.

He foraged for his supper while she assumed her natural form and grazed on the rich grass growing here. She was catching up on sleep, too; she could graze while sleeping, which was a useful ability at times.

After he ate, he caught up on natural functions, then piled fragrant ferns and lay down, nominally to sleep. Actually he whispered the spell of separation. Stile had worked this out so that its evocation was virtually undetectable; it was largely internal magic, not the external magic that used enormous power. When he conjured himself from place to place, the magic made a splash that could readily be detected by those alert for it; when Stile conjured one of Bane's butterfly forms to another spot, the splash occurred at the site of the conjuration, not of arrival, so there was no alarm. But he had done about all he could with butterflies; now he hoped to do more with his spirit.

He drifted out from his body. He could see, hear, smell and even feel, despite having a center of awareness that was insubstantial. He saw his body, seemingly sleeping; he saw Fleta grazing; he saw Naughty Nautiloid foraging in the nearby ocean.

He moved on through the water, looking for the Translucent Adept. The man was in a palace that appeared to be made out of water: bricks of water kept firm by magic, forming walls and arches, with beams of water supporting the upper levels. There were large windows with panes of water, and furniture shaped from yet more water.

Translucent was relaxing, watching a water-mirror in which an image of the isle was reflected. There was Bane sleeping, and Fleta grazing. So their suspicion was correct: they were under constant observation. Probably Translucent could hear their dialogue, too. The Adept had offered sanctuary for Mach and Fleta, and freedom, but had never guaranteed privacy. He did not interfere with their activities, but he knew of them, in every detail he cared to.

But watching the Adept watch the isle would not accomplish anything. Bane wanted to know the exact plans of the Adverse Adepts, so that his father could counter them specifically. He could not depend on overhearing significant conversations; he had to find records or other indications.

There seemed to be no records. Whatever Translucent knew or planned was in his head. That was a place Bane could not go.

His spying effort here was a failure. He could not even be sure that Translucent was planning any treachery; the limited evidence was that the other Adepts were planning it, for the time when Translucent's more liberal policy of accommodation failed.

He passed the Adept again—and discovered that the

water-screen had changed its picture. Now the Tan Adept was on it, talking to Translucent.

". . . she'll be there tomorrow afternoon," the senior Tan was saying.

"I like this not," Translucent answered. "I gave mine oath, and I mean to break it not."

"An they be truly the rovot and the 'corn, with their triple Thee, she will have no power o'er them," Tan said. "An they be the other pair, thine oath applies not. My daughter can capture Bane, then, and the whole of it be ours."

"I yield to thee on this point only to establish their legitimacy," Translucent said, obviously irritated. "Thereafter, I want interference not from thee. There be a smell about this I like not."

"Agreed." The Tan Adept faded out.

So he had gained some information anyway! Tania was coming here tomorrow, to verify whether it was the right couple on the isle. The Adepts' suspicion had been aroused, so now they were checking. Translucent was hewing to the letter of his word, and Bane respected him for that, but the man had to allow this test.

Bane did not want Tania to try her evil eye on him. He could counter it only by the full exercise of his own magic—and that would give away his identity on the spot, because Mach had only clumsy powers of magic. But if he did not counter her, he would fall prey to her, and that would be worse. They were in trouble!

He returned to his body. He had less than a day to figure out a way to pass this challenge.

He pondered for a while, and drifted off to sleep. He could not talk to Fleta, knowing he was being watched; he had to act completely naturally.

In the morning Fleta changed back to girlform and approached him for a kiss, as she would have done with Mach. "What news?" she whispered.

He nuzzled her ear. "We be watched, as we thought. Today Tania comes to test us."

"The e'il eye!" she breathed, tickling his ear. "I like that not!"

"Mach's triple Thee would be proof against it. But we be the wrong partners; that oath exists not between us."

She drew back her head. "Not before breakfast, thou sex fiend!" she exclaimed. "Give me leave to think on't."

He let her go. How cleverly she answered him, without arousing suspicion!

They foraged for breakfast, and this time she remained in girlform and ate with him. As they finished, she leaned toward him. He caught the hint and grabbed her for another kiss. It would not do to have Translucent realize that only Fleta initiated such activity.

"Canst leave before?" she whispered.

He had thought of that, and rejected it. They were theoretically here so that they could love each other without restraint, in perfect security and comfort. They would not depart except for good reason—and they weren't supposed to have any notion of the impending visit. "Would give us away," he replied.

She wriggled away from his grasp. "Not before washup!" she protested.

Bane managed to convert a smile to a grimace. Any watcher would be convinced that he was constantly trying to get her into sex, while she was endlessly coquettish. Despite his knowledge of her rationale, he found himself responding, wanting her in the manner she pretended he did. Pretense of this nature could be treacherous!

They washed up at a freshwater spring on the isle. It was amazing how Translucent had set this up! They stripped, setting their apparel out of harm's way. Fleta insisted on washing him, using her hands to splash the water on him and to rub him down. Naturally she brought him to arousal. This was not entirely mischief on her part; Mach would have reacted exactly this way.

"I think there be only one way to deceive Tania,"

she whispered as she gaily splashed water at his eyes and ears. "We must be amidst it as she comes."

"But that be only sex!" he protested. "Her power could still move me."

"Why use it, an she sees how true we be to each other?"

And that just might be the answer. Magic was not cheap for any practitioner. Tania could only use a particular variant of her evil eye on a particular person once. She would not care to waste it on a subject likely to be immune—as Mach would be, because of his absolute love for Fleta. The triple Thee, vindicated as it was said his had been, could not be overridden; indeed, it had overridden Adept magic itself. So if Tania were satisfied that she saw Mach, she would let him pass unchallenged.

He had known that he would have to make love to Fleta, and had felt his mixed guilt about that. Now he realized that he would have to do it for an audience, and make it thoroughly convincing. His mission, and perhaps his freedom, depended on it.

"Aye," he whispered.

She wrestled herself away, managing in the process to slide her slippery breasts almost the full length of his body. "Nay, Mach! Not till we be at the proper place!"

What a tease she was! Surely Translucent, if he were watching at this moment, was chuckling.

So it continued through the morning, Fleta always putting him off on one pretext or another, he always yielding with decent grace. Then it was time for lunch, and then for a nap, she claimed. But she kissed him, and whispered in his ear: "Canst see her coming, now? Needs must we know exactly when."

He nodded. He fashioned a partial shelter from boughs and ferns so that the sun would not burn him, though its light was filtered through the water above the dome and really was not fierce. Then he lay down for his "nap" and used a variant spell to separate his spirit again. He floated out to Translucent's water-brick house—and there she was already! In only a few minutes she would be at the isle.

He hurried back to his body. How lucky that Fleta had had him check!

He stretched as if waking. Then he reached out and caught Fleta by the arm. "Damn it, filly—you have been teasing me all day!" he exclaimed. "Now you are going to get it!"

"Now?" she asked, her eyes flicking about as if searching.

"Any minute now," he agreed. "Just let me get that cloak off you!"

"Nay!" she protested, laughing. "That were too brief a nap!"

"The hell with the nap!" he exclaimed, rather enjoying the Proton mode of swearing; it had a certain magic of its own. He wrestled with her, pulling ineffectively at her clothing.

"O, here, thou'lt ruin it," she complained. She drew off her cloak herself. Then she undressed him.

But when he sought to embrace her, she resisted. "Thou didst teach me thy way, remember," she said. "Not like my way, for when I be in heat and care not what member be in me, so long as I be bred. Slow, and with love."

She was still stalling, for Tania had not yet shown up. But she was also correct: he had to play this scene convincingly, and that meant that sex was only part of it.

He looked into her eyes. "I love you," he said. There was no ripple around them, of course; this was a line from a play. In fact, this was very like a game in the Tourney of Proton, in which the participants had to emulate a scene of perfect love-making. It was an open question whether two players ever got into such a match randomly.

"And I love thee," she said, with similar lack of ripple. That was not necessarily cause for suspicion; the splash showed only at truly seminal declarations, and like other magic tended to fade with repetition.

Now he sought to embrace her more intimately, but still she demurred. "Hast forgotten thine own mode of play?" she inquired teasingly.

Was she still stalling, or trying for perfect realism? He wasn't sure, but realized she was right either way. Tania still had not arrived, and regardless, Translucent was probably watching on his water-screen.

Translucent? Tania could be watching it too! Why should she come here physically, when she could learn what she needed at a distance?

He stroked her breasts. Oh, she was well formed! He had seldom really looked at her recently, and now appreciated in a rush how nicely she had shaped her girl-form. He kissed them, then moved up to kiss her ear. "I think we be on stage now," he whispered.

"Ah, Mach, how I have longed to hear thee say that!" she replied aloud with a straight face. Then she became an animal indeed, hugging him, kissing him, stroking him, rubbing her torso against his, wrapping her legs around him, mimicking the height of passion, human style.

This was the same body he had embraced when Agape occupied it. Now it became confused in his mind, and he feared he would cry out Agape's name and betray himself.

"Mach! Mach!" she cried, but it sounded like "Bane, Bane!"

"Fleta!" he responded, keeping it straight. Then, overwhelmed by the passion of the moment, he took her, not quite caring in that instant who it might be.

And the guilt surged up as his passion ebbed. *He had felt too much.*

But it seemed that his demonstration had been effective. Time passed, and Tania did not show up. She must have been satisfied that he was Mach, after she saw his demonstration.

Fleta still lay in his embrace, and he could not tell

her to go. He had to be consistent to his role. But what was that consistency costing him? What was it costing her?

Tormented by his uncertainty of feeling, he lay for a time, then drifted into sleep.

Later they woke. Fleta did not look happy, but in a moment she assumed a cheerful expression. "Mach, thou didst promise me a foal," she said.

He was silent, not certain what she was leading up to.

"Now thou art back," she insisted. "Now be it time to do it."

"Fleta, this is no simple matter," he demurred. Was she serious?

"I know thy magic be not yet great," she continued. "But the Red Adept doth have the Book o' Magic, and methinks a spell might be there. My time o' heat be coming in due course, and if thou couldst breed me then—"

A pretext to visit Trool the Troll! Now he had the gist. "If I promised, I promised," he said. "We shall ask the Red Adept for a spell."

"Aye, I thank thee!" she exclaimed, and kissed him with such conviction that he realized this was no ploy. She really did want Mach's baby, and thought she could get it.

On the following morning they set out, Fleta in her natural form, Bane riding. Translucent did not interfere; the Adept was satisfied that Mach was in his camp regardless where he might travel. That much was true, and when Mach returned, he would continue to represent the Adverse Adepts. Bane really had no quarrel with that—and none with Translucent, who was behaving decently. Had Tania caught Bane in his masquerade, it would have been fair play: he had tried a deception, and paid the price.

In Proton, Citizen Blue knew of the masquerade, but would not try to hold Mach captive; that was understood. This was a ramification of the truce: to let things be until they could be better resolved. Bane hoped that Mach was not having too much trouble maintaining the pretense with Agape.

And what if he was? It was no bad thing, making love to Agape! Bane could not hold that against his other self any more than Mach could hold Bane's act with Fleta against him. It was understood that this was necessary.

Still, it bothered him. Not the act itself, but his attitude about it. He had tried to make himself believe that it was Agape he embraced, but he had known it was not. He had made love to Fleta, and it had been wonderful. That was the problem. Exactly why had it been so good?

She had been his companion in childhood, and in young adulthood. He had always liked her, and she had liked him. But he had never loved her. She was, after all, an animal.

Now Mach had fallen in love with her, and she with Mach. That caused Bane to see her differently. In what way was Fleta inferior to a human woman? He needed no thought to answer that: the answer was no way. Just as Agape was not inferior to a human woman. Perhaps he loved Agape as an unconscious analog to Fleta: the nonhuman creature who seemed human.

Now he was back with the original, his emotional barriers down. Had he merely done with her what he had always wanted to do? Had he used this masquerade as a pretext to do it?

What had he accomplished in his spying mission? Only the discovery of Tania's threat—which would have been no threat at all, had Mach been with Fleta. In short, he had accomplished nothing—except sex with his alternate's beloved.

So Bane's thoughts ran, as he rode the unicorn from the Translucent Demesnes. He had no doubt of Fleta's constancy; she had done only what she agreed to do, her heart not in it. But his own was suspect. He might as well have raped her.

No, even that was not the whole of it. The sex had been a concomitant of the mission, supposedly of little importance in itself. Certainly Fleta had no use for it, when not in heat, except as a way to please her lover or to maintain a masquerade. It should have been little more for him: a pleasure of the moment, done for other than emotion. Instead he had been eager for it, and had found it not only physically satisfying, but emotionally fulfilling. As though he had truly meant the words of love he had spoken to her.

Was he falling in love with Fleta?

Bane closed his eyes, trying to drive away the specter of that forbidden emotion, but could not. He knew he should never have undertaken this foolish spying mission; he should have stayed well away from his other self's chosen. Now it was too late.

Fleta turned her head, glancing back at him with one eye. She was aware of the reactions of his body, and knew that something was bothering him.

And what could he tell her? Nothing! She was innocent; he could only bring her grief by expressing his illicit passion. So he simply petted her shoulder. "You are a truly good creature, mare," he said. "I would not cause you harm for all the frame." That much was true.

They camped for the night near a stream. Instead of grazing, this time, Fleta became the hummingbird and filled up on the nectar of flowers, while he made a fire and roasted wild potatoes he dug out. Then she assumed girlform and came to join him for sleeping.

"But I thought thou wouldst graze," he protested weakly.

"Nay, I prefer to be with thee, Mach," she said, removing her cloak and spreading it as a blanket for them.

Another night with her body warm against his? He owed it to her and to his other self to avoid that! But what could he say? The Adepts were surely still checking on them.

Unable to find sufficient reason to demur, and uncertain whether he even wanted to, he acceded. He lay down with her, and she embraced him, nuzzling his ear.

"There be spoor," she whispered. "There be scent. We be followed."

This was completely unexpected. She had had reason of her own to get close to him! Her attention, at least, was where it should be.

"Canst make love to an unconscious man?" he whispered back.

"Aye." She chuckled.

He smiled. Any Adept watching them would have no concern; they would be obviously engaged in romance. Meanwhile, he would find out what was going on.

He murmured a spell of separation, and his spirit traveled up out of his body. He looked down: yes, it certainly looked like active sex from here! At least he need have no guilt for this; it was none of his doing.

He oriented, making a swift circuit of the region, and in a moment he spied it: a party of goblins camped not far away. But why hadn't he been aware of them? He had not been paying proper attention.

He moved close up—and discovered why. There was Adept magic protecting the party—a spell of concealment. Fleta, being a unicorn, was resistive to magic practiced on her, so had been able to pick up hints, while Bane had not. However, his spirit was not subject to the same limits as his body. He could perceive the shimmer of the magic force; indeed, he passed through it with extreme caution, for his presence could disturb it, alerting the Adept who had set it.

This party could only be here to spy on Mach and Fleta. The Adepts were not merely watching, they were keeping a force close by. Why?

He infiltrated the main tent. There was a goblin chief. He was settling down for the night. Goblins were more at home in the dark than the day, but since these were evidently following Bane and Fleta, they had to match their schedule to that of the day-dwellers; otherwise they would get no rest at all.

That meant there would be no real activity while he spied. He could not learn why these goblins were following him. Surely they had better reason than just keeping track of his whereabouts, that the Adepts could do more efficiently from a distance!

He considered a moment, then decided to go for double or nothing. The Adepts were taking an extraordinary step, having a physical presence near him, protected by their magic, so it had to be worth his trouble to find out why. Maybe they just wanted to protect Mach and Fleta from possible harm—but maybe they had some treachery on their minds.

He returned to Fleta. She was still working over his inert body. Well, almost inert; it seemed that certain reactions could occur even in the absence of consciousness, and she was evoking one of those.

"Fleta!" he said.

She did not hear: he had no voice in this state. But if he returned to his body to talk to her, he would lose the rest of his spell, which would be a waste of one-time magic.

He drew close and overlapped her head. "Fleta!" he said.

She jumped, looking wildly around.

"It's me, Bane," he said. "In spirit. I need thy help."

She stilled. "Bane," she whispered. "I hear thee."

"A party of goblins is tracking us. I need to know why. Canst get up and cause them to react while I listen? Mayhap they will utter what I would hear."

"Aye," she whispered. "This body be not much fun, anyway."

"Good thing, tease! Thou dost not want me in love with thee too."

She looked thoughtful, and he feared he had said too much. Then she drew herself up, picking up her cloak. "Do thou wait here, beloved," she said aloud. "Must needs I go do what none can do for me." She became the unicorn.

"That way," Bane said, overlapping her head again. "I think they mean us not harm, but push not thy luck. If thou canst make them stir, to avoid discovery—"

She made a nicker of acquiescence and set out for the goblin camp.

Bane hurried back to the camp ahead of her. In spirit form he could fly, for his spirit weighed nothing; whether he could travel more swiftly yet, but imagining himself there, he wasn't sure, and wasn't inclined to experiment at the moment. This was magic his father had devised: he did not grasp all its aspects.

He entered the chief goblin's tent and hovered. Suddenly he wondered: could he overlap the goblin's head, as he had Fleta's, and read its thoughts? Probably not; he had not read Fleta's. All he might do was give away his presence.

A goblin sentry burst into the tent. "Kinkear!" the sentry exclaimed. "The 'corn be coming toward us!"

Kinkear roused himself with a start. "Why?"

"She has a load to drop."

"And she's going to drop it here?" Kinkear cried. "What a mess, an she blunder across us by sheer chance! Our whole plan could be discovered! The spell be not effective an a 'corn step straight into it!"

"Aye. What must we do?"

"Alert the others. Break camp instantly. Stay clear o' her!"

The sentry disappeared. Kinkear hastily rolled up his bed and hauled down his tent. "Just my luck," he muttered to himself. "She drops dung, and my mission be in deep manure! Tan'll tan my hide, an I bungle his trap!"

So the Tan Adept was behind this! Already this device was paying off. But why should Tan be after Mach? His daughter had already verified Mach's authenticity to her satisfaction; it was Bane she was after.

Now he heard Fleta. She was coming through the

grass, evidently looking for just the right place to do her job. She sniffed the air. This camp was downwind from Bane's body, by no coincidence, and the unicorn's coming in this direction was no coincidence either; who wanted to spend the night in the breeze from her own manure?

"Get it o'er with, mare!" Kinkear muttered. "Return to thy stud, let him screw thee to the turf—and when he change back to his opposite, then shall we screw *him* to the turf."

So it *was* Bane they were after! They wanted to be on hand after the exchange, and catch him. That was exactly the treachery he was looking for.

The goblins had dispersed through the field, leaving no sign of their camp. But in so doing some of them had strayed beyond the limit of the concealment spell. Fleta, with her sharp senses in the unicorn form, had to have spotted these, but she gave no sign.

She wandered over to a spot where one goblin cowered under a tangle of grass. For an instant it seemed she would stumble over him. Then she turned around, set herself—and let go her dung directly on top of him. He couldn't even curse, lest he give away his presence.

Satisfied, perhaps in more than one sense, she walked back toward her camp.

The goblins busied themselves reforming their camp. They all had a good chuckle over the fate of the unlucky one. Their crisis was over.

Bane heard no more key remarks. But he had already heard enough. This effort of spying had been worth it!

He returned to his body. Fleta had changed back to girlform, and was lying with his body under her cloak.

"They be setting a trap for Bane, when he returns," he whispered. "Tan be behind it."

"Then mayhap will they conjure Tania to eye thee, in the moment thou dost return unguarded," Fleta whispered back. "That must they do just then, for thou wouldst be else caught not. With Mach loving me, and thou loving Tania, then have they both."

"Then have they both," he agreed. "But how can I foil their plot?"

"An thou dost, will not they then know how thou didst know?"

Excellent point! "But an I foil it not, I be trapped, for I fear Tania's power. She could not hold me long, but she might coerce me into what would compromise me."

"Such as making love to one thou dost love not?" Fleta asked.

"Such can happen, on occasion," he said wryly.

"An I be not in a position to know better, I could have thought thy words to me, a day agone, were true," she said.

Did she suspect? "Just so the Adverse Adepts think so."

"Aye." Did she sound disappointed?

"But whate'er I said about thy body, that were true," he said. "It be sheer delight."

"Aye." This time she sounded satisfied.

They did not resume their effort of love-making; the purpose of that had been accomplished. Bane relaxed, relieved on two accounts, concerned on the third. One: he had finally justified his spying effort by uncovering an enemy trap. Two: Fleta did not suspect his true feeling. Three: how could he withstand Tania, if his love for Agape was not secure?

Fleta made good time, and on the third day they reached the Red Demesnes. The goblin party continued to track them, falling behind by day, catching up in early evening, evidently assisted by magic, for no goblin could keep pace with any unicorn otherwise. Apparently the goblins had to keep close enough to be able to pounce the moment Mach exchanged with Bane. They had, it seemed, tried to capture Agape before; failing that, they were taking no chances with Bane.

A bat flew out to meet them as they approached the castle. In a moment lovely Suchevane stood before them.

Fleta changed to girlform, giving Bane barely time to dismount. The two young woman forms embraced. "Be thou Fleta?" the vampire asked.

"Dost know me not?" Fleta asked, laughing.

"Last I met Agape, in thy body. I owe her."

"I know naught of this."

Suchevane cast down her gaze, coloring slightly. "I be resident at the Red Demesnes, now. To assist the Adept."

Fleta surveyed her, comprehending. "Thou dost have a thing for . . . ?"

"Aye. It were Agape put me on it, speaking the common sense I saw not for myself. And now—"

Fleta hugged her again. "O, Suchy, how glad I be for thee!"

"And not for him?" Bane inquired. He knew the Red Adept to have been the strongest and most lonely of creatures, surely eager to have a creature like Suchevane near, if she but showed the slightest inclination.

They laughed. Then Suchevane escorted them into the castle.

Bane had not been here for some time, but he recognized improvement. Suchevane had evidently wasted no time in setting the castle in order. Even the old troll looked better; his red robe was clean, and he stood with a certain pride he had not evinced before, despite his enormous magic. A woman could do that for a man; Bane was in a position to know. He had never anticipated such a combination, but it seemed that Agape had engineered it.

"We come on business," Bane said. "I be Bane, not Mach; we have maintained a masquerade to ascertain the threat posed against thy side by the Adverse Adepts. But Mach promised, and so did I, to seek a way that Fleta might breed with a man and bear a foal. Fleta has helped me in my mission; now I would help her in her desire, and for this I ask thy help."

"Thou shallst have it," Trool said. "What be the threat against us?"

"They mean to smite me with the evil eye, and enamor me of the Tan Adept's daughter, that I may change sides and work with Mach for them. They know not that I be not Mach, at the moment."

"Thou hast practiced deception," Trool said. "That were a violation of thy truce."

"I think not," Bane said. "I be on thy side; I made no deal with Translucent. Mach still honors that."

"Thou art on my side, agreed," Trool said. "Therefore to me falls responsibility for this abridgement o' the truce."

"But they be abridging it also, by setting a trap for me!" Bane protested.

"Aye." Trool walked in a circle, pondering. "I had thought not Translucent would do that."

"Translucent agreed only to let Tania test me," Bane said. "I think he be not part o' this scheme."

"If I may comment?" Suchevane said cautiously.

"Always," Trool told her, not bothering to conceal the delight he had in her presence.

"Methinks it best to know exactly where the guilt lies," she said. "An Bane go into the trap, and spring it, then mayhap those behind it will be revealed. Then will we know who keeps the truce, and who does not."

"Aye," the troll said. "Then can I deal with those who kept it, to make it right."

To Bane it seemed that this was quibbling over a technicality. But Trool was vital to the cause, so he said nothing. He would have to face Tania. The others assumed that he could withstand her, because his love for Agape was true; how could he tell them otherwise?

"Now will I research on breeding," Trool said. He shuffled from the chamber.

"He will be a while," Suchevane said. "Come, eat, rest; I will see to the amenities meantime."

She did so, and their comfort was complete. They no longer had to maintain the pretense of being lovers.

But Bane's gloom continued. Not only was he uncertain about his emotion, he was now in doubt about his integrity. He and his father had worked out the masquerade, to spy on the plotting of the Adverse Adepts. This had seemed justified—but it was evident that the Red Adept did not consider it so. The more Bane mulled it over, the more it seemed to him that he had allowed his standard of integrity to be governed by that of his enemy, and the less he liked it. Yet had he not spied, they would not have known about the enemy's marshaling of forces for physical action, or about the plot against him personally. Could it be right to hold to a standard that ensured defeat?

Tormented by the ethical riddle, he went to see Trool. The troll was deep in the Book of Magic, doing the research he had promised. "If I may . . ."

The troll looked up. "It be possible for dissimilar species to breed, but not easy," he said. "I be on the details now."

"That be gratifying, but that were not my concern."

Trool merely looked at him.

"I came to apologize for putting thee in an awkward position," Bane said. "I thought what I did to be right, but now I fear it be not. I would make amend, an I knew how."

Trool nodded. "I be of a species with a little concept o' right," he said. "It fell to me to make up for wrongs done by my kind. I did it only by dedicating my life to the right I perceived. Do thou that likewise, and thou hast no further apology to make."

"I know not whether I can," Bane said.

Trool closed the book. "The mare?"

"I know not whom I love," Bane said. "It were Mach who swore the triple Thee to Fleta; I ne'er did to Agape. Not in Phaze, where the splash—"

"The mare loves thee not," Trool said.

"Aye. She be true to her own. But I—what o' me?"

"Love be not a thing I understand," Trool said. "It be yet too new to me. Still, I suspect that love unreturned cannot be true, and must needs be based on other than it seems."

"But I must face Tania, who will strike at my emotion," Bane said despairingly. "An my love for Agape not be true, I be vulnerable! Mine inconstancy can doom me—and our side."

Trool nodded. "I tell thee again, I be no expert in this realm. I thought no woman would care to associate with me, and least of all the loveliest. But it be in my mind that thy doubt of heart be not normal. I met Agape, and if there be one who be the match o' Fleta, it surely be she."

"Aye, Agape be more alien than Fleta, and a fine person, and I do love her. I feel great guilt at this doubt, that I know should not exist."

"Exactly. Do thou allow me then to test thee for a geis."

"A geis? I have no geis!"

The troll rose and fetched an amulet from a crowded collection on a shelf. "Do thou hold this a moment."

Bane took it. The small carved charm resembled a wooden flower, intricately carved. But as he held it, it glowed.

"There it be," Trool said. "There be a geis on thee."

"But I be near-Adept! How can there be magic on me, and I not know it?"

Trool took back the charm. "I think thou dost know it."

"A love-geis!" Bane exclaimed. "Only partially effective, because of my own power, but insidious! Enough to—"

"The Adverse Adepts have set a trap for thee when thou dost return to Phaze. Could they not have prepared it before?"

"And when it worked not well enough, they set a worse one!" Bane said. "When I exchanged before, with Agape—"

"Whom they thought would be Fleta," Trool finished.

"*I* thought her Fleta!" Bane said. "At first. Then did I learn she was not."

"So the impact of the spell was blunted, leaving thee with a partial passion of Fleta that thou didst not recognize. But the geis remained there, drawing thee toward her."

"And mayhap I devised this masquerade, that I might—"

"A geis can be insidious."

Bane nodded, immensely relieved. "Canst banish it?"

"Aye." Trool brought another finely crafted amulet; the troll had a real talent for carving. This one resembled a wooden heart. "Invoke it as thou willst."

Bane took it. "I invoke thee!"

The amulet flashed brightly. The light encompassed him, and drew in to him, centering on his heart.

"Wouldst take Fleta to bed?" Trool asked.

"Aye, an it be required."

"Dost love her?"

Bane smiled. "As a person, aye. As a lover, nay. I respect her and cherish her, but I would not seek her to wife."

"And Agape?"

"I seek her to wife."

"Then the geis be abated," Trool said. "Thou canst now face Tania."

"Aye!" Bane said with his first real confidence. "Ah, Adept, I thank thee! What a burden thou has lifted from mine heart!"

"I do it because it be right to do," the troll said. "But it pleases me that it also assures the welfare of the one who helped me gain mine own love."

"But that she must hide aboard her own planet, to escape the Contrary Citizens," Bane said, sobering.

"Until an accommodation be achieved. Mayhap that will come soon."

"Soon," Bane agreed fervently. "Ah, long I to be with her again!" Then his thought turned to another aspect. "Which Adept put that geis on me?"

"It seems to have been an elixir-spell. There be deep

enchanted springs in the mountains, and if the Purple Adept had cause to oppose thee—"

"He did! And he could have had a demon or goblin deliver the elixir the moment we exchanged, and depart unseen."

"And when they learned that Agape exchanged with thee, they thought the geis lost," Trool said.

"So they set up for a more effective ploy. Now at last does it all make sense!"

Trool smiled. "I shall have thine other answer tomorrow."

Bane took the hint. "I thank thee for both, Adept!" He retreated from the chamber as Trool reopened the Book of Magic.

Next day Trool presented that answer: "The mating must be done thrice, once in each of the 'corn's forms, when she be in heat. A spell o' fertility must be invoked at each occasion. The forms o' the breeders must match. Their love must be true, and their desire for offspring true. In this manner can crossbreeding be accomplished."

"Mine heat comes upon me in mere days!" Fleta exclaimed. "Must needs I have Mach back in time!"

"Aye, it be time to exchange back," Bane agreed. "But I fear thou canst not achieve it on this occasion."

"Why not?" she demanded.

"I have just learned the manner of form-changing. It be Adept-quality magic. I fear it be beyond Mach."

"O, aye," Fleta agreed, crushed.

"But mayhap in time can he master it," Suchevane put in.

"In time," Fleta agreed, brightening somewhat. "Yet would I be with him for mine heat. It be the only time I truly crave what delights him always."

"Aye," Suchevane murmured, understanding exactly.

"But that must come only after the mock-exchange, to seem to bring me to Phaze," Bane reminded her.

She smiled somewhat perfunctorily. "Aye; we have labored at a masquerade to deceive the Adverse Adepts! How glad I be to see the end o' that!"

"Aye," Bane breathed, knowing that his own relief was other than hers.

"But must needs I confess," she continued after a moment, "that an I could, I would return to Protonframe for the Tourney."

"The Tourney!" Bane exclaimed, amazed. "What would a unicorn do in such a thing?"

"Ah, what indeed!" she agreed, sighing. "Yet have I a foolish longing for the thrill I found in that contest, so like the Unilympic yet so different too. At first I liked Proton not, but as I came to know it . . ." She spread her hands. "Grazing the plains be just not the same, anymore."

So she, too, had been struck by a certain illicit longing! That made Bane feel better.

Bane located Mach, coming toward the Red Demesnes, and knew that his other self was ready for the exchange. He approached a rendezvous with mixed emotions. He knew that this would spring the trap, and that the goblins would not seek to harm him or Fleta, but that when Tania appeared his love would be truly tested. The abolition of the geis had returned his emotional strength to him, and abated his gnawing guilt and doubt—but how strong *was* his love for Agape? He would soon know, and if it faltered even a little—

Mach had cried out the triple Thee to Fleta, and removed all doubt from all the frame of his commitment. But even in the absence of the geis, Bane feared his own love to be of lesser merit. What tragedy could befall them all, if—?

But he had to put it to this test. It was the only way to play out the masquerade, and to stop the Adverse Adepts without revealing how he had spied on them. If he prevailed, their chances against the Adverse Adepts and the Contrary Citizens would still be no better than even. If he did not, then all that his father had worked for in Phaze, and all that Citizen Blue had worked for in Proton, was in peril.

But he had to put aside such speculation. He had a lot to explain to Mach, in a very brief interval!

Bane elected to make the contact almost in sight of the red castle, so that Trool's appearance would not be questioned, when the trap manifested. He walked to an open spot with Fleta, who was in girlform. He could feel the near approach of Mach. It was time.

He embraced Fleta. "I will return to you when I can, beloved," he said, playing the role of Mach. Her body was as lovely as ever, and he liked her as well as ever, but the guilty tinge of sexual and possessive desire was gone; she was only his animal friend, as she had always been.

"Take care of thyself, Mach," she replied. Then, with an impish smile: "And be not distracted by alien creatures."

He had to laugh. That was the least of his worries!

"You remain here, while I exchange," he told her, disengaging. "We don't want another four-way crossover!"

"Or to find ourselves in the wrong lover's arms."

She was being very pointed. He nodded, and turned, and walked about fifty feet, coming to the spot where Mach waited. Then he slowed, as if not quite sure of the exact spot, and passed through it without stopping.

Mach! he thought as they intersected. *Exchange not yet. There be a trap for me here I needs must spring.* Then he was out of phase.

He turned, as if reorienting, and walked back into Mach. *Understood,* Mach replied. *I will wait.*

Bane stopped just beyond intersection, spread his arms as if in discovery, and put a dazed expression on his face. He blinked, and began to lose his balance. Then he looked up, as if reorienting on the landscape of Phaze after being in a chamber of Proton. He opened his mouth.

Tania appeared immediately before him. "Bane," she said. Then she hit him with her power.

The effect was emotional rather than physical, but it was potent. Suddenly she seemed to glow, to become the ultimate and eternal woman, perfect of form and feature, phenomenally desirable. Her tan tresses shone with a golden luster, and her tan eyes bore on his magnetically. It was as if the entire frame were dissolving, becoming unreal; the only reality was here.

And she *was* beautiful. He could not deny that, objectively. She was not creating the illusion of appeal where none existed, she was enhancing a formidable base. Her face had seemed relatively plain, but her body was excellent, and now that her expression was animated, even her face was good. But that was merely physical. He had seen her destroy the little bird; he had seen her cruelty. He knew she was no prize.

More important, he was not vulnerable. His love was not uncertain or compromised. "Agape," he murmured. And saw the faint splash.

The ripple spread outward, almost invisible. But when it passed Tania, she screamed. She knew in that moment that she had lost, and that the trap had been for nothing. She had tried to exert her power on a man whose love was true.

The Translucent Adept appeared, floating in his watery bubble. "What be this?" he demanded, staring at Tania.

"That wench tried to fascinate me," Bane said. "Be this the way thou does honor the truce?"

"I had no part in this!" Translucent cried angrily. "I knew of it not, nor was it mine intent." There was another faint splash as he spoke, vindicating him. "The wench was to test only Mach's identity, lest there be deceit; thereafter she was to have no part of this."

The Red Adept appeared. "There was deceit on both sides," he said. "The Adverse Adepts set goblins to track the couple, to capture Agape, and to bring Tania to catch Bane. This be the proof o' that."

"Then be mine oath compromised," Translucent said grimly.

"But it were Bane who went last to thy Demesnes, and spied on thee," Trool continued. "Thus be mine own oath compromised, by the dealing of mine associates. I learned o' this late."

Translucent gazed at him. "Dost proffer offsetting injuries?"

"Aye."

"Accepted. Let us have no more o' this."

"No more o' this," Trool agreed. "Needs must we fashion an end to this standoff, that the issue be decided fairly and openly."

"Aye. But how?"

"The Tourney!" Fleta called.

Both Adepts glanced at her in surprise. "What dost thou know o' that, mare?" Translucent asked.

"It be the fairest way in Proton to settle an issue," she said stoutly. "First be the Grid played, wherein be strategy, but none may know ahead what game can come o' it, then be the game played, and the victor be determined by skill or luck or agreement as may be, but none may know ahead for sure who will prevail. Settle the issue with a tourney!"

"But this be Phaze," Translucent protested. "There be no tourney here."

"There be contests," Fleta said. "The Unilympics, the Werelympics—"

"Animal shows," the Adept said disparagingly. "But in any event, this be a matter between frames, not to be settled by a contest in one. And we can not have a contest between frames."

"We could," Tania said, speaking for the first time since her failure.

Translucent turned on her a look of irritation. "Be thankful I banish thee not to the depth of the sea, wench!" he snapped. "I'll have no input from thee!"

"I cheated too," Fleta said. "I knew I was with Bane, not Mach, in thy Demesnes. I be guilty as she."

"Then let her speak," Trool said, intrigued.

"There be only two who can communicate between frames," Tania said. "Or maybe four, but only two on their own. One sides with us, the other with Stile's forces. They be alternate selves, inherently even. Let them vie with each other, one in each frame. Let the loser join the side o' the victor."

Translucent looked at Trool, who looked equally amazed.

"And let their loves assist them," Fleta said.

Trool spoke to Bane. "Dost thou concur?"

"I be not apt at the game," Bane said.

"But thy potential be Mach's, in his body," Fleta said. "And his be thine, in thy body. An we exclude not magic from the games, with Mach a duffer there—"

"Training," Translucent said. "Go to experts of Proton for training. They will do their honest best."

"Better yet," Trool said. "Go to the Oracle."

Now Bane was stunned. The legendary Oracle! The magical entity that had guided his father's career in Phaze. The Oracle knew everything—and it was now in Proton, in the guise of a computer, guiding Blue's dominance of that frame. If he could not prevail with the Oracle's help, he could not do so at all. "Aye."

"But the equivalent in Phaze be the Book of Magic," Translucent said. "And that be not in our power."

"An Bane be trained by the Oracle," Trool said, "I will lend thee the Book of Magic, for the training o' Mach only."

This time it was the Translucent Adept who was stunned. "That be the mainstay o' thy power!"

"Aye. Canst make oath to abuse it not?"

Translucent considered, and there was a faint shimmer about him. "Nay. Canst give me access to it in thy Demesnes?"

Now Trool the Troll considered, and the shimmer was about him. "Aye," he said at last.

"Then can I agree," Translucent said. "Troll, we be

on different sides, but I would be friends with thee."

"Aye," Trool said.

Translucent stepped out of his bubble, and it dissolved into vapor. He walked across to Trool, extending his hand. The troll accepted it.

Then Trool turned back to Bane. "Does Mach agree?"

"Ask him," Bane said. He stepped back into overlap. *New challenge,* he thought. *They will explain.* Then they made the exchange.

10

Filly?

Mach felt the change, and knew it was now Agape he held. She had returned to her proper frame, and could return also to her own world of Moeba.

He disengaged. "I had better acquaint you with recent events here," he said.

"Aye," she agreed.

He looked at her, startled.

She laughed. "No, I am Agape. I have a story of my own to tell." She looked around the chamber. "But is it safe to talk?"

"It's supposed to be." But now he remembered how Citizen Purple had caught on to Fleta's identity. Had it been a good guess, or had information leaked from this chamber? The Game Computer could overhear everything, of course; Mach had trusted its discretion, but Citizens did have extraordinary powers.

She read his doubt. Then she hugged him. "Let us whisper, in that case. I have learned things about enmity."

"You are in the Tourney," he whispered in her ear.

She drew back her head and looked at him again, startled.

"It was the only way to protect Fleta from the Contrary Citizens—and even then, it was close. But you need not worry; you can lose and be shipped home to Moeba. You know the planet better than she does."

She smiled, agreeing.

There was a knock on the entry panel. Both of them glanced at it, startled. Who would knock, instead of using the screen to communicate?

Mach went to the panel and opened it. There stood a cleaning machine. Since when did such service devices knock?

The machine's speaker murmured a code. Then Mach understood: this was a self-willed machine masquerading as a mindless one. It extended a tiny package.

Mach took the package and folded it into his palm. Then the machine rolled on down the hall, and Mach closed the panel and turned to face Agape, making a small gesture toward his lips with a finger: silence.

She understood. She shrugged, and went to the food dispenser. He quickly opened the package, removed the electronic chip inside, and slid it into an aperture that opened under his left arm.

The message was stark: CONTRARY CITIZENS WILL CHALLENGE AGAPE AS FALSE ENTRY, DISQUALIFY HER, TAKE HER INTO THEIR CUSTODY. SHE MUST DEMONSTRATE SHE IS FLETA. TAPES OF THE CHAMBER TO BE REQUISITIONED AS EVIDENCE FOR HEARING. ACT ACCORDINGLY.

Assimilation took only an instant. Now he understood why the contact had been physical and masked: a communication through the screen would have become part of the requisitioned evidence. The Contrary Citizens were still after Agape, and would not let her get to her home planet, now that he had nullified their trap there.

She had to prove she was Fleta? Evidently the Citizens had caught on, but did not know that the girls had exchanged back. He trusted the judgment of his kind; he would do as they recommended.

Meanwhile, Agape was about to operate the food controls. He hurried over. "Fleta, you should know better than to try to work that thing yourself; you'll foul it up. Let me do it. What would you like?"

She masked her surprise. He put his hands on her shoulders and gently urged her to the side. As he let go, he tapped the spot under his arm where he had inserted the message chip. She nodded almost imperceptibly. Fleta might have been confused, but Agape understood his machine nature.

"The usual," she said. "I thank thee."

She was cooperating quickly and well! His experience on Moeba had increased his understanding and appreciation of her kind, and now he saw things about her that made him see how his other self could have come to love her. The tiny amoeba in the laboratories of Proton were far from intelligent, but those of Moeba were advanced, and every bit as clever as multicellular life. To think of a microscopic amoeba as the model for Agape was about as accurate as thinking of a single on-off switch as the model for Mach.

He fixed her the usual: a bowl of nutritious mush, that she could digest with her feet. He reminded her of this matter-of-factly, as if bored by it, but the information was important. Agape would not otherwise have known how Fleta had adapted to the amoeboid body.

After she had eaten, he guided her to the bed and lay down with her. Her look of uncertainty was only fleeting; she knew he had reason. He hugged her, and spoke quietly into her ear.

"Message chip. They mean to challenge your legitimacy as a Tourney participant. You must prove you are Fleta."

"But I don't know how she played, or anything!" she protested.

"Evidently my kind believes you can authenticate it.

But the tapes of this chamber will be requisitioned as evidence. That means—"

"Aye, I know what it means," she replied.

"I'm not sure you do. You see—"

"A moment, Mach, while I change into something more comfortable," she said.

He waited, not sure what she had in mind. What he had been trying to tell her was that Mach would have made love to Fleta, and if she was to prove she was Fleta, now, when supposedly unobserved, this was a necessary step. As a robot, he could do what was necessary, without compromising his love for the real Fleta. But could she—?

Her body was melting and changing. Her hair turned black, and a button appeared in her forehead. Her features—

"Fleta!" he exclaimed, amazed. For she was assuming the exact likeness of the unicorn girl, in her human form.

How could she have known that form? Then he chided himself for his doubt: Agape had just spent a good session in Fleta's body. Of course she had come to know it!

It was evident she also understood the rest of it. Agape loved Bane—but she had just been with Bane, and knew his plan to spy on the Adverse Adepts. She knew that Bane would have to treat Fleta as Mach would have treated her. Now she was ready to emulate that action here: Mach and Fleta, with the female being the pretense-identity, instead of the male. Perhaps there was a certain justice to it.

She smiled at him. "Come, my love. Do what thou must, and I will help thee. I would sleep soon, for I have a game on the morrow."

She looked like Fleta. She sounded almost like her. She knew his body, because of Bane's occupancy. She understood the rationale. She was a worthy person. But she was not Fleta, and he could not blank out that knowledge.

Could not? What was he thinking of! He could do just that, with a little spot reprogramming. He did it now, setting up a bypass so that for the next hour he would believe that what he saw was genuine. As a machine he could do that deliberately; he knew that living creatures could sometimes do it unconsciously, blanking out portions of their memory or instilling delusions that seemed real.

"Fleta," he said, accepting the presence of his love in this frame. He remembered the delight he had had of her in Phaze, after she had learned to accommodate his kind of love-making. He remembered his oath of love to her.

After that, it was easy.

Next day the challenge came: Citizen Purple levied it against Agape. "I submit that this is not the creature from Planet Moeba, but another creature in her body," he declared. "As such, she is not qualified to participate in the Tourney. Her apparent victory over me must be nulled, and she disqualified and turned over to me for compensation."

Such a charge would have been dismissed as nonsensical, had a serf made it. A Citizen was another matter. Agape was required to report to a hearing chamber for a settlement with the Citizen.

"But the evil man will grab me!" she protested. "I know not the ways of thy frame, but I know the ways o' the Adverse Adepts!"

Mach's temporary circuit had been eliminated; he knew her identity. But how like Fleta she was acting! That time in Phaze had really prepared her.

"The Citizen cannot take you as long as the Game Computer retains authority," he said. "All you have to do is demonstrate that you are properly entered in the Tourney." But he was nervous, because he had not been with Fleta when she qualified; he had stayed clear, deliberately, and gone to Moeba. He trusted the word of the self-willed machines, but he had no idea how pretending that Agape was Fleta would get her through this challenge. He had rejoined her after she had qualified; he had told her, in the guise of routine reminding, of the four matches Fleta had won. But he hadn't thought to look up the records on her qualifying matches—and in any event, it might have cast doubt on her authenticity if he had asked for those records.

They went to the prescribed chamber, following the line of the floor. Citizen Purple was there, glowering at Agape. "See—she doesn't even try to conceal it any more!" Purple exclaimed. "She's got the unicorn button!"

"Aye," Agape said.

"Hearing as to the validity of the qualification of Fleta for the Tourney is now in progress," the voice of the Game Computer said. "Challenger will present specifics."

"It was supposed to be Agape of Moeba," Purple said. "I want to verify the record of her qualification. What name is it under?"

"Record of subject's first qualification game displayed," the Game Computer said. A screen on the wall lighted. On it was printed:

PLAYER ONE: SHOCK OF KOLO
PLAYER TWO: FLETA OF UNI

The Citizen gaped. "She registered as a unicorn?"

"Transcript of dialogue at console," the Game Computer said. On the screen appeared:

"HI! I'M SHOCK. MY HAIR, YOU KNOW."
"HI. I'M FLETA"
"WELCOME TO THE LEFTOVER LADDER. I'M SECOND FROM THE BOTTOM. I LOVE THE GAME, BUT I'M NO GOOD AT IT, SO I'M EASY TO BEAT."
"LADDER?"
"OH, YOU NEW HERE? FROM ANOTHER WORLD?"

"NEW. FROM ANOTHER WORLD."
"SAY, THAT'S GREAT! I'M A KOLOFORM MYSELF. WELL, I MEAN MY FOLKS CAME FROM KOLO, SO IT'S MY BLOOD. I WAS BORN HERE, BUT I CAN ONLY STAY TILL I'M TWENTY-ONE, NEXT YEAR, YOU KNOW. THEN I'M EITHER A SERF, OR I HAVE TO GO TO KOLO. WHAT'RE YOU?"
"A UNICORN."

So that was it! Fleta had indeed registered as Fleta the Unicorn. Mach knew what had happened: she had automatically given her correct identity when talking with the other player, and the Game Computer had picked that up and made it official. She had proceeded to qualify for the Tourney under that identity. She was legitimately entered.

Citizen Purple hesitated, and Mach was sure he was going to demand to see the tapes of their chamber. But evidently the man changed his mind, knowing that they were on to his ploy and that nothing in those tapes would prove she was not Fleta. Certainly the tapes from before the exchange would not; then she had indeed been Fleta. The Citizen had challenged her as being an impostor for Agape, assuming that she would have been registered as Agape or under a phony name. Had he been able to requisition the records before making the formal challenge, he would have discovered his error, but all qualification records were sealed during a Tourney, to prevent cheating.

Citizen Purple strode out without further comment. He had lost—again. But Mach knew that they would have to maintain the pretense that she was Fleta until she was safely out of the Tourney and offplanet, lest she be disqualified for *not* being Fleta the Unicorn. The message of the self-willed machines had been timely!

That afternoon her next match came up. This was for Round Five, relatively rarefied territory for the Tourney. Fleta had done amazingly well, turning out to be a natural games-creature; Agape would not be able to match that level.

But he had, in the guise of a few private caresses, advised her: she could afford to lose, now, but she had to play in the manner of Fleta. A win in the manner of Agape would lead to the pouncing of the Citizens, and disqualification would put her into their hands. A loss in the manner of Fleta would enable her to be deported to Moeba safely. For the Tourney she was Fleta, but legally she remained Agape.

Mach could not join her at the console, of course. He watched her from their chamber, on the screen, as he had when Fleta played.

Her opponent was someone he knew: a man in his twenties who was a veteran player. His name was Sharp, and he was especially skilled at physical combat with sharp things: swords, knives, needles. He was not as good at intellectual things, and that was fortunate, because if Agape had the numbers she would put it into the mental category. If she had the letters, she would go for Machine-Assisted, avoiding the chance of direct physical competition. That was the strategy they thought Fleta would go for, avoiding animals because others would be expecting her to go for animals.

Evidently she did get the numbers, because the first selection on the grid was 2B, Tool-Assisted Mental.

The second grid was 5G, Separate and General: obviously she had had the numbers again, and chose to keep the two of them apart, as an uncertain unicorn would. This category contained such things as origami (paper-folding), crosswords, cryptograms and other noninteractive paper games. The assisting tools were pencil or paper or both, nominally; actually it was all done on the console screen.

The final determination was Cryptogram: the interpretation of a set of symbols that represented a quotation in English. Mach didn't like this; Agape could handle it, but Fleta would have real trouble. Unicorns had no literary education to draw upon, and indeed, it was sheer luck that Fleta was even literate; most did not go to that extreme when adapting to the human form. The danger was that Agape would play too well, and reveal her nonunicorn nature.

RULES: the screen said, for the contestants and for the private viewers, such as Mach. EACH NUMBER STANDS FOR ONE LETTER OF THE ALPHABET. SPACING AND PUNCTUATION ARE NORMAL. TO PLACE LETTERS, TOUCH NUMBER AND LETTER SIMULTANEOUSLY; TO MAKE CORRECTION, TOUCH AGAIN. A FULL LIST OF QUOTATION AUTHORS IS AVAILABLE, OR AN AUTHOR MAY BE REQUESTED BY DESCRIPTION. CONTESTANTS WILL WORK INDEPENDENTLY ON IDENTICAL QUOTATIONS. WINNER IS FIRST TO COMPLETE QUOTATION AND AUTHOR CORRECTLY. PLAY COMMENCES WHEN BOTH PLAYERS SIGNIFY READINESS BY TOUCHING "READY" SQUARE.

In a moment, the screens appeared on Mach's screen: Agape's on the left. Sharp's on the right. The players would not know who was doing better, but the watchers could see it plainly. There was a row of letters across the top, and other directives at the bottom. Each screen looked like this:

A B C D E F G H I J K L M N O P Q R S T U V W X Y Z

123456! 4758 975830'94

{11}{12} 32{13}26{14} {15}4 4729 758{16}:

{12}6{14}3{15}60 7{15}47 6{12}{12}0 5{17} 47{12}{12}!

{18}2332{15}1 {18}5{16}09{18}5{16}47

LETTERS NUMBERED FROM 1 TO {18} AUTHORS: LIST DESCRIPTION

Mach was experienced as a gamesman, and would have been happy to tackle this challenge. He would have started by touching AUTHORS and DESCRIPTION and requesting a selection of authors with first names of seven letters and last names of ten; that could have given him an immediate break, though the computer tried to foil that approach by having a number of authors for every such combination, sometimes too many to make it feasible. But neither contestant tried that.

Sharp knew some of the basics. He counted, and discovered that there were eight 7's, more than any other letter. He knew that E was the most common letter used in English, so he filled in E's above the 7's. That gave him a quick start, but Mach wasn't sure; in short quotations like this, distribution could be atypical, and Mach noticed that five of those 7's were preceded by 4's. Why were so many locked together like that? It was certainly possible, but not usual.

Agape, trying to think like a unicorn, was having more trouble. She did not count letters, she just pondered the whole, biting her lip. (He assumed that last detail; she was not shown on the screen.)

Sharp, buoyed by his success with E, pondered the doubled 12's near the end. He tried MESS for the last word, but that gave him –SS– for the third one from the end, and he didn't like that. So he changed the last to TELL, and that gave him –LL– for the other. He struggled with that, and was in the process of coming to the conclusion that he could not make it with that E; but he obviously did not want to give it up.

Agape, meanwhile, in a fit of inspiration calculated to convince everyone that she was Fleta, however badly she might lose the game, suddenly touched letters rapidly and filled in that last word as THEE. Mach had to applaud the genius of that; of course that was the way a creature from Phaze would see it!

Now she filled in her E's, T's, and H's, and suddenly she had a lot of notions to pursue. She found the second word beginning with TH and immediately filled in THOU, as Fleta would, and followed through with the O's and U's elsewhere in the sample. The word following THOU was –HOU––'–T; she had no hesitation about completing it as SHOULD'ST and filling in its other letters elsewhere. Her display now looked like this:

```
  L T O     !   T H O U   S H O U L D ' S T
1 2 3 4 5 6 !   4 7 5 8   9 7 5 8 3 0 ' 9 4

 E         L         T              T H   S  H O U
{11}{12}   3 2{13}26{14}  {15} 4    4 7 2 9  7 5 8{16} :

 E         L       D   H      T H      E   E   D   O        T H  E   E   !
{12} 6{14} 3 {15}6 0   7 {15} 4 7   6 {12}{12} 0   5 {17}   4 7 {12}{12} !

     LL            O    D S    O    T H
{18}2332{15}1  {18}5{16}0 9{18}5{16}4 7
```

Mach stared at it. Could she actually be on the right track? This certainly seemed to have possibilities! Sharp, meanwhile, was still agonizing over the loss of his easy E. That was a mistake; he was wasting time, being emotionally committed to an approach that wasn't working.

Fleta—no, Agape, he corrected himself—filled in the a for HATH, which also gave her AT. This was definitely falling into place!

She filled in F for FEED. Unicorns were always interested in that. But that made the first word --LTOF, which was awkward.

Then she stalled.

Mach agonized as she pondered, while Sharp tried one thing after another. Sharp would find the key, if she didn't do something!

Then Mach reminded himself that her objective was not to win, but to play like a unicorn. That she was accomplishing!

Then she evidently reread the options at the bottom of the screen. She touched AUTHORS: DESCRIPTION.

TYPE DESCRIPTION, the screen printed, and displayed a keyboard.

She went at it hunt and peck: A U T H O R S E N D I N G I N {TH}.

Stroke of genius! In a moment she had WILLIAM WORDSWORTH. The letters checked, and she had a number of new ones—and she hadn't had to draw from her memory a name Fleta would not have known. Now her cryptogram looked like this:

```
MILTOF!   THOU   SHOULD'ST
123456!   4758   975830'94

     E     LI      IF      AT    THIS  HOUR:
{11} {12}  3 2{13}2 6 {14} {15}4  4729  758{16}:

E F      L A F D    H A T H   F E      E D    O       T H E      E !
{12}6{14}3{15}6 0   7{15}4 7  6{12}{12}0     5{17}   4 7{12}{12}!

W I L L I A M        W O R D S W O R T H
{18}2 3 3 2{15}1    {18}5{16}0 9{18}5{16}4 7
```

She pondered, then filled in B above {11} for BE. Then she put N over {17}, making ON.

FEED ON THEE? Mach doubted it, and so, evidently, did Fleta. (He knew it wasn't her, but she was playing the role so well, he kept slipping.) She pondered, then in another fit of brilliance reversed F and N, making it NEED OF THEE! She corrected her bad F's elsewhere, and now the quotation was almost complete:

> MILTON! THOU SHOULD'ST BE LI–IN– AT THIS HOUR:
> EN–LAND HATH NEED OF THEE! WILLIAM WORDSWORTH

Sharp, meanwhile was starting to get on track; he had asked for the AUTHORS list, and after a tedious search from A to W had spotted Wordsworth. Had he chanced to start from the other end of the list, he would have been there much faster. He had no trouble with MILTON, but couldn't make sense of THOU and THEE.

Fleta filled in LIVING, and suddenly, to her surprise, she had won. She had no notion what kind of creature

ENGLAND was, but that wasn't necessary. What a perfect portrayal of the unicorn!

Then it occurred to Mach that Agape probably didn't know England either; it was not part of her heritage. Neither was Wordsworth, or Milton. She might have proven herself to be Fleta—by being herself.

Next day she was up against a young serf woman of about her own apparent age. Agape got the letters, so chose C. MACHINE. The other woman chose 3. CHANCE. They wound up with the game of number bracketing. This required three players, but the Game Computer simply generated random numbers for the third person.

The object was to choose a number from 1 to 100 that was between the two numbers chosen by the others, or, if two numbers matched, to be the odd one out, the one that didn't match. It was a very simple game, but a nervous one nevertheless. Obviously the best strategy was to go for the center, because the fringes were losers—but every player had the same notion. Thus it might be better to choose one near the edge, and let the other two jam up in the center, perhaps duplicating their numbers and yielding the victory. But every player would reason that way, too. What was the better strategy?

But it wasn't Mach's decision to make. He did not like games of chance, as was the case with most competent players; chance was the refuge of incompetence. At least there was no problem about unicorn strategy here; the game was too simple.

Agape chose 1, and the other player chose 50. The random number was 22, making it the winner. Therefore they played again.

This time Agape chose the other player's prior number, 50, while the other took 75. The random number was 63. Again they had no decision.

The third time Agape went for 75, taking her opponent's last number again. The other, gambling that she would do just this, took 74, bracketing her toward the edge. But the random number was 90, and Agape won. It was of course sheer luck—but the other woman had elected to win or lose by chance, and had paid the price, when she might have won by skill.

Agape had now won the sixth round, and would compete next in the seventh—one of only sixteen survivors in the Tourney. Mach was amazed: how far would this go? Suppose—just suppose—that her luck continued? Four more victories would make her the winner of the Tourney, and she would become the first unicorn Citizen. What then?

Her Round Seven match was against another Citizen; not one of the Contraries, just a game buff who enjoyed the challenge and the privilege of dashing the hopes of serfs. He was a healthy man in his forties who was the most dangerous of players: the kind who truly understood the Game. He would make no mistakes and would have no mercy. Mach, watching from his chamber, felt the dread of likely loss; Agape was about to be put out of the Tourney.

She got the letters and chose TOOL, following her set strategy. He chose PHYSICAL, craving the greatest immediacy. In the subgrid she chose COOPERATIVE, while he went again for immediacy and challenge; FIRE, or variable surface.

They settled on a "team" sport—that was how COOPERATIVE translated here. In this case it was a variant of mountain climbing, with five-person teams roped together, descending into the rumbling crater of a volcano.

Well, he thought, Fleta was fleet of foot. She could navigate any slope with confidence. Except that this wasn't really Fleta, and she wasn't alone. She had four android teammates who were "neutral": neither apt nor clumsy. What would count was teamwork: how well she organized and directed them for the descent into ever-more-challenging territory. The victory would go to the player who brought his party safely to the bottom first. If any teammates were lost, that was a liability but not necessarily defeat, depending on the state of the other team.

The screen showed the crater: a truly impressive setting. The walls of the upper inner rim were almost vertical, the slope modifying below and finally becoming level. But there were ridges and irregularities, and vents issuing smoke and steam, and sometimes lava. The whole thing shuddered at irregular intervals, and there were occasional mini-eruptions of rocks and dust and gas. Verisimilitude was excellent; on the screen, it really did seem like a living volcano crater.

There were four established paths of descent: north, south, east and west. These varied in detail, but had similar hazards, and had been established as equivalent in difficulty. Lot determined the assignments. The Citizen's team was given the north slope, and Agape had the south. Mach's screen could be set up to watch the whole crater, with the tiny figures at either side, or to watch one at close range, or split to watch both parties at intermediate range. He checked the AUDIENCE indicator, and discovered without surprise that it was huge. There were relatively few games being played now, and the unicorn had captured the public fancy; also, the volcano was always popular.

Mach knew that the Citizen would have played this course before, many times, and would have every path memorized. The Game Computer changed details with each game, to prevent this kind of advantage, but there was only so much it could do. The advantage of knowledge of the course was definitely with the Citizen.

Agape looked down her path, then took a daring and most unicornlike step: she detached herself from the safety rope. A unicorn, of course, would prefer to climb alone, regarding the other members of the team as a liability rather than an asset.

She started down, using chinks in the rim-wall for handholds, until she could stand on the less formidable slope below. She found a safe-seeming vantage by a projection of solidified lava, and called directions back to her remaining team. She had to get them down safely too; she could not leave them behind. They followed her route, descending in order, until they rejoined her. It was a decent start.

Meanwhile the Citizen was proceeding conventionally and efficiently. He too led his party, not trusting the androids to be good judges of the route. He barked orders to each, moving them along. His team made the first "landing" before Agape's did.

Then the first shudder came. The rocks shook, and several fragments of rock became dislodged and slid down. No damage was done to either party; it was merely a warning.

Agape went ahead again, spying out the best descent. She had a choice at this stage: one reasonably safe but long path, and one short but treacherous one. She gambled as a unicorn would, taking the shorter one. The Citizen took the safe one. That made Mach nervous; the Citizen surely had reason.

That reason soon manifested: there was another tremor, worse than the first. Gas hissed up from vents—and there were more such vents along Agape's fast path than along the Citizen's slow one. But Agape had had her team wait again while she explored, and she was watching; she lay flat as the vents expressed themselves, and had no trouble. Then she jumped across a minor crevasse, found another staging point, and brought her team down. She was now ahead of the Citizen.

Was there an upset in the making? The Citizen, seeing himself behind, hurried his team—and one of his androids misstepped and fell. The safety rope prevented him from being lost, but he took an injury, and now was limping. That was another point for Agape: all her teammates were safe.

But as she explored for the third leg of her descent, a lava vent just behind her spewed out molten rock, splattering her body. It was not real lava, of course, but jellylike emulation. Nevertheless, she had received a direct strike on the torso, and was deemed to have been burned beyond the ability to continue. The Game Computer issued a STAY IN PLACE directive; Agape was not permitted to go on.

If the Citizen suffered a similar mishap, then points would be assessed and the winner determined. But he did not. Relieved of any need to hurry, he took his time, and brought his slightly incapacitated party safely to the bottom. Thus, anticlimactically, Agape lost the match, and was out of the Tourney.

Mach felt a pang of regret. He reminded himself that she had done it correctly, playing the way a unicorn would; moving alone, gambling with her own safety rather than that of her teammates. Had she sent an android ahead, and had the android taken the incapacitating lava-splat, she would have been allowed to continue. The Citizen might have taken a greater loss of personnel, giving the victory to her. But she had done it Fleta's way, and lost, and that was the right way to lose.

Still, Mach wished she had won. He knew that the great majority of the audience felt the same.

Agape was returned to her planet, banned from Proton because of her loss in the Tourney. She had made it safely, and Mach knew the Contrary Citizens had no trap remaining there. The administration of the Tourney seemed to have no concern for the fact that if she really had been Fleta, as she had "proved" herself to be for her qualification as a player, this exile would have been inappropriate at best. But what of her relation to Bane?

He had no acceptable answer for that. In order to communicate or exchange with Bane, Mach had to overlap him geographically, and as far as he knew, that could only be done on this planet. If Agape was forever exiled from Proton, how could Bane get together with her?

There were two answers, as he saw it. Either Bane would have to make frequent trips to Planet Moeba, or

Agape would have to be allowed to return. Suppose they worked out a compromise: cooperation with the Contrary Citizens, in exchange for this exception to the law of Proton. Would Bane go for that? He wasn't sure.

Now, belatedly, he realized that the Contrary Citizens had never challenged Fleta's identity, after challenging her registry in the Tourney. That meant that the tapes of the chamber had never been requisitioned. Now she was safely back on her own planet, and it no longer mattered. He had not had to make love to her, to preserve the pretense.

Still, Agape had done such a good job of imitating Fleta that he was satisified to leave the recent past as it was. For an hour he had just about been with the filly. What others might think of the situation he wasn't sure, and didn't care.

The Tourney proceeded, and a serf woman won it, becoming a Citizen. How nice for her, Mach thought. But what of Agape? Neither she nor Bane deserved this enforced separation.

He spent his time doing research in the computerized Proton Library. Could a machine breed with an amoeba? Suppose a genetic pattern were crafted in the laboratory, living tissue modified to fit the attributes of a living man who occupied the body of a robot . . .

But why do that, when Bane had his own genetic pattern? What was needed was to send Agape back to Phaze to—

No, for then she would be in Fleta's body. There seemed to be no way to get the physical Agape together with the physical Bane. Or the physical Mach together with the physical Fleta. No way except magic.

No way except magic. And that existed only in Phaze, while one partner in each couple was physically locked here in Proton. There was the intractable problem.

Then, abruptly, Bane contacted him. The touch was fleeting, but he got the gist: do not exchange yet. Bane was trying to spring a trap, and needed just a little more time.

Mach waited, wondering what was happening.

Then Bane contacted him again, with news of a new truce. The picture had changed significantly in Phaze. If the rival factions of Proton agreed, they would have a way to settle this matter, and the two couples could be together regardless of the way it went.

That appealed to him. He agreed without hesitation. He knew Agape would feel the same.

11

Magic

Mach found himself standing near the Red Demesnes, with Fleta nearby, and three others. One was Trool the Troll, the Red Adept, whom he had met when he sought Fleta, to prevent her from committing suicide. The second was the Translucent Adept. The third was a sharply pretty young woman who looked familiar. In fact, it was Tania, the sister of their employer in the office in Proton! There she had been naked, and cold; here she was attractively clothed in a tan gown, and that made a significant difference. What was she doing here?

None of them spoke. Evidently they were waiting for him, being uncertain whether he had yet exchanged with Bane. "I am Mach," he said. "I gather something has happened here, and that there is a new agreement, but I don't know what it is."

Fleta approached him. "Be it truly thee, Mach?" she asked. She looked concerned.

"Thee," he murmured, letting his love for her come through. He had wanted her so much, in Proton, and Agape playing her role had been only a suggestion of the real person. How good it was to be with her again!

A trifling wave passed through her hair: the suggestion of the splash. Then she was in his arms, hugging him almost painfully hard. "Thee!" she echoed.

Translucent glanced at Trool. "Tomorrow?" he asked.

"Aye, Adept," the Troll replied.

Translucent glanced at Tania. Abruptly a watery ball enclosed her. It lifted from the ground, carrying her with it, and floated rapidly westward. Then Translucent himself vanished.

"Welcome to be guests of the Red Demesnes, an the two of ye prefer," Trool said. "Or not, as desired."

Mach hesitated, not knowing what was involved. "We thank thee, Adept, and accept," Fleta said.

The three of them walked toward the red castle. "I know only that there was a trap Bane sprung," Mach said. "And a new arrangement, that will make things easier. I would like to know more."

"The Tan Adept's daughter attempted to fascinate Bane, thinking him newly arrived," Trool said. "This were a breach that countered Bane's breach in deceiving and spying on the Adverse Adepts. Translucent knew not of it, nor I of Bane's device, prior. Now will Translucent and I work to train thee in magic, that thou mayst rival thine other self in a private tourney, and the victor will determine for whom the two of ye work."

Mach had trouble assimilating this. "I am—to play against my other self? Against Bane?"

"Aye. Thou for the Adverse Adepts, and he for Stile and Blue."

"But you are with Stile!"

"Aye. Yet do I honor the pact. This matter must be settled, and the imbalance between frames corrected, lest great harm come to all."

Mach nodded. "I am conversant with the Game, in Proton. But Bane isn't. And since the two of us can never meet in the same frame—"

"Thou willst rival him across the curtain, thou with magic, he with science."

"But I hardly know magic, and he—"

"Translucent will train thee, with the Book of Magic,

and Blue will train Bane, with the Oracle. We deem it fair."

Mach was silent. He wasn't sure it was possible, let alone fair. But if the two sides were satisfied, then he could not disagree.

They reached the castle and entered it. A woman came to meet them, stunningly beautiful. "Suchevane!" Mach exclaimed, remembering her from his canoe trip. "What are you doing here?"

"What, indeed," the troll murmured with fond awe.

"I be keeping company with the Adept," she said demurely. "Thy creature friend from Proton did help me broach him, and her do I now call friend."

Agape had had a hand in this? There had indeed been much she hadn't told him! He remembered how Suchevane had brought him to this castle, when he was in pursuit of Fleta, and how the Adept had reacted to the vampiress. Evidently Suchevane had been similarly struck by the Adept.

They had a meal together, the four of them, and Mach felt completely at home. Suchevane and Trool had helped him rescue Fleta; it seemed fitting that they be together now. There had been much mischief in the conflict between Adepts, but also some benefit, and this was that.

Fleta brought him to a private chamber for the night. "And how was the amoeba filly?" she inquired with a slight edge.

Mach's jaw dropped. Then she laughed, and he realized she was teasing him. "And how was Bane?" he returned.

"I love thee," she said, abruptly sober. "But I like him, and would help him how I could. He had need to seem to be thee—"

"And Agape had need to seem to be you," Mach said.

"Aye. So what we said, and what we did—it were merely words and deeds, n'er the truth. Canst accept that?"

"Agape made herself look and sound exactly like you," he said. "She knew you, because she had used your body. I—there are devices of circuitry I can use, in my own body—"

"And so I came to thee again, in her body. And thou didst come to me, in his, e'en as now. Mayhap we best think no more on that."

He nodded. They knew the situation, and knew it had changed. "But I wish I could always be with you." He hugged her, and kissed her.

"Thou mayst be with me more than thou dost like," she said with a certain impish malice. "Mine heat be nigh upon me. I can stave it off somewhat with herbs, but wish that not. I would breed with thee—"

"Uh-oh." He had tried to satisfy her insatiable breeding lust, the last time, and had had to use magic to do it. Sex was ordinarily a game with her, a game she played with increasing aptitude and delight, but when she came in heat it was savagely serious.

"In all my forms," she concluded.

"What?"

"The Red Adept looked in the Book of Magic, and learned how we could be fertile. There be spells, methinks, but also needs must we breed in mine human, equine and avian aspects."

"But I cannot—!"

"Thou must change form," she said. "The Book will tell thee how."

"It better!" he muttered. "And I'll need a new perpetual potency spell."

"Why, Mach," she said with disarming innocence. "Be I not attractive to thee?"

"You're an infernal nuisance to me!" he exclaimed, wrestling her into position for an explosive love-making while she giggled.

Then they talked, lying embraced, and caught each other up on the recent events of their frames. Fleta was pleased to learn that "she" had won two more games in the Tourney, but disappointed with the concluding loss. "But I will coach thee so thou dost not lose thine own tourney," she swore.

In the morning, Translucent appeared. Trool conducted him and Mach to his study, where the great Book of Magic lay.

"But—" Mach protested, out of sorts.

"First we shall teach you the magic of form-changing," Trool said. "Be not concerned; thou willst be ready for the filly."

"That, too," Mach said. "But—I am the son of Citizen Blue, and my sympathy is with his side. I only went with the Translucent Adept because he gave us sanctuary for our love. I agreed to serve their side for information from Proton. I never expected actually to fight for the Adverse Adepts."

"This do we understand," Trool said. "But this matter be beyond such preferences. An the matter not be settled, the frames be in peril. *Any* settlement be better than none. The need be for fairness in coming to a compromise. Thou dost represent not thine own view, but an instrument in a settlement that can no longer be denied."

"But how can I do my best for a side with which I disagree? I mean, psychologically I will want to lose."

"Bane had need to hide his identity," Trool said. "He did what was needful to keep that secret. Didst thou face a similar challenge in Proton?"

"Yes, but—"

"Didst find thyself unable?"

"No, but—"

"Canst not do what be needful to effect settlement?"

Mach hesitated. Did he have a double standard?

"Where lies thine honor?" Translucent asked.

Honor. To do his very best for the job he agreed to do, regardless of his personal sacrifice. He found that his internal conflict, when viewed that way, disappeared.

"I can do it," he said. "But I should think that you would question—"

"Mayhap some do," Translucent said. "I have put my trust in thee. An thou dost betray it, I be lost in more than my cause."

"I suppose I must be like a paid mercenary," Mach said. "I must do the job I am committed to do. My private feelings have no bearing."

Both the others nodded affirmatively.

"Still—"

"Methinks thou shouldst consult with the Blue Demesnes, and be satisfied on this," Translucent said. "I will conjure thee there."

"But—"

Then Mach was standing outside the neat blue castle that was evidently the residence of Bane's father. This was the first time he had seen it.

The Translucent Adept had conjured him here. The man had extraordinary confidence!

Yet perhaps it made sense. Translucent had asked him about honor. If he was going to betray the agreement he had made, this was the person with whom he would do it: his father's other self. It was better to settle this private matter now.

"Halooo!" he called.

In a moment a woman came to the bridge at the moat. She was a lovely creature in blue that he knew immediately was Bane's mother. "Why Bane," she said, surprised. "Back again, without thine alien friend?"

"I am Mach."

She gazed at him, taking stock. "Then where be Fleta?"

"She is at the Red Demesnes. I—the Translucent Adept conjured me here, to talk with Stile."

"He be not here at the moment," she said. "But come in, Mach; I will talk with thee."

Agape had visited here, and not seen Stile. Where was the man? But perhaps the Lady would do.

"Thank you." He walked across the drawbridge.

The Lady's hair was fair, and her eyes blue. She was of course of a different generation, and her age showed as he saw her close, but she remained as lovely in her way as his own mother, who was literally ageless.

The Lady turned and escorted him into the central courtyard. There were flowers and a number of animals, evidently ill or injured, recuperating. The Blue Demesnes, he knew, had always been close to animals.

"I love an animal," he said abruptly.

She took a seat at a table in the shade, beside a pleasant pool, and gestured him to the other seat. "We say naught here against Fleta."

"But you want an heir."

"Aye, Mach. We lose ground slowly to the Adverse Adepts, who would o'erturn what we have done, and make o' this frame a kingdom o' their own. We hoped Bane would hold them at bay, and his child after him. Without that, we will surely be defeated, and it matter little whether it be now or in the future."

"But I mean to find a way to breed with Fleta, and for Bane to—"

"An thou dost breed with the unicorn, thou has not a human being for a child, but an animal crossbreed. That be not sufficient, for the animals have not the talent for magic that the human beings do."

"But Bane also might breed with Agape—"

"And have an alien child, confined to Proton-frame," she said. "Mach, think not we oppose thy happiness, or Bane's! Nor would we hurt Fleta—or Agape—for anything. We be merely aware of the loss entailed. Where be thy happiness an the frame be ruined?"

"You know that I have agreed to represent the Adverse Adepts, because they support my union with Fleta," Mach said. "Where are you if power is achieved by those Adepts *now?*"

"Stile be working on that," she said. "That be why we see him not here."

"What would you have us do?" he asked, anguished.

She gazed at him levelly. "We would have thee return to thy frame and stay there, and find a woman there. Perhaps Agape; she be a fine creature. And Bane stay here, and marry a woman o' Phaze."

"How can you speak so lightly of the disruption of love?"

"Nay, I speak not lightly," she said. "I married Blue for love, but lost that love, and came to love Stile, his other self. Then did I have to give up Stile and return to Blue, for the good o' the frame, and to that did I accede."

"But—"

"The Brown Adept, then a child, drew a spell at the end from the Book of Magic, reversing Stile and Blue," she said. "Thus did Stile come here to me, when he had thought to be confined to Proton, and Blue went to Proton instead. Thus was our happiness snatched from our resignation. But I had done what I had to do, for the frame, and so had Stile. We both put the frame ahead o' our private happiness. We expect no less o' thee and Bane."

Mach shook his head. "Bane may be resigned to that, but I am not. Fleta tried to facilitate your position by throwing away her life. Even if I did not love her, I would not purchase the good of the frame at such a price. The end does not justify the means."

She looked at him, her eyes glistening, then overflowing. She put her face in her hands. "Ah, I am torn!" she cried. "There be unbearable evil on either side!"

Mach felt his own eyes going. "I must do what I must do," he said. "I must represent the side I have chosen. Bane remains on your side; if he wins, you will have your heir." Then he rose and left the castle, knowing there was nothing more to be said.

Beyond the moat, he called out: "Translucent! Bring me back!"

There was a wrenching, and he was back in the chamber with Translucent and Trool. "You're right," he said abruptly. "There is no way to settle it but this."

Trool opened the Book of Magic. "There be this, too," he said. "In this volume be magic such as to govern all the frame, an it be invoked. When thy mother-machine used it, she became Adept in mere hours, while others built to it all their lives. I be but a troll, unable to practice magic o' the level o' the human kind, with little natural talent for it. I can use only a tiny part o' this power—yet that part makes me equivalent to other Adepts."

He focused on Mach with a disquieting intensity. "But thou dost be human—or at least, in human form. Thy potential for magic dwarfs mine own. E'en without training or experience, thou didst conjure a boat like none crafted before, to travel in. Thou didst save thy filly from death by o'erriding the spell I put on her. That be Adept-level magic. Thou dost be untrained, but with time and training thou couldst be a full Adept; the signs be plain. That be why the Adverse Adept feared thee, and tried to capture thee, and when that failed, why Translucent took over and made a deal with thee to join them. Mayhap thy potential be but the reverse face o' Bane's, and he be no slouch either. But with the aid of this Book, and proper guidance, thy power can become most formidable. That be why we want thee to comprehend thine honor."

Mach saw that the troll was quite serious, and so was Translucent. "You mean that I could become a stronger Adept than either of you?"

"Aye. Than any. No human being before has had the power o' this Book. We must make thee strong enough to represent the side thou be on as well as can be done. But after that, thou willst remain more formidable than any other, an thou remain in Phaze. We want not to see that power abused."

"But I must leave Phaze, when this is done," Mach said. "Because of the imbalance. Or at least agree to equal time in Proton, so the imbalance can be limited."

"Aye. But an thou choose not to depart, no other could make thee."

Mach's understanding was growing. "You don't want to solve one problem and create another," he said. "Maybe a worse one."

"Aye. Therefore we ask thee to use this power only for the purposes we seek. Thy service is to make the settlement. Thy reward is to have successful breeding with Fleta. Seek no more than these, and there be no problem."

Mach's awareness seemed to be spinning. "But what of the issue between Adepts? If Bane and I cooperate to link the frames for one side or the other, won't that generate a similar power?"

"Mayhap. But that be limited by the narrow conduit through which it must pass. We deem that the lesser evil."

Mach sighed. "I hope you are right!"

Then they went to work, explaining to him the nature of the relevant spells in the Book, and how to invoke them. They were of all types, not limited to the mode of any single Adept; he had no need to speak or sing them, or to draw them, or use any other particular mode. He could implement them any way he chose; all modes were one, in this amazing Book. Many were complex; without the help of the two Adepts, he would have taken much longer to assimilate their significance and application, let alone master them.

In minutes he understood that the power of magic in these pages was greater than any he had guessed at. In hours he saw that in those minutes he had vastly underestimated the case. By the end of the first day, his awareness of the nature of the universe had changed fundamentally. Reality had assumed a new dimension.

By the end of the second day, he was able to perform magic consistently of the level of the Adepts, and to counter spells made by either Trool or Translucent.

On the third day he went beyond. He learned a spell to invoke his robot information storage capacity in his human frame, so that he could instantly memorize spells without understanding them. That meant that he could ponder them at leisure, without using the Book. He learned other spells to enhance his comprehension and applications, so that he could make far better use of magic than any ordinary person could.

On the fourth day he studied organization and discipline, so that he grasped precisely what magic was appropriate when, and understood without having to reason it out when minor or no magic would do the job as well as a major invocation could. Now, with the most minor spell, he could accomplish what might require the full magic of an Adept. This magnified his power in another way.

On the fifth day he studied the philosophy and responsibility of magic. This was a necessary concurrent to the power he had developed.

He was truly becoming the Robot Adept.

Fleta came into heat. The first time he had encountered this, she had demanded copulation several times an hour for several days and nights, until her animal nature had completed that aspect of the cycle. Had any of the efforts taken, her heat would have abated sooner, but his human body had been unable to fertilize her equine nature. She had remained in human form, but that was superficial; man was genetically incompatible with unicorn.

This time he invoked magic that in effect translated the language of his seed to the language of her egg, enabling them to communicate and merge. Even so, they differed, much as a man differed from a unicorn despite their ability to converse with each other. Only a part of the union could occur while she was an imitation human woman. But another part could occur in her natural form, while he was an imitation unicorn, and the completion could be accomplished when both were in avian form. Trool had seen that, without possessing the magic to enable it. Mach now possessed the magic.

He mated with her in human form, and it was a deeply gratifying act, because it was for love *and* procreation and pleasure. Then he applied a spell to himself that gave him continual potency, but allowed no actual seed to be expelled, because that was needed for the next stage. Because she was not yet bred, her ardor continued; he sated her lust continually through the day and night, his pleasure more of accomplishment than of sexual fulfillment. They snatched bites of food and gulps of water in the few minutes' respite between sieges, so as not to suffer deterioration of health.

After the full day/night cycle, they left their bedroom chamber and went to a private garden. He made a spell to transform himself to the form of a unicorn stallion. She reverted to her natural form. Now the odor of her need smote him, and he found he required no instruction to do what was necessary. In a moment he had expended the seed of the past day, and invoked another seed-conservation spell.

They snatched mouthfuls of hay that Suchevane had thoughtfully provided, between bouts of mating. They drank from the water of a clear fountain. Mach would have enjoyed the experience of being a unicorn, had he not been kept so busy with the breeding. As it was, the matter became somewhat tedious. He had to use subsidiary magic to abate the soreness that was developing. How did a Herd stallion manage?

He discovered that he could speak to her in horn talk. His horn sounded like a bassoon, and was actually quite versatile. But more than that, his spell of form-changing had included the whole of the unicorn anatomy and potential, including knowledge of the language of their music. Suddenly he appreciated an enormously significant aspect of unicorn nature and culture. It was true that horn talk was relatively limited, compared to human language, because unicorns had more limited interests; indeed, when they had complex matters to discuss, they tended to shift to human form and use the human language, which was competent to handle it. But for most purposes, horn talk was adequate, and it could also be understood by the werewolves and vampires. He resolved to spend more time in this form, after the business of the moment was done, when he could appreciate it for itself.

As their day and night of equine breeding came to its end, they played a duet, bassoon and panpipes. Actually it had three or four parts, because of Fleta's ability to play her own counterpoint. Then she changed to her hummingbird form, and he matched her, becoming a male hummingbird.

They mated, and expended his past day's production of seed. Then they flew to the garden and sipped the nectar of the flowers. This, too was a pleasure—but in just a few minutes, because of the swift metabolism of the form, they had to mate again.

But after a few matings, the intensity of her desire eased, and the spacing stretched out. Then her interest faded out. Her period of heat was over.

They changed back to human form. "I worry," she said. "Mine heat be normally longer than this."

"Maybe it was cut short because the breeding was successful," he said.

"O, how I do hope so!" she exclaimed, hugging him.

They were naked, and in love—but at the moment had no temptation at all to make love. Instead they retreated to their chamber and fell into weary sleep.

They would not know whether the effort had been successful until the time of her next heat. If it manifested normally, it would mean that this one had not taken. He might have ascertained her status sooner by magic, but he did not want to interfere in any way, lest that same magic destroy what it had achieved. He wanted nature to take its course, now.

It was time to go into training for the contest with his other self. Mach received a "visit" from Bane, confirming that the separate Citizens of Proton had agreed to the mode of settlement, and that they had decreed that it should be done by Tourney rules. They wanted to make it two out of three rounds, with three games per round, so that chance would not play too significant a part.

Mach discussed it with the Translucent Adept, who checked with his compatriots. They agreed, but wanted the selection of games done in advance, so that there would be time to prepare properly for particular types. Mach relayed that, and in due course got agreement, with further qualification: the advance choices would be for only one round at a time, with a thirty-day training period for each after the game was determined. They were concerned that Bane, having been raised apart from Proton society, would otherwise be at a serious disadvantage because of his lack of experience with the breadth of games available. With intensified specific training they could ameliorate this liability, making it a fair contest.

To this stipulation the Adepts agreed. The contest was now established. All they had to do was decide on the first set of games.

They set up a special console. Trool carved it from stone, and animated it by magic: it now had an operative screen just like one in a Game Annex of Proton. A similar, but science-animated, console was set up at the same spot in Proton. But Bane and Mach did not stand on opposite sides; they stood on the same side, overlapping each other, so that what one did was known to the other.

The Game Computer operated the console in Proton, and the two selves relayed the signals so that the same information appeared on the one in Phaze.

The grid appeared:

PRIMARY GAME GRID

	1.PHYSICAL	2.MENTAL	3.CHANCE	4.ARTS
A. NAKED				
B. TOOL				
C. MACHINE				
D. ANIMAL				

PLAYERS: MACH—NUMBERS
BANE—LETTERS

It felt just like home!

Mach wasn't sure that a physical game could be played between the frames, so he touched 2. MENTAL. After a brief pause, Bane evidently made his choice, for B.TOOL developed a highlight. The box for TOOL-ASSISTED MENTAL GAMES brightened and expanded to fill the screen.

SECONDARY GRID: TOOL-ASSISTED MENTAL GAMES

	5.SEPAR	6.INTERAC	7.PUZZLE	8.COOPER
E. BOARD				
F. CARDS				
G. PAPER				
H. GENERAL				

Mach had the letters this time, so he touched E. BOARD. Bane chose 6. INTERACTIVE. The 6E square expanded.

Now it was time to assemble their own grid. There was the usual list of choices down the side. Mach had the first choice, so he touched CHESS, OCCIDENTAL and put it in the center of the nine-square array. He had played many variants of chess, and liked them all; he had many standard strategies filed in his memory. Bane probably had not put the same type of time into it, though he certainly could be familiar with the game. But Bane's chances of mastering a sophisticated chess variant in only one month were minimal.

Bane put GO BANG in a corner. That was a relatively simple game in which each player tried to be the first to set five stones in a row.

Mach put SHOGI next to Bane's choice. That gave

him two choices in a row. Shogi was Japanese chess, like Occidental but with extra pieces such as "silver" and "spear" and extra motions and strategies. For example, castles and bishops could be "crowned," or promoted, taking on additional abilities, and captured pieces could be made to fight for their captor.

Bane put CHINESE CHECKERS in that row, preventing Mach from having three of his own choices there. Had he gotten that, and then had his choice of rows rather than columns, he could have been set!

Mach put POLE CHESS in the center of the bottom row. This was a minor but intriguing variant developed in the last centuries, first as a joke, then seriously.

Bane put FOX AND GEESE, one of the hunt games, in the center of the top row.

They continued, Mach with variants of chess, Bane with simpler games. At the end they chose their line and column, and Mach got one of his choices: POLE CHESS. He had a definite advantage; he had played the grid to win, and now was in a fair position to do so.

But Fleta had a question. "Thou willst play here, in Bane's body?"

"Yes. But my basic knowledge of the game carries over."

"And Bane will play in Proton-frame, in thy body?"

"Yes, of course."

"And has he not access to all thy memories and skills?"

Mach froze. She had just identified a critical flaw in his thinking! Of course Bane had all the robot memories and skills; they were inherent in the nature of the machine and its programming. He, Mach, had even made a recording of his experiences on Planet Moeba for Bane to enjoy. *Bane could do anything as well as Mach could!*

All his savage strategy had been wasted. Citizen Blue and the Oracle would see that Bane started at Mach's level, and proceeded from there to a higher level. In fact, the infallible machine brain could probably play chess better than the fallible human brain, for it would not make the kind of error Mach was not prone to. Such as this one, of forgetting the elementary liability of his strategy!

"I'm in trouble!" he muttered. "I outsmarted myself."

"Magic will enhance thy capacity," Translucent said. "That is why we have made thee an Adept. Thou willst play better than ever thou didst as a machine."

"So will Bane," Mach responded glumly.

"I meant not to cause thee distress," Fleta said contritely.

At that he had to smile. "Good thing you brought me to my senses, filly!"

12

Oracle

Bane was in a chamber in Vamdom, and Agape was not with him. That drained much of the delight he had had in this frame. But with this new compromise, he should be able to bring her back.

He went to a communication screen. "Citizen Blue," he said.

Almost immediately, the man who so resembled his father came on the screen. "Ah, Bane," Blue said.

Bane hadn't even spoken directly to him yet, and the man recognized him! How was it possible, when he was in a robot body? "Aye, Citizen. I bear news o' a new deal. Mach and I needs must play a tourney of our own, three rounds, and both serve the side that does prevail. The Adverse Adepts be training him, with the Book o' Magic, and I may train with the Oracle. Dost agree?"

Blue did not even hesitate. "I agree. Let me contact the other side. Meanwhile, go to the Oracle."

"Aye. But if Agape may now return—"

"If the Contrary Citizens allow it."

"Methinks they will."

"We shall know in a moment."

Blue's face faded from the screen. Immediately a new

one formed. This was a young android woman, evidently a secretary. "You have business with the Oracle?" she inquired.

Already! "I be Bane, of Phaze. Needs must I oppose mine other self in a tourney, and if the Oracle will train me for that encounter—"

"If you will report to the nearest Game Annex, the Oracle will be in touch."

"Game Annex? But—"

"The Game Computer permits this use of its facilities," she explained. "The location of the Oracle is private."

So that the Contrary Citizens would not interfere with it, he realized. The Oracle was the mainstay of Blue's power in this frame.

He made his way to the Vamdom Game Annex. Soon he was sealed in a chamber with a holo unit.

Color developed in the air, swirling diaphanously. "The Contrary Citizens have agreed," a melodious voice said. "Agape will be recalled from Planet Moeba, on the technicality that she was never in the Tourney, but served only as the host for the unicorn who was, so cannot be deported for the unicorn's loss. She will join you here in due course. In the interim, I need to learn from you what has occurred in Phaze during the past fifteen years."

"I will try to tell thee—"

"Your present body is a machine. Plug in your brain, and I will take a full readout."

"Readout?" Bane was baffled.

"There is an access panel behind your left ear. Connect this." A multipronged plug appeared, extending from the wall.

Bane found the panel and slid it open. He plugged in the plug. His awareness changed.

First he felt a kind of draining, as if his mind were pouring out through the connection. Then he felt a return flow, as if other material were entering. He knew he was not losing his own identity; the information was merely being called up and copied. But the process was interactive, and the act of reading his mind generated a lesser return flow, so that he perceived, as in a dream, the memories of the Oracle. At first he resisted; then he realized that this was a remarkable opportunity, and sank into the dream.

There were levels and levels of it, a memory within the dream. Bane, confused, sought the beginning—and found himself in a vision of ancient Earth, when magic was there. In the ambience of magic, things occurred that were not possible with science, such as instant shape- and mass-changing, and the crossbreeding of divergent species. Indeed, crossbreeds flourished, and many such species had stabilized. Their magic was internal; they limited their effects to set form changes and particular talents, such as carving rock. They retained their potency thoughout their lives.

But every act of external magic—that which was not natural to the species—depleted the store of magic on the planet, and so its power inevitably diminished. The vacuum was slowly taken up by a new system, later codified as science. At first science was weak and unreliable, but it gained strength in direct proportion to the diminution of magic. In sum: magic waned, science waxed. Those who practiced the new discipline came to doubt that the old one had ever had validity, because they assumed that the fundamental forces of the universe were unchanging. That was their folly—but on Earth it could not be disabused. The old texts of magic were systematically destroyed, for their spells no longer operated.

But in the larger universe, magic remained, and though it was losing its effect throughout, certain nuclei retained their potency. These came to shine like beacons in the thinning ambience, and drew the devotees of the old disciplines who were by their specialized arts able to detect them from afar. One of the strongest was the planet Phaze, where enormous magical energy had imbued its specialized nether rock.

Earth was becoming inhospitable. An oracle, or

prophecy, told of a distant locale where magic would be safe. So certain creatures fashioned a great wicker boat they called the Craft of the Oracle, or Coracle. Those who were ready to risk their lives for the sake of such a dream boarded it and set sail, leaving the more conservative majority of creatures behind. The Coracle passed through the fluxes of the universe and came at last to its destination, bringing to this planet the first unicorns, werewolves, harpies, vampires, dragons, elves, goblins, ogres, demons, trolls and others, leaving behind the centaurs, rocs, merfolk, sphinxes and others. The creatures spread out to fill the ecological niches of Phaze, and flourished; in due course there were many herds of unicorns, packs of werewolves, flocks of vampires, hordes of goblins and conclaves of elves. They achieved a certain equilibrium, each dominating its chosen habitat, generally hostile to each other when there was competition for particular territory.

Then, hundreds or perhaps thousands of years later, man came to Phaze. Magic had been all but exterminated on Earth, and the crossbreeds remaining there were extinct. Some had been vicious creatures whose disappearance was little loss, but some had cultivated the best traits of their ancestor species, and their demise was a tragedy. The centaurs had been too arrogant to settle for any region less than Earth itself; now not only Earth but the universe existed without their civilization. Instead it suffered the ravages of man.

Man came technologically, and brought the infectious seed of science with him. He set about colonizing the planet, calling it Proton, burning its forests and slaughtering its creatures. The animals had never been exposed to the horrors of science, and though they tried to fight back, they were being decimated. The goblins mounted a savage counterattack, wiping out several colony settlements, but the humans reciprocated by bombing the goblins' camps and warrens and nearly wiping out several tribes. It was evident that all too soon the creatures here would go the way of their cousins on Earth.

But not all the invaders were vicious or uncaring. Some few appreciated the nature of Phaze and sought to preserve its unique environment. These managed to deal with the elves to create a barrier between the frames of science and magic, separating them. This had an immediate effect, because the weapons based on science no longer worked in the magic frame, and magic no longer worked in the science frame. It effectively isolated the two factions, though they actually shared the territory. They were out of phase with each other. This was the origin of the name of the magic realm: Phaze.

Then a peculiar effect manifested. The two frames assumed an equivalence in more than geography. Human beings who were born and raised on the planet began appearing on either side of the curtain, mirror images of each other. In some interaction between science and magic they had cloned, the parties on either side living similar lives, but utilizing different modes. It was possible for newcomers to the planet to cross the curtain, though not always easy. Clones could not; the presence of their other selves barred them. Thus the frames were increasingly separated. But this meant that only those who knew least about the opposite frames could cross to them, and this meant trouble.

Some long-time residents developed formidable powers of magic, and became known as Adepts. The potential for magic was in every creature, but the Adepts acted ruthlessly to restrict its application. Those whose powers were less soon learned to avoid the use of magic almost entirely, so as not to seem in any way competitive with the Adepts. They settled into innocuous village life, while the Adepts became like distant lords. The Adepts took it upon themselves to protect Phaze from unwarranted intrusions across the curtain, using magic to detect and eliminate most of those who crossed.

But the Citizens of the developing hierarchy of Proton were in no mood to brook such interference with their rights of exploitation. They used their computers to prepare an exhaustive analysis of the mechanisms of magic, and developed a computer that could invoke this magic without error or waste. Because a computer could not operate in Phaze, they digested these principles into a comprehensive Book of Magic that any person could use with devastating effect. The conquest of Phaze by Proton was about to resume. This of course was incipient disaster, and the more sensible elements of both cultures opposed it implacably.

A compromise was achieved: the Book of Magic was confined to Proton and hidden, so it could not be used, and the computer was put across the curtain into Phaze, where it was given limited animation as the Oracle: an entity that would answer any question once. References to Phaze in the literature of Proton were extirpated, and in a generation it was as if the other frame did not exist. But the Citizens knew of it, and some of their secretaries learned. Surreptitious crossings still occurred, but there was a conspiracy of silence about the matter. The Citizens who had other selves in Phaze could not cross, and did not want others to do so.

So it was for three hundred years—until the extensive mining of Protonite in the science frame generated an imbalance that threatened to tear the fabric that separated them and destroy both. The Oracle understood this, but could not act directly to allieviate it. Its only power was answering questions directed to it, and not many of those. Therefore it used that power to cause the Blue Adept to be murdered—

Bane snapped out of the vision. "What?"

"You have assimilated the history of the frames," the Oracle said.

"*Thou* didst cause Blue to die?" Bane demanded.

"Only one person seemed likely to be able to do the necessary job," the Oracle replied. "That was Stile, in the frame of Proton, the Blue Adept's other self. He knew nothing of Phaze, and could not cross. Therefore I devised a plan to free him for crossing, and to acquaint him in due course with this mission. This is a story whose general gist you may already know."

Bane did indeed! The Red Adept had murdered the Blue Adept, whose soul had taken refuge in his harmonica: then Stile, Blue's other self, had crossed the curtain and taken Red out, replacing her with Trool the Troll. Stile had married Blue's widow, the Lady Blue, and begotten Bane. Blue, meanwhile, had crossed to Proton, animating Stile's body. Stile was actually using a golem body crafted by Trool, animated by magic; he was a golem with the soul of a man. Or, in Proton terms, very like a cyborg. Bane had actually been conceived before that shift of bodies; there could be none conceived thereafter. All this Bane understood—but it seemed that there were aspects he had not been told.

"The permanent separation of frames was intended to prevent any further imbalances from developing," the Oracle continued, its light still swirling. "But it seems that there is after all imbalance."

"Because Mach and I exchanged frames," Bane said.

"That should not have been possible."

"For an entity that is supposed to know everything, thou dost seem to be short some information."

"True. I lacked news of the developments in Phaze. I must ascertain what changed," the Oracle said. "I have the transcript of your life experiences, but this is not enough. I must know *how* you exchanged."

Suddenly Bane was back in the dream, but this time he was himself. He was in the retreat he had fashioned, really only a rock in a glade, communicating with his other self. He had not at first realized that this was what he was doing; he had been drawn into this glade for no reason he could ascertain, and now felt the odd presence. "Who be ye?" he asked, and felt it echo in alien language, *Who are you?*

I am Mach! the answer came, definitely not his own thought. Then: *Let's exchange places!*

The notion intrigued him "Aye—*for a moment.*" He improvised a quick spell, and sang it, to facilitate the process, whatever it might lead to.

Then, with an abrupt wrenching, he had found himself in the frame of Proton, and his remarkable adventure had begun.

"Amazing!" the Oracle exclaimed.

"Thou dost be just a computer, a thinking machine," Bane said. "Dost feel surprise?"

"Yes. We machines can experience emotion when our design permits, as is the case with Mach. I have discovered the source of your ability to exchange. It is because the connection between the frames was never completely severed. You and Mach tuned in to that open channel, and used it, and later your friends did too. Now that channel is broadening with use, complicating the imbalance—but the imbalance has been building slowly throughout the life of that channel. I never thought to check for such a thing!"

"A channel between the frames? But how came that to be? Methought all connection was severed before my birth."

"I recognize the psychic pattern. It is that of your father—Stile."

"My father? But he ne'er—"

"Not consciously, no. But it seems that this is something more fundamental than consciousness. He originated in this frame. He now inhabits a golem body. The life-force derives from Proton, and retains a connection to its origin. Ever since the frames separated, that lone connection has existed—feeding a slight but detectable imbalance. You are his son; you resonate to his life-force, for you derive from it. You used his channel."

"Then needs must I agree: amazing!"

"I shall have to consider this discovery. It may be

that a complete separation of the frame is not feasible without cutting off the life-force of Stile."

"Nay!"

"Have no concern, Bane; I would not cut that connection, had I the means to do so. Stile and Blue have been my instruments, and you and Mach are becoming my instruments."

"Yet hast thou been known to kill thine instruments!"

"Not permanently, as it turned out."

Bane removed the plug from his ear. "Thou dost strike me as a creature of expedience, without scruples."

"Granted. I am not even a creature, but a thing, possessing no more life than does your present body."

Which felt alive to him. Bane knew how Mach had felt, and how Mach's robot mother Sheen felt. The Oracle was reminding him of the capabilities of its state of existence. "Point taken, machine. But I trust not thine expedience."

"But you can trust my logic. If that psychic connection between Stile and his living body is broken, he may die or lose his sanity or suffer no measurable malaise; we cannot know. But if that line ceases to exist, the channel by which you and Mach communicate and exchange places will be gone, and all that you contemplate will end, and my chance to rectify the accumulated imbalance will abort. Therefore I value Stile's life and your own, and will not act to imperil them."

Bane wasn't sure about that, but accepted it for the time being. Except for one bad thought: "An that line be cut, there be no problem of linking of the frames. Canst thou not solve it most readily by cutting the line?"

"No. The imbalance exists. It must be redressed before the connection is severed, or mischief to both frames can result."

"So thou dost seek to correct it, *then* cut the line?"

"That would be the sensible thing to do."

"And thou dost expect Mach and me to help thee cut us off from our loves?"

This time the Oracle paused before answering. "I perceive that that could be awkward."

"Awkward, hell, thou stinking golem thing! It be unacceptable."

The Oracle was unmoved by his invective. "What would you find acceptable?"

"Do thou find a way to fix the imbalance and preserve contact between the frames, that I may remain with Agape and Mach with Fleta."

"This may be a difficult thing to accomplish."

"An thou dost wish to work with me longer, needs must thou bide by it."

"As I understand it, the frames must either be completely separated, with no interaction between them, or completely overlapped, so that any imbalance corrects instantly. You evidently prefer the latter course."

"Aye," Bane agreed grimly.

"Since I need your active cooperation, I am constrained to accede to your terms."

"An thou find a way to work without my cooperation, thou dost mean to renege?"

"I am reluctant to be bound to a fixed course in a changing situation."

"Then work without me, machine!" Bane said, and faced the exit.

"But without the knowledge and training I offer, you will most certainly lose your contest with Mach."

"And with what result?" Bane retorted rhetorically. "We keep our loves!"

"Perhaps it is unrealistic to expect mature behavior from juveniles."

"Aye, thou calculating device!"

"Perhaps a compromise?"

Bane had learned the advantage of dealing. "Make thine offer."

"I am supposed to train you for your encounter with Mach. Because he is long conversant with the Game procedures to be employed, and has trained in many of the games, you are at a severe disadvantage. I can at one stroke restore parity. I will do this for you now, if you will accede to a partial commitment on the handling of the frames."

Bane considered. He would do his side little good if he went into the contest unprepared and lost badly. Despite his angry words, he did intend to do his best for his father. He did need the Oracle. "In what manner partial?"

"I will make my primary effort the unification of the frames. Only if that proves to be impossible will I seek to separate them completely."

"Unification—"

"Means that you would be able to join Agape physically—in your own body, and Mach would join Fleta in his own body."

That seemed so good as to be suspicious. In a moment Bane saw the flaw. "But with unification, all alternate selves would unite. Stile and Blue would be but one person, and Mach and me. That be no solution!"

"I think not. You have had time to develop separate identities despite your initial cloning. Identical twins are the parts of a single person, but their lives make them separate. In addition, there are formidable distinctions between the bodies: Mach's is machine, while yours is flesh; Stile's is golem, while Blue's is flesh. I doubt there would be mergence of that nature, this time, though there could certainly be formidable disruptions as individuals are replaced by pairs of selves in a common framework. This is why I regard this as the less desirable alternative. Nevertheless—"

"Agreed," Bane said quickly. He was ready to handle the awkwardness of individual duplication, for the sake of interacting with Agape in his own, living body.

"Then restore the connection, and I will activate Mach's experience."

"Wait. I want to know exactly how thou dost mean to make me equal to Mach, in an instant."

"You occupy his body. Your personality has taken over his general functions, but does not invoke his total experience. I shall activate the remaining circuits, that contain his complete knowledge of Proton and the Game, and his expertise as a player. You will then be able to utilize any or all of it at will."

Something nagged at him. In a moment he realized what it was. "But an thou restore the whole of Mach, then will not I be Mach, not Bane?"

"I can alleviate any such effect by excluding the region that establishes your personal identity. Your consciousness is largely random-access memory, evoked from a file that does not exist in this host: your living body in Phaze. Similarly, your personality and awareness and memories are damped out by Mach's awareness. It is fortunate that your two systems are compatible—but perhaps this is not coincidence, because of the parallelism of the frames."

Bane considered. "Very well—but do thou do it carefully. Methinks there be treachery in the likes of this." He plugged the cable back into his ear.

There was a soundless click. Nothing obvious changed, but his awareness of his situation seemed to clarify. He knew exactly where he was, and how to get anywhere else.

"That be it?" he asked.

"Try remembering Mach's Game experience," the Oracle suggested.

He tried—and abruptly experienced a flood of memories going back to Mach's childhood. Every game Mach had ever played was filed in his memory banks—and he understood the strategies for each, too. He knew that he could play any game as well as Mach could, because in this respect he had become Mach.

He could compete; there was no question about it. He did not even need to train; his robot body did not lose skills by disuse the way human flesh did. Citizen Blue would be pleased, and so would Agape. Fleta was not the only one from Phaze who could play the—

Fleta? He reeled, internally.

He was in love with the unicorn.

"Oops," the Oracle said, in a surprisingly unmechanical way.

"That love spell!" Bane exclaimed, chagrined. "It followed me here!"

"Not so. I did not exclude the emotion-circuit that activates that interest. That is Mach's love, not yours. I shall exclude it from your compass."

Abruptly it was gone. Bane loved Agape, not Fleta. But he was shaken. The depth and power of that love—

He removed the cable. "He came to love her in my body. Could that love—"

"Develop a resonance in you? Certainly, if strong enough. Flesh is less defined in such matters than machine circuitry; it would be surprising if there were not some sympathetic carryover."

"Then mayhap it was not merely the love spell that addled me," Bane said thoughtfully.

"Nor merely the spell and resonance combined," the Oracle said. "I perceive by your memories and my observations in Proton that she is a very fine creature. But so is Agape. Perhaps you should invoke Mach's experience with her."

"Nay, that were snooping!"

"When she emulated Fleta," the Oracle prompted.

The thing understood him too well! Bane called up that memory—and was impressed. Agape had assumed the aspect of Fleta, in form and voice and attitude, so perfectly that even he, Bane, almost doubted that it was not she. And Mach, knowing, had loved her—even as Bane had loved the real Fleta, for a moment.

He banished the memory, and the mixed emotions it aroused. "Truly, they both be great females," he said. "And we both be somewhat guilty." But he felt less guilty, now.

"You could each have settled for the one in your own frame," the Oracle said. "Had you not each been blinded to the familiar by the lure of the unfamiliar."

"Aye. But then would we not have exchanged. Seek not to reverse us now, machine; we have a deal."

"We have a deal," the Oracle agreed. "I will train you in the specific games you select to play against Mach, so that your skill improves beyond his. But this is no guarantee of victory."

"Why not?"

"Because there is always an element of chance in the playing of the grid and of any game, even those of greatest skill. Because he will be trained in magic by the Book of Magic he will have the advantage in any game involving magic."

"Then I will choose not that kind."

"But he will try to choose it. The grid gives you equivalence, and your skill in playing it will be similar. You must prevail in science, for you will likely lose in magic."

"I be no slouch in magic myself," Bane reminded it.

"You cannot prevail against the Book. I know, for the Book is but another aspect of me. The verdict of this contest is in doubt."

Bane pointed a finger at the shimmering light. "Do thou find a way to merge the frames, and the contest be meaningless."

"It will be easier for you to prevail in the contest than for me to merge the frames," the Oracle said.

"And if I win—what then o' our loves? My father, Stile, does oppose our unions, because they lead not to a suitable heir. I be resigned—but Mach be not resigned. I favor my father o'er my love, but Mach does not. There be that in me that be uncertain whether victory be best."

"Let me acquaint you with the nature of the Adverse Adepts and the Contrary Citizens," the Oracle said. "You will appreciate that they must be denied control of the frames."

"Aye, I know already! But also I know love, and this be no easy choice."

"Win, and you will know you have done right. Then perhaps I will succeed in unifying the frames, and you will have love too, as your father did."

"And if I win, and thou dost not succeed?"

"You are young. You will find in time that you can love again, a woman of your own frame."

"I believe that not—nor do I want to!"

"You are young," the Oracle repeated.

Agape returned, and they had a somewhat diffident reunion. "I had to do what—" she began.

"I know. As I did with Fleta. We need no more o' that."

"Yet—"

"I have Mach's memories now—and in mine own living body, some of his feelings. They be not mine, but they be ones I understand. I apologize to thee for putting thee in such an unkind situation; it were my fault."

"But—"

"Must needs I contest with mine other self, to settle who shall benefit from our communication between the frames. An I win, we shall serve my father, and Stile, and I think I must resume mine own body and be in Phaze and find a damsel there with whom I may generate an heir to the Blue Demesnes. An I lose, mayhap I can be with thee—but the frames will be ill-served."

"I understand that," she said. "And I agree. I love you, but I would not destroy what your father has done for the sake of that love. But what I was referring to—"

"Thou didst make Fleta for Mach."

"Aye," she said, with a quirk of a smile.

"And so thou didst protect him from possible discovery when he emulated me, and perhaps protected me also when I emulated him. Even as Fleta did in Phaze. Now I can see how he does love her, and he can see how I do love thee. Can we not consider that it were as it seemed, and no harm done?"

"If you wish."

"Aye, I wish." He looked at her. "Agape, an thou

couldst have whate'er thou didst wish, what would that be?"

"To be with you in Phaze," she said without hesitation.

"I have made a deal with the Oracle to merge the frames, an it prove possible. Then mayhap we can be together, each in our own bodies, in either frame. And Mach and Fleta too. Then could she play the Game at will, and thou couldst learn magic. And—"

"We could reproduce," she concluded.

"Aye. But as that be no certain outcome, must needs we do it now. I did learn how Mach and Fleta could do it in Phaze, and Mach did study how we two could do it here. Dost understand how Mach was crafted?"

"Yes. He started as an infant-robot, and moved to larger body and capacity in the way a living person would grow, until he reached adult status."

"I have it from Mach's memory: we can craft a cyborg with a body like mine and a mind like thine. It be not a perfect solution, but I be not a living man, in this frame. So if thou wouldst be interested—"

"I would," she said.

"Mach learned that Moebites have learned to fission unevenly, so that one retains identity while the other must immediately merge with another to gain enough mass to survive. If thine merges with the machine, for life support—"

"Yes. I have met the cyborg girls, and they can be quite interesting, if you like that type."

"Girls," he repeated. "It had not occurred to me, but robots be female too, and cyborgs. Mach's mother, Sheen—"

"Yes. We shall have a female child."

"But an I win, and we must separate—"

"The child of our union will remain," she said firmly. "She must remain here, where the facilities exist for growing and learning."

"Aye. But an I return to Phaze—"

"I will remain here, and care for her until she is of

age. This can be justified as continued experience in the bisexual mode, that my folk need to know."

"Must needs we name her."

"After you—"

"And after thee—"

"BA for Bane, AG for Agape?"

"Baag? Forget it, alien!"

She laughed. "Maybe the last letters, NE—"

"And PE."

"Nepe," she said.

"Nepe," he agreed.

They kissed.

In due course Bane played the grid with Mach, across the curtain, and they settled on a board game called Pole Chess. "I know it as well as Mach does," he said. "By definition. This be a fun game."

"I do not know of it," Agape replied.

"It be Occidental chess, with a piece added, invoked after the first piece be lost on either side. Serious practitioners play it not, but it does have its points."

He had a month to prepare. The Oracle trained him in the nuances of this specialized variant, but expressed concern. "You now inhabit the mind of a machine. Machines are excellent at storage and manipulation, but are not as creative as living creatures. If error-free playing suffices, the advantage is yours, but if not, it is his."

"He has been limited all his existence," Bane pointed out. "Can he now become creative?"

"That remains to be seen. He has strong motivation."

Bane nodded. Mach's motivation might well be stronger than his own. Yet he had to make his honest best effort.

"Teach me some aspects of this game that Mach knows not," he said. "And teach me flawless defense. I like not winning a game as it were by default, but this be the way methinks I should play it."

"True."

And while he explored the special wrinkles of the game, Agape ate voraciously to increase her mass so that she could fission, and the lab designed a cyborg unit that would support, not a human brain, but a Moebite entity.

13

Pole

"There be only so much magic can do, in a game like chess," Trool said. "Thy powers of perception and thought be now enhanced; thou willst play thy best, and make no direct error. But ultimately the victory must go to the one with the greatest experience and vision. Thou must have practice against excellent players."

"Who are the best in Phaze?"

"Stile. The Silver Elves. The Eldest Vampire."

"Damn!" Translucent exclaimed. "He cannot play them!"

Because they were all on the other side. "I thought I was so smart, angling for a variant of chess," Mach said ruefully. "I only got myself in trouble."

"There be other players," Translucent said. "And ye be committed to a variant. Mayhap there be other experts in that variant. Some among our forces."

Mach brightened. "I can make a spell to locate the finest available player of Pole Chess."

He did so. In a moment he ascertained that the Silver Elves dominated this variant also, but that there was one outstanding player among the snow demons. His name was Icebeard, and he was a chief of a White

Mountain clan. He seldom played in tournaments, because he could not tolerate any warm location, so his skill relative to that of the Silver Elves was not known, but it was suspected that it was equivalent.

"I will go see Icebeard," Mach said.

"But the demons eat normal folk," Fleta protested.

"I can protect myself, now," Mach reminded her. "And you, if you want to come."

"Methinks I had better," she said. "They may be thine allies now, but an thou sleep, it be best to have a guard."

Translucent nodded. "I will acquaint him with thy situation. But trust him not behind thy back. Our alliance be jury-built. Conjure thyself to the base of the mountain range, then climb them afoot, that they may recognize thee."

Mach conjured himself and Fleta to the base of the White Mountain range. The White Mountains were as massive as the Purple Mountains of the south, but more formidable because they were cold.

"One thing amazes me," Mach said. "The frames of Proton and Phaze overlap, geographically; every feature of one is mirrored in the other. Yet Proton is a planet, a sphere, while Phaze is a flat surface. How can this be?"

"Methinks the folk o' the other frame suffer from illusion," Fleta replied. "They think their world must be a ball, while we know it for what it truly be, a circle."

He glanced at her, uncertain whether she was serious. "Proton has a north and south pole, while Phaze has an east and west pole. How can those be reconciled?"

"By playing Pole Chess," she replied.

He considered that. Pun or wisdom? Then he saw her laugh bubbling up from her belly to her bosom. He grabbed her and kissed her before it could reach her mouth. "Silly filly!" he exclaimed.

And found himself kissing the unicorn. She had changed form, leaving only her lips touching his.

He changed to his stallion form, snorting. If she wanted to play it that way—

She became the hummingbird, her slender bill touching his nose. He became another.

She returned to girlform. "Ah, I forget thou be Adept now!" she exclaimed. "My Rovot Adept! Methinks I like thee better as a helpless man!"

"Tough manure, bird brain," he said with mock gruffness as he joined her in manform. "I accepted you as a unicorn; now you have to accept me as an Adept."

"O, sigh," she said, not sighing. "What shall we name him?"

"What?"

"Has thou not paid attention, sludge brain? Our foal, an we conceive."

She changed subjects as readily as she changed her form! "Aren't you counting chickens before—" He saw her laugh bubbling up again, and corrected himself. "Foals, before they hatch?"

"I ne'er yet saw a foal hatch," she remarked. "An we make a name for him, he will have to step into it. So what be the name?"

She had already decided on the sex, and now was working on the name. He reached for her, seeking another kiss, but this time she eluded him. "Mayhap combine our two names?"

"Mach, Fleta," he said, considering, "MA, FL. Mafl?"

"That be more like a sneeze!" she protested. "Mayhap the hind ends?"

"TA, CH," he said. "Tach?"

"That be more like cloth ripping! Mayhap one of each?"

"FL, CH—Fletch or Flatch?"

"Flach," she decided, pronouncing it with a soft C.

"Flash?"

"Watch thy language, rovot! Flach."

"Flach," he agreed, not changing the pronunciation. Then she stepped up for her kiss.

Now they started up the trail that Mach's magic told

him led to Icebeard's den. They had to approach slowly, so that the demons had a chance to recognize them; it seemed that the demons were suspicious, hostile folk.

Fleta assumed her natural form, and Mach rode her, deciding that he needed to remain recognizable. He kept alert, though; demons were known to like starting snowslides.

Sure enough, they had not progressed far before there was the rumble of an icy avalanche starting.

Mach snapped his fingers. The sliding snow became white fog, that flowed past them without impact. They proceeded as if nothing had happened.

Farther along, five snow tigers appeared, pouncing in unison. Mach made a tiny gesture, and they became five snow birds, who spread their wings and flapped wildly, not understanding what had happened.

They crested the first foothill, and moved on toward the larger range. A horrendous snowstorm swept in, stirring white tornadoes from the drifts, and hailstones the size of human heads began pelting down.

Mach lifted his gaze and squinted, and the tornadoes lay meekly down on their sides and expired. The hailstones slowed, becoming translucent, and bobbled in the air like balloons, finally popping into nonexistence. The storm thinned to the semblance of a canopy, and slid away to the side, leaving the sky clear.

Fleta snorted musically through her horn. Mach now understood horn language. Her sentiment translated, approximately, into: "Methinks that will teach them not to mess w' rovot Adepts."

They moved on without pause. They were approaching the region of the ice caves, where the snow demons lived. Fleta played a merry ditty on her horn, theme and countertheme on the panpipes, as if the two of them had not a care in the frame. Indeed, it seemed they had not; Mach's Adept magic was proof against all the demon malignance.

A snow demon appeared at the mouth of a cave. His whole body seemed to be made of ice; parts of him were even transparent. "Go 'way, freaks!" he called in the demon fashion of welcome.

Mach lifted his left little finger. Fire blossomed behind the demon, cutting off his retreat and causing him to leap forward before he melted. He plunged into a snowbank for protection.

"How's that?" Mach inquired innocently.

"Go melt thy buns in a furnace, flatlander!" the demon snapped.

The snow puffed into steam, leaving the demon exposed. He scrambled up the slope to reach fresh snow.

"We have come to see your leader," Mach said. "Will you lead us to him?"

"Ne'er!" the demon exclaimed.

A panel of quartz appeared beneath the demon's feet. Beneath it could be seen the leaping flames of some subterranean conflagration. The snow above it began to melt.

The demon started to retreat, but more panels appeared, surrounding it. "Well, maybe . . ." he said doubtfully.

The panel beneath him developed a hinge. Slowly the quartz eased down, about to slide whatever was on it into the inferno below.

". . . it would be best if I did that," the demon concluded.

"How nice of you," Mach said graciously. The quartz ceased its motion, turned opaque, and frosted over.

They followed the demon to the mouth of the largest cave. But he stopped there. "No 'corns allowed," he said.

Fleta assumed girlform, huddled in her black cloak. "Do I look like a 'corn?" she inquired.

"Listen, mare. I just saw thee change!"

A small ball of fire appeared in the air, like a star that had fallen too low.

The demon eyed it nervously. "Look, it's Icebeard's law! No animals inside!"

The fireball brightened, resembling the sun on a foggy morning.

The demon reconsidered. "Come to think of it, she looks not much like a 'corn." He led the way into the cave.

It had been cold outside, but it was colder in the cave. Mach made a spell to warm them both without affecting anything else, and Fleta gave him a glance of appreciation.

A glow developed in the icy walls, providing wan light that became adequate as their eyes adjusted.

Then the demon leaped ahead. The ceiling cracked, and ice dust sifted down. The tunnel was collapsing!

Mach grimaced. The falling particles became floating motes of fire, that moved forward through the tunnel as if propelled by a stiff draft. As larger chunks came down, they too ignited and shot forward. Whatever was ahead would become quite warm, quite soon.

The ceiling stabilized.

Mach turned to Fleta. "Do you know, the demons seem to live in rather shaky passages. I worry that the entire mountain might fall in on them unexpectedly." A rumbling developed, and indeed the mountain did seem to be shaking. "If I ever got the suspicion that any of this were deliberate, I might be inclined to hasten that collapse." The shaking increased, making that collapse seem imminent. "It isn't smart to annoy an Adept, as I'm sure these demons know." The shaking became horrendous, so that even Fleta flinched.

The demon reappeared. "Icebeard will see thee now!" he cried.

The mountain was instantly quiet. "I thought he might," Mach said.

The tunnel opened into a chamber whose walls were curtained with icicles. On a frozen throne sat the leader, whose beard was indeed formed of ice. "So nice to see you, Adept," the demon leader growled.

"I came to play Pole Chess with you. Do you by chance have time for such a game?"

Icebeard considered, scowling. A distant rumble started. The demon's aspect changed. "Yes, of course. The Translucent Adept informed me that thou didst wish to practice, and the cause be worthy."

"Whether the cause is worthy is a matter of opinion, but the issue must be settled, and I mean to do my best. Since you are said to be the best player available to me, I want to practice with you."

"The best player," Icebeard said, evidently flattered. "Aye, we shall play." He glared at a demon messenger. "Frostbite, fetch the board and pieces!"

Fleta looked around, and chose a block of ice to sit on. All she knew of chess was what Mach had told her, but she wanted to watch.

Icebeard glanced at her. "Be thou not cold, filly?"

"Nay, thank thee; I be quite comfortable."

"Um," he said, disappointed.

The board and pieces arrived, and they set them up on a stand. The board was a cross-hatched sheet of ice, and the pieces were finely carved ice. Mach made sure his touch was cold, so that he would not damage the chessmen. The figures were elaborate: each pawn was a grotesque little goblin, the castles were coiled dragons, the knights griffins rampant, the bishops thin trolls, the queen a glowering ogress, and the king a crowned demon.

But this was Pole Chess, so there was one additional set of pieces: the poles. These were the tallest and most regular of them all, resembling the spiraled poles that ancient barbers once used as a signal of their operations. When all the other pieces were set up, the white and black poles stood to either side, just off the board, centered.

The pole could neither take nor be taken, except in one very special circumstance. It could only block. It could move to any unoccupied square on the board in one move, but did not have to be played. It was normally used to occupy a square that a player did not want his opponent's man to take, or to block the path of the opponent's man, or to shield a piece from attack. In the end game it could be critical in the defense of the king. Clever use of the pole could change the complexion of a game—but it was possible also to play through without ever invoking the pole. Thus it added an element to the game without any obvious corresponding sacrifice. Some players swore that Pole Chess was the best variant ever; others condemned it as a decadent offshoot. Mach himself was neutral; he could take it or leave it, and tended to be guided by his opponent's strength in it. A player who was good with the pole could trap himself when playing normal chess, forgetting that he could not abruptly block check. But a player who was not used to it could find his careful strategy negated at the end, when the pole interfered with the operation of his major attacking piece.

They played—and Icebeard humiliated Mach. The demon was a good player, all right!

They played again. This time Mach stuck to the most conventional opening and play, so that no surprises were likely, and played for a draw. He never got the chance; Icebeard overwhelmed him.

They played a third time. Mach went for innovative, risky play, trying to surprise the demon. For a while he seemed to be succeeding; then he made a foolish error, and Icebeard clamped down and never let go.

"I'm not in your league," Mach admitted ruefully.

"Obviously not," the demon said graciously. "I will make a deal with thee: get me a match with the Adept Stile, and I will train thee to win against any lesser player."

"But I thought you would train me for the benefit of your cause!" Mach protested.

"That, too, rovot," Icebeard agreed.

"I'm not sure that's fair," Mach said, and the mountain began to rumble warningly.

The demon pointed an icefinger at Mach's nose. "Listen, rovot, thou hast proven thou dost be Adept, and can bring this mountain down about our heads. I have proven I can play Pole Chess of a level thou canst only dream of. Causes be fine, but it be best to make fair exchange for service. Thou knowest that training thee will be a colossal bore to me. Dost think it fair that he who be mooted the best player o' the frame plays me not?"

Mach was taken aback by the force of this logic. "No, it is not fair. But it is Stile's son I must play against. How can I get Stile to play against you, knowing that this is your price for training me to beat Bane?"

Icebeard grimaced. "Thou dost have a point, rovot!"

Fleta spoke up. "Would Stile want his son to win 'gainst an untrained opponent?"

Both Mach and Icebeard looked at her, then at each other. "I'll try," Mach said. He looked at Fleta. "Do you want to come along?"

"The filly stays here!" Icebeard snapped.

"What is this? You think you need a hostage, demon?"

Icebeard reconsidered. "Nay, not for this. Old reflexes die hard! Let her go with thee."

"Nay, I will stay, an Icebeard show me how to play this game."

The demon stared at her. "Has thou any aptitude at all, filly?"

"I know not. But when I visited Proton-frame, I played in their Tourney, and won four rounds. Mayhap I will ne'er get to play again, but an I could learn more game skills, that would please me."

The demon softened. "Mayhap thou dost have potential. We shall shortly find out."

Fleta went to the table, and they were setting up the pieces as Mach conjured himself to the Blue Demesnes, slightly bemused.

He stood before the Blue Castle and hailed it, as before. Again the Lady Blue emerged. "I fear thou canst not change his mind, Mach," she said.

"Lady, this time I come to ask a favor of him."

"He will see thee not at this time, but I will talk to

thee." She showed him into the courtyard, and they took seats at the table, as before.

He gazed at her for a moment. "You know, my mother is a robot."

"Aye, the Lady Sheen. I know her."

"You know her?" he asked, surprised.

"In the old days it were possible to cross the curtain physically, an one's other self be dead. Mine other self—" She broke off, looking troubled; but before he could think of anything appropriate to say, she resumed. "I crossed and met her, and knew she was worthy, and asked Stile to marry her. But in the end he remained with me, and it were Blue who married her."

He continued to look at her. "You are a beautiful woman, Lady."

"What be thy business, Mach?"

"I am in training for the first match with Bane. I know it is not to your interest to help me in my effort to defeat him, but—"

" 'Interest' be defined in sundry ways," she said. "Bane represents the existing order, and there be good and evil in that. Thou dost represent a contrasting order, and there be evil and good in that. There be that in thy order that Bane craves, and that in our order that thou dost crave."

"Yes!"

"So thou dost represent a part of him—the part that would marry Agape and live in Proton-frame. He represents a part of thee—the part that would have our way govern, rather than the special interest o' the Adepts. Thou dost contest for part of his good, and he for part of thine. The victory o' either be neither comedy nor tragedy. There be nor right nor wrong in this. It be merely the settling o' an issue which else would destroy all."

Mach had been braced for hostility, open or covert, and ready to argue his case purely on the issues of pride and fairness. But the Lady Blue showed no condemnation, only understanding. This realization caught him off guard, and momentarily overwhelmed him. As a robot, he still got caught on occasion by the surges of feeling and emotion generated by the living state. "Oh, Lady, I love you," he whispered, feeling the tears come.

Then she was standing beside him, embracing him as he sat, her maternal bosom against his cheek. "We love thee too, Mach," she murmured, stroking his hair. "We know thou dost what thou must."

In a moment she returned to her place, but the sensation of her embrace lingered. What a woman she was! It was easy to understand how Stile had left Proton to marry her.

"What be thy business?" she repeated gently.

"I—I—the demon—" He took a breath and started over. "The snow demon Icebeard will train me in chess, if Stile will play him a match. He—he is an excellent player, and feels that Stile should at least play him once."

"Aye."

"So—"

"Stile will play him by correspondence, one move a day. Here be Stile's first move." She handed him a tiny scroll.

So they had known all along that this would happen! Mach was largely at a loss for words. "Thank you, Lady. For everything."

"Welcome, Mach. Do thou give my regards to thy mother, when convenient."

"I will." He found himself outside the castle, and conjured himself back to the cave of the snow demons.

Icebeard looked up from the board. "The filly be a natural player," he said. "Her could I more readily train than thee."

Fleta flushed in the human manner, pleased.

"Here is Stile's first move," Mach said. "Correspondence."

"Ha!" the demon exclaimed, immensely gratified. "Set up a permanent board," he called to another demon.

He unrolled the scroll and glanced at the notation. "The Lady gave thee this!" he exclaimed.

"Yes. How did you know?"

"It be the Queen's Gambit, in her hand. She moved for him."

Mach was dismayed. "I understood that—"

"Nay, an she committed him, Stile will play. Thou has made good thy bargain." He glanced at the demon setting up the other board. "Pawn to queen four," he called.

"Which color?" the demon called back.

"Idiot! White, of course!" He returned his attention to Mach. "That will be one interesting game! We see not many such gambits these days."

"Pawn to queen four, pawn to queen four, pawn to queen's bishop four, pawn takes pawn," Mach said. "I'd play either side of that."

"Thou wouldst lose either side o' that, too," Icebeard said. He glanced at Fleta. "Make thy move, filly, while I set up another for the rovot."

Soon a third board was ready, and while the demon leader instructed Mach, he also instructed Fleta, evidently deriving more satisfaction from her game than from Mach's. The training had begun.

They played on the console: the screen showed the chessboard and the positions of the pieces. To move, Mach had only to touch his piece, then touch the spot to which he wished to take it.

Mach had White, and he used the Queen's Gambit. He knew that his trainer opposed this; he could hear Icebeard's growly voice in his mind. "Stick to the tried and true, rovot! This gambit be dangerous for thee!" But after his session with the Lady Blue, he had to do it.

Bane responded immediately with the standard return, and they both followed through with the next set of moves. Then the real play began. Mach knew that others were reporting the progress of the game to all who were interested; the moves were being magically relayed to the White Mountains, the Purple Mountains, and the various Demesnes, including the Blue. Some were present in person: Translucent and Brown, the latter to see that Mach received no advice now from his trainer. The game between Stile and Icebeard was not yet done, but it was evident that it was a superlative one, and no one could yet judge the advantage. Certainly Icebeard's advice would be an unfair advantage for him. Bane was similarly limited, in Proton; a Contrary Citizen was standing over him. But Bane would have had the training of Blue, and that made Mach nervous. His father had always beaten him.

The game proceeded quickly to the end-stage. The two seemed evenly matched, which was perhaps no surprise. Bane checked Mach's king, and Mach used his pole to block it. He consolidated his position, and attacked Bane's king, but could not penetrate the defense. Finally they ground down to a draw. One of the liabilities of Pole Chess was that it facilitated draws, because the pole made it difficult to keep a king in check. That was one reason the duffers liked it, but in matches where clear-cut decisions were needed, it could be a problem.

The score was even: half a game apiece. The next game would be on the next day. Mach conjured himself and Fleta to the White Mountains to consult Icebeard.

"You were lucky, rovot!" the demon growled. "Had the boy been alert, he could have mated thee by the twentieth move."

"What? I saw no such opportunity!"

"He be right," Fleta murmured.

Icebeard set up the board. "You saw it, filly? Damn, I wish thou wast playing that match! Show him the move."

The board was at the fifteenth move. Fleta moved a black pawn up one space.

"There!" the demon said. "Dost see it now, rovot?"

Mach studied the position. "I see nothing so great about that."

"Nor did Bane, the dolt! How wouldst thou counter?"

"I wouldn't. I would attack. He has wasted a move, and given me the initiative."

"Make thine attack."

Mach made his move.

"Filly—"

Fleta moved a Black knight.

Mach considered the new position. "Oh, no!" he groaned.

"Next time, be on guard against all potential attacks, rovot," the demon said gruffly. "Luck strikes naught twice the same. Bane's mentor be even now chewing his rump to shreds for missing that, e'en as I chew thine for setting it up. He could have been one up on thee!"

He could have, indeed. Mach was mortified. He thought they had played an excellent game. They had not.

"Well, there be two games, yet," the demon said. "Filly, take him elsewhere and teach him aught. I have a move of mine own to study." He turned to the game he was playing with Stile, which was of a wholly different level.

Mach and Fleta went to the ice cave they were using for this period, and she made savage love to him. "On the morrow, play thou chess like that," she admonished him.

"I'll try," he agreed contritely.

Next day Mach had Black. He was set to play conservatively, but Bane opened with the Queen's Gambit, forcing it into more adventurous territory at the outset.

However, Mach kept his eyes open for opportunities, and managed to forge an advantage in the midgame—only to be foiled in the endgame by the pole. It was another draw. Now each player had one point, and the final game would decide it.

He expected Icebeard to bawl him out again, for

missing an opportunity, but the demon was grudgingly satisfied. "Thou didst play at thy level, consistency. In a conventional game, the victory would have been thine."

Mach breathed a silent sigh of relief. He had been almost more concerned about the demon's critique than about the game itself.

"But on the morrow, it be huffdraw," Icebeard reminded him sternly. "That be a new game, rovot."

Mach's nervousness clamped down again. That was indeed a new game! There would be no draw this time.

The demon turned to Fleta. "Filly, whate'er thou didst do yester, do it twice tonight, to put him in readiness for the morrow."

Now Fleta quailed. She had done her ultimate yesterday! She could not hope to match it, let alone exceed it.

But she tried.

Mach had White again. This time he started conservatively, with pawn to king four, and played conservatively, trying first to avoid any error that his nonrobot flesh might be heir to, and second to pick up any slight advantage he could. He understood, in retrospect, why Bane had overlooked the winning play in the first game; he was in the robot body, and imagination was hard for that to come by. But he would not overlook it again; he would have been reprogrammed to be alert for anything similar.

Unfortunately, it was Bane who picked up the small advantage. As they ground into the endgame, Bane was ahead by one point, but his position was stronger than that indicated and, for the huffdraw variant, stronger yet.

Huffdraw was a device that had come into play in the last few centuries, because too many tournaments were being stymied by frequent draws. Planetary championship matches had dragged on interminably, draw after draw, as each player settled for even rather than risking worse for the sake of better. This was hard on the players, and worse for the audience. Chess was in danger of fading as a competitive sport because of it. Huffdraw changed that radically. The term was borrowed from checkers, and the effect was roughly similar, but the execution differed significantly. There were several applications, depending on the type of draw that threatened. But the basic element was the removal of "dead" pieces: those that hadn't moved in some time. If that failed, then pieces started to be added back in, until there were enough in action to force a decision.

They came to a draw by perpetual check: Mach prevented Bane from winning by checking his king continually, forcing him to protect the king rather than closing in on Mach's. Bane used his pole to block each check, but Mach simply moved to a new position for check. This repetitive motion caused the board to assume the same configuration for a third time, by definition a draw.

At that point all chessmen of either color that had not moved during the game were to be huffed, or removed from the board as if taken. There were none, so the huff proceeded to those who had been longest without moving, as traced by the Game Computer in Proton, without regard to color. This proceeded until either the position was freed, or it proved to be impossible to free it in this manner. In this case, it was freed—but it left Mach in a weaker position than before.

Play resumed, but he was in trouble. Bane's small advantage in pieces was looming more formidably. Mach saw a chance to play for another draw—but saw also that the resultant huffing would make him yet more vulnerable. Only if he could achieve a draw whose breakup would benefit him could he afford to take it. He used his pole increasingly, which meant he was moving his other pieces less often, and that made them vulnerable to huffing. If he could only get Bane to neglect his pieces—

But he could not. Bane had evidently drilled in this,

and was playing with machinelike conservatism. He made no errors, simply letting his advantage operate.

Mach tried a desperate strategy that he knew was flawed, hoping that Bane's machine mind would not perceive the flaw. But the effort failed, and Mach's position became hopeless.

He had to resign. He had lost the game, and the first match.

14

Chase

They played the grid again. This time it did not seem remarkable to Bane that he could match against his other self through the console; the three grueling chess games had made it seem natural. But this time he intended to stay well clear of board games; Mach's experience in that regard was far greater than his, and it had been mere luck that he had learned chess from his father, Stile, and been able to add that experience to Mach's stored knowledge and the advice of the Oracle. If he encountered a game in which he was inexperienced, he would not be able to upgrade sufficiently to be competitive. It had been close, as it was.

He had the numbers, so he chose 1. PHYSICAL. That eliminated the major region of danger! He had had a lot of experience with physical games of all types. Mach had too, of course, but Bane now had Mach's physical body and could match any of his experience by opening the appropriate memory file. He wasn't sure how they would be able to play a physical game, but the Oracle said it would be arranged. Soon he would discover what the Oracle had in mind.

Mach chose A. NAKED. So it was to be man against

man, unadorned. The man in the machine body against the robot in the living body. Bane was ready, if the framework could arrange it.

The second grid appeared on the screen:

	5. SEPAR	6. INTERAC	7. COMBAT	8. COOPER
E. EARTH				
F. FIRE				
G. GAS				
H. H_20				

He had the numbers again. He chose 6. INTERACTIVE, becoming more interested in the challenge to the system than in the game itself, for the moment. A separate game would be easy enough: they could race against a common clock, or lift similar weights, or do individual dives for rating on a common scale. But Interactive meant that they had to touch or at least be affected by each other, as with Hide and Seek. How could they do that, physically, across the frames?

Mach chose H. H_2O. So it was to be a water sport! Bane had no fear of that; he had swum joyfully since infancy. Were they going to stretch a pool across the frames?

But as it turned out, the H category was more than water; it was a catchall for all the surfaces: Flat, Variable, Discontinuous and Liquid. The list of qualifying games included one as simple as splashing, and one active as water tag, and—

Bane gaped. The magic games were there too! Levitation Tag, Conjuration Dodge—how could these be played in the frame of Proton? If he tried to make himself float magically, he would get nowhere; if he tried to conjure a snowball to hurl at his opponent, none would appear.

But there had to be a way, or the grid would not be showing these choices. This gave him the chance to select a game with which Mach had no experience!

They assembled and played the third grid, and the result was Transformation Chase. Bane had never actually played that one, because of the number of form-changing spells required; a single game would have exhausted his spells for months. But he had always liked the idea of it, and envied the unicorns who could play it with their natural magic, changing forms effortlessly. Human magic was versatile, but limited to one invocation for any given spell; the animals could do their particular magic without limit. In that way they were superior to man. But they could not do any other magic.

The game was set. There would be a month for training. But Bane could hardly wait to talk to the Oracle, and ask: how? How could he transform his body into the several animal forms that would be required for the proper playing of this game? Mach would have no trouble; they could teach him the necessary spells. But this was Proton!

"Mach is in 1A," the Oracle explained. "You are technically in 2C—Machine-Assisted Mental. He will transform directly; you will transform in emulation."

"I be in Machine-Assisted Mental? But the grid—"

"This is a special situation. What he can do directly and physically, you cannot. But the emulation will make it equivalent."

"How can we know that? Mine emulated figure could have powers my physical one has not."

"The emulation will exactly match the powers of your physical body. There will be no advantage physically. You will have to convey game information to Mach so that the Red Adept can set it up there, but this will be no problem."

"But magic—transformations—"

"Your consciousness will be attuned to the game setting, and to Bane's mind. It will be as real to you as your current existence is, and as accurate."

Bane realized that the Oracle knew more about altered states of reality than he did, but still he argued. "Look, if we are to play this chase game properly, one o' us must be the Predator and the other the Prey. When the two come together, the Predator be the victor; an we complete the circuit without that happening, the Prey wins. So we can overlap not during the game itself. Therefore there can be ne'er any connection then. So—"

"The connection will be maintained," the Oracle explained patiently. "The awareness will be displaced. Your body will pace his throughout, but your awareness will be with your representation in the game. Have no concern."

Bane gave it up. His lifetime in Phaze simply had not prepared him for the peculiar convolutions of science. "If everyone else be satisfied . . ." He shrugged.

He joined Agape. "I think I have a few hours off before training for the next round starts. What be good for relaxation?"

"Normally it does not require so much effort for you to think of your favorite relaxation," she said with a smile.

He had to smile back. "Thou'rt so certain we males have but one interest!"

"Not so, Bane. You have but one interest *at a time,* in the manner of an animal. That's not quite the same."

"Let's go walk in the park."

They took a conveyor to the park. This was designed to resemble a wooded region of Old Earth, with fair-sized trees spreading their branches overhead, and ferns growing below. It was arranged to seem considerably larger than it was, because of the premium on space within the dome, but the illusion was effective. Stray breezes wafted through, making the leaves quiver, and butterflies flitted randomly about.

That reminded him of his spying missions. He regretted those, now, despite the importance of the information gleaned. Would it have been better not to have done it? That would have meant falling into Tania's trap, and also he would have avoided the need to be with Fleta, when—

"There be much in this I like not," he muttered.

Agape did not misunderstand. "But also much to like. I will always be glad for the visit I was able to make to Phaze, and the folks I was able to know there, though I had to borrow Fleta's body."

"Aye. But what future have we? An I win, we be soon parted. An I lose, the frames be in peril. What choice be that?"

"It would be easier if your kind was like mine in this respect," she said. "With no set sexes."

"And no love between them," he agreed. "Is that the way you prefer it?"

"No."

They went on through the park. It had not changed, but his mood had improved.

Next day he overlapped Mach and relayed the information about the arrangements for the game. The Game Computer had worked out the basics and compressed them into a few code words for Mach to tell Trool. They would overlap again in a few days for verification.

Then: *I wish we were locked not in this struggle between ourselves,* Bane thought.

The issue must be settled, one way or the other, Mach responded. *It would have arisen elsewhere, if not with us.*

And that was probably true. *Dost know that the source of our exchange be the lingering connection between Stile and Blue?*

Mach was surprised. *It's not because we are alternate selves?*

Nay. Other alternates can do it not, only us—because we relate to our sires.

And our loves relate to us, Mach concluded.

Aye.

That was all. They separated.

Bane reported for the first game of Round Two. "Plug in," the Oracle directed.

Bane plugged the cable into his ear.

Suddenly he was standing in Phaze. Mach was standing beside him, and there was a little collection of chairs in which Fleta, Agape, Trool, the Translucent Adept and the Brown Adept sat. Before them was a shimmering curtain concealing the setting of the game, reminiscent of the historical curtain between the frames.

Trool rose and walked to them. "Thou knowest the nature o' this contest?" he asked Bane.

"Aye, Adept," Bane said. "But not the nature o' this dream!"

"It be no dream, Bane," the troll assured him. "Only thy presence here be a vision and that o' thine alien friend; all else be real. Do thou play the game to win."

"Aye, Adept." The Oracle had told him it would seem realistic, and it was! It seemed that his body was overlapping Mach's, but his awareness was being projected to the representation of his body here. Thus he saw everything that Mach saw, here in Phaze—without actually being here. He was actually in the Game Computer's mock-up of the scene, and the mock-up was based on the actual scene of Phaze. Technology was emulating magic.

"Thou knowest the nature o' this contest?" Trool asked Mach.

"Yes, Adept." Mach was in Bane's body, so looked like Bane. Bane glanced down at himself: it was the robot body.

"The machine in Proton-frame has made Bane the Predator, this time," Trool continued. "Mach be the Prey. An the Prey lap the course three times, he be victor; an the Predator catch him first, the Predator be the victor. The Prey be given a five-second start. Ready, players?"

"Aye."

"Yes."

"Then begin."

Mach stepped forward, into the setting. He disappeared.

Bane glanced at Agape. It was incongruous to see her here in Phaze in her own form, but of course with magic any vision could be crafted. He waved to her, and she waved back. He wondered whether Agape and Fleta were talking together, and if so, what they were saying.

"Go, Bane," Translucent snapped.

Bane stepped through the curtain.

He found himself on four feet, in a solid, striped body. He was a tiger! His passage through the curtain had triggered the first of the transformations, rendering him into the predator animal.

The setting was an irregular landscape with projecting rocks and descending gullies. There were a number of trees; in fact, parts were as solid as a jungle. This would be a good region to hide and pounce—but he knew he could not afford that. He had to run down the prey, lest it lap the course before he catch it.

He sniffed the air. He smelled mongoose. That would be the Prey form, for the moment. As a tiger, he could readily kill it; the problem was running it down. On an open plain, in real life, that would be simple, but this terrain offered many hiding and dodging places; it would be hard to catch it here.

In fact, that five-second head start made the task of location a problem, let alone the task of catching. The mongoose could be through this region and into the next medium, while the tiger was still trying to sniff out the trail.

So he played it smart. He bounded directly across,

going for the lake he saw in the distance ahead. If he could get there first, and cut off the mongoose—

But as he ran, bounding along the highest ground, he peered into the low regions, noting which ones offered the best protection and clearest access for a mongoose. This was a vital part of the game; what he overlooked could cost him the victory.

He had almost reached the water when he heard a splash. The mongoose had raced right through to the next medium!

Bane charged for the lake, trying to catch up a little. In this game, the traveling velocities of the creatures were identical, whatever they might be in life. The Predator gained only by cutting corners or by taking advantage of opportunities like this, when he knew the location of the Prey. This slight advantage of the Predator was unlikely to make up for the five-second delay of the start, in the course of any one medium, but would inevitably close the gap a little each time. All he needed to do was to make no error, and the Prey would be his.

He did not step into the water, he leaped into it, trying to gain another fraction of a second by entering it at speed. He came down with a horrendous splash—and found himself in the form of a dolphin.

Ahead was a shark. A shark might not be considered prey to most creatures, but in life a dolphin could kill a shark by knocking it with the snout. Thus the shark fled the dolphin, in this situation.

The water was not deep. Aquatic plants were rooted in its sediment, reaching their stems up to the surface, forming patterns of thin columns where they clustered. Sponges were grouped on rounded nether rocks. Some rifts showed below, partially filled with sediment, and a few dipped into dark holes that might be blind caves or might be tunnels. Small fish darted about, giving way to the far more massive dolphin.

Bane forged after the shark. But the lead was still too great; he knew he could not catch up within the limit of this lake. Rather than expend his full energy trying to do so, he kept the pace and watched the surroundings, mentally mapping the terrain. The thickest growths of plants offered concealment, but also slowed progress of larger swimmers. Velocity of the contestants was equivalent, but not if they moved foolishly; he would feel better about plowing through those plants if he were smaller. As for the bottom—he paid special attention to the darkest holes, so that he would be able to spot them without faltering when he came this way again.

The shark moved toward the bottom, and swerved around a greenish rock. Bane remained higher, and so was able to cut across above the rock, gaining another fraction of a second. He knew the shark would have to come up again, to enter the next medium, so in this, too, he was saving time. The fact was that Mach was not managing his forms perfectly. That was probably because a month's training for this game was not enough to compensate for a lifetime as a robot. Mach was simply not acclimatized to the nuances of the motions of wild creatures. But he would probably catch on rapidly enough, with this experience.

However, the shark was doing the right thing, overall: swimming swiftly ahead, never pausing or looping back, so that the dolphin could not close the gap significantly. While the Predator could always gain by proper management, the longer he took to close the gap, the more chances there were for something to interfere. It was best to catch the Prey as quickly as possible, to reduce the element of chance or error.

Now the lake was turning shallow. They were approaching the far bank. The shark swam up, as it had to; there was nowhere else to go, without turning back. Bane gained another bit of distance.

The shark shot up to the surface, and through, and disappeared. Bane angled up too, breaking into air—and he was winged, with feathers and beak. In fact he was a hawk, flying strongly: a predator bird, a raptor.

Ahead of him, ascending the sky, was a black bird, a crow. The Prey.

The day was clear, with a few fleecy clouds. But on the horizon was a darkening cloudbank. A wind was stirring; if a storm were brewing, it was coming this way. That could complicate things for flying but the hawk was a better flyer than the crow. In a storm, Bane could gain on his Prey. But the storm was not close, and they would be through this medium of air before it arrived. All he could do was keep flying, and try to close the distance.

The horizon did not recede as they moved. This was the game setting, not reality; it was limited. As the crow flew, the line of the sky descended, heading down to touch the ground, sealing off further progress. The Prey had to seek the next medium.

The crow plunged through the limit, just above the horizon, and disappeared. Bane swooped down to a similar level, because it would not do to turn landbound too high in the air, and went through also.

He was back in the first medium, as he had known he would be. But this time he was not the tiger, he was the mongoose. The forms did not repeat for a player, they only progressed. That was why he had studied the layout the first time through: so that he could handle it well as the mongoose.

Ahead a big snake was slithering out of sight, probably a cobra. A mongoose could handle a cobra, being swift enough in close quarters to avoid the poisoned strikes. But in this situation, he could not run any faster than the snake could slither.

But he could take a more direct route. The snake's fastest travel was along the ground, while the mongoose could bound over some obstacles. Bane bounded, slowly closing the gap. By the time they reached the water he was only two seconds behind.

In the lake, Bane was now the shark—pursuing a squid. The squid was almost as large as the shark, and its trailing tentacles made it longer. But its body was soft, and the shark's teeth were hard; a few chomps would sever the tentacles and render it helpless, and soon the squid would be consumed. So it fled, jetting water behind so that it shot forward as swiftly as a fish. Its motion was jerky, because it had to pause to take in more water, but the overall velocity was the same as that of the shark.

Would the squid dive, and seek refuge in one of the dark recesses at the bottom? That would be risky for it, for if it entered a blind cave, it would be trapped. There would be no caves that the shark could not eventually penetrate; the game allowed no indefinite hiding. If it had located a tunnel, it might swim through and out the far end, while the shark hovered at the near end; that would gain the Prey the time it needed to complete the course unscathed.

Mach did not take the risk. He jetted straight across, and out the far side. Bane followed, perhaps a second and a half behind.

He was now the crow, and Mach was an owl. The theory for the game was that the owl was a nocturnal creature, at a disadvantage by day, so the crow harassed it, flapping about just out of reach and interfering with its hunting so that eventually it starved. The hawk would not do that; if it came at the owl, it would dive straight in, and the owl, being larger would simply grab it and destroy it with talon and beak. Bane doubted that interaction like that ever occurred in nature, but that hardly mattered here; the crow chased the owl, and if they looped through the course again, the owl would chase the hawk in the vicious circle that was the hallmark of this game. It was a good game, even in mock-change form, and Bane had always liked it.

Mach took a moment getting oriented in owlform, and Bane gained a full second before their flights became straight. The end was close—if nothing happened.

They plunged through the sky-curtain. Bane readied himself before he crossed, curling his crowform into as tight a ball as he could, passing through like a stone and plunking into the ground.

This time he was the cobra, and though he wasn't

coiled, he was bunched. He launched a strike at the nearest object even as he landed, having judged the Prey's position by the passage through the curtain. If there were that moment of reorientation, before the run began . . .

He caught the tail of the tiger. His fangs sank in, delivering the poison—and the game was over. The Predator had caught the Prey.

That night he did make love to Agape, but it was not enough to take his mind from the situation. "I have beaten mine other self in the first round, and I am ahead in the second. An I win again tomorrow, it be over—and I lose thee and he loses Fleta. Mayhap there be justice in it, but I like it not."

"But the benefit of the frames—" she started.

"Aye, I know, I know! My mind does claim I be doing right—but mine heart be doubtful. What be his crime? That he loves the 'corn? Fleta be worthy o' love! That did I see when—" He broke off, embarrassed.

"Bane, I understand," Agape said. "I occupied her body, I learned her life, her ways, and her land, and came to love them all, as I love you. Of course she is worthy of love! Of Mach's love, or yours."

"A love I would sunder!" he said bitterly. "Damn, would I could honestly lose this match!"

"No, you have to try your best, and win it if you can. That is where your honor lies."

"Aye, aye! And try I will, though I fear success!"

"That is all anyone can ask of you," she said.

He hugged her tightly. "Ah, alien creature, I do love thee! Would I could get closer yet to thee, to be a part of thee, and thee of me, forever!"

"It can be done," she murmured. "Not forever, but for a time."

His eyes popped open. "What meanest thou?"

"I hold human form because that pleases you, but it is not my natural one, as you know. It is possible to embrace you amoeba-style, though I fear that might repulse you."

"Thou dost in no wise repulse me, Agape! Embrace me thy way!"

"As you will. Speak if you change your mind; I will hear you."

She lay on top of him, on the bed, her breasts and thighs pressing on him. She kissed him, once, then put her head to the side. She started to melt.

Bane lay still, feeling the change in her flesh. Her breasts lost cohesiveness, and so did the rest of her. She became like a huge pillow, warm and yielding. Then more like a water bag, and then like loose jelly. Her body spread out, making contact with all of his upper surface. The strange effect caused him to develop an erection; her melting protoplasm surrounded it warmly. She sagged, then flowed around him, between his arms and his body, between his legs. She became a padded wetsuit, a layer of warm wax all around him, and as far under him as his contact with the bed permitted. He raised his arms and legs slightly, and she completed the enclosure there; then he pushed back his head and hoisted his torso up, and she flowed around it and merged with herself.

From his neck to his feet, he was encased by her, and it was the most comfortable feeling he could remember. His body, in Proton, was of metal and plastic; it did not matter, for now it felt Alive. Every part of him except his face was in her, and now she crept around his head and across that too, stopping only at the eyes, mouth and nose.

"In this body, I need not to breathe," he reminded her. "Complete it."

She closed the remaining gaps. Now he was cocooned by her substance, and it was like floating in warm water, only better, because she pulsed gently against every part of him, as if he had a heartbeat. He drifted in that wonderful alien embrace, and it seemed like an eternity.

Truly, he was in her, and if it could only be for an hour, it was a phenomenal hour.

In the second game of the round, Bane was the Prey. He did not know what animal he would become; that was a surprise to both players. How Trool and the Oracle had managed to come to an understanding of such details without either Bane or Mach knowing was hard to guess, since they were the conduits for the information. Perhaps they had code phrases that had meaning only for computers and trolls.

He stepped through the curtain. He was on a broad plain, with a rocky escarpment to the north, that descended from a mesa. He was a monkey. He started running immediately, knowing that whatever form Mach took would be able to destroy the monkey.

Sure enough, in five seconds a panther appeared behind him. He ran straight ahead, giving the big cat no chance to gain on him by cutting corners. But he watched the escarpment. Some of it was clifflike, and some was a jagged slope. From this distance he could not be certain, but he suspected there would be caves. If he could reach a cave, next time around . . .

What form would he be in? What would lose to a monkey, but overcome a panther? He could not come up with an answer at the moment, but he decided to make for the caves next time, and if his form could take advantage of them, he would do so. He did not slow or swerve to get a closer look; he wanted to give his opponent no hint of whatever strategy he might have in mind. But he considered options. Go directly to the escarpment, circle it, and pop into a deep cave? Climb to the mesa? If he climbed, he might just lose time, but if there were a good cave entrance that could not be seen from below . . .

He reached the shore of a wide river and plunged in. The river flowed toward the north, curving in a broad meander toward the escarpment and disappearing behind it, but it should be possible simply to swim across it and enter the medium of air quickly. He still had his five-second lead.

He was a sting ray. He swerved to swim downriver, wanting to explore the section that brushed the escarpment. He hoped the Predator would assume the Prey was swimming straight across, and lose a second or two.

No such luck. A walrus appeared upriver, and immediately reoriented and stroked down. But at least he had not lost any time.

He veered to the left, angling up. The walrus matched him, cutting the corner. Then he veered right and down, deep. As a ploy it was no good; the walrus merely matched the maneuver, cutting the corner again, picking up a bit of time.

Then Bane saw what he was looking for: a weed-shrouded cave, underwater in the right bank. It could be blind, but it could also lead to the mesa, or somewhere amidst the escarpment.

He swerved back to the left, as if trying once more to shake the pursuit. Once more, it didn't work. This time he carried across to the left bank, and angled up and out, sailing into the air.

He was a four-winged insect—a dragonfly. He zoomed over a great field of flowers, but they did not tempt him; dragonflies were predators in their milieu, not pollen eaters.

Behind him, by about four seconds, a bat sailed up out of the river. He could not fight that! He flew straight, maintaining his lead, until he plunged through the horizon, completing the first lap.

He landed on the plain as a skunk. So that was what would balk the panther! But why not the monkey?

He angled for the mesa. The ground soon became rocky. Behind him the monkey appeared and pursued.

When the monkey encountered the stony section, it paused just long enough to scoop up a stone. Bane discovered this when that stone came flying past his head. *That* was how the monkey stopped the skunk—by catching it from a distance! Those stones were heavy and sharp; his skunk body was vulnerable. He needed more than four seconds' distance, to get out of range. Meanwhile, he would have to dodge, which would cost him time. The chase was heating up!

He reached the foot of the escarpment and scooted up. Monkeys were better climbers than skunks were, but he had scouted this terrain from a distance the first time through, and was on the gentlest part of the slope. He found a series of ledges that ascended along the south face of it, working up toward the mesa-top.

He encountered one gravel-strewn section, and scraped with his four feet, sending gravel and pebbles sliding down into the face of his pursuer. That gained him a second or so, and he made it to the top with above five seconds' leeway.

He ran directly toward the river, watching for openings. There were none; the mesa was grassy and even. Soon he came to the brink, and scrambled over it, sliding and tumbling down the steep slope.

Then, down near the river, he spied it: a rock-blocked cave entrance. His skunk body was small enough to wedge in between the rocks, and he squeezed inside before the monkey caught up.

He didn't pause; he followed the cave down into darkness. Then he found water. He slid into it quietly, and became an eel. Good enough: the walrus could crush the sting-ray, the sting-ray could sting the eel with its tail, and the eel could shock the walrus. There was the endless circle.

If his strategy worked, the Predator would not realize that the cave went through to the water, and would waste time either pulling away the rocks that blocked it, or waiting for the skunk to emerge, or throwing stones down into it. There was always a way for the Predator to get through, so there could be no impasse, but that way was not always obvious. Bane had gambled that the cave connected to the one he had spied below the water level of the river, and had won.

He swam across the river. There was no pursuit. It

had worked! He had gained enough time to ensure completion of the course without being caught.

Unless the monkey waited, and devised a trap for him. That was within the rules; it was possible for Prey to nab Predator if the Prey had time to set a clever snare that injured or delayed the Predator so that it could not complete the course.

He emerged from the river and became a mosquito. Now how could a mosquito put away a bat? By stinging it, and giving it some lethal disease. Far-fetched, perhaps, but viable for the purpose of the game. All these animal sets were only analogies for the root game: scissors/paper/stone. Scissors cut paper, paper wrapped stone, stone crushed scissors, making the circle. No doubt many current games derived from similarly obscure originals. A mosquito stinging a bat was as realistic as paper demolishing a stone by wrapping it.

He flew swiftly—more swiftly than any genuine mosquito could have—across the field of flowers, and came back to the land medium. Now he was the panther. He had lapped his opponent, and that made him the Predator. It did not give him the victory automatically, but it certainly gave him the advantage.

But, wary of a trap, he walked to the foot of the escarpment, and climbed it as carefully and quietly as he could. There was no sign of any trap. Perhaps it had been set in the lower plain, where he might be expected to run; by choosing this route, he might have foiled it.

He came to the cave entrance. The obscuring stones had been pulled aside, so that a creature the size of a monkey could enter it. Apparently Mach had decided it was a blind cave, and gone down to catch the Prey. Indeed, that would have been the correct decision, had the cave not gone through to the river! It would have been smarter for Mach to go directly to the water, and watch there to see whether any new fish appeared; indeed, he could have lain in ambush, for the Prey could win only by completing the full course, and that meant crossing the river at some point.

He sniffed the region. The smell of monkey was definitely there—but was the monkey still inside, or had it—

He heard a noise just above him, on the slope. He looked up—and the blast of the skunk caught him in the face, blinding him.

Too late, he realized what had happened. He had not lapped Mach; Mach had followed, one medium behind, keeping out of sight, and come up on him while he was distracted by the cave. The slope of the mountain had concealed the Predator, so that he needed only a few seconds' distraction time to get close enough. Bane had given him that time, and lost the game.

All he had had to do was keep moving, completing the course. Mach could never have caught him. But, wary of the nonexistent trap, he had fallen into a worse one: the trap of incaution.

"I saw it," Agape said. "The Game Computer puts the games on holo. We saw him following you, and creeping up on you at the end."

"What a fool I must have seemed!" he lamented.

"It is always easier to judge the play when you aren't in it," she reminded him. "We knew he had not remained, so could not be caught by your lapping him and putting him away so you could finish the course. But you did not know, and we knew that too."

But his chagrin went deeper than that. "Could it be that I dawdled because I wanted not to win? That I betrayed my cause?"

"You wouldn't do that!"she protested.

"How can others be sure? How can *I* be sure?"

She paused, considering. "There is another game tomorrow."

"Aye. Needs must I prove therein I be no malingerer."

"You will," she said. But she could not ease his doubt.

• • •

Bane was Predator again for the third game. This was the critical one; if he won, the match was over.

Mach stepped through the curtain. Five seconds later, Bane followed.

He was a dragon. Not a fire-breather, not a flying creature, but nevertheless a dragon, with horrendous teeth and claws.

Ahead of him was a salamander. That was a far smaller creature, but formidable enough in its own right, because it could set fire to any vegetation it touched, and burn most other creatures. Dragons, however, were immune to heat, because so many of them were fire-breathers; even those who were not, like himself, possessed enough of the fire-resistant scales and mouth armor to resist the efforts of the salamander. Thus the dragon could chomp the salamander, and the salamander was the Prey.

The landscape was fantasy too: exotic enchanted plants grew high, bearing blossoms that natural flowers could never manage. Bane recognized poison sprayers and sleep weeds and illusion spikes. As a dragon, he had little to fear from these, but a man would have had, literally, to watch his step.

However, there could be aspects of this setting that could damage a dragon, such as clefts in the ground covered by illusion. He would have to watch the path taken by the salamander, and if he saw anything strange, be warned. Meanwhile, because of the prospects for illusion, he could not afford to let the Prey get out of his sight; he could lose critical time trying to locate it through the fog of illusion.

They wound through a forest whose trees supported monstrous webs. The hidden giant spiders could not hurt either contestant because only a contestant could harm a contestant, but they could impede progress significantly. If the salamander got entangled, the dragon could catch it; if the dragon got caught, the salamander could gain vital time.

The trees thinned out, and they came to the water.

This was an inverted lake: broadest at ground level, with the water extending up instead of down in an irregular dome. Effects like this did not exist in Phaze; this magic setting was crafted of imagination rather than reality.

The salamander plunged in. Bane followed. He was now a sea serpent, chasing a kraken. The kraken was a monstrous magic weed whose stems and branches were tentacles. They had little stickers that stung and poisoned the flesh of ordinary creatures, but the hide of the sea serpent was too tough to be affected. If he caught up with the kraken, he would simply bite off its tentacles, making it helpless.

The kraken was aware of this, and propelled itself through the water by stroking with flattened tentacles, making the same speed that the serpent could by threshing its coils. The two of them churned the water, generating myriads of bubbles that sank quickly to the bottom surface.

Bane was gaining. The kraken could move as rapidly as the serpent, but it took Mach a while to catch on to the most efficient use of his paddle-tentacles. By the time he plunged out of the far side of the lake, Bane was ony two seconds behind.

In air, Bane was a roc: a monstrous predatory bird, said to be able to carry an elephant aloft in its talons. Bane believed that was an exaggeration; nevertheless, very few creatures on land or in the air debated territory with a roc. Mach was a wyvern: a small fire-breathing flying dragon. He was of course no match for the roc, but dangerous to most other creatures.

They flew through colored clouds: red, green, blue, yellow, black. These might be harmless, but could also be nuisances; the wyvern brushed by a green one, and its substance adhered, stretching like taffy, fouling a wing. The wyvern whipped back its snout and blew fire at it; the green taffy shriveled and smoked and let go, but Mach had lost time. Bane was now only one second behind.

Thereafter they both skirted the clouds. Most were probably just vapor, but neither player could afford to take the chance that it wasn't. Time was at stake, and a shift of a single second could make the difference.

They plunged through the horizon, and now Bane was the salamander, chasing a basilisk. There was the completion of the circle: the basilisk was a small lizard, but its glance could stun or kill other creatures. It could not hurt the salamander, because the salamander could engulf it in a wave of fire, obscuring its glance in smoke and flame and cooking its body. But it could stun the dragon, who lacked the fire.

But with only one second separating them, the basilisk had no time to turn and glare back, and the salamander no time to start a fire. They simply ran, both maintaining the pace, keeping to the same path as before, avoiding the devious plants.

They reached the inverted lake and plunged in. Now it was Bane who was the kraken, and Mach was a siren: a creature with the body of a mermaid and a voice that could lure ships and large creatures to their deaths against great rocks in the water. That would be bad for the sea serpent, who would naturally have a taste for so soft and lovely a creature, and who would be charmed by her eerie voice. But the kraken was tone-deaf, and its appetite was too ravenous to be charmed away by prey, and rocks did not affect its streaming tentacles. It would simply squeeze the siren to death, then suck the body dry.

Bane knew how to use the tentacles to move the creature forward, but Mach was having no trouble with the siren, so the distance between them did not narrow. They forged through the water and out to the air.

Bane became the wyvern, and Mach was a harpy. There, again, was the circle: the wyvern could blast the harpy with fire, if it ever got close enough to remain in range while it took a deep breath, but the harpy's poisoned talons could poison the roc.

They followed their curving route between the clouds,

which had not moved, neither risking any deviation. Mach, again unfamiliar with the dynamics of the new creature, lost another half-second before attaining full velocity. Then they proceeded to the horizon, and through.

Bane was the basilisk, and Mach the dragon. Now the basilisk could glare forward—but the dragon could not be stunned from the rear, only from the front. Impasse, again.

But the dragon snagged a claw on a root, and stumbled. The basilisk almost caught up, but still could not get a line on the head, because of the mass of the serpentine body. They plunged on.

This was the last circuit; if Mach could survive the next two media, he would make it through, and win. But Bane was now within chomping distance. The next medium was the lake, and he would be the siren; she could charm from behind, because it was her voice that did it. Deep in the water, that voice would be distorted, but actual contact would undistort it. Touch the tail of the serpent, sing—and the serpent would be charmed into destruction.

The dragon dodged to the side, sideswiping a stout tree by the inverted bank, and lunged ahead. Bane, much smaller, gained time by making a leap to the water. He sailed surprisingly high.

And, in midair, he saw the dragon whip its tail around the tree. Its body reacted like rope; it snapped about, smacking against the other side of the tree.

Then Bane landed in the water, and became the siren. He was ready; he had actually gotten in ahead of the other!

And Mach did not follow.

Then Bane realized that he had been tricked. Mach had let him come deceptively close—and balked. Bane had been tricked into the one-way transformation, and could not return. He could not make the circuit, lapping his opponent, as he had tried to do before; he would be out of the game, because he would have gone through every form in every medium. All he could do was wait for the other to come through—and the other would never do so, now. It was an impasse—and that meant victory for Mach, because he had not been, and could not be, caught.

Bane had lost the game, and the round. The very closeness of his pursuit had done him in, denying him the reaction time he needed to stay clear of the lake. Mach had won by using his mind.

Bane experienced relief. He knew that he had done his utmost, only to be caught by a trick that would have surprised all the watchers too. He had lost with honor.

But there was one more round to go. Nothing had been decided yet.

15

Table

Mach stood at the console. He had the numbers, so he chose 1. PHYSICAL; he trusted that more than the others. Bane chose B. TOOL, evidently not trusting NAKED after his loss in the Chase. The truth was, that had been a very near thing; had Mach's desperate ruse not worked, Bane could easily have won, and finished the match.

He had the letters on the subgrid. He chose H. H_2O, having found that general-surface category compatible the last time. Bane chose 6. INTERACTIVE.

The square opened out, and the list of games appeared; a number of ball games wherein more than a ball was used, such as tennis, Jai alai and bowling, so that they wound up in this catchall grouping; water games like pedal-boat bumping and underwater volleyball (wherein the ball had to be propelled *under* the net); and string-ball games such as tetherball.

They assembled the nine-box grid, and played it, and came up with what each was evidently well satisfied to play: table tennis. There were several variants; Trool consulted with the Oracle, with Mach and Bane relaying the messages, and decided on three variants, one for each game. The first game would be standard, with identical equipment on both sides. The second would be freestyle, which meant the individual paddles could be of any type. The third was to be doublet, generally considered to be the most formidable challenge of a player's capacities.

Mach was familiar with them all, and good at them all. But Bane now had his expertise, as well as the sureness of the machine body. Could Mach, in this fallible living body, match that? He doubted it. Therefore his month's training would be critical. He had to come up with strategy and skill that could defeat the person he had been in Proton.

Meanwhile, there was the separate challenge of enabling the games to be played. Trool and the Oracle had made the chess games work, and the chase games; but table tennis was a physically interactive game of another nature. How could they hit a ball across the barrier between the frames? He was sure it would somehow be arranged, though.

He turned to look at the Translucent Adept. "Who are the best players of this game?" he inquired.

Translucent scowled. "Stile, and certain vampires in manform. We be hoist again."

"I have to find players better than I am, who can teach me things, and drill me in new techniques."

"We have resources, but thou mayst like them not."

"It doesn't matter whether I like them! I can't win unless I improve significantly, and even then the outcome will be in doubt, because Bane will improve too, and he won't make errors."

"Aye, thou must practice," Fleta agreed. "There be naught distasteful in that."

"One who can show thee much be Tania."

Fleta's ears flattened back, though she was in girlform. "That creature has shown thee already too much!"

Mach had to smile, though he too was startled. "No, that was Bane she showed," he said.

"When he were emulating thee!" she returned, as if

that made Mach culpable. "And in Proton-frame—"

"But it was Tan who was making you—"

"So Tannu be bad for me, and Tania for thee!"

Translucent nodded grimly. "I realize that neither of you be partial to those of the Tan Demesnes. But Tania alone has what thou dost require."

"What has that harpy that I do not?" Fleta demanded, one hand bunching and moving as if to paw the ground.

"A magic paddle."

Mach's interest quickened. "A magic paddle? To play table tennis?"

"Aye. It be a rare device, that she charmed from an elven craftsman of the carbon clan. Methinks thou must in turn charm it from her."

"O'er my dead carcass!" Fleta snorted.

But Mach was already dazzled by the notion. "A magic paddle, of elven craftsmanship! That would be something very special!"

"Aye. So do thou come to terms with thy filly, and I will make arrangements for thee to visit the Tan Demesnes."

Fleta did not seem to be in any mood to come to terms. "This may take a while," Mach muttered.

It did. Unicorns were known to be stubborn creatures, and Fleta showed her mettle in this respect. She did not want Mach going near Tania! But finally he persuaded her that if he did not take advantage of every opportunity to improve his game, he would lose, and then the two of them would be separated. "But the only reason I yield," she said grudgingly, "be because she be also in Proton, and I would be not there to safeguard thee from her clutches."

"Good reasoning," he said, relieved.

But it was not easy, when they went to the Tan Demesnes. Fleta insisted on carrying him there herself, in her natural form, theoretically to save his magic for more important things, but he suspected she was motivated more by the extra time it took this way.

Tania was resplendent in a fluffy tan cotton dress that fitted closely about her torso. Her hair was tied back with a tan ribbon and bow, and her feet looked tiny in tan slippers.

The grass here was excellent, but Fleta was not about to change back to unicorn form and graze.

Tania smiled brilliantly, flouncing her hem so that a petticoat flashed. "How nice to see thee, Mach! Hast come to play a game with a real woman?" Mach heard something like a squeal in the back of Fleta's throat.

"A game of table tennis," he said carefully. "The Translucent Adept said you have a magic paddle."

"Aye, and that be not all, rovot." She delivered a brief but intense glance, and he felt the power of her evil eye. Fleta's head moved slightly, as if orienting a horn for action.

"I brought a good paddle carved by the Red Adept," he said. "It has perfect heft and balance, and I can play well with it."

"We shall see," she said. "Let me change into something more comfortable." She spun around, her skirt flaring, showing her legs up to the thickening region of the thighs, and walked to the tanion tree. Mach, accustomed all his prior life to naked serfs, was amazed at how much a little clothing could do for a woman. Tania had not looked nearly as enticing naked in Proton.

Fleta's foot came down, just missing his toe. "What be thou looking at, machine?"

"Uh—"

"She knew we were coming," she hissed. "Why did she change not before?"

"Remember, I'm supposed to get her to lend me the paddle," Mach said. "I have to *seem* interested, though of course I am not."

"Thou couldst have fooled me," she muttered.

Soon Tania reappeared, garbed in tight tan shorts

that made her nether portion seem almost bare, and a translucently loose blouse. "This be better, methinks," she murmured.

"Shethinks!" Fleta sniffed.

After a moment Mach noticed that Tania carried a paddle. She was evidently ready to play.

There was a chamber in an alcove of the tree, and the table was there. Tania took a stance at one end. "Do it to me," she invited.

"Nay, an I could . . ." Fleta breathed wrathfully.

There was a ball on the table, wedged by the net. Mach fetched it, and served it. He had not played this game in this body, but his motions were good; either his experience or Bane's reflexes made the play easy.

Tania jammed her paddle at the ball somewhat jerkily; it was obvious that she was not an apt player. But the ball came back; she had made the return.

He struck the ball again, getting the feel of it and the paddle and his body. Again she was somewhat awkward, but returned it. Obviously she would soon miss, though.

He struck it the third time, angling it across the table. She stretched, almost losing her balance, and he thought she was going to hit the ball well wide—but it returned neatly enough.

Curious, he slammed it off the right corner. She blocked it in a pure reflex of self-defense—and the ball looped back to the center of his side of the table, another fair return. How had she done it?

In the course of the next several volleys, he discovered that no matter how awkwardly she moved her paddle, the ball always made a good return. He finally missed his own shot, trying too hard to make her miss. The skill was not in her, but in the paddle: that was its magic. It would not miss a point.

He lost the game, winning no points at all. He could not prevail against the magic paddle.

Tania smiled as she won. "What wouldst thou give

for this paddle, rovot?" she inquired, her bosom heaving. "To use 'gainst Bane in thy tourney?"

She had a double score to settle with Bane, he realized: he was on the other side, and he had resisted her attempt to fascinate him. She would lend Mach the paddle; she was just trying to see what else she might profit from the transaction. Meanwhile, he had Fleta to contend with.

"Nothing, Tania," he said gruffly. "There will be three games; it could only win one of them for me. If I depend on magic, I will lose. I need to hone my playing skill, and you are unlikely to do that for me."

Tania's face transformed in the course of his speech from self-satisfied to furious. "Take it then, golem-brain; I care not!" And she hurled it at him.

He caught it. "If you insist, Tania."

She glared, evidently ready to use her magic on him. He snapped his fingers, and a full-length mirror appeared before her, reflecting her outraged visage back to her. Then he turned his back and walked with Fleta away from the table and the tree.

"Methinks that were not wise, Mach," she said, satisfied.

"Better an angry woman than an angry unicorn," he said. "She was supposed to demonstrate the paddle, not try to vamp me. I tried to be polite, but she pushed her luck."

Fleta was silent, but her anger was gone.

Mach found practice with the animal heads. Most of these supported Stile, but one aberrant faction did not, and one of the best table tennis players of the frame was a member of that faction. This was an elephant head, who held the paddle in his trunk, and manipulated it marvelously well.

Against Eli the elephant head Mach used his regular paddle, the one Trool had carved. It had no magic, but was an excellent instrument. Mach played well, very well, for the reflexes of Bane's body were good. But

Eli tromped him; his control was superlative. This was the one who could teach him improved play without magic.

But Mach used magic, not to make returns, but to improve his own perception and stamina. To enable himself to learn, to become a better player.

They played again. At first Mach, distracted by the nature of his adversary, had made easy misses. But pride soon caught up with him, and now he played with better precision—and still lost points. That trunk was so limber and controlled that the paddle seemed like a living part of it. The spins it imparted seemed magical, though they were not. When Mach tried to analyze them, he missed worse than ever. Eli's serves were especially bad; Mach could handle them only by playing extremely conservatively and defensively, which only set him up for further trouble.

Little by little, he discovered the key: Eli's paddle motions were complex, shifting direction and angle with blurring facility. Sometimes the paddle literally spun in his grasp, so that it was difficult to tell which side struck the ball. Since the two sides had different surfaces that imparted different qualities to the flight of the ball, this could be devastating.

"I must learn to do that," Mach said.

"Aye," Eli agreed. Rather, he snorted musically through his trunk, making the affirmative; human speech was difficult for him.

They played constantly during the following days and weeks. Eli had the patience of a pachyderm, and the endurance, and was pleased to have such a willing student. He demonstrated all his best shots, and showed Mach how to counter them. Mach, realizing that he would be up against a high-tech Proton paddle in at least one game, was happy to work on his defense. A good defense could not win the game for him, at this level, for it left the initiative to the opponent; but that defense had to be tight before he could score with his offense. The best defensive players took the offensive the moment a suitable opportunity offered; their opponents knew that it was folly to ease up, and so were under pressure that could cause errors.

By the time the month was done, he was giving Eli some excellent games. He was vastly improved, and ready to tackle his other self in any of the three games. He had not used the magic paddle, as that was pointless; it was already incapable of making a bad shot. In fact, he felt slightly guilty, knowing that this was one instrument Bane could not match. Only by winning both the other games could Bane prevail.

Meanwhile, Fleta had special news for him. "Dost remember my heat?" she inquired diffidently.

"Oh, no—is it coming again?"

"Nay, hast not noticed it came not again?"

Mach paused. "You mean—?"

"Aye. I be with foal."

Mach had no idea how to react, so he simply reached for her and embraced her, so cautiously that she laughed. She was a mare; her condition did not make her delicate. She was as happy as he had ever seen her.

But she was not willing to let it rest at that. "This be my compensation, an I be separated from thee. But how much better will it be if we separate not."

"If something can be worked out," he agreed. "To save the frames, and still be together."

"Aye. And raise our foal ourselves."

"To be perhaps the best of unicorns—"

"Or the best of men."

"Perhaps like both: able to change form freely, yet able also to practice magic."

"Flach, the Unicorn Adept!" she exclaimed.

Why not? "Why not unite our species with a truly superior composite?"

"And needs must we set up a house, for I fear the Herd will welcome him not."

"Why not a castle? I am Adept now; I can make what I choose. Our son should have the best."

"The Rovot Demesnes," she said, smiling.

She wasn't serious enough, so he kissed her again. Whatever the outcome of this round, they would have that success together.

It was the day of the first game. Now at last Mach discovered how they were going to make it possible to play across the frames. As before, the two selves would overlap, standing together at one end of the table. Each would play his side. But the ball, instead of passing through the no-longer-existent curtain, would fly across the net to a simulacrum of the other player at the far end.

To Mach, it looked as if Bane were standing there, paddle in hand, in Mach's robot body, but it was probably a golem provided by the Brown Adept. The golem would not literally play; it would merely emulate Bane's motions.

But the ball could not physically cross between the frames. What would the golem be striking?

This might be an irrelevant detail, but Mach wanted to know, as it could affect his attitude and therefore his play. He didn't want to ask openly, which he realized was foolish; he was adapting increasingly to living ways, as he spent more time in this living body. Living creatures had awareness of pain, both physical and mental, and tended to be much more careful about things they did not quite understand than machines were. Mach was now far more sensitive than he had ever been in Proton, and he liked to believe that was an asset. So he wanted to know whether a hornet's nest was inhabited without getting stung during the investigation, and to know the exact nature of the appearance of his opponent without suffering any embarrassment about his naivete in asking. So he practiced another aspect of personality that came more readily to the living than to the machine: innocuous deception.

He went to Fleta for one more embrace. "Is that a golem?" he whispered to her ear.

Her ear twitched. She did retain some unicorn mannerisms in her human form! "Nay, it has no smell," she replied. "It be a wraith."

"Thank you." So the whole thing, ball and player, was merely an image, a projection from the information coming through him. Trool's spells from the Book of Magic could readily accomplish that; indeed, Mach himself could do something similar, at need.

"That be all thou dost want of me?" Fleta inquired.

Oops. "All I can ask in public," he said, giving her backside a squeeze.

She sniffed, but she was mollified.

He returned to the table and took up his paddle. It was the standard one that Trool had made for him, without magic. In this first game, the equipment was equivalent, with each paddle meeting set specifications. The idea was to see how well each played with no advantage of equipment. "Let's rally a little first," he suggested.

"Aye," Bane agreed. "This be a strange arrangement."

Suddenly Mach wished that the two of them could be together like this when not opposing each other. That they could do without illusion what now required illusion. Maybe, after this contest was settled, they could see about that.

He picked up the ball and served it, throwing it up from his left palm in the prescribed manner, so that it was evident that his hand imparted no spin to it. It bounced on his side of the table and crossed the net. He knew that it became illusory at that point, transformed by magic to an image, while in the frame of Proton the Game Computer introduced a physical ball with the exact velocity, azimuth and spin of the one in Phaze. In Proton Mach was the image, generated holographically, seeming as real as Bane did on this side. It was an amazingly sophisticated interface, to make the appearance of an ordinary game.

Bane returned the ball, seeming at ease. It crossed back over the net. Was there a flicker as it did so? Mach could not be sure. In any event, he should not allow himself to be distracted by the intricacies of the system; he had to play as well as he could. If he even started wondering how he could move freely about, to play the ball to either side or far back from the table, without losing his overlap-contact with Mach, he would start fouling up! How much of his own motion was also illusion?

They played for a few minutes, becoming acclimatized. All was in working order. "Time for business," Mach said, with both excitement and regret.

"Aye." Bane caught the ball in his hand, put his hands behind him, brought them out closed and held them just below the level of the table. Mach pointed with his paddle to Bane's right hand. Bane lifted it: empty. That meant that Bane had the first serve.

Bane served. The ball came across the net, low and fast, striking Mach's right corner. Mach fielded it with a chop, using a short, sharp downstroke to return the ball with a backspin. This tended to slow its progress, causing it to drop to the center of Bane's table rather toward the back edge. But the backspin did more than that. It changed the nature of the bounce, so that the ball tended to lift and fall short; an incautious player could have misjudged it and missed it for that reason. And more yet: when the other paddle touched it, the spin would tend to carry the ball down, perhaps into the net, for a miss.

But Bane now knew all that Mach did about the dynamics of play. He met thc ball with a chop of his own, that countered and reversed the spin, sending the same kind of shot back.

Mach, ready for this, touched the ball lightly with his backhand, so that it bobbed up over the net and down just the other side: a shot that could be far more troublesome than it appeared, because normally a player stood back from the table.

But Bane was there, and with a quick flick of his wrist plunked the ball down and to Mach's right, so that it bounced near the edge of the table and dropped to the side. Mach leaped to intercept it, but the table was in the way, and he could not get there in time to do more than flip it way up in a high arch over the net.

That, of course, was a setup. Bane slammed it off the far side, and Mach had no way to return it.

One–love, for Bane. Now the game was truly under way!

Mach recovered the ball and tossed it back. Bane caught it in his hand and took his stance for the next serve.

This one was backhand, cutting across to Mach's left side. He returned it the same way as he had the first, with backspin. Mach's return was similar again; the machine body and mind tended to stay in familiar channels. That was apt to be a weakness.

Mach followed through with the same sort of shot he had made at this point in the first rally, flipping the ball gently over the net to the center of the table. And Bane replied as he had before, with the dropshot to the side, only this time to Mach's left. Again Mach was caught in a squeeze, and made a poor return, and got it smashed past him. Two–love for Bane.

But Mach was verifying what might be weaknesses in his opponent; that was more important than the points, at the moment. Mach had qualities of imagination he had lacked as a machine, and now he was using them for what he hoped would be his advantage. If he charted Bane's weaknesses, he could exploit them before the game was done.

Bane's third serve was forehand, to Mach's backhand. One forehand crosscourt, one backhand crosscourt, one forehand downcourt—the next should be backhand downcourt, and the fifth a new variation. If so, Mach would know what to expect later in the game, and that would help immensely.

He returned it with a high looping sidespin shot, the kind that could utterly befuddle a neophyte but would be a lost point against an experienced player. Sure enough, Bane compensated for the spin and slammed it off the corner. Three–love. A lost point, but confirmation of the reaction. It was not possible to put ultimate spin on a ball with the standard paddle surface, but in a later game it would be another matter.

However, he could not afford to get too far behind. He played to win on the fourth point. As anticipated, Bane served the ball backhand, to Mach's forehand, and because he was ready for it, he slammed it right back where it had come from. It was a beautiful shot, and it caught Bane by surprise; the paddle was late, and the ball went flying to the side, out of play. Three–one.

Bane's fifth serve was a drop shot, as Mach had thought reasonably likely. He dropped it back, and gained the initiative, which in due course won him the point. Three–two.

Now it was Mach's serve. He tested Bane's reactions on different types, and verified that Bane's skill was basically Mach's own—before he had come to Proton. He was thoroughly familiar with that style of play, by no coincidence, and knew its strengths and weaknesses. A defensive game would never prevail, because the robot made no unforced errors, and would outlast any other opponent. But the right kind of offense, initiated at the right occasion, could force errors. Mach was about to find out whether what he had learned fom Eli the elephant head was the right kind.

It was, but not by much. Mach found that by making wild alterations in his play he could cause Bane to lose track momentarily and become vulnerable—but that same wildness made Mach's own shots unreliable. He missed more than he should have, by taking risks, playing low-percentage shots. As a result, the score seesawed. He caught up at 9–9, fell behind to 13–10 (the server's score was always given first), went ahead at 16–17, and tied again at 19–19.

It was make-or-break time. Mach, as the robot, would not have gambled; Mach, as the living creature, did. It was his serve, and he had no better occasion to seize the initiative. He used the Eli special, thinking of his right arm as a flexible trunk, using it to put on the backspin that looked like a topspin. He spun the paddle; both sides were the same, for this game, but the spin helped mask the particular angle and motion as it contacted the ball. If it fooled Bane the way it had himself—

It did. Bane's return smacked into the net. He had countered for topspin, and sent the ball wrong.

Now for the real gamble. Mach had not repeated shots since his experimentation early in the game; Bane should be expecting a different serve. Mach used the same one, spinning the paddle again. This time Bane, more cautious, did manage to return it—but his volley was unaggressive. Mach played it aggressively, gained the initiative, and forced the rally to its conclusion. He made the point, and won the game, 21–19.

But he knew he would never catch Bane that way again. This ploy had been viable only at the end of the game, only for two points. If he ever tried that serve again, Bane would know what to do with it, and that, combined with error-free play, would suffice. Robots did learn from experience, and learned well.

"Good game," Mach said.

Bane nodded. "Until tomorrow."

But tomorrow was freestyle. Mach would have the magic paddle. *This* had been the key game, setting up for the sure win tomorrow.

Bane faded out, along with the far side of the table. Mach turned to Fleta, who seemed to materialize almost in his arms. "I took him on skill," he said, well satisfied.

"Don't get cocky," Translucent said. "He's as good as you are, and you won't take him again this way."

"I won't need to," Mach said.

But the Adept did not look confident.

16

Decision

Bane shook his head. "He learned tricks he never knew before! I'm in a position to know. I could have finished the match by being smarter in the Chase, and now one more loss can finish it the other way. I know not we'er I have really been trying."

"You tried," Agape said. "You were ahead, but then he used those peculiar serves."

"I know not who could have taught him those," he said. "I played the game all my life, but ne'er could match my father, and knew of none other could. Stile would not have trained him, and—" Then a thought caught up. "The renegade animal heads! They played not with others, but there were stories of an elephant head who were marvelously dexterous with his trunk! That could be it!"

"That, and the natural skill of your human body," she agreed.

"Aye, it be a good body," he said with a certain resigned pride. "This machine body makes errors not, but also can handle complex surprises not. He caught me often enough with shots I could calculate not in time. He knew my limits, as he should. It were his body longer than mine."

"But you can adjust."

"Aye. He can catch me once or twice with a new shot, but thereafter I be attuned to the device, and it be useless. I will be stronger for the next game, and stronger still for the third. In only a month, he cannot have mastered enough new things to compensate for that."

She changed the subject. "Let's go look at Nepe." She meant their child, who did not yet exist. But there was daily progress in the construction of the robot body, to be like that of a human baby, and the development of the particular programming required to enable that body to interface harmoniously with a partial Moebite, while being closely patterned after that of his body. Agape herself was gaining mass, eating voraciously, preparing for the time of fission. If Bane won the contest, and the two of them had to separate, they would delay long enough to get Nepe started. That, at least, they intended to salvage from victory.

Next day Bane was ready. This was freestyle, and he had prepared diligently. The key was in the paddle. Technology was able to produce a wide variety of sizes, substances, weights and surfaces, and he had tested them as thoroughly as he could. He now had a paddle that was virtually magical in it propensities. The touch of finger or thumb on the controls near the joining of blade and handle could change the hardness of the rubber (it wasn't rubber, but tradition called it that) all the way from diamond to marshmallow, and the adhesion from glass to glue. The paddle could hold the ball so that it would not drop off, or be so slippery that the ball bounced away with its spin unaffected. It could completely damp out both the force and spin of an incoming ball, or put on devastating force and spin of its own. Because the nature of the surface was exactly what he specified it to be, without changing the appearance, the other player would have little notion what was coming. He could make an obvious gesture, applying phenomenal spin, but set the paddle on null so that none of that spin was imparted, and the other player would miss by compensating for nonexisting spin. Such paddles had been illegal for centuries for tournament play, but popular for trick play.

Mach had never used one, preferring to hone his skill within tournament regulations. Adaptation to such a paddle could spoil a serious player for tournaments, because his reflexes were wrong. Only the mediocre players tried to shift back and forth between types; the top ones settled on legal variants and perfected their technique with these. Indeed, a top player could defeat any of the special-paddle players, because surface was only part of the nature of the game. Skill and training and consistency counted for more.

That was one reason that Bane had not played his best in the first game: he had adapted to the specialized paddle for the freestyle, and so not been in perfect tune for the standard paddle. He had invoked a different program for the other, so that he did play well, but he could have played better had he put all of his energy into perfecting his technique with it. Instead he had settled for the level of skill Mach had developed, and put his energy into the special mode. He expected to win this second game, because he knew that neither Mach's prior experience nor that of his own body prepared them for the type of play and deception this paddle offered. A good player with a conventional paddle could handle a mediocre one with a special paddle—but he was now a good player with a special paddle. That made it a new ball game.

Indeed, he had practiced against some of the ranking players of Proton, in special matches. They had used their legal paddles, and regarded it as an intriguing challenge to meet the special one. A number of them were clearly superior to Mach, as he had played before, but the paddle added considerably to Bane's effectiveness. He had taken them, in the early games, then lost again as they learned how to compensate, but all admitted that he was a more formidable player this way. They doubted that any player on the planet could take him in the first game, this way; the difference was too striking. It was hardly possible to learn in the course of a single game what he had spent a month mastering, and it was not easy to do in several games.

So Bane was confident. Mach, attuned to the conventional mode of the first game, would find himself up against a totally different creature in the second. He would compensate—but hardly before he had lost the game.

Yet as they stepped up to their ends of the composite-image table, Mach seemed oddly confident. Had he devised a similar paddle, and practiced against it? That seemed unlikely, because the tricks he had learned with the conventional paddle should have taken most of his training time.

They rallied, as before, and things seemed normal. Mach had a different paddle, but of course so did Bane. He did not try any special shots, preferring to save them for the game. Soon they were ready, and Mach caught the ball and hid his fists under the table.

Bane guessed right, and was right; he had the serve. Now was time for the surprises.

He started with a fierce crosscourt topspin, the rubber softened and rendered tacky so that it imparted far more spin to the ball than would ordinarily have been the case. Mach, judging by the prior surface, would fail to compensate sufficiently, and the ball would fly well beyond the end of the table.

Mach returned it, and the ball did loop up, but the force was gone, and it plunked down in the center of the table. Obviously he had been caught by surprise, but had a lucky shot. Table tennis was a game of skill, but luck played its part, as it did in every game to some extent. That was part of the excitement: the invocation of chance.

No problem. Bane smashed it down the center, an easy put-away shot. The first point was his.

Except that the ball looped up giddily, and somehow managed to catch Bane's side of the table again. Was the frame translation mechanism malfunctioning? No, the arc was true; Mach had just somehow managed to aim it right, obviously with no certainty on his part. Sometimes it happened.

Bane made sure it would not happen again. He thumbed his paddle to maximum force, producing a surface that had all the thrusting power of a trampoline, and smashed the ball down with such velocity that Mach would have to retreat far back from the table to have any hope of returning it.

But Mach remained up close—and the ball, crazily, came back, in another shaky but fair return. It seemed impossible, but there it was. How could it have happened?

Bane, shaken by this freak series, tried a trick shot. He wound up as if for the hardest slam yet, then dinked the ball down just over the net with a heavy backspin that damped it almost to a standstill.

Mach, though, was ready. The tip of his paddle caught the ball and flipped it to the side, forcing Bane to dive for the return—and then, of course, Mach slammed the setup to the other side, winning the point. Love–one.

But Bane knew that freak shots could not be depended on. Mach had been extraordinarily lucky in his returns, then pounced on the opportunity that offered when Bane changed the pace. Had Mach been playing well back from the table, in anticipation of a slam, he would never have caught up to the dink shot.

He served again, this time putting on backspin so heavy that though the ball started fast, it slowed dramatically and failed to clear the table for the second bounce on the far side. Bane returned it without even trying to counter the spin; as a result, the ball sailed up in an invitation for another smash.

Bane of course accepted the invitation, and slammed

it off Mach's backhand corner. But Mach took it on his backhand without effort, and again it looped back.

Bane slammed it off Mach's forehand corner. Yet again Mach intercepted it in what should have been a return that careered wildly, but again the ball simply looped back to strike at the center of Bane's table.

This was crazy! Mach wasn't even trying to play offensively; he was simply making fluke returns! What was he up to? No one could play that way for long without losing the point; human reflexes were not swift enough or good enough to handle slammed balls up close.

This time Bane softened his rubber and sliced, so that the ball curved visibly in the air before striking the table. The sidespin did not have much effect on the bounce, but would be very strong against the opposing paddle. The shot was hard enough so that Mach would not have much time to analyze or compensate.

But Mach didn't try. He simply poked his paddle at the ball—and the ball looped back in another of those high, amateurish returns.

This time Bane had been watching that paddle closely. *The angle had not even been correct.* By rights the ball should have flown off the table, a lost point. Yet it had flown fair, to the center of the table. It was like magic.

Magic! Suddenly Bane caught on. Mach had gotten hold of a magic paddle! That possibility had never occurred to him. There had been no magic paddles in Phaze, because there was no point to them; why use magic to foul up a game of skill? But evidently someone had crafted one, perhaps simply for the challenge of it, and now Mach had it.

Bane tried to slam the ball again, but his realization about the paddle distracted him, and he missed the table. Love–two.

Obviously the paddle was enchanted so that any shot it made was fair. If no effort was made to guide it, the ball returned in neutral fashion: a high arc to the center of the table. If Mach made a more aggressive shot, then it went where he sent it—but wouldn't miss if he sent it wrong. Thus he could try for the most difficult shots with the certainty of making them. Or not try at all, and still get the ball back. He could not miss.

How was he, Bane, to win the game—when his opponent could not miss a shot? All his preparation with the special paddle had been nullified in a single stroke! Only in Phaze would magic work—but Mach was playing in Phaze. Since the validity of a shot was determined at the point of the ball's contact with the paddle, it didn't matter that there was no magic on Bane's end of the table; the ball was correctly guided there.

If they had set it up to exchange courts at the halfway point of each game—but in this special situation that wasn't feasible. So Mach would have the magic throughout the game.

Bane had thought he would win this game readily. Now, suddenly, he faced defeat and loss of the entire contest, because he had overlooked this possibility.

He glanced at the audience. They were watching, in Proton and in Phaze, but would not speak to him in the midst of the game. What advice could anyone give him, anyway? It could not remove the enchantment on Mach's paddle!

He was behind by two points, a trifling amount, yet he felt like resigning, to spare himself the humiliation that was coming. Could he win even a single point?

But battered pride kept him going. He would play his best regardless, so that everyone would know it. He would not give up just because the game had become hopeless.

He tossed up the ball for the third serve, and tried for a horrendous slice.

And missed the ball entirely. That was the danger in trying too hard; the angle was so sharp and the speed of the paddle so great that the tiniest misjudgment could become devastating.

Love–three. When the server made his pass at the

ball, that was the serve. He had missed his serve and forfeited the point. Some brave try that had been!

Missed the ball entirely . . .

That was not supposed to happen to a robot; it was an unforced error. But the body was governed by Bane's mind, and he had overridden it to try his own extreme technique. By going beyond the body's parameters, he had enabled it to err. Yesterday Mach had used trick shots that caused the computer brain to miscalculate; this time he had done it to himself. But that was of lesser significance.

Suddenly he realized how he could give himself a fighting chance. This game was not yet over!

He served again, making the paddle surface hard and fast, applying minimal spin, just enough to help control the ball. Spin made limited difference now, because the magic paddle nullified it; the balls Mach returned were spinless. But speed and placement counted, because Mach had to get the paddle to the ball. He now needed spin only to help control his shots.

Mach returned it with that familiar loping shot that was the paddle's default. Ready for this, Bane smashed it back. Mach's second return was higher, a perfect setup.

Bane decided to test the limit of the magic. He set his paddle for maximum hardness, and smashed the ball down as hard as his metal arm could do it. The ball flattened significantly against his paddle, then rebounded with such force that when it caught the edge of the table it broke, with half of it dropping down the side of the table while the other half dragged after.

But Mach's paddle was there, jabbing at it. And the tip of the paddle caught the crushed remnant and hooked it over the net so that it plopped in the center on Bane's side.

The point did not count; the broken ball had to be replaced. But another type of point had been made: the magic paddle could return anything at all, even a demolished ball. As long as it touched it.

Bane served again, the same way. Mach returned the same way. A very similar shot offered, and Bane wound up for the same smash. But this time he bent his wrist sharply back and slammed the ball off the opposite side of the table.

Mach, caught by surprise, did not even try for the ball. The point was Bane's. One–three.

The magic paddle could not return what it did not touch. As far as it was concerned, the ball was out of play. It was up to Mach to get it there in time.

And up to Bane to see that Mach could not get it there in time.

The remainder of the game was grueling. The robot body that made no unforced errors, and the magic paddle that never missed its shot. Bane played every shot for maximum motion on the opponent's part, getting Mach off balance, putting the ball where he did not expect it, so that his living-body reaction was strained, and errors occurred. Mach had been a machine all his life and still tended to depend on the automatic reliability of it; but now he was living flesh, and the flesh was fallible. He could not always get to the ball, and each time he failed, Bane won the point.

But Bane's body was healthy, and the magic paddle made returns easy. He did not readily miss the ball. So the rallies were long and hard, and only when Mach tired did Bane score. That was the final key, however: Bane's body did not tire. He was able to keep the pace indefinitely.

So inevitably, the final point was his. Bane had beaten the magic paddle, and won the game. The score was tied, one game apiece.

"I think some thought you were not trying hard to win," Agape said when they were private, after the grueling game. "That doubt is gone."

"It be strange," Bane said. "When it looked hopeless, and I thought there was no point in continuing, that was when I had to try hardest to win."

"Tomorrow will decide it," she said.

"Tomorrow will decide it," he agreed. "He won the game I thought he would lose, because the flesh can play not as reliably as a machine—but the flesh managed to strain the limits o' the machine through innovative play. He lost the game methought he would win, because o' the magic paddle—but the machine managed to strain the limits o' the flesh. Tomorrow—I think no one can know the outcome o' that game."

"No one can know," she agreed.

"But an I win, and we must separate—"

"There will still be Nepe," she said. "We can surely delay that long."

"Aye. But an Mach return to this body—"

"Where else?" she asked with a wry smile.

"It would please me if thou didst play Fleta for him, again. I oppose him, but I hate him not, and his love for the filly be true."

She did not answer right away. "I thought never to play that role again," she said at last.

"Aye. But an I deprive him o' her, what do I owe him in return?"

"And what of Fleta? What do you owe her?"

That returned him to reality. "Must needs I find another way." He got up. "I will talk with Blue."

"And I," she said.

They went to Citizen Blue, who met them graciously, with Sheen. "On the morrow, mayhap I will win the match," Bane said. "And deprive myself and Mach o' our loves, and the alien and the filly o' theirs. That be no easy thing."

"The imbalance must be corrected," Blue replied. "But you will be able to visit the frames, while we work to find the key for correction."

Bane took a deep breath. "Methinks we have the key already. It be between thee and my father."

Blue arched an eyebrow.

"The Oracle learned it," Bane continued. "There be a line between ye two, and that be the line Mach and

I followed. Methinks thou couldst exchange, an thou didst try."

Blue whistled. "And lose *our* loves, even as we have asked of you."

"I thought o' it not that way!" Bane protested.

"But it may *be* that way," Blue said grimly.

"Unless there be another way. The Oracle be studying that."

"What way is that?"

"To end the separation o' the frames, and merge them again."

"But that separation is for a reason!"

"A reason that accomplished not its purpose. The imbalance remains."

Citizen Blue nodded. "That would be a whole new game!"

"A game that leaves all of us our loves."

"We must explore this! If you and Mach—"

"First must I win the game tomorrow. Then will Mach work with me, and with thee. Then can the root of this be explored."

"Yes. Win tomorrow, and the essential tool is ours. The Oracle and the Book of Magic, reunited—"

"Aye," Bane said, feeling better. Now he could do his utmost, and believe that the best would come of it.

The final game was Doublet: played with two balls and four paddles. It was not popular with serious players, because it tended to get wild, but dabblers liked it, as did some specialists.

Each player had one standard paddle, and one freestyle paddle. Play was not required to alternate between them; rather, each ball had to be played with its own paddle. Thus this represented two separate games, played simultaneously. It could be a formidable challenge.

Bane had the first serve, which meant one pair of balls. He was required to serve the standard one first: the yellow ball, with the standard paddle. The second had to follow not before the first cleared the net, and not after the first returned; the window was while the opposite player was playing the first. Thereafter there was no set order; the balls were simply played as they came.

Bane had the standard paddle in his left hand. He tossed up the yellow ball with his right, his fingers also holding the other paddle, and struck it with the correct paddle. Then he tossed the red ball with his left hand, and struck it with his high-tech paddle. Both balls were served crosscourt, requiring Mach to orient on the extremes rapidly.

The first was coming back as he completed his serving pass for the second. He played it back to the same court he had served the red one, and with a shorter stroke, so that it gained somewhat on the other. But Mach played them back to opposite courts. Whether it was better strategy to play them to the same court or to opposite courts was an open question; it depended on the player and the situation. Already Bane felt his robot intellect being extended; this was no easy task for it, tracking two at once.

Now the two balls were crossing oppositely. Theoretically there was the danger of them colliding, and that was a complication in regular play. But for this game there was no problem; the yellow and red balls were on different planes of reality, and would pass through each other without interacting. In fact, that applied to the paddles, too: the wrong one could not touch the ball, literally. Thus there would be no question whether the ball was returned with the wrong paddle; if it returned at all, it was by the right paddle. Bane wasn't quite sure how this worked; perhaps the seemingly solid balls were mere images, extensions of the images on the far side of the table. They *seemed* solid, but he had learned not to believe everything that had seeming, in either frame.

Bane played conservatively, concentrating on one ball at a time, so that he could devote his whole competence to it. He put intricate spins on the red ball—only to see them nulled by the magic paddle Mach used. He went for speed and placement with the yellow ball, because the standard paddle was not as sharp on spins. But Mach could handle such straightforward play.

Mach played slow on the red ball, retreating from the table to return it late, and fast on the yellow one. As a result, the two soon came into alignment. Bane tried to separate them in space, if not in time, angling the red one right and the yellow one left.

That was his tactical error. Mach slammed them simultaneously, crosscourt, and Bane was unable to field them both. He had to let one go, and chose to sacrifice the red one. He returned the yellow one.

Love–one. Now it was down to a one-ball game, with standard equipment. Mach had won their prior such game—but Bane had zeroed in on the new tricks and was ready for them. Deceptive spin would not catch him. Also, Mach could no longer use the magic paddle, so could fail to return the ball. This was better for Bane. He played hard, moving the ball from side to side and front to back, until Mach's fallible living body made the error of sending too gentle a return, and Bane put it away for the point. One–one.

Now it was Mach's serve, both balls. Because of the special nature of this game, the serve changed each time, so as to prevent a facile combination of serves from generating too great a run of points. He served the yellow ball fast, crosscourt, and the red one slow, downcourt. He was trying to get the two aligned again, so as to catch Bane in the same split as before. But this time Bane had a trick of his own to play.

He returned the yellow fast and the red slow but not easy. He set his paddle to max-tack and sent what was known as the double loop: a high shot with extremely potent topspin. It came down on Mach's side almost vertically, and bounced away almost horizontally, retaining formidable spin. That would be an extraordinarily difficult shot to return, if it were not for the magic paddle.

Meanwhile, the yellow ball had lapped the red one, and he played it before the red one landed, slamming it to the far corner. Mach knew that if he went for it, he would never get to the red one. So he let the yellow go, losing the point, and caught the red.

It was one-ball table tennis again—but this was the variant Bane had proven he could win. He smashed the ball again and again, until he maneuvered Mach out of position and placed a shot he could not reach. One–three, Bane's favor.

That set the complexion of the game. Bane had greater reliability when the game was down to one ball; Mach had the advantage with two, because his living body was more flexible and his magic paddle gave him one sure return. After the initial points, neither tried to align the two balls; it gave too much of an advantage to the one who had the first chance to make simultaneous slams. Mach won the first ball more often than not, and Bane the second. The lead varied, and changed often, but it was basically even ball.

Thus it was that they came to the conclusion neither had wanted: a 20–20 tie. Now it would be sudden death; the first to gain an advantage of two points would win the game and the match.

Bane was torn: should he play conservatively, or draw on a special shot he had saved for emergency use? If he played conservatively, they would probably continue splitting points, and the game would drag out interminably. If he gambled on tricky but risky play, he could win quickly—or lose as quickly. It was his set of serves; the initiative was his.

As a robot, he knew that his best chance was conservative. Mach, in the volatile living body, could make mistakes, magic paddle notwithstanding. But as a living being who was merely housed in a machine, he felt that his best chance was to take the gamble. At least it would be over quickly.

He gambled. He served the yellow ball low and fast, so that Mach would not be able to do more than return it. He did the same with the red one. The magic paddle would return it regardless, but if he served it easy, Mach could take the initiative and make an aggressive shot, and Bane did not want that.

The yellow came back. This time he sent it in a phenomenally high shot, a towering trajectory that sent it as far aloft as the crown of a tree. That effectively put it out of play for a few seconds. Meanwhile he returned the red one with a backspin so strong that the ball actually bounced backward, back across the net, rather than on forward for Mach's return.

Would Mach be so surprised that he let the ball go? If so, he would lose the point. Then Bane would have the lead, and the advantage on the remaining ball.

Mach stepped around the table and went for the red ball. This was legal; a player could strike the ball on the opponent's side of the table, if its natural impetus carried it there. Many players did not know that, but of course Mach did. But how would he play it—when he was unable to cross the curtain? That was the question, and because Bane did not know the answer, it was the essence of his gamble.

Mach stepped forward, across the midline—and disappeared. He was now entering the magical representation on the other side of his table. No provision had been made to project his image, here. He was in limbo.

Abruptly the red ball changed course, taking off at right angles, crossing the table, bouncing, and sailing off the far side near the net. Bane had no chance to get it. He had lost the gamble; Mach had struck the ball he saw in his frame, and the question of its nature in Proton now was answered: it was illusion, and was affected by Mach's stroke.

Twenty–twenty-one. Bane was behind, and now the yellow ball was coming down. Mach reappeared, circled the table, and set up for a left-handed slam. The element of surprise had failed, and now Mach had a setup to put away. Bane might return it, but he had lost the initiative, and the point would almost certainly be Mach's.

Mach slammed it—and it touched the corner of Bane's side and veered crazily away, an unplayable ball. Mach had taken his own gamble, striving for a placement ordinarily beyond human ability, and won.

Won everything.

And Bane, knowing that he had tried his best, honestly, and lost despite it, was relieved. He had given Citizen Blue the key to a possible reversal of the situation, while he was on Blue's side; now he was on the other side, by the terms of the deal, and was no longer free to provide such information. The Contrary Citizens and Adverse Adepts had no more wish than Adept Stile or Citizen Blue to see the frames destroyed; perhaps some mutually satisfactory accommodation would yet be worked out. So it was not necessarily the end of decency.

Or so he hoped.